Praise for Nicola's previous HQN titles

"Ms. Cornick is first-class, queen of her game."
—*Romance Junkies*

"A rising star of the Regency arena."
—*Publishers Weekly*

"Nicola Cornick creates a glittering, sensual world
of historical romance that I never want to leave."
—Anna Campbell, author of *Untouched*

"A wonderfully original, sinfully amusing
and sexy Regency historical by the always
entertaining Cornick."
—*Booklist* on *The Confessions of a Duchess*

"Fast-paced, enchanting and wildly romantic!"
—*SingleTitles.com* on *The Scandals of an Innocent*

"Witty banter, lively action and sizzling passion."
—*Library Journal* on *The Undoing of a Lady*

"RITA® Award–nominated Cornick deftly steeps
her latest intriguingly complex Regency historical
in a beguiling blend of danger and desire."
—*Booklist* on *Unmasked*

"If you've liked Nicola Cornick's other books,
you are sure to like this one as well. If you've
never read one—what are you waiting for?"
—*Rakehell* on *Lord of Scandal*

"Cornick masterfully blends misconceptions,
vengeance, powerful emotions and the realization
of great love into a touching story."
—*RT Book Reviews*, 4½ stars, on *Deceived*

NICOLA CORNICK

MISTRESS *by* MIDNIGHT

HQN™

Recycling programs
for this product may
not exist in your area.

ISBN-13: 978-0-373-77488-3

MISTRESS BY MIDNIGHT

Copyright © 2010 by Nicola Cornick

This edition published by arrangement with Harlequin Books S.A.

For questions and comments about the quality of this book
please contact us at Customer_eCare@Harlequin.ca.

® and TM are trademarks of the publisher. Trademarks indicated with
® are registered in the United States Patent and Trademark Office, the
Canadian Trade Marks Office and in other countries.

www.HQNBooks.com

Printed in U.S.A.

Author Note

Like the other books in this trilogy, *Mistress by Midnight* is inspired by real-life events. In this case, the London Beer Flood of 1814, when a vat on top of the brewery in Tottenham Court Road exploded, flooding the nearby streets with beer and claiming several lives. One of those was a man who died of alcohol poisoning from drinking too much of the flood.

Mistress by Midnight tells Merryn's story. The younger sister of celebrated society hostess Lady Joanna Grant, Merryn is a bluestocking whose scholarly activities hide a secret life working for the private investigator Tom Bradshaw. Merryn also has a vendetta to pursue against Garrick, the new Duke of Farne, the man responsible for her brother's death. When the Beer Flood traps Merryn and Garrick together and they are in fear of their lives, a new sort of connection develops from their bond of hatred— this time a bond of wild passion. But will it outlive the terror of the flood?

I have adored writing these three books in the Scandalous Women of the Ton series and there is much more background history and exciting detail to explore on my website at www.nicolacornick.co.uk. Look out for more in the Scandalous Women of the Ton series. Coming soon!

For my mother, Sylvia

MISTRESS *by* MIDNIGHT

"Ah Love! Could you and I with fate conspire
To grasp this sorry scheme of things entire
Would not we shatter it to bits—and then
Re-mould it nearer to the heart's desire!"

The Rubaiyat of Omar Khayyam, verse 108,
translated by Edward Fitzgerald

CHAPTER ONE

"WE WERE NOT expecting you, your grace," Pointer, the butler, said.

Garrick Northesk, Duke of Farne, paused in the act of loosening his greatcoat. The raindrops on the shoulders glittered in the dim candlelight of the hall like dusty diamonds before sliding down to splash on the tiled floor.

"Lovely to see you again, too, Pointer," he said.

The butler's expression did not waver. Evidently, Garrick thought, his late father had not been given to jokes with the servants. Of course he had not. The eighteenth Duke had been famed for many things but a sense of humor was not one of them.

"We have had no time to prepare your chamber, your grace," Pointer continued, "nor is there any food in the house. I only received your message a few hours ago and there was no time to engage any staff." He gestured at the shrouded furniture and grimy mirrors. "The house has been closed. We have not had the opportunity to clean."

That was manifestly obvious. Long cobwebs trailed

from the chandelier in the center of the vast hall. The dust and grit of the London streets crunched beneath Garrick's boots as he crossed the floor. The ghostly covers on all the statuaries and the veiled furnishings only added to the sense of Gothic mystery. A mere two candles burned in the sconces, throwing long shadows. And it was cold, very cold. Garrick wished he had kept his coat on.

"I don't require anything tonight, thank you," he said. "Only a candle to light me to my bed and some hot water."

"You have no luggage, your grace?" Pointer's long nose, so appropriate to his name, twitched with disapproval.

"It follows," Garrick said briefly. No carriage could have kept up with his hell-for-leather ride.

"And your valet?"

"Gage follows, too."

Garrick took a candle from the sconce, leaving Pointer fluttering around in the dark hall like a monstrous moth. He was tired, exhausted really, the fatigue bone-deep, his limbs aching from riding hard all day. He had buried his father only five days before in the family mausoleum at Farnecourt on the west coast of Ireland. Trust the old devil to choose to be buried on his Irish estates with all pomp and circumstance and maximum inconvenience to his family. The late Duke had never cared a fig for Farnecourt in his lifetime, deploring the beautiful Irish countryside as barbarous and the people as heathens.

It was no wonder that few people other than his closest family had turned out for the funeral and those who did had probably only come so that they could be sure the old man really was dead. Well, the vault was sealed now and not even the eighteenth Duke could come back from beyond the grave.

He was Duke of Farne now, with no son to follow him.

Nor would there ever be one.

His first marriage had been disaster enough. He had no inclination to try again.

Garrick paused halfway up the shallow staircase that led to the first floor. The intricately inlaid parquet steps were dull with dirt. The elegant curls and swirls of the iron banisters were festooned with thick white cobwebs. The house was like a tomb. How appropriate.

His father, the eighteenth Duke, had been furious to be dying in such an untimely fashion, with half his life's ambitions still unfulfilled. He had railed against his mortal illness, a reaction that had in all probability carried him off all the quicker. So now Garrick was master of this mausoleum and twenty-six other houses in ten counties, plus an obscenely large fortune. It was more than one man had any right to possess.

Out of habit rather than choice, Garrick pushed open the door of the sixth bedchamber on the left-hand side down an endless corridor that stretched away into darkness. On the rare occasions that he had stayed at his father's house in London this had always been his room.

It was smaller than the state chambers albeit not one whit cozier. Farne House had been designed to awe and impress not to welcome. It would be possible for a small army to be lost in the labyrinth of passages for a number of days. The grate was empty and the whole room cold and inhospitable, although there was an odd scent of smoke in the air as though the candles had recently been snuffed out. A copy of *Mansfield Park* lay on the floor. Garrick picked it up absentmindedly and returned it to the table.

There was a knock at the door; a housemaid with blessedly hot water. Evidently Pointer had managed to drum up at least one servant to help him. The girl placed the ewer of water carefully on the side table and dropped him a frightened curtsy. Her wide-eyed gaze searched his face before sliding away when he turned to thank her. Perhaps she was afraid of him in case he was like his sire. Rumors of the late Duke's behavior must have made their way into every servant agency in London. Garrick's father had seen the rape of the maidservants as one of his privileges rather than as a heinous crime. The eighteenth Duke had beaten his servants and kicked his dogs, and vice versa. Garrick felt his stomach cramp with disgust and revulsion at the memories.

Once the girl had run away he eased off his boots with a heartfelt sigh. As he had no valet to attend him it was fortunate that he was no dandy. He liked fine leather but he did not want a pair of boots that were so tight they had to be removed by brute force. Nor did his jacket require coaxing from his shoulders. He had even mastered the art of tying his own neck cloth with tolerable ease. It had always struck him as supremely impractical to be incapable of dressing or undressing without help, like a child or an invalid. Besides, for many years he had lived and traveled in places where not even the most devoted servant would ever follow.

The hot water removed the dirt of his journey and made him wish suddenly for a bath to ease his saddle-sore body, but it was late and he had no intention of disturbing the servants again. Tomorrow he would have to start the tedious business of mastering his father's affairs. That was his duty. Being a Duke was a privilege, or so he had been told from the cradle. It was a pity, then, that he saw it as a monstrous burden. He would not shirk it, though. He understood all about duty and service. Now, though, he wanted nothing more than to sleep.

There was a decanter on the dresser. On impulse he poured a glass of brandy, hoping it might warm him a little. It did more than that; it burned fire down to his stomach, reminding him he had not eaten for at least a day. No matter. He refilled the glass, knocked the liquid back again, once, twice? The combination of strong drink and weariness set his head spinning but now at least he might be able to sleep.

He expected the bed to be damp but to his surprise the sheets were cool and smooth but quite dry. He slid between them with a heartfelt sigh and turned his head against the softest of down pillows. A scent arose, elusive, sweet, the smell of a summer garden with shifting perfumes of bluebells and honeysuckle. It filled his senses, heating him from the inside out, awakening urges that were as unexpected as they were unwelcome. Suddenly the silken slide of the sheet felt like a lover's caress against his bare chest. He could taste temptation, sweet, dark and provocative. His body hardened into arousal.

He was dreaming. Fantasizing.

With a groan Garrick rolled over and willed his errant body into submission. Mind over matter. It was easy. He had done it a hundred times before. But this time the desire was too strong and it had come upon him too hard and fast. It swirled about him sinuously until he was helpless in its grip. He lay back and breathed deeply but that merely filled his lungs with that wistful scent of flowers. If it had not been so fanciful he would have sworn that someone had been sleeping in his bed, a wraith, a ghost, imprinting her very presence on him.

It was a trick of the senses. It could be no more. He was tired and drunk, and he had not had a woman in a long time and now his body was rebelling, reminding him of all that he had rejected.

Once, before his marriage, he had been a rake and after his wife had died he had returned to that life for a while. He had tried to drown his grief and guilt in debauchery. It had not worked. Now he lived like a monk. Some physical frustration was therefore inevitable. Or so he told himself.

The ton gossiped about him. They had done for years. He knew it. He ignored it.

Garrick Farne, the man who murdered his best friend, his wife's lover.

It was twelve years but even now he could not remember without a lurch of the heart and that familiar drag of guilt and grief. Which was as it should be. Penance was not meant to be easy.

As he rolled over to blow out the candle the book caught his eye once more. It had a deep red cover and black lettering. Below it, on the nightstand, was tucked a small pair of spectacles. Garrick raised his brows. Had Pointer used this room to escape with a good book? Garrick thought it unlikely. The very proper butler would surely not make free with the ducal bedroom, nor would he approve of fiction for that matter.

He took the book in his hand and turned to the flyleaf. There was an inscription there, the initials *M* and *F* entwined, and from the pages came the same elusive scent of flowers. Garrick laid the book aside on the coverlet and thought vaguely that he should perhaps check beneath the bed or inside the wardrobe for the spectacle-wearing, bluebell-scented intruder, but he was too tired. Tomorrow…tomorrow he would make a thorough search, but for now he wanted to slough off all the responsibilities of rank, forget his father's grim legacy and sink into unconsciousness.

He was about to do so when the door opened again, most unexpectedly and without the courtesy of a knock first. In the doorway stood a vision of beauty. From her elegantly coiffed dark curls to her pink satin slippers she exuded sophistication and an unmistakable air of raw sexuality. Garrick shot bolt upright with an oath.

"Harriet? What the devil—" He was fiercely aware of his huge erection, which had not been roused by Harriet's appearance but by his previous unrestrained imaginings. Thank goodness he had retained his trousers. He had no wish for the evidence of his physical state to be tenting the bedcovers.

"What the hell are you doing here?" he demanded. He should have locked the door, he thought. Except that this was his house and he had not expected a seduction.

He had last seen Harriet Knight five days ago at his father's funeral, when she had been swathed from head to foot in irreproachable black rather than lightly dressed— or rather, undressed—in this thistledown confection of pale, transparent pink. So much for his belief that he had outrun the rest of the family in his headlong flight back to London. Harriet, his late father's ward, was before him. And she really *was* standing before him, allowing the gown to fall from her shapely pale shoulders, down over her full breasts and lushly curved hips, to stand beside the bed in all her glorious nudity. Garrick's head spun with drink, tiredness and shock. He had known Harriet was a minx, probably worse than a minx, but he had not thought her quite so brazen.

"Garrick, darling." Her voice—that throaty, seductive

purr—washed over him. "I've come to welcome the new Duke to his new…position."

Harriet, Garrick thought, had long wanted to be the next Duchess of Farne. She had made no secret of it. She simply had not previously resorted to such sledgehammer tactics.

She stepped up to the side of the bed and he was almost knocked flat by the powerful scent of her perfume. It banished the other softer, sweeter scent of bluebells with the subtlety of a mallet. He almost fell over against the pillows.

"Did Pointer let you in?" he demanded. "At this time of night? Dressed like that?"

Of all the foolish questions… A naked Harriet was sitting down on the edge of the bed, a foot away from him, and he was discussing issues of etiquette? He was disorientated, drunk and disturbed. Harriet's left breast brushed his bare arm and he flinched. He was getting confused now. He was weary and more than a little cast away, and he was aching for a woman who was not this one, a woman who was no more than a wraith, a dream. But Harriet was all too real and she did have magnificent breasts…

She also had an enormous desire to be a Duchess and he was in extreme danger. He eased away from her beneath the sheets. She wriggled voluptuously in pursuit.

"Where is your chaperone?" he demanded, breathlessly. "I cannot believe that Mrs. Roach would countenance this—"

"I'll send for her if you desire a threesome." Harriet's narrow green eyes glittered like a feral cat. "Darling Garrick, shall we celebrate?"

"My father's death is hardly a matter for celebration," Garrick said. His mind was spinning. "Harriet, no—"

"On the contrary." She had thrown one thigh over him now and was pinning him down. Her moist warmth seared him through the sheet. "We are all absolutely thrilled that he has died," she said. "Why pretend? And now you and I can have our own, very special little reunion, Garrick." She slid a hand down over the bedcovers until it met his erection. "Oh, good, you have started already."

She wriggled down upon him, simultaneously pressing her lips to his. "Brandy," she murmured. "Delicious."

She, in contrast, tasted a little sour. Garrick felt as though he was being smothered by a cushion. He groaned in protest. Harriet seemed to interpret this as enthusiasm. Her hands were all over his naked chest now, her lips clinging to his, her thighs gripping him through the bedcovers. In a moment she would surely slip under the sheets, slide down on top of him, and then…

And then there would be the most almighty scandal and Harriet Knight would be Duchess of Farne and his life would be ruined a second time over.

To have one unfaithful wife could be construed as a misfortune. To have two would be worse than careless. He did not want a wife with fashionable morals. He did not want a wife at all.

Suddenly Garrick was very awake and very sober. His body might desire Harriet—it could be very indiscriminate at times—but his mind most certainly did not. He had had enough of mechanistic, emotionless couplings and he was not going to be trapped into marriage via another one.

"Harriet, no." He took her arm and pushed her away from him with more force than finesse. She gave a little bounce and a squeak as she tumbled from the bed onto the floor.

"You do me too much honor," Garrick said smoothly, leaping out after her and scooping up her negligee. "I understand your need for comfort after the shocking death of your guardian. I am privileged beyond measure that you thought to give me your virginity—" *God forgive him for two lies in one short sentence* "—but I cannot take such a sacrifice. You are distraught."

He wrapped the gaping beauty roughly in the diaphanous material and gave her a shove toward the door. But Harriet was stubborn.

"I shall tell Mrs. Roach," she said, glaring. "I shall tell your mama. I shall tell *everyone* that you seduced me."

Garrick shook his head. "I don't think you will, my dear." There was steel in his tone now.

She stood staring at him for a moment. Garrick wondered what she could see in his eyes. Was it the coldness of a man who had long ago ceased caring?

For a moment Harriet looked frightened.

"Damn you, Farne," she said.

Garrick shrugged. "If you wish."

Harriet whirled around and slammed out of the door. Silence settled again.

It was then that Garrick heard the sneeze.

UNDER THE LARGE tester bed, Lady Merryn Fenner lay with her face pressed against the dusty floorboards. She had been trapped for a half hour. In a short but varied career working for the private investigator Tom Bradshaw she had never been in a situation quite like this one. She had never been caught before.

Merryn had been reading when the Duke of Farne had entered the bedroom and had had a bare few seconds to take cover. She had hoped to escape when he fell asleep. Then the woman had come in. Merryn had heard the husky seductive tones, seen the robe fall to the floor, felt the bedsprings give and had known she was in for a thorough education in a matter in which she had previously been in almost total ignorance.

She had rolled over, pressing her face against the floor, eyes screwed tightly closed. She had shoved her fingers in her ears and prayed that Garrick Farne's ardor would be both quick and exhausting, that the lovers would wear themselves out swiftly and fall into a sex-induced stupor. The sounds and the movements she could not *quite* block out had made her feel very hot and bothered. She could feel her body radiating a warmth that was part embarrassment but also something else infinitely more disconcerting. Her clothes felt tight and restraining and she wanted to squirm. It was most odd.

Then she had inhaled a cobweb and the harder she tried to hold back a sneeze the more it tickled her before it burst out with explosive force.

Oh, dear. There was no escape now. That would have disturbed even the most ardent lovers.

Sure enough, a second later, someone reached down, grabbed her arm and dragged her from under the bed. She was hauled roughly to her feet. Eyes watering, another sneeze threatening, she drew herself up to her full five-foot height.

How to explain? No, forget the explanations, how to escape?

"My bedroom seems an unconscionably popular venue tonight," the man before her drawled.

Garrick Farne, best friend to her brother Stephen. Her brother's murderer...

Merryn shivered. Once—pitiful to remember now—she had had a schoolgirl crush on Garrick Farne. He had been like a god to her, a creature who inhabited a different world. While Merryn and her sisters had lived a circumscribed life, educated at home, their existence bounded by the village of Fenridge and their parents' immediate acquaintances, Stephen and his friends, including Garrick, had studied at Oxford, gambled their patrimony away in London, lived, according to the gossip, for women and drink and vice. Oh, how she had lapped up that scandal. It had all sounded frightfully exciting to a thirteen-year-old girl who had never traveled farther than Bath in her life.

Garrick had never noticed her, of course. Why should he? Merryn had two beautiful elder sisters who drew all the eyes, all the attention and all the compliments. Besides, Garrick had been betrothed from the cradle to Kitty Scott, the daughter of his father's political friend and ally; it was simply a matter of when Kitty and Garrick wed, not if they wed. Kitty was a beauty, too, the toast of the town. Which was no doubt why Stephen had fallen in love with her, too…

A shock ran through Merryn now, like lightning, like recognition, setting her shaking as though she had an ague. Garrick Farne. His name had become a byword for evil in her family, a murderer, a man who had ruined her life and those of her father and her sisters. While he had been abroad, in exile, it had been just about possible for her to put him from her mind, to ignore, if not forget, the events of that hot summer so many years ago. Then, fifteen months ago, Garrick had come back, back to a society that instead of trying him for murder had welcomed him like a hero; back to be lauded as the most handsome, wealthy and eligible nobleman in the ton.

In contrast it seemed to Merryn that no one remembered her brother Stephen at all. He was gone, irrelevant, forgotten. They had not one single memento of him left, for every picture, every possession, had been swallowed up to pay off the debts when their father died. The Earldom of Fenner was extinct, the family lands lost while

Garrick Farne was wealthy, titled and, most importantly, *alive*. Garrick's return to England had sparked something within Merryn, awoken all those unbearable memories from the time that Stephen had died, and suddenly the past was real and painful to her once again, as raw and ragged as when it had first happened.

Merryn rubbed one hand across her streaming eyes and looked around for Garrick's mistress, the woman with the husky voice, imaginative ideas and overpowering perfume. But it seemed that they were alone.

"Oh!" she exclaimed involuntarily. "She has gone!"

Garrick raised one dark brow. "Did you not hear me throw her out?"

"I had my fingers in my ears," Merryn said. "I did not want to *hear* anything, thank you. Being squashed by the bouncing of the bed was quite bad enough."

"I'm sorry," Garrick said politely. "Had I known that you were there I would, of course, have ejected her all the sooner." His gaze swept over her, lingering on the cobwebs.

"It is very dirty under your bed," Merryn said defensively.

He bowed ironically. "Again, I apologize. Next time you plan to take refuge there I shall ensure the room is swept clean."

"That would be appreciated," Merryn said.

Why are we having this conversation? she thought. This was quite wrong. This was not how she had imagined an encounter with the Duke of Farne would be.

She looked at him. Actually she had not imagined any encounter, at least not here and now, which was why she was so frightfully unprepared. She had thought Garrick would be safely out of the way in Ireland for at least a further week. He had buried his father less than seven days ago, after all. It was perfectly reasonable to assume that the house would remain empty.

Garrick was standing between her and the door. He looked enormous. In part that was because she was quite small. It was also because he was over six foot and he had a powerful physique—she could see that quite clearly since he was half naked. His chest was broad and bare, and his trousers were molded to muscular thighs.

At least he had his trousers on. Thank God.

Merryn felt quite faint with relief as she realized it. Light-headed, she closed her eyes for a second. After the scene with his mistress she had expected him to be completely naked...

"Are you quite well?" His voice cut through her mental image of what a naked Garrick Farne might look like and her gaze flew up to meet his own sardonic one.

"Perfectly, I thank you," she said.

He had dark brown eyes under straight black brows, high cheekbones and a very hard line to his jaw. It was an austere face, Merryn thought, cold and remote, enough to make one shiver. The rest of him was russet and gold—smooth golden skin, tousled auburn hair, an intriguing scattering of more wiry dark red hair across his chest, and down toward the band at the top of his trousers.

Merryn found she was staring. She had never seen a man in a state of undress before. It was fascinating. She felt the urge to touch so strongly that she was already reaching out a hand toward him before she realized it. She turned scarlet and hoped the dust on her face would conceal her embarrassment. In the same instant she remembered that she hated him.

A shudder racked her.

"Well? I await the explanation of your presence here." Farne's voice was as sharp as a lash and Merryn jumped. She really had to get out of here before matters got any worse. Because of course she could not tell him her purpose in searching his house. She could hardly say, "I discovered three weeks ago that you lied to everyone about my brother's death. It was bad enough that you killed him…I hated you for that. But now I know you covered up the truth as well and I want justice. I want you to hang…"

No, indeed. It would not do to alert Garrick Farne to her purpose.

"I beg your pardon," she said. "I did not realize that you required an explanation. You had not said."

Garrick's mouth curled up at the corner into a beguiling smile. Chill ripples ran across her skin. *Revulsion,* she thought. *That is the effect he has on me now. Hatred. Disgust…*

"My good woman, any right-thinking person would demand to know your business." He paused. "Or should I call you a girl rather than a woman? You do not look very old—" Before she had chance to escape him, he had raised a hand and brushed the cobwebby dust from her cheeks. His touch was gentle. She shivered again, stepping back.

"I am five and twenty," she said with dignity. *Why am I offering this information? Why am I even speaking to him?* "I am not a girl."

"Woman, then." That disquieting smile in his eyes deepened. So did the curl of heat in her stomach, the one that she wanted to attribute to hatred.

Concentrate. You have to get out of here.

"I suppose," she said hastily, "you think it odd in me to be in your room."

"I do." He had not taken his eyes from her face once during their encounter. "I am fascinated to hear your explanation."

"Well, I…" No useful lie sprang to mind. Merryn was not very good at dissembling. She never normally needed to bother. No one ever noticed her because she took pains to appear small, plain and insignificant. No one ever really *saw* her.

"I thought the house was empty," she said. "I needed somewhere to sleep."

It was partially true. She had been sleeping in Farne House for several nights while she made a leisurely search of the premises, hunting for something, *anything,* which might throw fresh light on the circumstances of her brother's death. At first it had happened by accident. She had been exhausted and had dropped off to sleep in an armchair in the library, waking hours later both amazed and amused that she had not been discovered. She had known that a skeleton staff of servants lived in the house but they had not troubled her. No one had even realized that she was there. Farne House was huge and had been neglected for months, ever since the late Duke had been taken ill on his Irish estates back at the start of the year. And so the idea had come to her that she could stay at Farne House while she hunted for the evidence to incriminate Garrick Farne. In an odd way sleeping in Garrick's house had made her feel closer to him. It had fed her hatred and hardened her determination to find out the truth.

Farne's brows had snapped down at her words. "You broke in here because you are destitute?" He rapped out. "Homeless?"

"Yes." Merryn thought that she might get away with the story. London was full of tumbled down and abandoned houses. It was common knowledge on the streets that if you had no roof over your head you would be able to find shelter under the cover of the Fleet Market or in the abandoned workhouse in Dyot Street. But there were those beggars who were more daring and who squatted in the houses of the nobility. Plenty of these mansions were barely used, closed when the family was out of London, neglected and empty.

It seemed, however, that Garrick was not convinced. He took a step closer to her. His hand was on her shoulder. She flinched, but he was only fingering the fine wool of her gown, testing it. Unfortunately the dust was insufficiently thick to conceal its quality.

"A good try." He sounded grimly amused. "But this is not the attire of someone who is down on their luck."

Devil take it, he was sharp.

"I stole it." Now she had started with the deception it seemed she had a more vivid imagination than even she had thought. "From a washing line."

He was nodding thoughtfully. "What a fine liar you are. Most imaginative."

Damnation. He had not been taken in even for a second. But he had at least moved away from the door.

"Who *are* you?" he said. "Why are you here?"

"I cannot tell you that," Merryn said, reverting to her true character after her brief and unsuccessful foray into deception.

"You mean that you do not *want* to tell me." He had his head on one side, still watching her. Those brown eyes were very perceptive. She felt a little dizzy. Discovery felt a little closer.

Concentrate. Three steps to the door...

"That's right," she said. "I do not want to talk to you at all."

"Yet you are not in a position to refuse."

"That's debatable."

He laughed. "You want to debate?"

"No," Merryn said. "I want to leave."

He shook his head. "I should hand you over to Bow Street for housebreaking."

"And then you would still get no explanation whatsoever."

His eyes gleamed. "A fair point." He shrugged those broad shoulders. "Then there is nothing for it than that I keep you here until you tell me the truth."

Merryn glanced around. He was going to keep her imprisoned in his *bedroom?* The big tester bed, so wide, so inviting, seemed to mock her. She remembered the cool smoothness of the sheets and the yielding softness of the mattress. For one scalding moment she had a vision of Garrick's naked body bearing hers down into that silken embrace, of his hands against her bare skin, of his caresses… She looked from the bed to Garrick. He raised his brows a fraction of an inch and Merryn felt her body suffuse with heat. .

"You could read your book," he said gently, "to pass the time." He held out her copy of *Mansfield Park* to her.

"Thank you," Merryn said. She put out a hand to take it. He held on to it. She gave it a little tug. Garrick allowed her gesture to bring him a step closer to her. Their fingers were practically touching now on the deep red cover, hers slender and pale, his tanned and strong. She remembered his touch against her cheek and closed her eyes on a long shiver.

He took the final step. They were very close now. He was frowning, his gaze fierce beneath the dark brows. And then he leaned closer and *sniffed* her, delicately, as though she were a flower.

"Bluebells," he muttered. He shook his head, sniffed again; looked up again, incredulous. His gaze had narrowed to an intense black stare.

"Have you been sleeping in my bed?" he demanded.

"I…" Suddenly Merryn's mouth was dry and her wits seemed to have gone a-begging. "Yes, I have…" She licked her lips and tasted dust. His gaze had gone to her mouth and fastened there, his eyes darkening with an intensity that had her stomach knotting.

"An extraordinary intimacy," he murmured.

Merryn had never been kissed but she knew with an instinct deep as time itself that in another moment Garrick Farne would kiss her, cobwebs and all. The fierce heat she could see in his eyes trapped and held her. Her heart hammered.

He closed the remaining distance between them and his lips brushed hers. Soft, so soft, and barely a touch at all and yet the caress seemed to awaken something fierce and burning inside her. Her head spun. She could smell his masculine scent and for some reason it made her knees tremble. Her whole body was alight with a sensation she had never experienced. Her lips parted on a little gasp of shock.

Garrick stood back, a look of stunned surprise on his face. Merryn seized the moment. She grabbed *Mansfield Park* from out of his hand and hit him squarely with it on the side of his head. Garrick gave an oath. The spine of the book was fragile and the pages came loose, showering him in paper like confetti, blinding him for a moment. It was all that Merryn needed. She whisked through the door and out into the passage. The key was in the outside of the lock. She turned it.

And then she ran.

CHAPTER TWO

"POINTER," GARRICK SAID, sitting at his father's desk the following morning, "do you think it would be possible to break into Farne House? Is it vulnerable to intruders?"

"Your grace?" The butler sounded faintly anxious.

"I only ask, you understand," Garrick said, "because I found a strange female in my room last night."

"Lady Harriet—" the butler began.

"Ah, yes," Garrick said. He had packed Harriet and her chaperone off to stay with his mother in the country. Since the Dowager Duchess's household would be in deep mourning for the foreseeable future, this seemed punishment enough for the promiscuous minx.

"Pray do not admit Lady Harriet to my presence again, Pointer," he said. "Not under any circumstances."

"No, your grace." Pointer sounded subdued. "I did try to stop the lady but she was the late Duke's ward and is much given to following her own desires."

"She is indeed," Garrick said. "Lady Harriet can be very persuasive. But this other woman—"

He stopped. What could he say?

I found a woman under my bed. She was small, with blue eyes that glow like agates and pale golden hair like a swatch of silk. She smelled of bluebells. I kissed her and she tasted of dust and innocence, and I have never wanted to bed a woman more in my life...

No, decidedly he could not tell Pointer his thoughts. Such vivid fantasies had no place in the life of a Duke shackled to duty and responsibility. Nevertheless Garrick shifted as he remembered the shape of the girl's lips beneath his, the tiny gasp she had given when he kissed her, the shocking sensation of wanting to catch her in his arms and tumble her onto his bed and strip those cobwebbed clothes from her to discover the pleasures of her body beneath. He wanted to taste that tempting mouth again, to kiss her senseless. He felt his body harden into arousal.

Hell and the devil.

Pointer cleared his throat and Garrick jumped.

"Your grace..."

"Pointer?" Garrick said.

"Perhaps she was one of the servants, your grace, come to make sure you were comfortable," Pointer said. He looked shifty. "I will ask the housekeeper to tell the maids not to trouble you."

"That would be appreciated," Garrick said. He knew his intruder had not been a servant. She had spoken with the instinctive confidence of a lady regardless of her pretense to be a waif from the streets. This morning he had found other evidence of occupation in his bedroom, too. There were the charred remains of a letter curling in the grate. There was a stick of striped candy on the dresser, wrapped in a twist of paper. He had found that rather endearing. There were even some female unmentionables neatly folded on a shelf in the wardrobe. Those had given him pause. How long had she been making free with his property and sleeping in his bed?

Pointer was waiting. Garrick sighed. "To return to my original question. Is the house secure?"

"I will check, your grace." Pointer sounded very stiff at the suggestion that he was not in control of every aspect of security at Farne House. "If there is nothing more, your grace, I shall go and do so at once…" Garrick knew the butler was mortally offended. They had already disagreed once that morning. The first thing Pointer had offered to do after breakfast was to visit the employment bureau in order to recruit more staff to open up Farne House again. When Garrick had told him that he did not intend to use Farne House as his London home, he had thought Pointer might well burst with disapproval.

"But, your grace—" the butler had forgotten himself sufficiently to protest "—Farne House is the…the *flagship* of your Dukedom, the very pinnacle of your position! It is the feather in your cap, the summit of your status—"

"Farne House is ugly, old, draughty and expensive," Garrick had said. "I do not care for it, Pointer. I shall not be entertaining, nor do I have a Duchess who requires a social setting. I will return to my own house in Charles Street as soon as I have set my father's affairs in order."

"Charles Street!" Pointer had said, as though Garrick had suggested he would be returning to the London stews. "That may have done very well for you when you were the Marquis of Northesk, your grace, but you are the *Duke* now. You have a dignity to uphold. Your father—" He had fallen silent as Garrick had pinned him with a very hard look.

"I," Garrick had said, "am not my father, Pointer."

Now he waited as Pointer retreated, outrage evident in every stiff line of his figure.

When the door had closed behind the butler, Garrick turned back to the desk and sorted methodically through the papers, making a note of the people he needed to contact and the actions he needed to take. Regardless of the dislike in which he had held his father—actually, hatred would probably be a better word—he had to give the late Duke credit for being extremely well organized. All the papers were in order, the income from the Farne estates was up-to-date and clearly notated and everything appeared to run like a smoothly oiled machine, a tribute to the late Duke's rather vulgar grasping after every last penny that could be squeezed from his lands.

The clock on the mantel chimed twelve. Suddenly restless, Garrick got up and walked across to the dirty window. Dusty drapes shuttered the room. His mother, who might well have taken Farne House in hand, had not been to London for years. Tired of her husband's famously indiscreet infidelities, she had become a dowager before her time and had retired to a house in Sussex.

Garrick wondered vaguely how she would greet the arrival of the ungovernable Harriet on her doorstep. No doubt she would have the vapors. It was her usual mode of response to any crisis.

Outside the day was bright and clear, the sort of November morning that had slanting sunlight and scurrying white clouds. Garrick felt as though he were trapped here in this cobwebbed mausoleum. He wanted to take his stallion and ride out, not in the park among the chattering crowds, but somewhere wild and empty where he and the beast could both let go of all restraint. He had lived abroad for many years and had a taste for empty spaces and the hot blue skies of Portugal and Spain. And though he had been back in London for over a year, still the city felt cramped and cold and strangely repressive to a man who only really thrived in the open air.

Duty called him back to the pile of estate papers. He was Duke of Farne now and regardless of how disappointing he was as upholder of the family dignity, he could not escape his responsibilities. He had had that drummed into him since he was a child. He strode back to the desk. In his study in the house on Charles Street he had plenty of work waiting, too, research relating to his academic studies into seventeenth-century astronomy, documents to translate for the War Office. He had worked for Earl Bathurst, the Secretary of State for War, during his time in exile. He had also done plenty of other, less official, work for the government as well. It was one of the reasons that his father had raged against him, the heir to the Dukedom of Farne, trying and consistently failing to get himself killed in the service of his country. But what was he to do? For years he had carried the burden of taking a life, that of Stephen Fenner. He had tried to give his own in reparation, but the gods appeared uninterested in taking it.

He picked up his pen. He put it down again. What he *really* wanted to do, he found, was to discover the identity of the woman who had penetrated his house and his defenses, his midnight visitor, she of the vivid blue eyes and the porcelain fair skin. She had run from him like a fairy-tale Cinderella.

He wandered over to the oak bookcases that lined two walls of the study. Here he paused, the hairs on the back of his neck rising with a curious feeling of awareness. Someone else had perused these shelves, and recently. There were tiny marks in the dust, as though someone had carefully drawn out the books and replaced them without wanting to leave a trace.

He turned back to the desk. Had she been rifling through the papers here, too? If so, what could have been her purpose?

He wondered how, in the whole of London, he might find one elusive lady. There were always the inquiry agents, he supposed, though he could give them precious little to work on. A physical description, based on all the things he had found so seductive about her, would not be particularly helpful.

Shaking his head in exasperation, Garrick resumed his work, untying the red ribbon that held the next set of estate papers.

"Title to the estate of Fenners in the County of Dorset…"

Garrick felt chilled. Icy memory trickled down his spine. He had had no idea that his father had bought up the Fenner estates. He ripped the ribbon away and sifted through the papers. His father, it seemed, had purchased not only the house of Fenners but also the land and all associated coal-mining rights. He had done so ten years previously when the estate had been broken up after the last Earl had died. The mining had proved lucrative; it had brought in a sum approaching a hundred thousand pounds.

The cold hardened inside Garrick, deep and dark. His father had profited by the death of Stephen Fenner and the subsequent extinction of the Earldom. While he had been trying to atone for Fenner's death his father had been turning it to financial advantage. How utterly typical it was of the late Duke to act with such vile cupidity. Garrick felt sick and revolted. It was intolerable to inherit an estate that had come to him through violence and bloodshed, even more so when it was blood that he himself had shed. With a sudden burst of anger he brought his hand down and scattered the deeds across the floor.

He threw himself down into his chair and tried to think. He had been back in society for fifteen months, long enough to know that the eldest of the Earl of Fenner's daughters was the famed hostess Joanna, Lady Grant, married to the equally famous Arctic explorer Alex Grant. The middle sister, Teresa Darent, was notorious, a widow who had run through four husbands already. Naturally enough he had not met either Lady Grant or Lady Darent socially; they would scarcely invite to their balls and routs the man who had murdered their brother in a duel. Ton society might be extraordinarily flexible, but it was not *that* flexible. He thought there was also a third girl, the youngest, but he knew little of her. She was unmarried, reputedly a bluestocking, almost a recluse, if gossip was to be believed.

Garrick reached for pen and ink and began to write. After he had finished the letter, sealed it and addressed it, he picked up again the papers relating to the Fenner estate but after a moment he let them drift from his hand down onto the desk before him.

Stephen Fenner had been his best friend at Eton and Oxford. He had been a rake, a gamester and a noted whip. His handsome face and winning charm had allowed him to cut a swath through the bedrooms and boudoirs of a number of ton ladies. It had been amusing to be one of Stephen's friends, part of a dazzling raffish crowd who had lived for pleasure. Garrick had been seduced by the glamour of it all. It was such a far cry from the life of service and obligation that he had been raised to embrace. But then Stephen had chosen

Garrick's bride as his latest conquest and friendship had disintegrated into betrayal and disgrace…

There was a knock at the door; Pointer, Garrick thought, had evidently overcome his disapproval sufficiently to resume his duties.

"I have ascertained that a window in the east wing has been forced, your grace," the butler said, looking with disfavor at the scattered pile of papers. "It is possible that an intruder may have found ingress into the house that way."

"She broke in through a window," Garrick said. "I see. Thank you, Pointer."

"I have made the house secure," Pointer finished grandly, "so your grace need have no further concerns."

"I am confident to leave the matter of household security entirely in your hands, Pointer," Garrick said. He held out the letter. "If you would be so kind as to see this is delivered to the offices of Churchward and Churchward, the lawyers, in Holborn please?"

"Of course, your grace," Pointer said, bowing with exquisite precision and proffering a silver tray on which Garrick could place the missive.

"And then," Garrick said, "I would like you to find me an inquiry agent."

Pointer's long nose twitched with shock. "An *inquiry agent,* your grace?" He repeated, as though Garrick had asked for something so outrageous he had no idea how to respond.

"Your esteemed father," he added, "would *never* have required such a person, your grace."

"I know," Garrick said, grinning. "You are going to have to get used to some changes, I fear, Pointer. If you could expedite the matter," he added, "that would be appreciated. There is someone I need to find urgently."

When he had found his midnight bibliophile, Garrick thought, he was going discover exactly what her business was with him. And this time he would not let her run away.

"THANK YOU FOR YOUR CUSTOM, Lord Selfridge. It was a pleasure to be able to provide you with the information you required."

Merryn sat in a dark corner of the waiting room while her associate, Tom Bradshaw, ushered the peer toward the stairs. Selfridge barely noticed her and certainly did not recognize her. Merryn would have been astonished if he had. In her daily life, as the frightfully studious bluestocking sister of Joanna, Lady Grant, celebrated ton hostess, she was practically invisible. She seldom attended the high society events that both her sisters loved and when she did she hardly ever danced. Those people who took the trouble to engage her in conversation usually regretted it because she was only interested in erudite subjects and chose to have no small talk. Most young men were afraid of her, bored by her, or both. She was known as the Simple Ton by those society fashionables who deplored her bookishness and her lack of social graces.

Such insignificance made it far easier for her to live as she wished, pursuing an interest in all manner of scholarly activities on the one hand and working for Tom on the other. If her sisters had known that she worked for a living they would probably have had the vapors. If they had known she was employed by an inquiry agent the strongest smelling salts would not have been able to revive them. And if they discoverd that sometimes she stayed out at night to do her work and invented fictitious friends to cover for her… But then, Merryn thought, they never would find out. They would not guess because such thoughts were unthinkable.

Except…except that she had made a mistake last night. It was the sort of mistake that could lead to the unmasking of what she liked to think of as her secret life. She had committed the cardinal sin of being caught, and by Garrick Farne, of all people. If there was one time that she should have been particularly careful, it was when she was working against the man who had killed her brother and ruined her family. But it was too late now. Farne had seen her. Farne had *kissed* her. A little of ripple of disquiet, mixed with something more deep and disturbing, edged down her spine.

"Are you coming in or are we to talk out here?"

Tom was holding his office door open for her, his head tilted inquiringly to one side, eyes bright, a smile curling his lips. He was cocky, but Merryn liked him for it. Tom, the son of a stevedore who had worked on the Thames loading ships, still kept his offices within a stone's throw of the river. He was one of the most successful inquiry agents in London, finding everything from missing heirs to servants who had absconded with the family silver. She had worked alongside him for the past two years.

Merryn uncurled herself from her seat and preceded Tom into the office. There was a chair but she knew from experience that it was uncomfortable so she remained standing. Tom propped himself against the edge of his desk.

"So did you find any papers relating to the duel?" Tom said. "Any servants paid off around that time, any proof of a cover-up, anything suspicious at all?"

"I'm very well, thank you, Tom," Merryn said tartly. "How are you?"

Tom grinned, his teeth a flash of white in his face. "You know I have no manners."

"Clearly," Merryn said. She looked at him. No one would mistake Tom Bradshaw for anything other than what he was: the self-made son of a working man. The well-cut clothes could not conceal his innate toughness.

"No," she said. She turned her face away. "I didn't find anything."

Three weeks previously Tom had come to her with some information that he had said he thought would interest her and when she had read it the shock and outrage had gripped Merryn like a vise. Tom's information had been a tiny entry from an obscure local Dorset newspaper. He said that he had found it quite by accident when he had been working on a different case. The paper was twelve years old and there, between references to pig rustling and theft at a country fair, had been the report of an inquest into the death of Stephen Fenner.

Merryn could remember the piece word for word. She thought she would never forget it.

"The coroner at the inquest into the death of Stephen, Viscount Fenner, reported that there had been two bullets in the victim's body, one in the shoulder and one in the back…" And then, farther down the page: "Daniel Scrope, gamekeeper on the Starcross estate, reported hearing an altercation followed by the firing of three shots…"

Merryn shook a little now as she remembered how she had frozen where she had sat, her gaze riveted to the tiny shred of news that contradicted all the official reports of her brother's death. Before he had fled the country to escape the exigencies of the law, Garrick Farne had left a statement giving details of the duel. He had sworn that it had occurred over the elopement of his best friend, Stephen Fenner, with Kitty, Garrick's wife of only a month. Two shots had been fired, Farne had maintained, one by Stephen, who had missed, and the other by himself, which had proved fatal. The doctor and the two men's seconds had supported his statement. Farne's second had even claimed that Fenner had fired early, an unforgivable piece of cowardice further blackening Stephen's name.

The case had never gone to trial and public opinion had been very sympathetic to Garrick Farne. He and Kitty had been married for barely a month. Stephen Fenner had clearly played his best friend false, seducing Garrick's wife, trying to entice her to run off with him and compounding his deceit by attempting to kill Garrick by firing before the flag was dropped. Besides, a duel was an affair of honor and society understood the rules that governed such cases. Garrick Farne was generally felt to have acted regrettably but understandably.

That had been appalling enough to Merryn, unforgivable, heinous, but when she had discovered that there had been three shots and two bullets in Stephen's body, she had been consumed with grief and anger. Garrick Farne had lied, there had been no duel, only an execution, and he should have hanged for murder. She had hated Garrick before, hated what he had done, despaired over the way his actions had wrought such unhappiness and ruin on her family. Now, though, her anger was transformed. If the truth had been buried she would dig it out. She would show the world that Garrick was a liar and a criminal, and she would strip him of all honor and respect. She would find the proof that would mean his life was forfeit.

Merryn had searched like a woman possessed to find any other evidence such as the original inquest report, the findings of the doctor who had conducted it, the original witness statements of the seconds who had allegedly been present at what she now suspected was a fictitious duel. She had drawn a blank. All papers were lost. All witnesses had vanished. Merryn had been disillusioned but hardly surprised. She knew that the Dukes of Farne were rich enough and powerful enough to pay their way out of such a scandal. But she could not give up now. If there were the slightest chance that she could prove that Garrick Farne had killed her brother in cold blood then she would expose him. She wanted him to lose everything that had been built on his lie. She had lost so much when Garrick had killed Stephen. She wanted him to understand how that felt.

"You found nothing," Tom repeated. He was looking annoyed, so irritated, in fact, that Merryn wondered if he might secretly have a client interested in her findings. It seemed unlikely but not impossible.

"You did search everywhere?" Tom persisted.

Merryn frowned. "Of course I searched everywhere. I'm not an amateur. I looked in the study, the library, the bedrooms—"

"In the bedrooms?" Tom said.

"I thought there might be papers concealed in a book," Merryn said.

Tom gave her a quizzical look. "I repeat, in the bedrooms?"

"People read in bed," Merryn said, a shade defensively.

"Do they?" Tom seemed surprised. "I don't. I have more exciting things to do."

Merryn rolled her eyes. "You and Garrick Farne both."

Tom raised his brows. "What?"

"I was under the bed," Merryn said, "when the Duke had a visitor. A voluptuous and eager lady called Harriet."

Tom pursed his lips on a soundless whistle. "Harriet Knight, his late father's ward?"

"I have no idea," Merryn said tartly. There was a squirm of something in her belly that felt disconcertingly like...*jealousy?* "They were obviously beyond needing surnames," she added.

"Poor you," Tom said. "There's nothing worse than voyeurism."

"I'll take your word for it," Merryn said. "Fortunately he threw her out before things became too embarrassing for me."

Tom started to laugh. "Farne threw an eager seductress out of his bedchamber?" he said. "He really has changed. I assume you were able to get away when he fell asleep?"

"No," Merryn said. She hesitated. It probably was not wise to tell Tom of her encounter with Garrick Farne. He would be furious because she had compromised not only her own safety but also his business. If Garrick were to discover her identity somehow and start asking questions he would discover that she worked for Tom and a powerful enemy like the Duke of Farne would be very dangerous for Tom's livelihood. Besides, she was not sure she wished to relive the encounter. The unexpected affinity she had felt for Garrick, the pleasure of their quick-fire conversation, the sweetness that had ambushed her when his lips had touched hers in that infinitely tender caress… She had not expected to feel any of those emotions. She should not.

Tom was watching her. He was quick; he'd seen her hesitation.

"Well?" he said.

"Unfortunately I sneezed," Merryn said, "and he dragged me out from under the bed."

Tom's reaction was predictable. There was a moment of silence and then he exploded. "Bloody hell, Merryn—"

"I know," Merryn said hastily. "But I didn't tell him who I was, or what I was doing there. You don't need to worry. He doesn't know I work for you. No one does."

Tom clenched his fists. "Merryn," he said, "the work you do is supposed to be secret. The clue is in the word."

"Of course," Merryn said quickly. "Sorry—"

Tom made a visible effort to get himself under control. He rubbed his forehead. "I warned you it was dangerous to go there," he said. "I told you to be careful."

"I *was*," Merryn said defensively. "It was just bad luck."

Tom gave a sigh. "Well, you have not been hauled up in Bow Street so evidently you got away," he said. His tone had eased a little. He even managed to give her a half smile. "Did you kick him in the balls and run away?"

"Something of the sort," Merryn said. She wondered how she had managed to retain any shred of innocence associating with Tom Bradshaw. Her vocabulary had certainly been broadened, if nothing else.

Merryn had never been quite sure how she and Tom had come to be as close as brother and sister. She had first met him three years before when he had broken into a house where she was staying. She had found him rifling through her host's study and had held him at sword point—there had been a medieval claymore on the wall—until he had revealed to her that the purpose of his illicit visit was to reunite the government with some very sensitive papers pertaining to the war. She had been frankly intrigued by Bradshaw's business and had thought it would be the perfect line of work to get into. She had a passion for justice, too little money, too much time and nothing to do that remotely interested her. Being a debutante was a tedious business; all the men she met wanted blandness in a woman, a pattern-card wife. Merryn, in contrast, did not want a man at all. She had never met one she preferred to her favorite books.

Tom had laughed at first when she had sought him out at his office and proposed that she work for him. Then he had remembered the claymore. And she had pointed out that she had the entrée into houses that he had to burgle. She could attend balls and routs, speak to people that he could not approach. They had been a partnership ever since.

Tom walked across to a side table that held a dusty crystal decanter and matching glasses. He gestured to them. Merryn shook her head. She was never quite sure what was in Tom's decanter and suspected that it was villainously bad sherry. Tom poured for himself, took a mouthful and then looked back at her.

"It might be better if you drop this whole matter," he said abruptly. "When I first found the reference I thought that you had a right to know the truth but now—" He shrugged uncomfortably. "I think it could get us all into trouble."

"No!" Merryn said. She felt panicked. "It was an accident, Tom. I promise to be more discreet in the future."

Tom did not answer for a moment. He sat down, placed his glass gently on the desk and leaned forward. "I think your determination to find out the truth leads you to take risks we cannot afford because you are obsessed with exposing Garrick Farne," he said. "It is not only dangerous." He took a breath. "It is unhealthy, Merryn. You should let it go."

Merryn wrapped her arms about herself. She felt chilled and her stomach lurched a little with sickness. She always felt like that when she thought about her brother Stephen and the fate Garrick Farne had meted out to him. The scandalous shadow had dogged her steps for over a decade. She had been thirteen when Stephen had died and it had felt as though the sun had gone out. Everything had changed, every keepsake of Stephen lost when the estate was sold, every link with him wiped out. Stephen had blazed across her life like a wayward star and when Garrick Farne had extinguished that light her whole life had been plunged into darkness. The grief had been like a punch, leaving her stunned with the force of the blow.

"It's not just about Stephen's death," she said. She rested a hand against the window glass. It felt cold beneath her fingers. Down in the alleyway below, two ragged children were playing with a hoop. "We lost our father as well, and our home. We had nothing left. Papa went into a decline and died because he was so broken to have lost his heir."

"Then he should have valued his daughters more," Tom said grimly. "He was a fortunate man to have other children, yet he did not appreciate it." He looked at her. "I do wonder, though," he added, "if your recollection of that time is quite accurate, Merryn. You were only a child—"

"I was thirteen," Merryn said. Her stomach did a giddy little swoop. "Old enough to remember everything."

She turned away so that Tom could not see her face. She had known exactly what had been going on between her brother and the newly wed Kitty Farne because she was the one who had carried their clandestine messages. She was the one who had led Stephen to his death. The old guilt stirred and she shuddered sharply, slamming the door to block out the memories and the pain. It was not her fault. She had never intended it to end in murder. She had to remember that she was not the one who had pulled the trigger and taken Stephen's life.

"You sound guilty," Tom said, frowning at her. "Why on earth—"

"Spare me your analysis," Merryn snapped, angry that he had been acute enough to pick up on her feelings. "I don't feel any guilt. Why should I? Farne was the one who killed Stephen. And if he did that in cold blood rather than in a duel then he has even less honor than I had thought and he deserves everyone to know it. This isn't just about revenge, Tom. It's about *justice*…" She stopped, gasping for breath.

There was a silence in the little room. "I'm sorry," Tom said. "I accept that Garrick Farne's actions were far-reaching." There was a note of impatience in his voice now. He pushed his chair back from the desk. "But I still think your feelings affect your judgment, Merryn." He gave a quick shake of the head. "I don't know… I suppose that I cannot stop you pursuing Farne if you choose since it is not an official case."

"No," Merryn said, "it is not. But I think that you have an interest in it all the same. I've thought so from the beginning."

Tom looked startled. "Why do you say that?"

"Because I know you," Merryn said. "Don't prevaricate with me, Tom. Is there a client?"

Tom stared at her for a moment and then shook his

head. "I cannot tell you anything," he said. "Client confidentiality—"

Merryn made an exasperated sound. "Tom!"

"Oh, very well," Tom said. He moved the files around on his desk. "There is someone who is interested," he said. "One of Farne's brothers. There is no love lost there."

"One of Garrick Farne's brothers wants to see him hanged?" Merryn pressed. She had known that Garrick was estranged from most of his family but still she was shocked. "Why on earth…"

Tom shrugged. "I don't ask questions like that. I simply take the money. But you see…" He paused, looked at her. "That is another reason why we cannot afford for Farne to know."

"I understand," Merryn said.

Tom ran a hand through his hair. "It is a pity that Farne saw you. He may start asking awkward questions. And he's a dangerous man to cross. He worked for the War Office for years when he was in exile."

"As a translator," Merryn said dismissively. "It's hardly the front line."

"It is when you are translating between the British and the Spanish guerrillas," Tom said dryly. "One might as well live on a powder keg. Farne was, and still is, a famed swordsman, a crack shot—" He stopped. "Sorry, that was tactless of me." He opened a drawer in his desk and took out a file.

"I have found out a little more information," he said.

"I checked out the seconds at the so-called duel. Farne's second was a man called Gabriel Finch. He went to Australia as a curate. And your brother's second was Chuffy Wallington and we all know what happened to him."

"He drank himself to death," Merryn said. "I remember Chuffy. He was a frightful soak."

"Easily bought off, I expect," Tom said. "As for the doctor, he is locked up in the Fleet prison for debt. I might well pay him a discreet visit."

"I'll go," Merryn said. "He will be more likely to talk to me."

"Possibly not," Tom said, "when he knows who you are." He closed the file softly. "I have to admit," he said, "that it looks very bad for Farne. Three shots, two bullets, one in the back... Reports suppressed and rewritten, witnesses disappearing, no doubt paid off... And he runs away abroad and then his father fixes it all with the authorities so that he never has to stand trial and can come home a decade later with everything forgiven and forgotten..." Tom shook his head. He paused. "Perhaps we should reconsider. We're stirring up a lot of trouble. All this was buried years ago. People won't like it."

Merryn shivered. A little ripple of anticipation mingled with apprehension fluttered down her spine.

"I'm not giving up now," she said. "I want to know the truth and I want Farne to face justice. But if he finds out..."

If Farne finds out there will be hell to pay...

She remembered the ruthlessness she had sensed in

Garrick Farne the moment she saw him. Tom had been right: he was no ineffectual scholar, he was a man with a dangerous past.

Tom was watching her face.

"You had better make sure he does not find out," he said, "but if you are too scared to do it—"

His tone was all the incentive Merryn needed.

"No," she said. "No, I will do it. It will be my pleasure."

CHAPTER THREE

"I HAVE FOUND YOU an inquiry agent, your grace, Hammond by name." Pointer, his nose twitching in a manner that indicated that he could not quite believe how low he had stooped, stood back to allow the ingress of a man into the library at Farne House. The late autumn evening was already drawing in, darkness dropping over the streets of London and creeping into the room. Garrick had forced himself to work for another four hours on the Farne estate papers, acquainting himself with all the dependents on the Dukedom, all the pensions to be paid, the widows and orphans, the servants, estate workers, the whole panoply of his fiefdom. It was terrifying how many people depended upon him.

Despite the presence of a full branch of candles the room looked gloomy and bare, the bookshelves standing like sentinels. Garrick stood up and stretched, only now aware of how stiff he had become poring over the books for hours on end. He shook the newcomer by the hand and gestured him to a chair. The long mirror that stretched along one wall reflected back their images. It was easy to see why Pointer disapproved, Garrick thought. In the butler's eyes the visitor would be categorized as most definitely not a gentleman. There was about him an indefinable air of seediness. It seemed soaked into his person, from the battered hat he held in his hand to the world-weary expression in his deep-set gray eyes to the cut of his clothes. He was the type of man Garrick had met on many occasions in his work in the Peninsular—the fixer, the intelligence man, for sale to the highest bidder, exactly the man Garrick needed now.

"Mr. Hammond," he said. "How do you do?"

"Your grace." The man did not bow. It was more a meeting of equals, Garrick thought. He needed a service Hammond could provide and the inquiry agent saw no need to be deferential.

"A drink?" Garrick offered. "Brandy?"

"Not on duty, thank you, your grace."

That, Garrick thought, argued a certain discipline. He nodded. "You will excuse me if I do?"

Hammond's smile indicated that he recognized this was merely a courtesy. He sat in one of the large wing chairs before the fire, his hat on his knee, politely waiting for Garrick to state his business. Garrick poured for himself—no sense in summoning Pointer simply to perform that function, although no doubt the butler would feel he should have preserved the formalities—and took the chair opposite, crossing one ankle over the other. Mr. Hammond raised an interrogative brow. Garrick paused, chose his words with care.

"I need you to find a lady for me, Mr. Hammond."

Hammond snapped open a notebook with such alacrity Garrick jumped.

"Is she lost, your grace?"

"No," Garrick said. "What I should have said is that I need you to *identify* a lady for me."

"Ah," Hammond said. "Semantics."

"Quite," Garrick said, warming to him. "There is a lady I have met, I do not know her name and I want you to find her and tell me who she is."

Hammond nodded. "Description?"

"Small, fair-haired, blue-eyed…" Garrick struggled. *A pocket goddess, beautifully rounded, soft, smooth skin, vivid blue eyes, hair like a tumble of golden corn…*

Get a grip on yourself, he ordered himself.

"Age?" Hammond's sharp gray gaze was unblinking.

"Twenty-five," Garrick said, "or so she told me."

Hammond nodded. "And you met…"

"Here," Garrick said. "She broke into my house last night. Or rather," he corrected himself, "I believe she might have been staying here for a little time."

"Lady Merryn Fenner," Hammond said.

Garrick blinked. "I beg your pardon?"

"Lady Merryn Fenner," the inquiry agent repeated. "Sister to Joanna, Lady Grant, and Teresa, Lady Darent, and daughter of the late Earl of Fenner. Your grace."

Lady Merryn Fenner.

Garrick felt as though someone had emptied a bucket of ice down his back. The woman he lusted for, the wraith who haunted his thoughts, was Stephen Fenner's youngest sister. In a flash he remembered the initials in the copy of *Mansfield Park,* the entwined *M* and *F.* He remembered her eyes and saw the vivid blue of Stephen's.

"How the devil," he said slowly, "did you know? There must be a hundred small, fair, twenty-five-year-old ladies in London. Two hundred. A thousand."

Hammond permitted himself a small, wintry smile that was nevertheless full of satisfaction. "Aye, your grace. Normally it would take me—" he paused "—oh, at least a day to come up with that information. But Lady Merryn Fenner works for Tom Bradshaw and we like to keep an eye on his business." He waited, then as Garrick looked blank: "Bradshaw the inquiry agent, your grace. A rival company." For a moment Garrick thought Hammond was about to spit but he clearly thought better of it in the ducal library. "Bradshaw's a cocky fellow," Hammond said. "Smooth as you like, but bent as a guinea note. A good job you didn't approach him with your inquiry, sir. He would have taken your money and spun you a line."

Garrick frowned. Oddly the thought of his midnight visitor working for a corrupt inquiry agent filled him with a strange sense of protectiveness. Merryn Fenner had seemed too innocent and too honest to be mixed up in crooked business. But clearly his instinct about her was wildly astray. She had broken into his house, after all, had been searching his library and his study and his bedroom. She was not a sheltered debutante. She was a burglar and very possibly a thief.

"So you knew," Garrick said slowly, "that Lady Merryn Fenner had broken in here last night because you were watching her?"

"One of my men reported it," Hammond said. "She's been here every night for the past five days."

Five days. Sleeping in his bed.

Garrick thought of the slide of the sheet against his body and Merryn's scent enveloping him, soft, sensuous, seductive.

Five days. Searching his papers.

She had nerve. He would give her that. He thought about what Lady Merryn Fenner might be hunting at Farne House. The conclusion was inescapable. The connection between the two of them was her brother. The object of her search therefore must be something to do with Stephen's death.

He got to his feet abruptly and strode over to the fire, stirring it to flame with his booted foot. The logs settled with a hiss.

He had feared this for twelve years. His father had told him that the matter was settled, all witnesses paid off, all evidence destroyed, all those who needed protection kept safe. The Earl of Fenner, Kitty's father Lord Scott, and the Duke of Farne had buried the matter so deep they had believed it could never be revived. Manifestly, however, that was not true. Something—or someone— had started to stir matters up. It could be Merryn Fenner herself, he supposed, embittered over her brother's death, bearing him an understandable and very real grudge. Or there could be more to this, someone else behind it, someone pulling Merryn's strings perhaps. For the sake of all those who depended on him, he had to find out.

He turned to Hammond, who had been watching him gravely and in silence.

"This Bradshaw," he said. "What do you know about him?"

Hammond laughed. "That he's a bad lot. Brought up on the streets, knows the rookeries like the back of his hand. Made a bit of money—best not ask how—set himself up in business, not too fussy about the cases he takes if the payment is right." He shrugged. "Rough, tough…"

"Dangerous to know?" Garrick said ironically.

"Without a doubt, your grace."

Garrick pulled a face. There was no immediately obvious reason why Tom Bradshaw should be interested in a twelve-year-old duel so perhaps Merryn Fenner really was the instigator in this.

"I need to know where Lady Merryn plans to be tomorrow," he said. Then, as Hammond nodded, "and I need to know more about Tom Bradshaw. Anything you think might be useful."

"Aye, your grace," the man said.

"Thank you, Hammond," Garrick said. "You have proved yourself invaluable."

Hammond grinned. It was startling and not particularly pretty. "Bradshaw thinks he's the best," the man said with satisfaction. "But he ain't."

"Of course, if Bradshaw spies on you as you spy on him," Garrick said gently, "he will know all about our meeting."

After Pointer had shown the inquiry agent out, disapproval in every quivering line of his body, Garrick went back to the desk and took out the papers relating to the Fenner estate, weighing them in his hand. Merryn Fenner would know that his father had profiteered from her brother's death by buying up the family estate. It would be another reason for her to hate everything that the name of Farne stood for.

Tomorrow, he thought, he would seek Merryn out. He would find out what she knew and what she intended to do. He swore softly under his breath. Merryn Fenner had been determined and passionate and, he would wager, a total innocent. There was no more dangerous combination than honesty and passion when it came to someone set on discovering the truth. And he could never allow that truth to come to light.

MERRYN SMOOTHED DOWN her plain blue pelisse and took a slightly tighter grip on the worn leather handle of her briefcase. This afternoon she was very much in her own character, bluestocking and avid student of literature. She had arranged to visit the Octagon Library to peruse the catalog of periodicals in the collection. Alongside his extensive collections of classical, English and Italian literature, King George III had a rather less august selection of newspapers and periodicals. It was in one such obscure publication that Merryn hoped to find another reference to her brother's death that might bear out the details in the Dorset newspaper Tom had found. Most reports she had read reported the official line on the duel but one or two might have written the truth—before the Farne family clamped down, suppressed the real version of events and paid off anyone who might have proved awkward.

"This way please, madam," the clerk said respectfully, gesturing her through a doorway on the right and into the most marvelous library she had ever seen. "Sir Frederick will be with you shortly."

The room was magnificent. Light fell from windows high in the octagonal white dome of the ceiling. On all eight walls the bookshelves stretched above head height with a wrought-iron balcony and further shelves on the first floor. Merryn had never seen quite such an impressive library. If she browsed for years she knew she could never be sated.

Sir Frederick Barnard, the King's librarian, came over to shake her by the hand and lead her across to a seat at the center table. She had already written to ask for permission to scrutinize the catalog and she saw that it was now laid out in front of her. Sir Frederick explained how the entries were compiled then left her to leaf through at her leisure. A deep peace settled over the room, the sort of reflective silence that one found in libraries, broken only by the rustle of pages and the soft footfall as Sir Frederick or one of his clerks trod quietly across from one shelf to another.

After about ten minutes, however, a gentleman took the seat opposite Merryn. He was tall and broad, no dandy but elegant enough in a plain jacket and pristine buckskins. His hair, an unusual dark red, was disordered by the wind rather than the ministrations of his valet, and as she watched he raised a hand and smoothed it down. Then he looked up and his eyes met hers. They were deep brown eyes and so dark that they were unreadable.

Garrick Farne. The Duke of Farne was here, in the King's Library.

Merryn's heart stuttered for an instant and then began to race. She tilted her head down deliberately so that the rim of her bonnet sheltered her face from view. She knew that she had blushed. Or perhaps she had turned pale; she was not sure which, only that she felt hot even though her fingers seemed icy cold. Her hands shook a little, sending the precious documents scattering to the floor. A soft-footed clerk came forward to retrieve them and she murmured an apology. She had to compose herself. This was foolish, to be disturbed simply because Garrick Farne was sitting opposite her. He could not possibly know that she was the woman who had been in his bedroom two nights ago. Then she had been covered in dust and cobwebs. He had not even been able to see if she were young or old. That was the beauty of her indeterminate appearance. She was completely unmemorable.

And if he challenged her she had simply to deny it. She was Lady Merryn Fenner. She did not disport herself in men's bedrooms in the dead of night.

Even so, it was the first time that anyone had come close to unmasking her and she felt anxious. Her fingers slipped and slid on the parchment and she found it unconscionably difficult to concentrate. She could walk out, of course. She could simply get to her feet, tell the librarian that she had a headache and would return on another occasion. Except that that would look odd given that she had been there only five minutes. And it was poor-spirited, and she was no such thing. She, Merryn Fenner, was scared of nobody and nothing. Gentlemen of the ton, in particular, held neither fascination nor danger for her. She had their measure. They never discomposed her. Only this man, with his perceptive gaze and his effortlessly authoritative presence, seemed to be able to disturb her, and that was only because for the past twelve years he had haunted her thoughts, and now that she knew that he had lied about her brother's death she wanted to take from him everything he had—friends, reputation, respect.

She tried not to look at Garrick and found it disturbingly difficult. How had he known she would be at the Octagon Library today? It could be no coincidence. He was already a step ahead of her. A horrid thought struck her. Perhaps Garrick had gone to an inquiry agent

like Tom and asked them to identify her. Merryn had
no illusions about the sort of information that could be
bought—or suppressed, for that matter—with enough
money. She had seen it happen time and again.

She risked a glance at Garrick underneath the brim
of her hat and then wished that she had not. He was not
reading. His book lay discarded to one side, his quill
idle on the desk.

He was watching her.

His gaze was thoughtful as it rested on her. It felt
oddly as though he were studying her, learning her by
heart. His eyes moved over her features, one by one:
her hair, beneath the dowdy blue bonnet, the curve of
her cheek, her mouth. He seemed to pause there for an
inordinate amount of time and Merryn felt tightness in
her chest and a constriction in her breathing. Her skin
felt too sensitive, prickling from his nearness. It was odd
and disconcerting. She kept her gaze on the page in front
of her although the words danced before her eyes and
made no sense. She knew even with her eyes averted that
he was still watching her; she could feel his gaze like
a physical touch, stroking her cheek, sliding along the
smooth line of her jaw, brushing her lips like a kiss.

She caught her breath on the thought and, unable to
resist the unspoken demand he was making, she looked
up and met his eyes.

He was not looking at her at all. He was writing with
every appearance of concentration. And as Merryn
drew back, frowning a little, her body still humming

with awareness, he glanced up and caught her staring. He raised one brow in a quizzical way Merryn could only categorize as insolent. A small smile tilted the corners of his firm mouth, a smile of such masculine self-satisfaction that she wanted to slap him.

Her face flaming, she bent furiously over the periodicals again. The *Dorchester Advertiser,* the *Bournemouth Intelligencer…* Not a single reference to Stephen's death. It was as though he had been eradicated completely, as though he had never existed. She felt enraged. There was nothing for her here.

Then she had a thought, a flash of an idea. She turned back to the London periodicals for July 1802 with their record of routs and parties, events and guest lists. The season had been ending, the last glittering balls taking place before town emptied for the summer. And there on the guest list for a dinner at Lord and Lady Denman's house on the night of July 25 was Chuffy Wallington, Stephen's friend, the man who was supposed to have been his second at the fateful duel, who could not possibly have been in Dorset during the afternoon yet at a dinner in London that same evening…

Merryn's hand shook so much as she scribbled down the details that her writing was barely legible. She closed the book carefully and got to her feet. She felt exhausted, her head aching. It was only a tiny scrap of evidence but it felt monumental to her, another fragment in the jigsaw that painted a very different picture of the events on the day of Stephen's death.

She shuffled the papers together and got to her feet, placing the precious piece of paper in her pocket.

"I apologize," she said to the hovering clerk. "I fear that I cannot concentrate further this morning. I will call to arrange another appointment. Good day and thank you for your assistance."

She turned to go. Garrick Farne had not moved, not shown by one flicker of a muscle that he had even noticed her departure. Merryn slapped her gloves into the palm of her other hand and stalked toward the door. She resisted the urge to look back at Garrick even though she was sure he was watching her. Her nape tickled with awareness and the goose bumps rose over her whole body.

She was within three feet of the door when Garrick stepped out from behind the nearest bookcase and directly into her path.

NOW THAT SHE WAS CLEAN and it was daylight, Garrick could see that Lady Merryn Fenner was everything that he had imagined the previous night. She was a perfect miniature, tiny, blonde, beautiful. And she had the most vivid blue eyes that he had ever seen. There was something fierce in them, a challenge that was curiously at odds with the shabby bluestocking garb she wore. Her strength of character and intense spirit made a mockery of the dull blue gown, the dowdy bonnet and the demure gloves and reticule. They were just local color, disguise even. Garrick could see through her at once. She was not a simple society miss.

She had told him the previous night that she was five and twenty. It surprised him. He thought she looked younger. She was a good actress, he thought. That night in his bedroom she had looked small and defenseless, like the waif from the streets she claimed to be. He had been halfway to believing her story that she was homeless and in need of shelter. Had it not been for the cut-glass accent and the high quality of her gown he might have fallen for the lie. She was like quicksilver, changeable, slipping through his fingers. She had run from him before. This time, though, she would not escape.

He could see that she had absolutely no desire to speak with him. The stiffness with which she held herself and her furtive glances toward the nearest exit told him she wanted nothing more than to flee. That was understandable. And this was not, perhaps, the best place to force a confrontation, in the august surroundings of the King's Library, with the King's librarian and his assistants watching avidly from behind a stack of books. But that was too bad. He could not risk her running out on him again.

Her scent, that elusive fragrance of bluebells, wrapped about him and made his body clench with longing. Even without Hammond's information Garrick thought that he would have known at once that she was the woman he had found in his bedroom, the woman who had slept in his bed, an intimacy that had haunted his thoughts ever since. He could picture Merryn between his sheets all too easily, her slight, lissom body lying where his had lain, her hair spread across his pillow, and her bare skin against the cool linen. He felt as though she had somehow imprinted herself on him and he could not break free.

She was looking at him with impatience and disdain, as though he was some importunate suitor or writer of particularly bad sonnets.

"I wanted to apologize," he said easily, "in case I was the cause of your distraction this morning."

He saw her bite her lip and knew that she was caught between the desire to give him a set down for his presumption and the equally strong desire to cut him dead and run away. The latter urge won out.

"I am sorry," she said, "that it is quite impossible for me to talk to a gentleman to whom I have not been formally introduced. Excuse me."

She made to pass him but Garrick put a hand on her arm. He lowered his voice and spoke softly in her ear. "Some might say that our informal introduction—in my bedroom two nights ago—would suffice as a basis for our acquaintance."

He saw that she was a little shocked at his direct approach. No doubt she had not expected him to be quite so blunt. Gentlemen, generally, did not speak so frankly to a lady. Her body stiffened, her blue gaze narrowed. Her perfect bow of a mouth pursed in a way that made Garrick want to kiss her. The urge hit him hard, squarely in the stomach. He felt as though the breath had been knocked from his lungs, felt a hot pull of desire that went straight to his head and also lower down as well.

Something of his feelings must have shown in his face for he saw the blue of Merryn's eyes heat and intensify for a moment as though responding to his need. Her lips parted on a tiny, startled gasp. He took a step forward, narrowing the distance between them to nothing. But already she was retreating, slipping away, the shimmer of desire in her eyes banished by cold disdain.

"I beg your pardon," she said, "but I think you mistake me for quite another lady." There was the slightest emphasis on the word *lady*. "I am not the sort of woman to be found in any man's bedchamber. That would be most inappropriate."

She turned toward the door again and Garrick leaned one hand against the jamb to bar her way. "You ran away last time," he said. "You are not going to do so now."

Her blue eyes flashed ice. "I do not take direction from you, your grace."

"So you do at least know who I am," Garrick said gently. "I thought you were claiming that we had never met?"

She looked irritated to have been caught out. "I heard Sir Frederick mention your name, that is all."

Garrick smiled. "How disappointing to discover that you did not deliberately seek to learn my identity," he murmured.

She flicked him a look of polite scorn. "I am sure that your grace's self-confidence will survive the blow."

"I know your name, too," Garrick said. "You are Lady Merryn Fenner."

Now there was no doubting her dismay. She stiffened. Her lips pressed together in annoyance. Then she raised her chin and looked him straight in the eyes. She did not deny it.

"I am," she said. "I am Merryn Fenner."

Garrick admired both her frankness and her intellect. In that second she had evidently weighed up the fact that he knew her true identity and she had decided that there was nothing to be gained in denying it. Garrick doubted, however, that he had won anything beyond that one point. Merryn Fenner, he was beginning to suspect, would be a stimulating adversary.

There was a silence, as though she was waiting for him to say something. Garrick wondered if she expected him to apologize. He regretted Stephen Fenner's death every day but any conventional words of condolence would seem at best hollow, at worst hypocritical. And he doubted that any words of his would make the slightest difference to Merryn's feelings. He had killed Stephen. She hated him for it. He could tell. He could feel the emotion in her, heated, dark, driven.

"What were you doing in my house?" he asked. "Were you telling the truth when you said you were homeless? Sleeping on the streets? Forced to take shelter where you can?"

For a moment his imagination presented him with appalling scenes of the Fenner girls destitute because of his actions all those years before. He had known that the Earl had died a bare year after his son and heir but he had not known what had happened to the daughters. He had been living in exile then, trying to come to terms with the fact that he had failed to save Kitty from the demons and the misery that had haunted her, trying to die in the service of his country and salvage some honor from disaster.

Merryn Fenner was looking at him thoughtfully with those blue, blue eyes. "It is true that my sisters and I lost our fortunes after our father died," she said, and the guilt that stalked Garrick's footsteps tugged at him again.

"But that is not the reason that I...borrowed...your bed," she finished. She turned away slightly, picking up a book from the stack on the table beside them, absently fingering the spine. "I was making a point." She cast him a glance under her lashes. "Farne House is defenseless, your grace, easily taken." Her voice was soft. If it had been anyone else Garrick would have thought she was making idle conversation but when she looked up and met his gaze her eyes were fierce. "You should be careful," she said, "that your secrets are not so... vulnerable."

Garrick straightened, his eyes narrowing. It was extraordinary that the conversation had moved so swiftly. Lady Merryn Fenner wasted no time. And she was very open in her hostility to him. He suspected that it was because she felt so strongly. He had met men who were as direct but seldom a woman. And with Merryn there was something else, some powerful bond between them that was as undeniable as it was unexpected. Perhaps it had been kindled by her hatred of him, but whatever the cause, it burned in her like a cold flame.

"Are you threatening me, Lady Merryn?" he asked slowly.

"I would do nothing so vulgar as to make threats." She gave him a proper smile this time. It lit her eyes, making them even more spectacular. "I am warning you," she said, "that those matters you thought were long buried are going to come out into the light and then…" She shrugged. "Well, you risk losing many of the things that you value, I think."

"And what do you think that I value?" Garrick asked.

He saw the tiny frown that touched her forehead as she realized that she did not actually know, that she had made assumptions. "Your title? Your fortune?" she hazarded. "Your life?"

"Your title, your fortune, your life…"

Garrick cared little for the Dukedom, beyond the fact that he had a responsibility to all the people who served it. He had often wished it away, thought that one of his younger brothers would have relished the role so much more than he, would have sat in the House of Lords and reveled in his own pomp. As for his fortune, it enabled him to do the things that he wanted and it would be an ungrateful man who did not value that. It also enabled him to protect those who needed him. And then there was his life… He smiled ironically. After Stephen Fenner had died he had thought his life worth nothing. He had tried to discard it on many occasions. He could find nothing to do with it, no matter how he tried. He wondered sometimes if that was his penance for killing a man—that no matter how he tried to atone, nothing would seem good enough, no purpose great enough.

"Do you intend to take those things from me?" he asked now. "Do you seek my death? Because I killed your brother and ruined your life?"

Merryn did not flinch at his deliberately brutal choice of words. She put the book back on the pile very precisely. "Yes," she said. "I loved my brother and I believe that he deserves justice." For a moment Garrick saw her glacial coolness splinter into a thousand tiny fragments of pain. "I want to take everything away from you, your grace," she said. "We lost everything because of you. You deserve to know how that feels."

Garrick kept his eyes on her face. "What do you intend to do?" he asked.

She raised her brows. "I intend to find out the truth," she said. "I know there was no duel. I know you shot Stephen in cold blood. I am going to find out what really happened and then…" She stopped and Garrick wondered if she really had the hardihood to go through with it, to see him hang. He saw her swallow hard, saw a tremor go through her.

"And then you will hand the evidence to the authorities and watch me swing on the end of a silken rope," he said.

Her gaze jerked up. "I..." She blinked. Her gaze locked with his. There was confusion in the depths of her eyes. She looked very young. Garrick felt the most enormous compassion for her. Merryn Fenner was brave and she was honest and she wanted justice and he admired that. But he also knew that if the truth came out she would be horribly disillusioned, all her memories tarnished and her life in ruins once again. Besides, there were others who deserved justice, too, others he had sworn to protect on that terrible day that Stephen had died. He could not permit Merryn to expose them to all the horror that the truth would bring.

"You won't find any evidence," Garrick said, and saw the softness fade from her eyes to be replaced by triumph.

"I already have," she said. For a moment her hand slid to her pocket in a brief, betraying gesture. "I have several pieces of evidence already and I will amass more. You may be sure of it."

The only thing that Garrick was sure of was that he had to know what she had discovered and he had to stop her. It was fortunate, he thought, that he had not lost all of his rake's instincts. Without any warning he pulled the ribbons of her bonnet and pushed it back off her head. She gave a little squeak of surprise, a squeak that was muffled against his mouth as he put an arm around her waist and drew her in for a ruthless kiss. Her lips parted on a gasp, opening beneath his. It was the response of an innocent who had never been kissed before. So he had been correct in his initial judgment of her—despite her somewhat unorthodox lifestyle Merryn Fenner was untouched. The realization shot Garrick through with a bolt of lust.

He made no concessions to her inexperience. The kiss was deep, irresistible, a possession. He slid his tongue into her mouth and felt her give a tiny groan. Garrick felt her heat and her response and for a moment he was so overwhelmed that he almost forgot what he was supposed to be doing. His world narrowed to the woman in his arms, the taste and the scent of her, the need to claim her with a primitive desire that all but shattered his control.

He pulled himself back from the brink, released her gently and watched as she opened her eyes. They were a deep, unfocused blue. She pressed her fingers to her lips. They looked plush and red and slightly swollen from his kisses. Garrick's body tightened further. On one level the kiss had not been the wisest move since it had inflamed his already heated desire for her. On another he had achieved exactly what he had set out to do.

Merryn looked dizzy. Then she blinked the dizziness away and a look of fury came into her eyes.

"I've never been kissed before," she snapped, "and I certainly didn't want you to be the first."

"I would apologize," Garrick said, "but that would be dishonest of me."

She gave him another look of searing scorn and he watched as she turned and walked smartly away from him, her heels tapping furiously on the marble floor. She went out and closed the door behind her with a sharp snap. Garrick moved across to the window. Presently she appeared again in the courtyard beyond, walking briskly away from the library. She had not replaced her bonnet and the autumn sunlight fell on her silver gilt hair, spinning it into bright, dazzling threads. She was rubbing her head as though it ached. The gesture gave Garrick an odd pang of compassion. She looked very small but upright, dauntless, brave.

Garrick did not take his eyes from her and after a moment she turned and looked over her shoulder, her gaze picking him out at the window. He saw her footsteps falter. For a second their gazes locked and then she raised her chin and turned smartly on her heel, whisking around the corner of the building and out of his sight.

"Your grace?" Barnard touched his arm, recalling him to the present. He was looking, Garrick thought, as flustered as a man might when a Duke had had the bad manners to kiss a lady in the King's Library. "Your grace," the librarian repeated, red in the face, spluttering. "Is all quite well?"

"My apologies, Barnard," Garrick said smoothly. "I did not intend to cause a disturbance."

Barnard shook his head. Garrick could tell that the

librarian was torn between upbraiding him for his appalling want of conduct and the fear of upsetting one of the premier peers in the realm.

"It is no matter, your grace," Barnard spluttered eventually. "I trust there is no problem with the young lady, though? I take it she *is* a lady? She had impeccable references so I had no hesitation in agreeing to her request for access to the catalog."

Garrick almost laughed aloud. Evidently Barnard's greatest concern was that he might have admitted a woman of ill repute to the King's Library by mistake.

"Lady Merryn is a noted bluestocking and most definitely a lady," Garrick said. "The unfortunate incident—" he cleared his throat "—should not be seen as any reflection upon her moral character or indeed her suitability to be permitted to use the King's Library. I am afraid—" he tried to look appropriately penitent "—that I have a great admiration for Lady Merryn and in that moment it overwhelmed me. The fault is entirely mine."

"Well," Sir Frederick said, "I trust that it will not happen again, your grace. Such a shocking thing!"

"Absolutely not," Garrick said. "My apologies once again."

After the librarian, partially mollified, had retreated to his desk, Garrick went across to a quiet table and took a seat. He retrieved the piece of paper he had taken from Merryn's pocket in the throes of their kiss. He unfolded it.

It was an entry from the *London Chronicle* of July 26, the day after Stephen Fenner had died, and it gave the guest list for a dinner at Lord and Lady Denman's house the previous night. Garrick immediately saw the name of Chuffy Wallington and recognized the significance. He knew Merryn would have known it, too.

Garrick felt his apprehension tighten. He was sure that if he asked Sir Frederick Barnard, the librarian would confirm that Merryn was searching through all the magazines and periodicals that related to the period around her brother's death. He wondered what else she had already found. He had thought that all the reports of the Fenner scandal told the same story. He had understood that his father, the Earl of Fenner and Lord Scott had made sure of it, suppressing all other reports. But it was so easy for something to be overlooked, for a detail to slip through the cracks. All it took then was for someone like Merryn, someone passionate about justice, to dig away and discover a discrepancy and for the whole house of cards to start to fall.

Garrick could see all the careful plans starting to unravel, all the innocents he had protected being exposed to the blinding light of scandal. Could he trust Merryn Fenner with the truth? The idea had a certain appeal because he knew instinctively that Merryn was an honest person and he wanted to meet her honesty with equal openness. He dismissed the idea reluctantly. It would surely be madness to trust her when she had expressed her desire to see him ruined, swinging on the end of a silken rope. No, the only thing that he could do was to continue to protect those who needed him and try to find out just what it was that she knew. Then he had to stop her pursuing the matter any further. He felt the apprehension tighten in his gut like a vise.

Garrick tucked the piece of paper into his pocket and went out. He could still hear Merryn's voice, soft but full of accusation.

"We lost everything because of you…"

He had not defended himself against any of her allegations. He could not. In one way or another they were all true.

CHAPTER FOUR

TOM HAD FELT RESTLESS after Merryn had left to go to
the Octagon Library. He had managed to apply himself
to several hours of paperwork but after a while he had
pushed the documents aside and had wandered across
to the window and stood looking out over the tumble
of roofs stretching away to the east. The sun had gone
and now the sky was a pearly-gray and the streets were
slick with rain. The river looked sullen and dark, and
evening was already closing in. Standing here, he could
see exactly where he had come from, see St. Giles's pier
and the ships tied up for unloading, see the thicket of
alleyways and narrow passages where once he had lived.
He had come a long way; the quick, observant child had
turned his talent for pickpocketing and shoplifting into
a skill for finding items and catching people, poacher
turned gamekeeper. But he liked to work here within a
stone's throw of the Thames. It reminded him of how far
he had climbed—and how far he still had to go.

There was a knock and then the outer door of the
office flew open imperiously. Tom turned to find himself
confronting a young woman of about three and twenty,
a very beautiful young woman, tall and statuesque.

Amazonian would probably have been the word Tom would have used had he been a quarter as well read as Merryn. As he was not, and was also a man who appreciated good-looking women, his response was less intellectual and more physical.

"Mr. Bradshaw?" the woman said. Her voice was husky. It seemed to promise all manner of erotic delight. Or perhaps, Tom thought a little hazily, that was simply wishful thinking on his part. She crossed the office to him and held out a hand. Her perfume enveloped him, making his head spin. She was beautifully and expensively gowned but there was something not quite demure about her style, her skirts clinging a little too closely to her thighs, perhaps, with the material sliding over her like a seductive caress. The neckline of her gown plunged low and a diamond brooch sparkled between her breasts, accentuating the deep V-shape. Tom said the first thing that came into his head.

"You should not wear jewelry like that around here, especially after dark. You are asking to be robbed."

She laughed. She did not seem remotely offended. "Good advice," she said. She leaned closer. Tom could feel the heat of her skin. "All my jewelry is paste," she whispered. "I sold the proper stuff years ago."

A counterfeit lady in more ways than one, Tom thought. He took a step back and tried to concentrate.

"How may I help you, ma'am?" he asked.

She liked the courtesy. A small smile played about her lips. "I hear you're the best," she said.

Tom smiled back. "That depends on what you want."

Her gaze swept over him comprehensively, making her needs quite explicit. "I've yet to meet a man who did not claim to be the best at everything," she murmured.

"I'd rather be an expert in one thing than master of none," Tom said. He held the chair for her then slid behind his desk. "I don't believe you introduced yourself," he added.

Her eyes gleamed. "I prefer not to do so."

Tom shrugged. He had her measure now. She was a spoiled little rich, and possibly titled, girl, who had been indulged—or neglected—when younger and as a result had run wild. She was used to getting her own way and she was probably nowhere near as sophisticated as she pretended. He wondered what her parents or guardians were thinking to give her so much freedom to get into trouble. But then, she was not so young that she should not know better and the moral guidance of gently bred young women was not his affair.

"So how may I help you?" he repeated.

She gave him a sideways glance from slanting cat's eyes. "I...need you to find someone for me."

"Man or woman?" Tom said.

She bit her lip. "It's a child."

"Yours?" Tom asked.

Her look poured scorn. "Please! I'm not so careless."

Tom was not sure he believed her. He could quite easily see her falling from grace as a young girl and being parceled off to give birth secretly. The baby would be given away, the matter hushed up. It was a story he came across often enough, secrets and lies, his bread and butter.

"Very well then," he said. "If not yours, whose?"

"The Duke of Farne's."

Tom almost snapped his quill in half. "I beg your pardon?"

She frowned at him. "I want you to find Garrick Farne's child."

"Garrick Farne doesn't have any children," Tom said.

"Precisely." She put her head on one side, looked at him. "I thought you were supposed to be good at this?"

"All right," Tom said. "You're alleging that Garrick Farne has an illegitimate child whose existence he has suppressed—for whatever reason—and you want to find out who the child is and where he or she is?"

She inclined her head. "That is correct."

"Why?" Tom asked.

She fidgeted. "I did not think I was required to explain my reasons to you. I thought I only needed to ask. And to pay."

Strictly speaking she was correct, Tom thought. He took plenty of jobs for the money and asked no questions, but in this case he was curious.

"Humor me," he said.

She looked at him, sighed. "Look, my name is Harriet

Knight and I am—I *was*—the late Duke of Farne's ward."

So this, Tom thought, was the woman Merryn said Garrick Farne had thrown out of his bedroom. He looked at the clinging silk gown, the straining breasts and the knowing glint in her eyes. Perhaps the rumors about Farne were true, Tom thought, that he had buried his heart with his wife, that he had renounced the reckless libertinism of his youth and that he lived like a monk. A man would have to be made of stone not to have some sort of physical response to Harriet Knight.

"Why do you want to find Farne's by-blow?" he asked bluntly.

She looked at him out of the corner of her eye. "To care for him or her?"

Now it was Tom's turn. "Please!" he said. "Do I look as though I would fall for that?"

She gave him a long, slow smile. "All right. The truth is…" She paused. "I'm curious. I heard things—about an affair, about a child. When Garrick's wife died I was only young, but I was inquisitive. I used to listen at doors. And I heard the Duke, my guardian, talking about a baby, finding a place for it with a respectable family, paying them an income… Even though I was only in my teens I knew that Garrick was a terrible rake." Her eyes sparkled. "Truth to tell, it made him most frightfully attractive to me." The sparkle died. She sounded sulky. "So I thought I would like to know what happened to it, one way or the other." She sat back and looked expectantly at him.

"Why now?" Tom said. "Why wait so long to ask questions?"

Harriet shrugged. "Well, I want to know because…" She fidgeted with the clasp of her reticule, avoiding his eyes.

"You want to know because it will give you a hold of some sort over Farne," Tom said. "You want to embarrass him for some reason."

Harriet looked pained. "That's very frank." Her eyelashes fluttered. For a second she was the perfect facsimile of the delicate society debutante. "I wanted to marry Garrick," she said. "He turned me down and sent me away. He thinks I am on my way to Sussex now to stay with his mother." Her lip curled. "Do I look the sort of girl who wishes to rot in the countryside with a dowager aunt?"

"Not at all," Tom said dryly. "How unappreciative of Farne to reject you." Harriet Knight, he thought, must have wanted Garrick Farne for a very long time, probably since those teenage days when she had had a *tendre* for him. No wonder she nursed such resentment. He stood up and came round to the front of the desk. "Take my advice, Miss Knight—"

"Lady Harriet," she corrected.

Tom grinned. "Take my advice, Lady Harriet. Seeking to get back at Garrick Farne through broadcasting information about his bastard child will not give you the satisfaction you crave, nor will it persuade him to marry you."

Harriet pouted. "It would make me feel better," she said. "I like revenge."

"You'll have to stand in line," Tom muttered.

Harriet's big green eyes opened wide. "I beg your pardon?"

"Nothing," Tom said. He sighed. "Surely the best revenge would be to show Farne what he was missing? Make a spectacular marriage, run off with someone else instead of hankering after him—"

"He wouldn't care," Harriet said sulkily. "He cares for nothing. I want him to notice me."

"Well, he will surely do that if you make him the talk of the ton," Tom said dryly. He shook his head. "Lady Harriet, please reconsider—"

She shook her head, silencing him. "If you do not help me," she said, "I will simply go to someone who can."

That, Tom thought, was a problem. The information that Harriet had provided was very interesting. It might prove useful to him. Her involvement, on the other hand, was a complication he could do well without. But Harriet Knight, he thought, was spoiled and willful and unused to people turning her down. If he refused her custom she would take it elsewhere, and just at the moment Tom really did not want another investigator digging into Farne's business. They might discover what Merryn was doing. They might even discover his own interest in the case. And then all hell would break loose.

"Very well," he said reluctantly. "I'll take your business."

Harriet gave a little, excited wiggle. There was no doubting that she was pleased.

"There is just one small thing…" she murmured. She stood up and came over to him, pinning him between her body and the desk. Her breasts pressed against his chest, soft and warm and very large.

"I can't afford to pay you," she murmured again, as Tom tried not to fix his gaze on her cleavage. "I have already outrun my allowance for this quarter. So—" she slid a hand down his chest "—we shall have to come to some other arrangement."

"That isn't how I do business," Tom croaked.

"Who said anything about business?" Harriet said. Her hand slid over his thigh, cupping his crotch.

"How lovely," she breathed hotly into his ear. "You are endowed with more than a quick intellect."

She kissed him before he could object again, her naughty tongue darting into his mouth and killing his protests, such as they were, stone dead. She kissed him avidly, insatiably, her hands roaming over his chest, slipping beneath his shirt, burrowing under the band of his pantaloons. Tom thought faintly that his initial assessment of her as more innocent than she appeared had been embarrassingly at fault.

After that it all became very fast, slippery, heated and, when Tom looked back on it, utterly unbelievable. Harriet pushed him back so that he was sitting on his desk and opened his pantaloons with such seductive efficiency that his cock sprang out, already rock-hard. She climbed on top of him, knees braced on each side of him on the desktop, and slid down, engulfing him in her tight, slick warmth. Tom's groan almost shattered the windows and certainly caused the sleeping seagulls to rise from the roof with angry cries. He quickly discovered that Harriet was wearing no underwear of any kind and she pulled down the neckline of her gown so that her generous breasts bounced in his face with each thrust and slide. She came quickly and jumped off him, leaving Tom almost speechless with thwarted desire. But then she turned and bent over the desk in mute invitation. Tom was not slow to take the offer. He pulled up her silken skirts and plundered her body deeply, the inkpot and quills flying as the desk rocked, the pile of client folders spilling all their secrets onto the floor in a cascade of paper.

Afterward Harriet gave him a little smile. "My guardian's groom first had me when I was sixteen." Her eyes gleamed. "I'm afraid that I have had a taste for the lower orders ever since."

Which, Tom thought, made his place explicitly clear.

She kissed him lingeringly and was gone.

It took Tom a fair while to recover the thinking part of his anatomy and even longer to tidy his office and mop up the inkstains, but when he was finally sitting at his desk again and drinking a restorative glass of brandy his mind returned to the idea of Garrick Farne's by-blow. If Harriet had been in her teens at the time of Kitty Northesk's death then the timing of the revelations about a baby must have coincided closely with the scandal of Stephen Fenner's murder. Tom had a good instinct for secrets and he felt strongly that the two scandals must be connected in some way. If the information on the child was as deeply buried as that relating to the Fenner duel it would be difficult but not impossible to find it out. Harriet had not been mistaken; he really was the best.

Tom wondered when Harriet would return for an update on his progress. He looked forward to exacting more payment. His body felt replete and even though his mind was telling him that mixing business with pleasure with the rapacious Lady Harriet was possibly the most ill-judged action of his life, he could not really regret it. He knew that he needed to keep a clear head for the Farne case, but Harriet had proved too tempting to resist. She had fallen into his lap like a gift in more ways than one and he had never been a man to turn down an opportunity.

He sat back in his chair and looked out across the river. He was sure he could manage this situation, complex as it was becoming. Merryn was investigating the circumstances surrounding the duel and it was easy to manipulate her because she hated Farne and wanted justice. Tom was not particularly taken with the concept of justice himself; he thought it was ridiculously idealistic. Still, it served to keep Merryn on his side. Meanwhile

Harriet had provided him with some additional information that he would look into and then he would keep anything useful for himself. And after that… Tom paused in contemplation of his grand plan. After that he might blackmail Farne if it served his purposes, or even allow Merryn to expose the Duke as a murderer if he chose. Having the power to decide, holding the Dukedom of Farne in the palm of his hand, would be the ultimate gift, all that he had ever wanted. He finished the brandy. It had been a very good day indeed.

MERRYN WALKED HOME quickly from the Octagon Library, the tap of her footsteps on the cobbles echoing the turmoil inside her. How dared Garrick Farne kiss her, and in such an abrupt, arrogant and utterly masterful manner that had, she was obliged to admit to herself, completely swept her away. The man was insolent and entirely disrespectful, following her to the library, unmasking her, challenging her over her plans to ruin him. He had expressed not one word of regret for Stephen's death. For a moment Merryn thought about that and it hurt her horribly. Garrick Farne was indifferent to the tragedy he had caused and for that, she thought, he deserved to be punished.

She had the evidence now, another little piece to add to the pattern that was starting to show a very different picture from the official version. She felt hot and triumphant. Garrick might discount what she was doing, he might confidently claim that she would find no evidence to prove him a criminal, but she knew otherwise. She slid her hand into the pocket of her pelisse, her gloved fingers searching for the little piece of paper with the newspaper entry recorded on it.

There was nothing there.

Merryn stopped dead, causing a young solicitor's clerk to cannon into her and rebound with an apology and look of surprise. She ignored him, searching frantically now, turning the pocket inside out. Nothing. The empty space mocked her.

Perhaps she had dropped the paper somewhere along the way, in the library, or out here in the street. Her heart missed a beat. What a confounded nuisance if she had. If it were in the library then there was an outside chance that Garrick Farne might pick it up... She stopped again.

"The low, despicable, devious, loathsome, odious toad!" she exclaimed. A lady and gentleman passing by, arm in arm, looked at her with some concern. Merryn stamped her foot. It hurt. It did not relieve her fury.

She could see it all now. Tears of anger and frustration stung her eyes. She replayed in her mind the exchange with Garrick.

You won't find any evidence...

I already have...

How had he known where to find the paper? Had he seen her slide it into her pocket in the library? But she had been so careful... She started to walk again, hands thrust deep into her pockets, her head down, shoulders hunched. It did not matter how Garrick had known. What mattered was that now he knew what she was doing. He knew she was gathering evidence and he knew her intention. As soon as he realized she was a threat he had moved to discover exactly what she intended. He had hired someone to identify her and then he had come after her.

Tom had been right. Garrick Farne was a dangerous man. She had underestimated him.

Merryn bit her bottom lip hard. It was still tender from Garrick's kiss and for a moment an echo of sensation coursed through her, heating her skin, making her burn with a mixture of hopeless arousal and complete mortification. She hated Garrick Farne but for a second she had thought, foolishly, wildly, that he might have kissed her because he wanted to. She had enjoyed it far more than she should have done and that had puzzled her. Now she felt fury as well as shame. Garrick Farne had once been a rake and he had used every ounce of that experience to trick her. He had kissed her with deliberate intent, to manipulate her—*to pick her pocket*—and she, silly little innocent that she was, had melted under his touch. She had been so distracted that she had not noticed what he was doing. She had responded to his practiced seduction and then she had stalked out, her senses full of nothing but him, her head still spinning at his touch, and he had gained exactly what he desired. He had won.

Merryn raised her chin. He would not find her so easy a target next time.

The cold wind tugged at her bonnet, stinging her cheeks. She wished she could anticipate Garrick's next move. In some ways he was a chameleon just as she was; she sensed a very different man under that cool, controlled exterior. He was unpredictable, enigmatic. There was also a forceful masculinity about him that she had observed in few other men. Her brother-in-law Alex possessed it, too, but Merryn had merely noted that— and noted the effect that Alex's powerful attraction had on her sister Joanna. Like all of her observations of life it had been objective, completely without emotion. But with Garrick… A shiver skittered across her skin. With Garrick that ruthless masculine appeal felt personal. It seemed to fill her with awareness. She could not explain it nor could she shake it off but it made her acutely vulnerable. She gritted her teeth. It was the reason that Garrick had been able to take advantage of her response to him.

She turned the corner into Tavistock Street. At the moment she was lodging with her sister Joanna and Alex in their rented town house. It was warm, comfortable and quiet. There were servants to attend to her every need. The only thing that was lacking was her freedom. Merryn was not accustomed to accounting to her relatives for her every move. It was one of the reasons she had invented various friends with whom she pretended to stay when Joanna was out of town. Her sister had never questioned her. Joanna had no notion of the type of life she really led and her work for Tom Bradshaw. She trusted Merryn. And until recently, Merryn had never felt guilty over her deception. Now that Joanna was back in town, however, and Merryn was misleading her on a daily basis, her conscience was starting to trouble her.

She had reached number twelve. A footman bowed her inside the house. A small white terrier threw himself on her with excited abandon and she bent to give him a hug. Merryn's sisters, Joanna and Tess, were in the sitting room reading, respectively *The Ladies Magazine* and *The Ladies Monthly Museum* or, more accurately, looking at the pictures. There was a library in the house but the only person who ever picked up a book other than Merryn herself was her brother-in-law, Alex. Merryn had sometimes wondered what it was that Alex saw in Joanna. Theirs had been an arranged marriage in the first instance but was now well and truly a love match. It seemed incomprehensible to Merryn that a man like Alex with broad scientific interests and a sharp incisive mind could possibly love her sister who had no interest in anything except shopping and was about as incisive as a sponge cake.

"Merryn darling!" Joanna cast aside her magazine and gave her sister a radiant smile. "Come over to the fire. You looked chilled to the bone! What have you been doing this afternoon?"

"I've been to the library," Merryn said, without bothering to specify which or what for.

"Well, how lovely, darling," Joanna said vaguely. "Would you care for some tea?"

Another cup was brought. Tess poured for her. Merryn let the heat of it warm her and the strong flavor revive her. Tess and Joanna were talking about winter fashions now. They were seated together on the sofa, heads bent. The firelight flickered over their glossy brown curls. Suddenly Merryn was transported back to the nursery parlor where two little girls were turned out as pretty as china dolls for visitors to admire. She could have made a third, perhaps, a pale imitation of their prettiness, except that she had already been up a tree, knees scraped, skirts torn, reading a book. Joanna and Tess, older, wrapped up in themselves and happy in each other's company, had never paid her a vast amount of attention. Neither had Garrick, on those rare occasions when he had been down from London with Stephen and the two of them had brought laughter and vitality and a sort of masculine vigor to the household that had felt so very different from the humdrum everyday life Merryn was accustomed to. Merryn remembered seeing them coming in, spattered with mud from riding hard, Garrick's auburn hair whipped by the wind, his face tanned brown. She remembered the impromptu boxing match he and Stephen had held in the paddock; Miss Brown, the governess, had clucked and shepherded all the girls away but not before they had all seen Garrick stripped to the waist, muscular and broad, much as he had been when Merryn had seen him that night in his bedroom… Merryn shifted in her chair, feeling a bolt of something fierce and wicked shoot through her. She bent her head over her teacup, aware that she was more than a little flushed.

Alex came in. He greeted Merryn warmly. She watched as he bent to kiss Joanna. For a second she saw a look in Alex's eyes, dark and intense, that mirrored the heat that had been in Garrick's when *he* had looked at *her*. Suddenly Merryn felt hot and breathless again as though the drawing room had been drained of air. Joanna had blushed, too, a pretty color that stung her cheeks and made her look very young. Alex was smiling at her. The atmosphere seemed to sizzle. Merryn felt supremely uncomfortable and quite out of her depth. For years she had viewed love as a literary phenomenon, something she read about on the page and analyzed with the same intellectual curiosity as she viewed philosophy or language. Yet now it was as though something had awoken inside her and could not be put back to sleep. She closed her eyes for a second and felt again the caress of Garrick's fingers against her cheek, his touch firm and sure, his mouth on hers, hungry, possessive.

She gave a little squeak and jumped to her feet. Everyone looked at her in surprise.

"I think I will go and rest," she said quickly. "I feel a little tired."

"You look rather flushed," Tess said. "Have you caught a chill?"

"No," Merryn said. "I don't believe so. I…" She stopped. *I do not understand what is happening to me…*

"There was a letter from Mr. Churchward this

morning," Joanna said, after a moment. "He asks us all to visit his chambers tomorrow morning as a matter of urgency."

Merryn paused, one hand on the door. "Must I go? I had plans for tomorrow."

A frown briefly marred Joanna's serene features. "It is a matter that affects all of us, so Mr. Churchward said. Something to do with our father's estate."

"Jo, do look at this design for a spotted muslin gown," Tess interrupted. "Do you think it too young for me?"

Joanna obligingly turned her attention to *The Ladies Monthly Museum* and Merryn was left with nothing more than a vague feeling of disquiet. It was Garrick Farne who possessed the Fenner estate now. Surely this could have nothing to do with him.

She went out into the hall. The nursemaid was bringing Shuna, Joanna and Alex's eighteen-month-old daughter, down the stairs. The baby held out her rounded arms to Merryn and for a moment Merryn hugged her close, breathing in her niece's baby smell and feeling something tight and warm clutch her heart. She watched the smiling nursemaid take Shuna into the drawing room then went slowly up the stairs. The servants were lighting the candles now and the house looked bright and light, full of color and the scent of fresh flowers, so unlike the cold mausoleum that was Farne House. She thought of Garrick alone in that place. It must be unconscionably lonely, all dark corridors and silent rooms, just as the burden of a Dukedom must be lonely, carrying the responsibility for so many people.

Again she felt a shiver of disquiet. Garrick Farne was a powerful man, a crack shot, Tom had said, a famed swordsman, a man who had walked alone in places she would have been afraid to tread with an armed guard. And now he was on her trail. She had a disquieting feeling that Garrick could be very dangerous to her indeed.

CHAPTER FIVE

"ARE YOU SURE, your grace," Mr. Churchward said, "that you are doing the *right thing?*" His tone, measured as it was, implied that he felt that Garrick might possibly have taken leave of his senses and should be clapped up in Bedlam.

They were sitting in the offices of Churchward and Churchward, lawyers to the aristocratic and discerning, in High Holborn. In fact they were in the inner sanctum, Mr. Churchward's own office, and the door was very firmly closed. Pale sunlight tripped through the window and danced across Mr. Churchward's imposing walnut desk, illuminating the deed of gift lying there. Mr. Churchward tapped it, impatient, unhappy.

"I am certain I am doing the right thing, thank you, Mr. Churchward," Garrick replied.

"It seems to me," Churchward pursued, "that you are giving away—" he took a deep breath "—a vast sum of money—" he put heavy emphasis on each word "—to the detriment of the Farne Dukedom."

"I am aware of that," Garrick agreed.

"One hundred thousand pounds," Mr. Churchward said miserably. "And a very fine property in Fenners."

"I have explained my reasons," Garrick said gently. It was anathema to him to own Fenners. The property should never have been his in the first place. He had known from the moment that he picked up the deeds that he would give it back, along with all the monies that had accrued to it over the past ten years.

"Your scruples do you credit, your grace," Mr. Churchward said, polishing his spectacles with great agitation, "but I do wonder if you may live to regret your generosity."

"I doubt it," Garrick said. "I am still rich beyond decency and if I have twenty-five properties rather than twenty-six I am sure I shall survive."

Mr. Churchward shook his head. "Sentiment," he said, "has no place in business, your grace. Your late father understood that."

"My late father," Garrick said, his tone hard, "did not set an example I wish to follow in any area of my life, Mr. Churchward."

"Well, perhaps not." The lawyer placed his glasses back on his nose. His pale eyes gleamed at Garrick through the thick lenses. "Your late father," he admitted, "could lack compassion."

"You have the most marvelous line in understatement, Mr.Churchward," Garrick said. "My father could best be described as an unfeeling bastard. I speak figuratively," he added, "lest you should be worried that someone might challenge the legitimacy of the Dukedom."

There was a knock at the door and the senior clerk

poked his head around. "Lord and Lady Grant, Lady Darent and Lady Merryn Fenner," he announced somewhat breathlessly.

Garrick stood up. He could feel tension in his shoulders, the strain making the back of his neck ache. He rubbed it surreptitiously. He had known that he had to be present for this meeting. Mr. Churchward could hardly be expected to bear the responsibility alone. But he was also acutely aware that it might cause Lady Grant and Lady Darent distress to be confronted by the man who had killed their brother. Merryn's reaction he was fairly sure he could accurately predict.

There was a commotion in the outer office and then Lady Grant and Lady Darent swept in. Garrick could understand why Churchward's clerks were behaving like chickens when a fox got in the henhouse; both women were extraordinarily beautiful, perhaps not in the classic sense, but they both exuded style and charm and warmth that could set light to a room. It was difficult not to stare. Apart they would have been considered incomparable. Together they were dazzling.

And then Merryn walked in. Her eyes met Garrick's and he found that he could not look away. Where Joanna Grant and Tess Darent had a cool, empty beauty, Merryn was all fire and passion. She stopped dead in the doorway so that Tess Darent almost walked into her.

"What the devil is *he* doing here?" she exclaimed.

Her loathing of him was completely unconcealed. It blazed from her blue eyes. There was antipathy in every

line of her slender body. Garrick thought she was about
to turn on her heel and walk out.

"You might have warned us, Mr. Churchward," Joanna
Grant said, with what Garrick thought was admirable
restraint.

"And then we need not have come!" Merryn snapped.

Garrick smiled at her and was rewarded with a glare
in return. He knew that it was not simply dislike that
motivated her. If he chose to reveal anything of their
previous meetings she would be in a very difficult situation indeed. He raised his brows in quizzical challenge
and saw her blush before she looked away. Her lips set
in a tight, angry line.

"Lady Merryn," he said. "A pleasure to see you
again."

That brought him another fierce snap of anger from
those blue eyes.

"I was not aware that you had met his grace of Farne
recently, Merryn," Joanna said mildly.

"We met at the library yesterday," Merryn said.

"And a couple of days before that," Garrick put in,
"in my b—"

"Bank!" Merryn said loudly. Everyone looked at
her.

"At the bank?" Joanna sounded surprised.

"Acre and Co. in the Strand," Merryn said. Her gaze,
equally as challenging as Garrick's own, held his for one
long moment. "I was admiring the architecture. Such a
fine design."

Tess Darent gave a little yawn, hiding it behind one languid hand. "Lud, Merryn, how very like you," she said.

Merryn smiled. Garrick saw the flash of triumph in her eyes.

"I bank at Coutts and Co.," he said gently, "for future reference, Lady Merryn."

"Then perhaps you were admiring the architecture, too," Merryn said sweetly. Her look dared him to go further, to expose her. He could see the defiance in her eyes. He could also see the pulse that fluttered in her throat. Merryn Fenner was nervous, he thought, for all her daring.

"I was certainly admiring something," he murmured. "I found our encounter most stimulating."

He dropped his gaze to her mouth. Merryn blushed, biting her lip, a gesture that only served to emphasize how full and luscious those lips were. Garrick felt a punch of lust, which was not, he thought, the appropriate physical or mental state to be in for a meeting with his lawyer.

Churchward cleared his throat. "Ladies, Lord Grant…" He ushered them all into their seats. Tess and Joanna arranged themselves prettily. Merryn sat bolt upright, her gaze pointedly turned away from Garrick. A glacial silence fell.

"If we might proceed…" Churchward said. "I must thank you all for coming at such short notice." He fixed his dusty spectacles more firmly on his nose. "And for your forbearance, ladies. I asked you here today because the Duke of Farne—" a thread of disapproval entered his voice "—wishes to make you an offer."

"Not of marriage, I hope," Merryn said shortly.

"Not unless you desire it, Lady Merryn," Garrick said smoothly.

"I'd rather you gave me the plague," Merryn snapped.

"Merryn," Joanna Grant said reproachfully, and Garrick saw Merryn grimace. A shade of pink came into her face and she fell silent.

"Let us not be too hasty." Tess Darent was sitting a little straighter in her chair and showing some interest in the proceedings for the first time. Her gaze inspected Garrick thoroughly. "I might be happy to add a Duke to my collection," she said.

"Not this one, Tess," Joanna said dryly. "He looks too healthy for you. He could not be relied upon to die within a year of your wedding."

"More is the pity," Garrick heard Merryn murmur.

"Besides," Joanna added, even more dryly, "he is too virile for your taste."

Garrick saw Merryn's gaze jerk up to his face and a wave of hot color stung her cheeks. For a second they stared at one another, captured in a fierce blaze of awareness, and then Merryn turned her head away again and her eyelashes flickered down to hide her expression. Garrick saw her knit her fingers tightly together in her lap.

"Ladies…" Churchward sounded reproving. Evidently, Garrick thought, he had had some previous experience of the shocking ways of the Fenner sisters. "No one," he said severely, "is offering to marry anyone." He turned to Garrick. "If you permit, your grace?"

"Of course," Garrick said. "Please proceed, Mr. Churchward."

Once again he felt Merryn Fenner's gaze on him. Her expression was dark now, unreadable. For a second, though, Garrick thought that she looked frightened and he felt a tug of emotion inside; he wondered what this meeting must be like for her, stirring up as it did feelings and memories she had clearly never overcome. Then she raised her chin, scorning the tacit sympathy he realized that he had offered, rejecting every vestige of comfort he might give. Her dismissal felt like a slap across the face.

"This is a deed of gift made on the eleventh of November in the year of our Lord eighteen hundred and fourteen," Mr. Churchward said precisely. "By this gift his grace Garrick Charles Christmas Farne, nineteenth Duke of Farne—"

"Christmas?" Merryn said, quite as though she could not help herself.

"I was born on the twenty-fifth of December," Garrick said, smiling at her, "to a very devout mother."

"How unfortunate for you," Merryn said politely.

"It could have been worse," Garrick said.

"The nineteenth Duke of Farne…" Mr. Churchward's stern voice bore them down "…freely gives in equal part the house and estate in the County of Dorset and the sum of one hundred thousand pounds to Joanna, Lady Grant, Teresa, Lady Darent, and Lady Merryn Fenner, to hold as their absolute right and dispose of as they wish, with his grace the Duke of Farne making no further claim upon the estate or the fortune accruing unto it. The estate," he added, "is in excellent repair."

There was an odd silence as Churchward finished, like the lull before the first bolt of lightning split the sky. Garrick saw Joanna and Tess exchange a look and then Merryn's chair clattered back with such sharpness that they all winced.

"Why?" she demanded.

Garrick could see that she was trembling. Her entire frame shook with the force of whatever anger or misery possessed her. Her eyes were huge. He could feel her passion and the pain beneath it, so raw and fierce it hurt. He put out a hand toward her, instinctively wanting to offer comfort again, and saw her recoil.

"Because Fenners should belong to you." He spoke directly to her, as though the others were not there. "I did not know that my father had purchased the estate. He should not have done so. It is rightfully yours. So I am giving it back."

She looked right into his eyes and Garrick felt the force of her gaze sweep through him. She was so transparent, so honest a person that nothing was hidden.

There was no artifice in Merryn Fenner and that meant she had no defenses at times like this.

"This is to ease your conscience!" Her words hit him with the force of a blow. She swept the deed of gift to the floor with an unsteady hand. "You killed Stephen and now you think that this will be recompense?"

"Merryn." Joanna had placed a restraining hand on her sister's arm. "Please…"

"It is in no way intended as recompense," Garrick said. "The death of your brother was—" He stopped, remembering the moment in the library the previous day. No words of his could ever give the Fenner sisters back what they had lost. There had been plenty of reasons to rid the world of a scoundrel like Stephen Fenner but he was not about to reveal them here. It would do no good. Merryn Fenner would never forgive him, no matter the truth. And once he were to start speaking of the tragedy he would put at risk all the people he had sworn to protect and all the secrets that had been so carefully hidden twelve years before. He chose his words with care.

"It is something that I regret every day of my life," he said. That at least was true but he saw from the flare of contempt in Merryn's face how inadequate the words were.

"The gift of Fenners," he continued, "is, however, a matter apart. It should not belong to the Farne Dukedom. That is wrong. So I am giving it back."

Alex Grant spoke for the first time. He had sat very

still and silent throughout, but now he shifted in his chair.

"That is…generous of you, Farne," he said.

"It is right," Garrick said shortly, "not generous." He felt Grant's perceptive gray gaze rest on him for a long moment. He wanted no credit for his actions. He simply wanted to be rid of the estate.

"One hundred thousand pounds to share between us," Tess Darent said. "How marvelous!"

Merryn turned on her. "Surely you cannot be intending to take it?" she demanded. "You are rich—you do not even *need* thirty thousand pounds!"

"I always need thirty thousand pounds, Merryn darling," Tess said calmly. "Any right-thinking woman would." She wrinkled up her nose. "You can have the house, though. I hate living in the country."

Garrick could see all the emotions chasing themselves across Merryn's face, bewilderment and disgust, closely followed by despair as she realized that her sisters, so much more worldly and, arguably, less-principled than she, were very likely to accept the offer. She looked intensely lonely, just as she had when she had walked away from him at the library.

"I won't take it!" She turned back to Garrick, fury igniting her gaze.

"You cannot refuse it," Garrick said gently. "It is a gift."

"I can try." She took an angry pace away. "I'll give it away."

"That is your privilege."

She gave him a look of such searing contempt Garrick felt it all the way to his soul.

"Damn you," she said distinctly.

Garrick thought of Harriet Knight. There was quite a queue of people wishing him in perdition. Interesting that he had cared not a jot for Harriet's dismissal of him. It had left him utterly cold, whereas Merryn Fenner's scorn raked him more deeply than he would have liked. He inclined his head. "Quite so, Lady Merryn."

"I think," Alex interposed, "that we had best discuss this matter in private." He stood up. "Mr. Churchward." He shook the lawyer by the hand. "We will be in touch. Thank you. Farne…" His nod was a shade more cordial than it had been at the beginning of the meeting.

"You will not buy me off," Merryn said through her teeth.

"Come along, Merryn," Joanna said, sounding like a governess.

They went out. Garrick could hear Tess Darent's voice fading away as she chattered to Joanna about the new winter wardrobe she would purchase with some of her thirty thousand pounds. He saw that Churchward had overheard Lady Darent, too. The lawyer grimaced.

"The late Lord Fenner's daughters are all very different from one another," he murmured.

Garrick thought that of the three, Tess was actually the one most like Stephen Fenner. Stephen, too, had been blessedly short of moral scruples when it came to money. Joanna, he rather suspected, had hidden depths. She might appear to be a society butterfly but she could not have attracted and held the love of a man like Alex Grant without some substance. As for Merryn, well, she was as transparent as glass, painfully honest and demanding the same integrity from all those that she met. He winced as he remembered her disillusion on hearing Tess's response to the deed of gift. Life could be very cruel to idealists. Which was another reason why to tell her of her brother's true character would be wantonly cruel.

He stood up, stretched, feeling the tension drain away from his body.

"Thank you, Churchward," he said, shaking the lawyer by the hand. "I appreciate your support."

"One hundred thousand pounds," Churchward mourned. "You are sure you will not change your mind, your grace?"

Garrick laughed. "Too late. Lady Darent will already be spending her share, I feel sure." He sighed, straightened. "Please let me know as soon as Lady Grant responds formally to the offer and please have all the estate papers ready to send over to her." He smiled. "Thank you, Mr. Churchward."

He went out. He felt a huge wash of relief to be outside in the fresh air. He resolved to ride out that afternoon. His ducal duties could wait a little. He needed space and speed and the opportunity to outrun his ghosts. Merryn Fenner filled his consciousness with her vivid passion and the sharp awareness that undercut every one of their encounters.

You will not buy me off...

He had not for one moment thought that he could.

"HAVE YOU A MOMENT, GUV'NOR?"

The man who had stuck his head around Tom's office door was Ned Heighton, one of the men who worked for him picking up information in the rookeries and coffee shops of London. A former Army Provost, Heighton had fallen from grace through some misdemeanor and been court-martialed and dishonorably discharged from the army. Tom had never inquired into the cause of his disgrace, although he suspected it was drink-related. Heighton could be a little too fond of the bottle. Still, the army's loss was Tom's gain. Heighton was a very sound man.

"What is it?" he asked, as the old soldier came in and shut the door.

"Your six o'clock appointment is here," Heighton said. "Nice-looking lady."

"Mrs. Carstairs," Tom said. "Her husband has absconded and she wants to find him."

Heighton shook his head. "Best leave him be. He'll have run off with an actress, like as not."

"Or he is at the bottom of the Thames," Tom said, reaching for a file from his drawer, "if my inquiries into his financial affairs are anything to go by." He raised his brows. "But you did not call in to act as my secretary, did you, Heighton?"

"No, sir." Heighton scratched his forehead. "There's something I thought you should know, sir. Someone has been asking questions. About her ladyship, sir."

Tom waited. Heighton always took his time in divulging information. Also he had a love-hate relationship with Merryn, whom he thought too grand to work for an inquiry agent. Heighton had strict ideas about rank. Interesting, Tom thought, that despite his disapproval the old soldier seemed to be on Merryn's side now.

"A rich cove," Heighton added eventually. "Titled, probably."

"The Duke of Farne," Tom said softly. Garrick Farne, it seemed, had not wasted any time.

"Nice clothes," Heighton said. "Expensive. But not a soft lad, oh, no."

"Soft lad" was Heighton's ultimate insult for any man whom he thought a bit of a dandy. Tom repressed a grin. "Go on," he said.

Heighton sighed. His eyes looked sad, like a dog left out in the rain.

"Took his business to Hammonds," he said dolefully, mentioning Tom's most successful rival.

"Well," Tom said, "he wouldn't come to us if he wanted information on Merryn, would he?"

"Might do," Heighton said surprisingly. "Looked the sort of cove who wouldn't mess around. Dangerous, if you ask me. He carried a pistol, Jerry said."

Jerry was one of Heighton's most useful informers and was correct nine times out of ten. Tom sighed. This was precisely what he had feared. Farne had got wind of Merryn's activities and was out to find out about her and, no doubt, scupper her plans.

"Any idea what questions he was asking, Heighton?" he said, a little wearily.

Heighton shook his head. "Jerry couldn't hear. Only heard her ladyship's name—and the sound of money changing hands. Big money, Jerry said."

"All right," Tom said. "I'll warn Merryn to be careful. Thank you, Heighton."

The old soldier paused. "One other thing, sir."

Tom looked up at the note in the man's voice. "Yes?"

"The rich cove—the Duke—was asking after you, too, sir."

Tom put down his pen very slowly. "Me?" he said. His voice did not sound quite right, to his own ears. He could feel cold fear crawling up his neck. "He was asking about me?"

Heighton was looking at him with concern. Tom swiftly rearranged his expression. "I expect," he said, "it was only because I employ Lady Merryn." He picked up the pen again, noticing that his hand was shaking slightly. "Thank you, Heighton," he said casually. "I will be out to see Mrs. Carstairs directly."

Heighton nodded and went out, and Tom paused for a

moment before getting to his feet, walking across to the decanter, pouring a glass of the vile sherry and drinking it down in one mouthful. He followed it with a second one.

So Garrick Farne was asking questions, about Merryn, about him. That was at best inconvenient and at worst could prove fatal. Tom returned to his desk, drumming his fingers on the pile of paper that reposed there while he tried to think clearly. If Farne discovered his connection to the Dukedom then everything would go spectacularly wrong. That was the reason he had been hiding behind Merryn from the start, using her, feeding her the information about her brother's death that he had known would set her off on this blind quest for justice. She did not know the full extent of his interest, of course, and he could never tell her. Equally he could not permit Garrick Farne to discover Merryn's purpose. The whole matter was delicate, poised on a knife edge. And there was a Dukedom at stake.

Tom ran his hand through his hair. He had already warned Merryn to be discreet and careful. She had thought it was because he was concerned for her safety. In fact it had been pure self-preservation. Unfortunately Merryn was easy to manipulate but difficult to control thereafter, because when she became inspired by a cause it tended to arouse such passionate fervor in her that everything else—caution, discretion, prudence—went by the board. Tom had seen it happen before when she had taken on cases where there had been a miscarriage of justice. In this particular case her personal feelings were involved and so the effect was twenty times the greater. She was proving more difficult to manage than he had anticipated, and he would have to think of a way to rein her in before Farne caught up with her and she ruined everything. If the worse came to the worst, he thought, he would simply have to cut her loose and use her as a decoy to draw attention away from him. He nodded. The idea had some appeal.

He went out into the waiting room. Mrs. Carstairs was sitting patiently, her fingers locked tightly together, a mixture of hope and fear in her eyes as she looked up at him. Tom sighed. On his desk was a fat file detailing her husband's spiraling debts and the mess he had got himself into trying to pay them off by borrowing from some deeply unpleasant moneylenders. Tom did not care much for his clients' pain. He had seen and done it all— thwarted eloping lovers, exposed bigamists, found lost heirs, even destroyed inconvenient evidence if the price was right. He had no sentiment left in him. It amused him that Merryn worked for him because she thought she was working for justice. In some ways, Tom thought, Merryn Fenner was extremely naive. But she had also been extremely useful to him. It would be a shame to lose her.

Now he turned his most compassionate manufactured smile on his latest client. Mrs. Carstairs was paying him enough money. The least he could do was give her his undivided attention and some apparent sympathy.

"Mrs. Carstairs," he said, "I am very sorry. You must prepare yourself for bad news…"

CHAPTER SIX

GARRICK DID NOT have an invitation to Joanna Grant's ball that evening. He would hardly have expected it. It would take more than one hundred thousand pounds and the handing back of the ancestral Fenner lands to make him welcome in Tavistock Street. But since he wanted to see Merryn again he had no choice other than to arrive uninvited. He left it very late, when all the guests had arrived and the footman on the door was wilting at his post, and then he simply walked in. No one stopped him. No one appeared to notice him at all in the crush.

Garrick went straight to the ballroom, where he saw Merryn almost immediately. She was dancing with a young sprig of fashion, dancing very badly moreover, and with the expression of one who was having a tooth pulled or perhaps whose slippers were pinching. Her partner looked grim and bored. Garrick could not help but smile. Most young ladies at least made a pretense of enjoyment when they were with the opposite sex. Merryn clearly saw no need to do so.

He took a calculated bet that she would soon tire of the ball, helped himself to a bottle of champagne and two glasses from an obliging footman and slipped out of the ballroom and up the stairs. He was aware that he was abusing Lord and Lady Grant's hospitality quite shamefully since not only had he not been invited, he certainly had not been given the freedom of the house. But he needed to discover how much Merryn knew. He needed to stop her quest for justice. And this was the quickest way.

The first bedchamber he came to quite clearly belonged to Joanna Grant and was lush with exotic drapery and scented with perfume. It had a connecting door standing open to her husband's dressing room. The second chamber was less easy to apportion to a member of the family and for a moment Garrick wondered if it was Merryn's. There was a set of very beautiful and very explicit pencil drawings spilling from a folder on the dressing table—nudes in various stages of debauchery with gods, satyrs and nymphs. The drawings were good—and extremely erotic. One of the nymphs, small, lush, curved, looked a little like Merryn. She was lying on a bench, her hair spread, her drapes sliding from her rounded limbs, a small cherub bending to kiss her breast. Garrick felt his evening dress tightening in various strategic places as he contemplated the picture. His breath strangled in his throat.

Concentrate.

This was not the time to be imagining Lady Merryn Fenner stripped of her clothes and lying small yet voluptuous, naked, perfect, among the tangled sheets of his bed. Despite that it was, Garrick admitted to himself, the image that had haunted him since the moment he had met her. Then he had not known her identity; he had known nothing but the blazing attraction that had drawn him to her. Now, even though he knew she hated him, even though he knew all the barriers that stood between them, the attraction was no less.

This was not Merryn's room, though. There were no books. Garrick closed the door softly behind him and wondered briefly if the rumors of Tess Darent driving all her ancient husbands to death with her incessant sexual demands were in fact true. He, accustomed to being the target of slander, had thought it nothing but idle gossip. Now he was not so sure.

The third room he entered was most definitely Merryn's. It was plain and tidy, almost austere. There were no exotic furnishings here: a bed with a simple white cover, a wardrobe, a table with a pile of books. French love poetry, in the French language, of course, jostled with Thomas Hobbes's *Leviathan*. There was an illustrated set of fairy stories and St. Augustine's *Confessions*. And on the top, a bound book that looked suspiciously like a diary. Garrick picked it up, settled himself in an armchair, opened the book and started to read.

Ten minutes later he heard the patter of footsteps on the carpet outside and the turn of the doorknob, and then Merryn ran into the room. Because she was not expecting him to be there Garrick saw her in a totally unguarded moment. She wrenched the rose-colored bandeau from her head and cast it aside, kicking off her slippers at the same time. Her movements were jerky and exasperated, almost angry. She put both hands up to cover her face, digging her fingers into her intricately arranged golden curls, scattering the pins that restrained them. She made a sound of relief and release that was so heartfelt Garrick felt a stir of sympathy. She dropped her hands and put her head back so that her hair tumbled over her shoulders and down her back like a silver river. Her eyes were closed and her eyelashes—very fair and not artificially darkened—were spiky against the curve of her cheek. The line of her neck was pure and tempting. Garrick found that he wanted to grab her and bury his face against that silken skin, dropping his mouth to the vulnerable hollow of her throat, inhaling her scent, burying himself in her. She looked lush, sweet and very seductive.

He must have made some involuntary movement because her eyes snapped open and she saw him. Her gaze widened with shock and she took a breath.

"Don't scream," Garrick said. "It would not do your reputation any good." He laid the book aside and got to his feet.

Merryn expelled the breath softly. He could hear a tremor in it though her voice was steady. "I never scream," she said. "Not for mice, not for pickpockets and certainly *not* for intruders."

She half turned aside from him, shielding her face, reaching for the shawl that was folded neatly over the back of her dressing table chair and wrapping it about her shoulders to cover the rose-pink ball gown. The room was hot, lit by a fire in the grate. Garrick thought she was wrapping herself up as much to add another layer of protection as for warmth. He could feel the withdrawal in her as she retreated from those moments when she had revealed so much of her feelings.

"I take it," he said, "that balls are not to your taste."

She shrugged a shoulder. "I only went to try to please Joanna. Your generous offer this morning—" scorn colored her voice "—has caused much trouble in this household, your grace."

Garrick could imagine. If Tess Darent wanted to accept the money and Joanna and Merryn did not, or worse if Joanna *and* Tess wanted to accept and Merryn did not, then he could see that the Fenner family would be split down the middle, wrangling over an issue that could not but wake painful memories.

"I am sorry if that is the case," he said. "Such was not my intention."

Merryn fixed him with a very direct stare.

"What was your intention then, your grace?"

"To give back something that should never have been mine," Garrick said.

He expected her to contradict him or at the least to make some derisive comment but she did neither. Her blue eyes searched his face as though she was weighing the truth of his words and after a moment she gave a tiny nod of acceptance. Garrick released the breath he had not been aware that he was holding. He felt relief and

something more, something that almost felt like gratitude, as though she had given him a present beyond price.
Then she straightened and the moment was gone.

"Were you looking for something?" she asked.

"Yes," Garrick said. He smiled. "As were you, when
you ransacked my bedroom."

Her gaze flickered. She stiffened a little. It was interesting, Garrick thought, how transparent she was.
Interesting, but extremely inconvenient for her. The lies
she had spun him that night in his bedroom had been
imaginative because she was clever, but deceit was not
her natural state. She would always prefer to meet an
enemy head-on.

She ignored his comment. "We must stop meeting in
bedchambers," she said. "It is not respectable. I suggest
that you leave."

Garrick smiled. "I am merely returning your visit,
as a courtesy," he said. "I don't believe we finished our
conversation at the library. I'd like to talk some more."
He phrased it politely but with iron beneath his words.
She heard the note in his voice and her head jerked up;
he felt her antagonism. It shivered like a mirage between
them. Her anger was palpable and with it bitterness, and
something more, something not so easily defined. Garrick knew she was acutely uncomfortable that he had
invaded her bedchamber, a space she had thought was
private to herself. And she was even more uneasy about
the fierce physical awareness that trapped them both.
Garrick knew that she felt it as much as he did and he

sensed that she, so much less experienced than he, did not understand their mutual attraction. Nor did she like it. But she could not deny it.

"I do not suppose that you were invited tonight," she said, her pansy-blue eyes considering him thoughtfully.

"No," Garrick said.

"Then you could at least have shown a modicum of courtesy and sensitivity by staying away."

"I could have done," Garrick agreed, "but I did not. This is too important."

Their gazes locked. The antagonism flowered again, strong and dark between them, once again with that undercurrent of something else, something hot and turbulent.

Garrick gestured to the champagne bottle resting on the table beside Merryn's pile of books. "Would you care to join me?" he asked.

She paused and then nodded. "Thank you." She motioned toward the glasses. "What a civilized intruder you are, your grace," she said. "You think of everything."

"It would be an insult to the vintage to drink straight from the bottle," Garrick said. He returned with two glasses and handed one to her. Their fingers touched. He heard the little catch of her breath she could not conceal as his hand brushed hers.

He poured for her and clinked his glass softly against hers in a mocking salute, two adversaries meeting and acknowledging that the game was going to be a fierce one. She waited for him to make the opening move. Garrick obliged.

"Does Lady Grant know that when you pretend to be attending lectures and concerts you are actually stalking innocent noblemen in their own homes?" he asked. "Does she know you have been sleeping in my bed?"

A hint of color, rose-pink like her gown, stole into Merryn's cheeks. "I don't stalk noblemen in the plural," she said.

"Then it's just me," Garrick said. "How flattering." He waited until she had taken the window seat then sat down opposite her and stretched out his long legs. The leather wing chair was comfortable, enveloping.

"So," he said again. "Does Lady Grant know?"

Merryn took a sip of her champagne. He knew she was buying time. A pulse beat in the hollow of her throat, betraying her nervousness.

"No," she said, after a moment. "She knows nothing of what I do." She looked up. Her eyes held a mocking spark. "What are you going to do about it?" she said.

"I could tell her," Garrick said thoughtfully. "I could tell everybody."

Merryn looked thoughtful. She caught her lower lip between small white teeth. "No one would believe you," she said politely. "I am Lady Merryn Fenner. I am a bluestocking. I am above suspicion." She held his gaze, her own steady and bright.

"Except that a woman's reputation is so vulnerable," Garrick said gently. "Was *vulnerable* not the word you used when you warned me at the library? A whisper of scandal and a reputation dies. Your reputation, Lady Merryn."

Merryn's gaze narrowed on him. "That is true, of course," she said. She dangled her half-full champagne glass between her fingers. "If you want to frighten me, though," she added, "you will have to use something more powerful than society's censure. I don't care for it very much."

A point to her.

"You don't seek to wed?" Garrick asked. "A tattered reputation might well put paid to your chances."

She flicked him a look of contempt. "I'd rather become a nun."

"I assure you," Garrick said, "that you do not have the least aptitude for it."

She blushed at his reference to her unrestrained response to his kiss but the look in her eyes was still one of deep disdain. "Oh, well," she said, "if I change my mind I am sure that your thirty thousand pounds will repair any *tatters* in my reputation, your grace." She shrugged. "That is if I find a man I prefer to my books. I confess I have not done so yet."

"You are meeting the wrong men, then," Garrick said.

She laughed. "Which is hardly surprising, I suppose, if I frequent the bedchambers of men like you." She gave him a very direct look. "And you, your grace? Do you seek to remarry?" She paused. "I suppose not. It is not exactly your forte, is it?"

Ouch. Two points.

"I wondered whether you wished me to return your possessions to you," Garrick said, upping the stakes. "Return the evidence of your midnight wanderings, if you like? Your book, your spectacles… Can you see without them?"

"Perfectly, I thank you," Merryn said.

"Then they are for disguise only?"

She gave him another pitying stare. "You have too vivid an imagination, your grace. My glasses are for reading, not for disguise. Fortunately I have two pairs."

"There is also your underwear," Garrick said.

She stiffened. "You have been rifling through my underwear?"

"You left it in *my* drawers."

"Then I think perhaps you had better keep it," Merryn said icily "I don't really want it returned secondhand."

"I haven't been wearing it," Garrick pointed out mildly. "Merely looking at it."

"How singular of you."

"Not really," Garrick said. "If you know anything of men, Lady Merryn—"

"I don't." She cut him off. There was something defensive in the way that she withdrew from him as though he trespassed on forbidden ground. Her voice was soft but her fingers, rubbing ceaselessly over the embroidery of the window cushions, betrayed her agitation. Merryn

Fenner, he suspected, was not accustomed to people getting close to her and stripping away her defenses.

"I know nothing of men," she said, "nor do I wish to know." Her tone eased a little. "My sisters… They are the ones to whom you should address your gallantries, your grace. They are wasted on me."

Garrick wondered if she resented being in the shadow of Joanna Grant and Tess Darent, both such beautiful, charming women. Had she deliberately taken this step back, refused all competition, made her world in books and libraries, lectures and scholarly research where they could not and did not want to follow? And could she not see that she, too, was beautiful and oh so desirable, like a tiny pocket goddess with her tumble of silver gilt hair and those wide blue eyes? It seemed not. Or perhaps she simply did not value good looks. Perhaps she did not even *want* to be beautiful.

He shifted in the armchair, studying her thoughtfully.

"What do you *really* do when you are pretending to attend your bluestocking soirees?" he asked. "And when you are not stalking me?"

She considered him for a moment. Her eyes were a smoky-violet in the shadowed room. "I lead a blameless life, your grace," she said. "I really do attend bluestocking soirees. I read and I study. I go to Professor Brande's lectures at the Royal Institution and to poetry readings and concerts." She took another sip of champagne. She sounded cool and amused.

Garrick smiled slowly. "You also work for Tom Brad-shaw," he said.

Merryn jumped. A drop of champagne fell on the rose gown, staining the material to a deeper pink. They had been fencing before, testing each other's defenses. Now the nature of their exchange had altered. Garrick sensed this was really important to her.

"How did you know that?" She spoke abruptly. Garrick was interested that she did not try to deny it, even for a second.

He shrugged. "I have been asking questions about you, of course." He tilted his head and studied her, watching her closely. "You know how the system operates, Lady Merryn. I pay someone to find out about you."

He saw her fingers tighten on the stem of the champagne glass. "You paid someone to do your dirty work for you," she said. Scorn tipped her words. "Yes, that fits."

"It's quicker," Garrick said. "Bradshaw is corrupt," he added. "But surely you know that?"

Her gaze flashed to his face. "He is not!" She sounded outraged at the slur. "Tom works for justice! He helps people—" She broke off, as though she realized too late that she had revealed too much.

"No," Garrick said gently. "That is why *you* work for Bradshaw." He paused. He could see it all, her blind quest for justice and the determination that drove her. She felt a burning need to set right perceived wrongs and he would wager his entire fortune that it had been initiated by her brother's death at his hands.

"It is, isn't it?" he persisted. "You do it because you believe in justice and fighting for what is right, and to help the underdog?"

"I do it for the money," Merryn said defiantly. She tilted her chin up, her look defying him to contradict her. He had trespassed, Garrick thought. Merryn Fenner's world had hitherto been a secret from all those she knew, even those closest to her. He had not only blown that wide apart, he had seen straight through her motives to the painful truth below. For a moment she looked small and defenseless and Garrick felt the most enormous compassion for her. He was a cad to do this to her, to force her to confront those truths, to strip away her defenses, and his only justification was that there were those even more defenseless who needed his protection. Twelve years before he had sworn to defend them. He had never imagined that the price would be so high.

"My reasons are not what matter here," Merryn said, after a moment, rallying. Garrick could see that her eyes were suspiciously bright but she faced him down. She was not, he thought, a woman who would resort to tears or to the vapors to get her own way. "What matters," she said, "is that you have chosen to challenge what I am doing. And you are doing this because…"

"Because you threatened me," Garrick said. "When someone indicates that they would like to see me ruined it concentrates my mind."

"Has that happened to you often?" Merryn inquired politely.

Garrick laughed. "More than once."

She flicked him a look. "I might have imagined so. A pity no one has as yet followed up on their threat."

"There's always a first time," Garrick said. The last time a man had threatened to take his life it had been in the Peninsular and it had ended very badly for his assailant. No need to tell Merryn that, though. She would probably pick up that cause as well and declare open season on him.

"You have been gathering evidence," he said. "That newspaper entry you found at the Octagon Library—"

He saw her eyes flash. "The one you stole from me? That was underhanded."

Garrick laughed. "I did not hear you protesting at the time."

The color fluctuated deliciously in her face. She looked infuriated, pink, cross, unwillingly aroused. "I should have guessed you would stoop as low as kissing me to achieve your aim," she said.

"It was no hardship," Garrick agreed.

She glared. "You are a rake."

"I was a rake," Garrick corrected.

"You are confusing your tenses." Merryn looked down her nose at him. "I do not believe that a man ever stops being a libertine."

Looking at her, with her shining fair hair as rich as silk and her cheeks stung pink with righteous anger and her bow of a mouth pursed with disapproval Garrick was tempted to prove that she was exactly right by grabbing her and kissing her to within an inch of her life.

"Forgive me," he said, "but you base your remarks on…what, precisely?"

She turned away. "Literature," she said. "Observation."

"Let me know if you would prefer to replace that with experience," Garrick said, and received another glare for his pains.

"We drift from the subject," Merryn said tightly.

"We do indeed." Garrick shifted. "From the piece of paper that I extracted from your pocket I surmise that you have found other items, little details that you think contradict the official record of your brother's death—"

She reacted to that, as he had known she would. "I don't think they contradict it," she said hotly. "They *do* contradict it."

"Guest lists can be notoriously unreliable," Garrick said. "Names confused, numbers miscounted—"

"Like the number of shots heard?" Merryn said sweetly. "The number of bullets in a body?"

Hell. She had discovered a great deal. Garrick felt the sweat break out over his body. A few more steps, a little more digging, and Lady Merryn Fenner would be perilously close to the truth. She would learn what an out-and-out rogue her brother had truly been, she would learn the appalling things Stephen Fenner had done, she would be heartbroken.

Not that he was blameless. Garrick rubbed his forehead. He should have dealt with matters differently, he should have kept his head, instead of sacrificing everything—life, honor, the future—in that one desperate moment that he had killed his friend. Yes, Stephen Fenner had been a scoundrel but a day did not go past when Garrick did not regret his death.

Merryn was watching him. She had, not surprisingly, misread his expression. Garrick knew that he had looked guilty as all hell because in many ways, in the matter of Stephen's death, he was.

"Can I appeal to you to let matters rest?" he asked. "I can look after myself but if you pursue this matter there are others who might be hurt—" He broke off, seeing again in her eyes that vivid flash of pain he had witnessed when they had spoken at the Octagon Library.

"Others often are," she said in a hard voice, and Garrick knew she was speaking of herself, of the thirteen-year-old girl who had had home and family and fortune ripped away from her.

"If you refuse to stop I will expose your work for Tom Bradshaw," Garrick said. "Taken together with the information that you habitually visit the bedrooms of noblemen, I think you will find that scandal more difficult to quell than a simple slur on your reputation."

There was a frozen silence. Merryn sat quite still, almost as though she had not heard him.

"You're trying to blackmail me," she said. "How immoral of you."

"I would do nothing so vulgar as stoop to blackmail," Garrick said, and saw her smile as she recognized her words to him at the library two days before. "I am merely pointing out to you the dangers of your situation."

"I am obliged to you," Merryn said ironically. She sighed. "The same argument applies as before, however. The worst you can do is ruin my reputation—" there was the shimmer of triumph in her eyes "—and that only matters if I care about it." She rubbed her fingers thoughtfully over the rim of her empty glass. "It would be a nuisance," she conceded, "to be the subject of scandal and gossip, but I am sure I would survive it."

"You would not survive with any of the things that you value left to you," Garrick said, and saw her gaze jerk up to his.

"What do you mean?" she demanded.

Garrick shrugged. "The other reason I think you work for Bradshaw is that you are bored," he said. "You are clever, and society has no use for clever women."

She was betrayed into a rueful smile. "Other than to laugh at them," she said dryly. "Or to make them conform."

"Exactly," Garrick said. "So with no work and a reputation destroyed, no freedom to attend all the academic events that you currently take for granted, nothing to do with your time…" He let the sentence hang. Her

life, he knew, would be an utter desert. She was too unconventional to conform and it made her vulnerable.

He waited while she thought about it and saw in the
widening of her eyes that she had reached the same
conclusions.

"You would take away all the things I value." She
looked stricken. "My work, my interests—" She broke
off. "Damn you," she said with feeling. "As if it was not
sufficient to rob me of everything once."

Garrick hardened his heart against the pain and disbelief he could see in her eyes. "It is your choice, Lady
Merryn."

She stood up so abruptly that the table rocked and the
champagne glass almost toppled to the floor. "I think it
is time that you left, your grace." She waited, drawn up
as tall as her diminutive stature allowed. "I should have
guessed that you would sink lower than I had could ever
have imagined," she added.

"I've only just started," Garrick said. "You will have
to broaden your imagination to keep up."

"Oh?" She raised her brows. "If I refuse to concede,
what then? Kidnap? Abduction? Marriage?" She smiled
faintly. "I doubt you could get away with murdering two
members of this family."

"The marriage option interests me more than the
murder one," Garrick said.

She laughed. "So that you could bar me from testify-
ing against you?"

"No," Garrick said. "So that I could make love to you."

The air in the room seemed to heat and catch fire. Merryn's eyes dilated in shock. She gave a gasp. A pink flush mantled her cheeks and she turned her back on him, hunting feverishly now for her slippers, the need to escape him evident in the tension enveloping her slim figure.

"You have outstayed your rather tenuous welcome, your grace," she said. "If you will not leave, I will. I should return to the ball anyway. My sister will be wondering where I am."

"A conventional excuse to escape," Garrick said. "I would have expected something more imaginative from you. Besides—" he took a breath, looked her over from shining fair hair to bare toes "—you cannot go back to the ballroom looking like that." His voice dropped. "You look far too disheveled. People would talk. You look as though we have already been making love."

Something flared in her eyes. Her lips parted. She looked innocent, frightened but also bewitched.

Garrick knew that he should not touch her. It was one thing to use whatever advantage he could to persuade her to give up on her quest. It was quite another to take the step of seducing her. Her innocence and her openness fascinated him, she called to every one of his long-buried rakehell propensities, but even he was not such an unscrupulous bastard that he would deliberately ruin her. Merryn Fenner was the last woman he could ever have. Twelve years ago, after he had taken her brother's life and destroyed so many other lives as a consequence he had sworn that the only way to redeem himself was through duty. He had given up his hard living. He had turned his back on those who had predicted that with his wife dead and so spectacular a scandal attached to his name he would go back to his debauched ways with a vengeance. He had proved them wrong because after Stephen's murder and Kitty's death, strength of character was the only thing he had left, the only thing that could save him. He had served his country and he had tried to atone for his past failings. And now what tarnished honor he had left did not permit him to pursue Merryn Fenner, innocent, untouched, a woman who had already been cruelly hurt. He could not be such an unmitigated scoundrel. Even so the temptation grabbed him by the throat.

Just this once…

He knew he was lying to himself even as he kissed her. If he tasted her response just one more time he would not be able to let her go.

He bent his head and his lips met hers.

That night in his bedroom it had been no more than a brief caress. At the library he had kissed her with ruthless intent. This time he did not hurry to force a reaction. This time he courted a response from her, teasing her lips until they parted to allow his tongue to slip into her mouth, tasting her, drawing out the pleasure. He felt her tremble and slid his arms about her to hold her still.

It was a thousand times more potent than Garrick had ever imagined. Her lips were soft and yielding beneath his, offering the sweetest of surrenders. Her tentative response, the hesitant way she touched her tongue to his, tempted him to deeper intimacies. Suddenly Garrick wanted to make love to her here and now, throw her down on the bed or take her on the rug before the fire, he who had not behaved like that with a woman in twelve years and had thought he never would again, the Duke whose emotions were ice-cold and whose only passion was for books and dry documents.

He deepened the kiss, plundering her mouth now, desire leaping to wild desire, passion laced with tenderness. He slid a hand into the bodice of the rose-pink gown and felt the curve of her breast against his palm, small and soft, the nipple tightening against his fingers. It was shattering, hardening his arousal to painful proportions. She made a sound deep in her throat, and her body seemed to quiver beneath his caress. Feral possession ripped at Garrick and set him gasping. He was within an inch of losing control and ravishing her body as fiercely as he took her mouth.

He fought a brief, violent struggle for self-control and let her go, stepping back.

And then he saw her face and almost dragged her back into his arms. There was a dreaming unawakened expression in her eyes and a little smile on her lips as though she had just discovered something new and so fascinating that she was enchanted by it.

It was there for a second and then reality smashed through her pleasure banishing the look of a princess in a fairy tale. Horror was etched on her face and she pressed her fingers to her lips as though to scrub the kiss away.

"No," she said. "Oh, no, not you!" And she turned and hurried away from him, her stockinged feet making a soft slapping on the floor that seemed to emphasize her agitation.

Garrick understood what she meant. If he had had a choice she would have been the last woman in the world he would have wished to be so attracted to. It was impossible. It was madness. And yet it seemed he had no choice.

MERRYN DID NOT STOP running until she had reached the sanctuary of the library. Halfway down the stairs she realized that she was running toward people, not away from them, but with Garrick in her room there was only one other place to go that could give her solace.

There were plenty of guests in the hall. She fled past them, seeing their faces, curious and speculative, hearing the titters of laughter.

"Lady Merryn is such an original… Running into the library with her hair down and no slippers…"

Damnation, this time it was her shoes she had left with Garrick Farne. First her book, her spectacles, her *underwear*… Soon he would have sufficient of her possessions to equip a whole room.

She braced her forearms on the table in the library—such a pretty room, designed to a yellow floral pattern by her sister Joanna—and stared at her face in the mirror facing her on the wall. She was horrified by what she saw there. Long blond strands of hair snaked about her face. Her cheeks were flushed a warm pink. Normally she had very little color. From childhood she had been accustomed to people commenting on her disparagingly as *"an odd, pale little thing..."* She had not minded particularly. She had always thought looks were overrated. What use was it to be beautiful, unless to make a good marriage? People had spoken approvingly of Joanna and Tess because they were such pretty girls, as though that was the most important thing in the world. Merryn, with her reading and the stories in her head and her imaginary friends, thought it was better to be clever than beautiful, though that did not mean that sometimes she would not feel a tiny bit jealous... Jealous of Tess's charm and dimples, jealous of Joanna's thick golden-brown hair and vivid eyes... Jealous of the admiration and approval that was withheld from her because she was different.

But now, looking in the glass, she saw that her face had all the color and vivid animation it had previously lacked. Her hair was all disordered profusion. Her eyes glittered with a fierce light so deep and blue, her mouth looked soft, pink and stung with kisses. She pressed her fingers to her lips again. She remembered her words to him at the Octagon Library:

"I have never been kissed before..."

Well, she had now. Wildly, passionately, *pleasurably* kissed by an experienced rake. She had been kissed until her entire body had risen to Garrick's touch.

It felt as though she could still feel the imprint of his lips on hers. An echo of primitive heat and tension clenched her stomach. The kiss at the library had shocked her, so brief and ruthless. This one had seduced her. It had been strange, something so far outside her experience, new and different. But it had also been so much more than that, a world she wanted to explore, a hunger awakened, a fierce desire stirred. She knew she would never be the same.

She backed away from the mirror and sat down heavily in one of the armchairs. How was it possible to feel like this? She had spent twelve years hating Garrick Farne with a clear, cold passion. Then she had met him and that cold hatred had become confused by a different sort of passion. Disgust and despair shredded her. She did not understand how she could so betray herself and all that she believed in. Yet she was still trembling from Garrick's kiss even as she despised herself.

She tried to tell herself that she would have responded in the same way to any man. She knew she lied. The thoughts cluttered her head, falling over each other. She ruthlessly demolished every justification with plain fact, too honest to deceive herself.

It would not have been the same with any other man. Two years ago, James Devlin, cousin to her brother-in-law Alex, had made his admiration for her very clear.

He had even tried to steal a kiss and she had rejected him. Dev was a wickedly handsome man, charming and dangerous. Many young ladies would have adored being the object of his attentions. Yet his handsome face and elegant address had left her completely unmoved. She had not for one second burned for him as she burned for Garrick Farne.

Garrick intrigued her as no man had ever done.

Garrick Farne had killed her brother.

It was hopeless, shameful. She would not, *could not,* allow herself to be drawn to Garrick. She did not understand how it could possibly happen. And yet she knew that there had been an affinity between them from the first moment that they had met. She could try to pretend that it was no more than a physical attraction, perhaps, although she knew little about such things and understood even less. But no matter how little experience she had, she would still know she lied. What she felt for Garrick was no mere infatuation. It was deeper than that. She lost herself when she was talking to him; he challenged her, he intrigued her. For a little while at least he made her forget who he was and what he had done.

She felt unutterably confused. Garrick had shown himself ruthless that night, as dangerous as she had feared, threatening to blackmail her, exposing her weaknesses. But her greatest vulnerability was her susceptibility to him. At the library he had exploited her attraction to him. Tonight—she trembled at the thought—he could have ravished her, taken her there and then, tumbled her on the pristine narrow bed in her spinster room, and she would not have stopped him. He had been a rake. He knew exactly how to provoke a response from her body. She shook harder as she thought of his mouth on hers, his hand against her breast. He could have seduced her, ruined her. She wondered why he had let her go.

If it were not so foolish, she would have said it was because he had some shreds of honor left. Her instinct told her it was so but surely her instinct must be mistaken.

Merryn shook her head to dispel such disturbing thoughts and went over to the bookshelves, taking a book down, a copy of *The Lives of the Twelve Caesars* by Suetonius. It was a beautiful volume, bound in leather, the pages smooth beneath her fingers. She started to read, concentrating on the words, willing herself to forget Garrick. Books were her friends. They never failed her. They soothed, cheered, distracted and encouraged her. She had used them to help her through the worst moments of her life and to celebrate the best. But tonight they could not save her. The words danced before her eyes. She could not concentrate. Her mind was full of Garrick, of his voice, his touch. Her senses felt inflamed. She was bewitched.

After ten minutes she put the book aside, baffled and upset. The ball was still in full swing but she was tired. She wanted to go to bed. She hoped Garrick had gone or she really would be obliged to call a footman and have him forcibly ejected, no matter the scandal.

She hesitated outside her bedroom door, aware of

the shivers of anxiety and anticipation running up and down her spine, but when she opened the door the room was empty. Her slippers lay just as she had kicked them off.

Something caught her eye—her journal, sitting not on top of the pile of books at her bedside but on the cushion of the chair Garrick had taken. She grabbed the book. A sheet of paper fell from it.

His writing was bold and strong, as she might have imagined.

"Love and war are the same thing and stratagems and policy are as allowable in the one as the other."

Cervantes. She smiled a little, despite herself, as she recognized the quotation. She had been harboring notions of war and revenge for years. She knew nothing of love.

Then her eye fell on the second line of writing.

"Pray do not waste your time in writing poetry, Lady Merryn. It is very bad indeed."

Garrick had read her poems. How dared he. She blushed with mortification. She had known they were bad. She did not need confirmation.

She thrust his note into the fire and watched it curl and burn.

It was as she was about to ring the bell to call her maid to help her undress that she saw the other book. It was not one of hers but was a new copy of *Mansfield Park*. There was a note in that one, too.

"Your other copy was damaged beyond repair, I fear, so please accept this replacement."

She wanted no gifts from Garrick Farne. She wanted nothing from him. She rather thought that she had made that plain in the lawyer's office that morning. Yet he had her now because she found that she could not throw a book away. It was impossible. Anything else she would have consigned it to the fire along with the note. The book she reluctantly placed on her shelf and she tried not to think too much of the man who had given it to her.

For the second night in a row she lay awake.

CHAPTER SEVEN

THE FLEET PRISON was not as Merryn had anticipated. Blessed with a lively imagination, she had thought that it would be infested with rats, the walls running with water, the inmates screaming in mad frenzy to be let out. It was none of those things. The floors were swept clean, the walls were dry and it was very quiet.

The unexpected trip to Mr. Churchward's office the previous day had delayed Merryn's plans but she was still determined to push ahead with them and seek out the doctor who had attended the duel between her brother and Garrick. He was the only witness she could find. She was sure he had been bought off and she was intent on uncovering what had really happened. Her encounter with Garrick the previous night had not dissuaded her. In some odd way it had made her even more determined to learn the truth. For now she was fighting against herself as well as Garrick, against her helpless attraction to a man whom she detested. She felt naive and stupid to have such a conflict of emotions, angry with Garrick, incensed with herself.

It was also pleasant, Merryn thought, to escape from the house in Tavistock Street as well, even if a visit to the Fleet might not be everyone's idea of a trip out. Garrick Farne's offer had caused deep divisions between her and her sisters. Merryn was barely speaking to Tess, who seemed incapable of understanding her rejection of Garrick's gift as blood money and was already merrily planning all kinds of expenditure. Merryn thought of Tess's greed, and tasted bitterness in her mouth.

That morning Joanna had agreed to take the money, too. Merryn found it easier to excuse Joanna because she knew she had her reasons; Joanna was deeply devoted to Fenners, not because she loved the house and the countryside, as Merryn did, but because it was their last link to their father and to Stephen. And Joanna and Alex were poor, unlike Tess, the rich widow. Alex had an estate in the Highlands of Scotland that ate money rather than generated it and he had his cousin Chessie, who was currently staying with relatives in Edinburgh, to provide with a dowry. So Merryn could understand why Joanna would accept Garrick Farne's offer, even as her sore heart rebelled against her sister's pragmatism.

Dr. Southern's cell was off the third-floor gallery. He was sitting alone, reading, when Merryn arrived. The light was poor and he was squinting. He looked like a plant that had grown in the dark: spindly, gray-faced and weak. There was a bottle at his elbow with a clear liquid in it and a stench of alcohol in the cell that hit Merryn like a wall. When the jailer ushered her in—she had paid him six shillings for the privilege—Southern looked up and his pale eyes rested on her gently but without focus.

There was nowhere to sit other than the pallet bed, so Merryn knelt beside his chair on the hard stone floor.

"Dr. Southern?" she said. "My name is Merryn Fenner." She hesitated. She had been hoping that the doctor would know her name but there was no recognition in his face. So she had no choice—she had to plow on with what she had come for.

"You may remember my brother, Stephen," she said. "Stephen Fenner?"

Even before he answered she knew it was hopeless and her heart swooped down to her feet. Southern's gaze slid away from hers blankly. He reached for the bottle.

"Stephen?" he muttered.

"Stephen Fenner," Merryn repeated. "You were the doctor present at the duel when he died."

"Duel?" The doctor was fumbling with the bottle, tilting it to his lips. Some of the liquid ran down over his chin and splashed on his shirt. It smelled sweet but sharp at the same time, catching in Merryn's throat.

"I remember no duel."

"Twelve years ago," Merryn said. "Stephen Fenner." She felt desperate. There had been two seconds at the duel, if duel it had been. One was dead, the other thousands of miles away, beyond reach. This man had been the only other witness present. Other than Garrick Farne himself...

"Please try to remember," she whispered.

"No duel," the doctor said and for a moment Merryn's hopes soared, until she realized that he was simply unable to remember anything. He was shaking his head, a little fretful, a little lost. His hand shook; the bottle nudged the book on the table and it fell into Merryn's lap.

There was a bookplate inside with a coat of arms, a mailed fist and the motto: *Ne M'oubliez. Remember me.* Merryn did not need to see the strong writing, the initials *GF,* to tell her whose book it was. She knew the motto well. It seemed appropriate.

She shivered. So Garrick Farne had been here before her. Had he paid for Southern's silence, with the gin in the bottle perhaps? For surely the doctor was going to give her no help. He was too drunk, too forgetful, too conveniently beyond reach even though he was sitting before her. For a second she felt an equal mix of fury and despair. Garrick had been a step ahead of her again. Was she forever to be outwitted, running after his shadow?

"The Duke of Farne visits you," she said lightly, placing the book back on the table.

"Often," the doctor said. His hands shook as he drew the book close in what was almost a protective gesture. "He bought me out of here," he added.

Merryn frowned. "Garrick Farne paid your debts?"

"I only fell into more." Southern was nodding gently, a whimsical smile on his face. "I try. I fail. I remember Stephen Fenner," he added, surprisingly. "He was a scoundrel. No good. No good at all."

Merryn smothered the instinctive protest that leaped to her lips. It was true that some people had considered

Stephen a rogue. He had been feckless, careless with the money they did not possess, a gambler, a drinker. She knew that he had argued with their father over his debts. She had heard them on the nights when she had crept downstairs after bedtime. Sometimes they had left the study door open and a crack of light had crept across the hall carpet and the words had spilled out, too, angry words between father and son. She, perched on the stairs in the darkness, had heard it all. But each and every time Stephen had smoothed matters out with his generosity and his winning charm. The servants had shaken their heads over his conduct but they had been smiling even as they deplored his bad behavior. And even if Stephen had been the greatest wastrel in the world it did not mean that he deserved to die.

"I am sorry you remember him so," she said stiffly. She got to her feet. Even after only a few moments kneeling on the stone she felt cold and sore, her heart colder still. There was nothing for her here.

The jailer met her at the door. This was a different man from the one who had admitted her. He had a thin face and a greedy gleam in his eyes.

"That'll be six shillings," he said, dangling the keys in front of Merryn's nose.

"But I paid six shillings to get in," Merryn objected.

"And now you pay to get out," the jailer said. "Unless you prefer to stay here with him." He jerked his head toward Dr. Southern, who was gulping gin from the bottle like a man possessed by the urge to find oblivion.

"I don't have the money," Merryn said.

It was evidently the wrong thing to say. The jailer took her arm in a grip that felt rather firmer than she would have liked. Suddenly the Fleet did not look quite as pleasant as Merryn had thought, a dark, cold, unfriendly, and alien place far removed from the world she normally frequented. She tried to wrench her arm from the jailer's grasp but he held her fast and leaned closer. He smelled stale and his breath was foul.

"Listen, miss, it's like this. Everything costs." His gaze appraised her, lingering on the lace at her collar, the swell of her breasts beneath the line of her coat. "Unless you want to pay another way—"

"How much?"

The voice was lazy, authoritative. If Merryn had not heard the undertone of steel in it she would have sworn he was indifferent. She closed her eyes. Garrick Farne, here. Well, of course. He would be. This was a cat-and-mouse game they were embarked upon. Garrick would have made sure that Southern was too drunk to remember anything useful and then to make absolutely sure, he would have waited outside the cell while she interviewed the doctor. She was sure he had been listening to every word and that he had paid a great deal more than six shillings for the privilege of spying on her.

He did not look like her idea of a spy, hiding in corners, listening at doors. For a start he looked too elegant, in a casual single-breasted morning coat, breeches and boots with a very high polish. Merryn thought he should be out riding, giving vent to all the banked-down energy and power she sensed in him. Their eyes met. He smiled. It was not an encouraging smile and Merryn did not for one second feel reassured. She thought that it would probably suit Garrick's purposes very well for her to be clapped up in the Fleet for a while. She looked at his hard expression and just for a moment she was afraid.

"You can buy her out for ten shillings, my lord," the guard said.

"It was six shillings a moment ago," Merryn said hotly. "And I do not even owe it!"

Garrick's dark, sardonic gaze considered her. "What are you in for? House-breaking?"

"I'm not a *prisoner!*" Merryn said.

"You surprise me," Garrick said, "given your penchant for crime."

Merryn blushed. "I am trying to get out."

Garrick took out his pocketbook. He looked at the jailer, raised a brow.

"Twelve shillings, your grace," the man said, estimating Garrick's rank upward and the sum of money accordingly. "And that's a bargain."

"I am not sure that it is," Garrick murmured, his gaze bringing the hotter color up into Merryn's face. "Believe me, you should be paying me to take her off your hands not vice versa."

"Don't pay him," Merryn snapped. She felt angry, torn. "I don't want to be in your debt," she said.

"You have made that quite clear before," Garrick said. He shrugged and slid the pocketbook back into his jacket. "As you wish." He turned to walk away.

The jailer smiled unpleasantly and tightened his grip. "Well, then, missy, I'm sure we can find a nice cell for you until *someone* chooses to pay up. Assuming that they do…"

"Wait!" Merryn called. Her heart was thumping. She saw Garrick pause but he did not turn. His back looked very broad and very uncompromising. "Please," she added, and there was rather more pleading than she liked in her tone.

Garrick turned back to her. A smile tugged at the corners of his lean mouth. "Are you going to beg?" he inquired gently.

"No!" Merryn said. She moderated her tone. "But I should be very grateful…" She stumbled a little over the words. Damn him for enjoying her discomfiture. She could have slapped him, she was so angry.

"Of course," he said courteously. With a sigh he took out his pocketbook again and paid the jailer, who let Merryn go with every sign of disappointment. Garrick offered her his arm.

"Permit me to escort you back to Tavistock Street, Lady Merryn."

"No," Merryn said. "I—"

"It wasn't a question," Garrick said, taking her arm and propelling her down the stairs. "It was an order."

They reached the first landing. Merryn stopped. "I will pay you back," she said.

Garrick slanted a look down at her. "How? I thought you said you had no money."

It was a fair question, Merryn thought. Tom paid her a generous amount but she had spent the last of her wages on a copy of Samuel Richardson's *Clarissa*. She had not enjoyed the book; now she wished she had the money instead. And she could scarcely ask Garrick to knock the sum off the thirty thousand pounds he had promised her—and she had rejected.

Garrick waited a moment, then smiled and urged her down the next flight. "I won't press you for payment," he murmured.

Merryn stopped again. "I'll borrow the money from Joanna," she said fiercely. "Or Alex. Or anyone. I'll go to the moneylenders. Anything not to be in your debt."

"Anything?" Garrick said. He grabbed her, turning her against the wall. The cold stone pressed against her back. He put one gloved hand against her cheek, tilting her face up to his. The leather of his glove felt cool and smooth against her hot skin. He kissed her.

This time Merryn was a little more prepared, not quite so stunned by something so utterly beyond her experience. Now, instead of discovery, there was an edge of wicked excitement and a heat that lit her from the inside out, burning her up, making her long for more.

She knew she wanted this. Garrick had shown her that there was a part of herself she had not realized existed, a wild, wanton side so different from the cool, rational Merryn Fenner whose life had been lived vicariously in the pages of books.

She opened her lips to Garrick and touched her tongue eagerly to his. He tasted delicious. She could not name the sensation that held her but it felt like temptation distilled. She was drowning in it, so potent, so hot. There was a tight, tense ache in the pit of her stomach. Her mind spun. The solid stone of the Fleet seemed to rock beneath her feet.

She felt Garrick groan deep in his throat. He laced his hand in her hair and gave her back all she asked for, more, deepening the kiss, his tongue moving against hers, demanding a response she barely understood. Merryn forgot where she was, forgot every last one of the rules that guided a lady's behavior and slid her arms about his neck so that she could draw him closer, pressing her body against his as though the layers of clothing between them simply did not exist. His tongue slid along the inside of her lower lip, his teeth closed about it, biting softly, and Merryn's body clenched tight as a fist, deep inside.

Someone laughed close by, a lewd sound, full of suggestiveness. There was a crash from near at hand and someone swore loudly and the sounds and smells of the prison slid back into Merryn's mind.

"Sure I can't hire out a cell to you so you can finish

your business, sir?" a voice said and Merryn pulled herself from Garrick's arms and turned to see the jailer leering at them.

For a second she caught Garrick's expression. His eyes were blazing and his face was taut with desire. They were both breathing as though they had been running. Then his face changed. The naked desire was gone, replaced by his habitual cool indifference.

"Consider your debt paid," he said.

"Twelve shillings," Merryn said. She was proud to be able to find any voice at all. "For one kiss. You are extravagant, your grace."

"It was worth every penny," Garrick said, "but I apologize that I chose to take payment in public."

Merryn shivered deep inside. No doubt a kiss meant little or nothing to Garrick, rakehell that he had been. She, in contrast, felt cast adrift, lost. The heat in her blood was cooling now and it left her feeling as bereft and alone as she had done the previous night. This was wrong, this desire she had for Garrick. So how could she feel it so intensely that it hurt?

Garrick drew her close to him, belatedly shielding her from the curious glances and the knowing stares of the inmates and guards. His face was hard and set, as though he was angry with her, or perhaps with himself. He said nothing else until they were outside the gates and even then he gave her no choice, practically throwing her into the carriage that was standing waiting, before jumping in after her and slamming the door. Tumbled on the seat, out of breath and dismayed, Merryn reached for the door only for him to catch her wrist and pull her back so that she was practically sitting on his lap.

"Forgive my presumption," he said, "but you will not leave my protection until I see you are safely home, Lady Merryn."

Thoroughly incensed, Merryn struggled to free herself. "I would in all probability be safer anywhere else than with you," she snapped.

Garrick laughed. "Let's not put that to the test."

He rapped on the roof of the carriage and the horses moved off. He sat back, watching her, crossing one elegantly booted ankle over the other knee.

"What were you doing in the Fleet?" he asked.

"I am surprised that you need to ask," Merryn said resentfully. "You were there before me, weren't you? You gave Dr. Southern the gin to render him so drunk he remembered nothing!"

She waited but Garrick did not deny it. A smile that was not quite nice curled his lips. "You would have to call before seven in the morning if you wished to see Dr. Southern sober, I fear."

"He said that you visited him often," Merryn said, "no doubt to make sure he is well supplied with drink and therefore insensible."

Garrick's smile deepened. "I do visit him often," he agreed. "For whatever reason."

"He also said that you bought him out of prison."

"Also true," Garrick said. "I paid off his debts on both

of the most recent occasions he was in the Fleet." He sighed. "Dr. Southern was physician to our family for many years. When I returned to England and found that he had ceased to practice because of his weakness for the bottle, I tried to help him. I paid his debts. I visited him in the Fleet." He shrugged. "I quickly realized that there was nothing I could do for him. He prefers to be in the prison because it is familiar to him. He feels safe. He is fed and housed. If I buy him out he only seeks its shelter again." His mouth thinned. "He is an unhappy man but *his* unhappiness at least is not on my conscience."

"He is in your pocket," Merryn said, "bought off by you, your creature." She felt bitter and frustrated and she could see something in Garrick's eyes, something of regret and pity that only made her all the angrier. "I'll go back," she said. "I'll find a way to get him to talk."

"I wouldn't advise it," Garrick said. "You saw what happened today. Next time you might get yourself into far greater difficulties."

"I would have persuaded them to let me go," Merryn said.

Garrick grabbed her without warning, his hands biting into her upper arms. His touch was fierce. It was so sudden and so shocking that Merryn could not hold back a gasp.

She had never seen this anger in him before. For a moment she thought he was going to shake her. His eyes were black with fury, his mouth a hard line. She could feel tension radiating from him.

"Persuade them?" he said. "With what?" He bit the words out. "You had no money. And you have only one other commodity to sell." His gaze raked her with insulting thoroughness. "Would it have been worth it—a few fumbled liberties—for your freedom?"

"Is that what you took from me?" Merryn said. She was shaking now. Her voice was shaking, too. "A few fumbled liberties?"

She heard Garrick swear under his breath. He dropped her onto the seat and pinned her there with one hand on each side of her. She pressed back into the plush cushions, trying to put some distance between them. His physical presence was overwhelming.

"You are too courageous and too stubborn, Lady Merryn," he said. "You never seem to learn that one day your persistence will get you into trouble."

He was very close to her. Merryn stared into his eyes. They were the deepest brown, flecked with gold and green and they held her gaze with absolute demand. She felt odd, light-headed. She knew she was an inch away from shifting her gaze to Garrick's mouth, and then he would kiss her again, or she would kiss him. It was inevitable; and there would be the same undertow of anger and longing and helpless desire in their embrace that there had been before. Her stomach felt odd, tingling with nerves, aching for something deeper.

"Tell me," she said suddenly. "Tell me about Stephen's death."

The change in Garrick was extraordinary. She saw

darkness fall across his eyes like a veil, thick, impenetrable, shutting her out. The line of his jaw was as hard as granite. He said nothing at all.

Merryn stared at him, baffled and frustrated, while outside the carriage the flow of people swirled around them, passed by in a blur of color, a moving pageant. She was locked into the still core of it, possessed by the ferocious tension she could sense in Garrick, trapped by the harsh misery in his face.

"Why don't you speak?" she burst out, after what seemed hours, goaded by fury and misery. "Why do you say nothing?"

He caught her wrists and pulled her close to him.

"There is nothing I can say." For all his harshness, his breath stirred her hair like a tender caress. She could hear pain in his voice as well as anger. "Nothing will put matters right. Nothing will give you your brother back."

His hands gentled on her, slid from her slowly, reluctantly. He sat back and Merryn felt shocked and alone, missing his touch, hating herself for feeling so bereft.

"You are home," Garrick said. "I'll bid you goodbye."

There did not seem to be anything else to say. Merryn looked at his face, at the unyielding line of his cheek and jaw and the cold distance in his eyes as they rested on her. He opened the door for her with studied courtesy and then Merryn was standing on the pavement watching the carriage disappear into the press of London traffic.

Garrick had said the previous night that he would stop her inquiries and so far he had been true to his word. He was always a step ahead. She felt so impotent. There was no one who could help her. The truth had been suppressed years ago. But her only alternative was to abandon her quest for justice and it had possessed her for so long that to forsake it now seemed unthinkable. It would leave a huge void in her life and she would not know how to fill it. Besides, that was what Garrick wanted. He wanted her to give in, to concede defeat, and if she did so she would never achieve the justice that Stephen deserved.

That justice would see Garrick Farne swing on the end of a silken rope, convicted for murder.

A long shiver racked her. She thought of Garrick, of his hands on her body and his mouth on hers, of the desire in him and the answering need in her. How could it be that an outcome she had so devoutly sought for twelve years now left her shuddering? For she had the strangest feeling that if she found the evidence she sought, if she held Garrick's life in her hands, proved him a murderer, she would not be glad, but sorry.

She turned and ran up the steps to the house trying to escape her thoughts. A footman opened the door and bowed her inside. As Merryn stripped off her gloves and unpinned her hat, she noticed a large bundle of papers, tied with ribbon, sitting on the hall table. The table, one of Joanna's decorative pieces of rosewood furniture that was intended for display not use, looked as though its spindly legs might collapse beneath the weight.

"Merryn, dearest!" Joanna was coming out of the drawing room, Max the terrier clasped in her arms, his velvet green topknot a perfect match for her gown. Alex was following, holding Shuna by the hand as the baby toddled across the marble floor.

"Where have you been?" Joanna said. "You missed luncheon!"

"Nowhere in particular," Merryn said. She knew that Joanna had no real curiosity and she had no intention of telling either of her sisters anything of her business. She nodded toward the pile of papers.

"What are those?"

"Oh…" Joanna waved a vague hand. "Mr. Churchward sent them over. They are the deeds to Fenners or something else monstrously dull. Alex can sort them out."

"I'd like to look at them," Merryn said in a rush.

Joanna looked faintly surprised. "Well, of course, darling," she said. "If you like. I'll have someone put them in the library for you."

Merryn put out a hand and touched the top sheet. It was smooth from age and use and it smelled faintly musty. The ink was fading brown but it felt magical, alive, the first link she had had to her childhood home in over ten years. Her breath caught in her throat and she felt the tears sting her eyes.

Fenners is rightfully yours… I am giving it back…

She could hear Garrick's voice like a whisper, like a promise. She looked at the writing, the word *Fenners* on the top of the document pile, a fragile link to another time.

She wished that Garrick did not always make it so difficult to hate him.

"OLD HABITS DIE HARD, FARNE."

Garrick glanced up from the brandy glass before him and into the mocking green eyes of the man who addressed him. How anyone had found him here in Mrs. Tong's Temple of Venus in Covent Garden, he could not imagine. Not that Owen Purchase was likely to have been looking for him. One did not come to Mrs. Tong's brothel for a conversation that one could have at White's or Brooks's club. If it came to that, one did not visit Mrs. Tong's brothel for any kind of conversation, other than the one where one handed over the money.

"Purchase," he said. He gestured to the bottle. "Care to join me?"

"Why not?" the other man said. He slid into the gaudy covered booth opposite Garrick. He looked oddly out of place there, Garrick thought, too hard, too masculine, amid the rich silk drapes and garish cushions. Owen Purchase was an American sea captain of legendary skill and no fortune. He had fought for the British against the French and fought for the Americans against the British and had ended a prisoner of war for his pains. Now that the war was over he was back in London looking for a commission and a ship. Garrick had met him the previous year when his half brother Ethan and Purchase had been prisoners together. It had been an unconventional start to a good friendship.

"Your brother recommended this place," Purchase said in his rich Southern drawl, looking around at the swinging Chinese lanterns and the shadowy alcoves where various ladies of doubtful virtue were plying their trade. "I hear he found his future wife here."

Garrick spluttered into his drink. "So he did," he said.

Purchase smiled. His thoughtful green gaze came back to rest on Garrick. "So why are you drinking this extortionately priced brandy," he asked, "rather than taking one of these willing harlots to bed? You could get drunk more cheaply in any tavern."

Garrick had spent the previous hour asking himself that very question. When he had arrived, Mrs. Tong had almost burst out of her low-cut evening gown with excitement. Her girls had flocked about her like so many brightly colored birds of paradise vying for the privilege of meeting his every carnal need. Although it was true that physical desire had driven him there, Garrick had looked at their artfully painted faces and had felt not the slightest flicker of lust. All he had was a deep urge to get very drunk very quickly, to forget, to drown the past.

Mrs. Tong had assumed that he was getting cold feet; that he was out of practice. She had given him a bottle of brandy and her best girl. The brandy had been of surprisingly high quality, the lightskirt less so and a great deal less tempting. After ten minutes Garrick had sent her away. Mrs. Tong had sent in another to replace her, a different girl, less obviously brazen, with more pretense of innocence. Garrick had felt repelled. When he sent that one out he had told her to tell the madam to leave him in peace with the brandy bottle. Mrs. Tong had sent a message back that it would cost him but as far as she was concerned, if he could pay he was welcome to drink himself to death in her whorehouse. Garrick had thought that was a fine offer.

But now Purchase was here and asking awkward questions. He watched as the man poured himself a glass of brandy and raised it in sardonic toast.

"You don't have to answer me," Purchase said conversationally, "but I want you to know I've noticed your evasion."

Garrick traced circles with his glass on the silken tablecloth. The brothel was busy. Every few minutes the door opened to admit another visitor. The girls fluttered past like showy butterflies. Purchase gave one of them a wicked smile and she looked at him, looked at Garrick, and raised her brows. Purchase shook his head and her mouth turned down at the corners in a pretty display of disappointment.

"Don't mind me," Garrick said. "I appreciate that you didn't come here for a chat."

"I can wait," Purchase drawled. He sat back in the booth, toying with his glass, his gaze keen as it rested on Garrick's face. "You know, Farne, if it did not seem so ridiculous I would say that you are suffering from unrequited love."

Garrick laughed. "Unrequited lust, more like."

He thought of Merryn Fenner. He had not stopped thinking of Merryn since that morning. In point of fact he had not stopped thinking of Merryn since he had dragged her out from under his bed. Love? It was not love, he thought, that hot, tight bond that held them so close. It was anger and frustration, an attraction that could not be denied, a force that impelled them together only to drive them apart. It was intolerable, like the chafing of a bond that could not be slipped. But the one thing that he could not dispute was that it was Merryn he wanted, not one of these Cyprians, no matter how prettily they might perform for him. He could take one of these girls and lose himself in forgetting for a little while, but then he knew his hunger for Merryn would come back and it would be sharper than before because what he was trying to substitute for it was hollow and worthless.

"It is Lady Merryn Fenner," he said.

He saw the amusement leap into Purchase's eyes. "Those Fenner girls," he said. "Born to drive a man to perdition."

Garrick paused in the act of refilling his glass. "You, too?" he said. "I did not know."

"Lady Joanna," Purchase said, nodding. "Or Lady

Grant as she is now." He shook his head. "A hopeless case but I have always been attracted to lost causes."

"There is another sister," Garrick pointed out. "Lady Darent."

Purchase laughed. "I know. I've heard about her. Who hasn't? Four husbands already." He tilted his glass to his lips. "Perhaps I should meet her. Or perhaps not if I want to keep my sanity." His amusement fled. "I've met Lady Merryn a couple of times. She is…" He paused. "Unusual."

"She's stubborn as all hell," Garrick said. "Never gives up."

Purchase grimaced. "Family trait." He raised his brows. "So what is the problem?"

"Even I am not such a bastard that I would seduce the virgin sister of the man I murdered," Garrick said.

Purchase almost choked. "Stephen Fenner," he said. "I remember hearing about that." He pulled a face. "I'll allow that's a difficult situation." He paused. "If you want her that much you could always marry her."

Garrick looked at him and then looked back at the brandy bottle. "Are you drunk already?" he said. "Lady Merryn would rather become a nun than marry me, or so she tells me."

Purchase laughed. "As I said, a difficult situation."

"That's an understatement."

"But not an impossible situation."

Garrick looked up. "It is a *completely* impossible situation for many reasons."

Purchase shook his head. His eyes were bright. "No, that's a challenge in my book, not an impossibility." He paused. "You must have had your reasons for killing her brother."

"I did," Garrick said. There had been many reasons to rid the earth of Stephen Fenner but he had not killed the man deliberately, in cold blood. Everything had unrolled like a horrible nightmare, too fast to think. The memories of that day swirled back around him, dark, choking. Fenner had betrayed him many times over. He had been such a scoundrel. Yet once they had been close friends. Garrick sighed, draining his brandy glass. He understood all too well the appeal of Stephen Fenner's friendship. Fenner had helped him to forget his duty as heir to a Dukedom. The drink, the gaming, the women, all those things had been rich and glittering temptations to him, a youth steeped from birth in the obligations of his inheritance. He could hear Fenner's voice even now.

"Duty? That's a damned tedious business, Garrick, old fellow! Time enough for that when your papa is dead and gone…"

And then they had gone out on the town and he had woken hours later in some female boudoir tied to the bed, his head aching, his balls aching more, and absolutely no idea how he had got there. That sort of experience, for Stephen Fenner, would have been a quiet night.

"Lady Merryn wants to know the truth about her

brother's death," he said and felt a clutch of grief and guilt at how disillusioned she would be if she ever knew.

"Then tell her, Farne," Purchase said. "She might be shocked but I'll wager she'll be strong enough to take it."

Garrick ran a hand over his hair. He knew he was drunk. It seemed to give his mind a curious clarity. He wanted to tell Merryn the truth even though he knew it would hurt her profoundly.

"She was only thirteen when her brother died," he said slowly. "She hero-worshipped him."

Purchase wrinkled up his face expressively. "Even so. She's not thirteen now. She's a grown woman. And sometimes…" He looked away. "Sometimes we all have to accept disillusionment."

"Yes," Garrick said. "If it was simply that…" He stopped. Could he trust Merryn when the lives of others were at stake? She was driven by a passionate desire for justice. She burned with the need to tell the truth. That very passion could see him hang and ruin lives a second time. The risk was enormous. Surely he would be a fool even to consider it. Yet the instinct to trust her was so strong.

"Twelve years ago I gave a promise never to tell," he said. His father was dead now. Lord Fenner was dead, too. Of the original men who had made that bond only Lord Scott, Kitty's old, embittered father, remained to hold him to his word and Churchward, of course. The lawyer knew everyone's secrets.

"Break the promise," Purchase said now. "If Lady Merryn is important enough to you, Farne, you will trust her with the truth."

"Would you trust a woman who wanted to see you hang?" Garrick asked.

Purchase laughed and refilled his glass. Some liquid splashed, rich and deep, in the candlelight. "It gives a certain spice to the relationship," Purchase drawled.

"I cannot wed again," Garrick said. "I have—" He stopped.

I *have nothing to offer, least of all to a woman as gallant and bright and brave as Merryn Fenner.*

He had nothing but failure behind him in the marriage stakes, nothing but tarnished honor and the endless duties of being a Duke. Merryn, with her dauntless spirit, deserved better than a man whose soul felt as old and worn as his. She deserved a man who could love her, for a start, not one who had lost the ability to love when he had lost his honor.

"You're a damned fool, Farne, if you let her go," Purchase said, but without heat. "At least I tried to win Joanna—and failed," he added ruefully. His eye fell on a redheaded girl who had drawn the curtain aside and stepped into the room. He put his glass down slowly.

"If you will excuse me," he said.

Garrick followed his gaze. "Of course."

As Purchase went out in response to the redhead's come-hither smile, the curtain parted again to reveal another figure, tall, austere, long nose twitching with disapproval. Garrick stared. Pointer had come to find him. No doubt the butler, like Owen Purchase, thought he was about to relapse into his old, wicked, rakish ways and forget all about duty and service and obligation.

If only he could.

Garrick stood up. The room spun. The butler placed a hand on his arm.

"What the deuce are you doing here, Pointer?" Garrick demanded.

"Your grace…" The butler was keeping his voice discreetly low. Everyone was looking at them but then, Garrick thought that was hardly surprising. Pointer, in his coat, cane and beaver hat, looked about as out of place as a…well, as a butler in a brothel.

"Your grace, you have a meeting with the land agent from the Farnecourt estate in precisely—" Pointer checked his watch "—three hours. I did not think you would wish to be late. It concerns the pensions for the widows and orphans and the payments to be made to other staff on your father's death—"

"Of course," Garrick said. "Of course it does. Widows and orphans… Duty calls."

A blonde harlot passed them, giving Pointer a luscious smile. The butler blushed.

"Tempted there for a moment, were you, Pointer?" Garrick said.

"No, your grace," the butler said. "I prefer a lady to be more rounded and less angular." He tucked his cane under his arm and politely held the curtain aside for Garrick to exit. "Mrs. Pond, the housekeeper, and I have an understanding," he added primly. "We are to wed next year when she retires. I would not like her to hear I had visited a brothel, your grace."

"All in the line of duty," Garrick said, "but she won't hear it from me, I give you my word."

Garrick gave Mrs. Tong a staggering sum of money for the brandy and went out into the night, Pointer trotting along at his side like a bodyguard, or possibly a jailer. He felt tired, his body taut with unsatisfied desire. It had probably been folly to turn down the offer of a few hours' forgetting in the skillful hands of one of Mrs. Tong's girls. She would have been able to give him fleeting pleasure and physical release. But it was Merryn he wanted, not a courtesan. And he did not want an hour or so of anonymous oblivion. Yes, he wanted Merryn in his bed, her body naked and exposed to his gaze and to his touch, her mouth eager and sweet beneath his. But he also wanted her innocence and her passion to illuminate his life. He had lived in the darkness for a very long time.

He wanted what he could not have.

Merryn Fenner. He knew instinctively that one way or another she would surely be his undoing.

CHAPTER EIGHT

MERRYN CAME OUT of the Royal Institution and shivered in the cold November breeze. The air had lost the last warmth of autumn and was cold today, the sky gray and sharp with an edge of sleet. She had enjoyed Professor Brande's lecture on the chemical elements very much. It was the type of event that she loved: esoteric, intellectual, peaceful, a far cry from the ballrooms and entertainments of the ton. There were few attendees, just a small group of medical students and a sprinkling of gentlemen with an interest in scientific matters. Humphrey Davy, Brande's predecessor at the Royal Institution, had been immensely successful and his lectures oversubscribed, but Brande was far dryer and less fashionable. Which was just the way that Merryn liked it. Her academic interests were, as she had told Garrick Farne, a refuge and an escape.

She did not want to return to Tavistock Street, where Joanna and Tess would either be out calling on their friends or entertaining guests and talking about something idle: the little season parties, the latest fashion in boots, the approach of Christmas. The thought of so much chitchat bored her. Her sisters had tried to take her shopping yesterday—for some reason they thought she needed some new clothes even though her current ones were not worn-out—but the idea of Belgrave House and the Bond Street emporia did not excite her. Instead she had spent the entire previous afternoon sifting through the Fenners estate papers, an exercise that was nostalgic but also practical. She knew it was folly to imagine that Garrick Farne would have overlooked anything remotely incriminating in the papers but she felt she had to look. Naturally enough she had drawn a blank other than to spot a reference to a meeting shortly after Stephen's death between her father and someone called Lord S and the Duke of F. It had surprised her that Lord Fenner had met with Lord Scott and the late Duke of Farne. She could see no purpose for such a painful meeting at all.

She took a hackney carriage to Grillons Hotel, an irreproachably respectable place where she had occasionally stayed when Joanna was out of town and wanted somewhere quick and easy from which she could come and go in her work for Tom. She ordered a luncheon of roast beef and watched the guests pass by. There was a clergyman with his wife and three pale, quiet daughters all dressed identically in sober gowns and dark bonnets. There was an elderly lady dripping with jewels who walked with a stick and raised a diamond-encrusted lorgnette to stare at Merryn for a full ten seconds. There were two country gentlemen who talked with their mouths full and drank copious tankards of ale, and there was a small, fair girl, governess or companion,

Merryn thought, who looked anxious, as though she was nervous to be out on her own.

Merryn ate her meal and ignored the curious glances of some of the other diners. She was accustomed to solitude. She preferred it. When her meal was over she went out into the pale afternoon, heading for the booksellers in the Burlington Arcade.

She was walking back along Bond Street when she saw ahead of her the tall figure of Garrick Farne cutting purposefully through the crowds. He disappeared into a saddlery shop across the street and Merryn paused, watching his reflection in the bow window. She was not quite sure why she was spying on him. Garrick himself was unlikely to lead her to anything that would be useful. He was on his guard against her, determined that she should discover nothing. Yet still she lingered.

"You must find me utterly fascinating, Lady Merryn," Garrick's dry voice said in her ear, "to follow me here and study me so intently."

Merryn jumped. The reflection had disappeared, scarcely surprising since Garrick was standing directly beside her, the elegant green superfine of his sleeve brushing hers. He removed his hat and bowed. The wind ruffled the dark red of his hair. An inexplicable shiver shot through Merryn, heating her from the inside out. She looked up into his eyes and met a most sardonic expression. Blushing, she shifted her gaze to his mouth. No, that was worse. She could not look at his lips without remembering his kisses, the warmth and the taste of

him, the way in which she had melted inside, soft and
sweet and yet burning with such a curious intensity like
a scientific experiment she had once witnessed where
copper had burned with a blue flame.

"Oh!" she said, her voice high and false. "I did not
see you there, your grace."

There was a silence just long enough to emphasize
her falsehood and then Garrick smiled. "In that case
you must have a particular interest in this shop, to be so
intently peering in at the window?"

"Oh, yes," Merryn said. "Yes, indeed."

She had not actually noticed what sort of shop it
was, having been concentrating on watching Garrick's
reflection but now as she turned back to the bow windows she saw it was a milliners. The window was full of
jaunty bonnets, ribbons and other accessories. Merryn's
brow cleared. She might have no interest in fashion but
she could pretend to one. Except…except that she was
observant, and what she was now observing was that the
shop was full of *men*. Which was odd. Unfathomable,
almost… Were they buying gifts for their womenfolk,
perhaps?

She saw one of the men follow a shopgirl through a
curtain at the back of the room.

"The ladies are not selling hats," Garrick said, even
more dryly, reading her mind. "They sell themselves,
Lady Merryn. The millinery is merely a front."

"Oh!" Merryn blushed bright red.

"First you take to sleeping in other people's houses,"

Garrick said, "then you are almost locked up in the Fleet for debt and now I find you studying the ways of the courtesans. Your financial situation must be parlous indeed if you are considering taking to the streets." His gaze dwelled on her face, bringing even hotter color into it. "You might do well. But I wouldn't advise it."

"I have no intention of becoming a courtesan," Merryn snapped. "I was merely—"

"Using the window as a mirror to watch me. Yes, I realize that." Garrick smiled at her. "You are following me for a change. How stimulating."

Merryn gritted her teeth. "I was not following you. I was walking home." She held out her parcel of books. "I have been to the booksellers."

Garrick fell into step beside her. "Poetry?"

"I did buy some Byron."

"Ah. To inspire you?"

"I imagine you think it would take more than that." Merryn was stung. She looked up at him. "You read my poetry journal that night in my bedroom. That was not the act of a gentleman."

"I apologize," Garrick said. He slanted a look down at her. Merryn wished he were not so tall. Not only did she almost have to run to keep up with his elegant stride, she could not see his face, nor judge his expression. "It was unhandsome of me," he agreed. "In mitigation, all I can say is that I was looking for your diary."

"Oh, well, then!" Merryn felt even more indignant. "I forgive you at once!"

Garrick laughed. "You would not have minded if your poetry had been good and I had praised you for it."

"This is not about the quality of my writing," Merryn said crossly. "It is about my privacy!"

Garrick's firm lips twitched. "Well, be careful of the Byron," he drawled. "It can be very inflammatory to the senses."

"My senses are in no danger of inflammation," Merryn said coldly.

"All evidence suggests the contrary," Garrick said. He stopped, put out a hand and lightly touched her arm. "Shall I demonstrate to you?"

"Farne. Lady Merryn." A group of people had come upon them unnoticed and now encircled them. Merryn, acutely conscious of Garrick's touch burning through the sleeve of her pelisse, shook him off and took a step back. She wished they had not been surprised just then, with Garrick looking down at her with that quizzical smile she was coming to know so well, his hand on her arm implying an intimacy she did not wish anyone else to see… She felt hot with mortification.

Nor were these acquaintances that she particularly wished to acknowledge. Merryn recognized Lord Ayres, an arbiter of fashion who practically worshipped Joanna but had never condescended to speak to her before, accompanied by his wife and Lady Radstock, another fashionable gossip. There was a younger man whom Merryn did not recognize but Garrick clearly did.

"Croft," he said coldly, giving the man an infinitesimal bow. "How do you do."

"Not as well as you, old fellow!" Croft raised his quizzing glass and ogled Merryn from top to toe in a manner that she found insolent and presumptuous. He let the glass fall from one languid hand. "Cunning move, what, to hand back the money and make yourself look good," he said. He smiled at Merryn, vulpine, eyes gleaming. "Let bygones be bygones, eh, Lady Merryn, for the sake of thirty thousand pounds?"

Merryn saw Garrick's eyes narrow. "Croft—" his voice was silky "—I do suggest that you think carefully about your next words."

"Or…what?" Croft laughed. "You'll call me out? There's been enough of that sort of thing, don't you think, old chap?" He slapped Garrick on the shoulder. "No, you are to be congratulated." His gaze swept Merryn again. "Especially if you keep a part of that sum in the family. Nice work, Farne!" He sauntered off down the street, offering his arm to one of the ladies, swept along in a wave of bright fashionable colors and loud fashionable laughter.

Merryn saw Garrick take a step after them and grabbed his arm. "Don't," she said. She realized that her voice was thick with tears. Lord Croft's derisive words rang in her ears.

Let bygones be bygones, eh, Lady Merryn, for the sake of thirty thousand pounds…

Everyone, she realized, knew about Garrick's gift to

them. No doubt it was the *on dit,* spoken of in every club, coffee shop and ballroom in London. Tess had probably boasted of it, told all her smart acquaintance of their newly acquired riches. A pain started in her chest. It was excruciating. She gave a little gasp. Her heart was pounding.

Everyone would think that she had sold Stephen's memory for thirty thousand pounds, that she had betrayed him and that she simply did not care that he had died. She felt hot and breathless, the misery clawing at her throat.

"Excuse me," she said, and her voice sounded high and tight. "I have to go now."

From a distance she could hear Garrick's voice calling her name and there was anxiety in it and urgency and some other emotion she could not place but she ignored it, ignored him, because all she could feel, all she could think, was that people were right: she had sold her brother, she had betrayed his memory, because she should have stopped Joanna and Tess somehow, she should have *seen* what would happen, should have known what everyone would think, and she would never forgive herself.

The late afternoon sunshine struck her in the eyes and she blinked. The noise of the street roared in her ears. Everything seemed too loud and too bright. Faces passed in a blur. She had a stitch in her side, she had been walking so fast. She stumbled a little, straightened, and tried to think. Her mind felt foggy. Simple matters, such as the way back to Tavistock Street, seemed impossible to grasp, so she set off walking again, quickly, to get away. She walked for ten minutes, blindly, thoughtlessly, until the coldness of the air started to penetrate her pelisse and finally made her realize that she needed to get home.

Merryn looked about her seeing her surroundings clearly for the first time. She had gone the wrong way for she was in Great Russell Street now which was not perhaps the most salubrious area for a woman to find herself alone, but it was only a step back to the main road and a hackney carriage home.

She turned on her heel, suddenly feeling exhausted and wretched and cold. Back in Tavistock Street Joanna and Tess would be preparing for a dinner that evening and no one would understand how she felt, no one would share her feelings, no one would in all probability notice that she was any different from normal. They would be happy because Alex could afford to make repairs to his estate now and give Chessie a dowry and Tess could buy yet more new clothes and nobody cared that Stephen was dead.

Her footsteps dragged on the cobbles. It was not much farther. As she reached the corner there was an extraordinary sound like the sharp crack of thunder overhead, then a roar that grew louder and louder until her ears rang with it and the ground beneath her feet shook. She could hear screaming and spun around, and in that moment something hit her with tremendous force, knocking her off her feet. She went down onto the cobbles, tumbled over and over like a rag doll, boneless, like flotsam on the tide. She was blinded by water; or at least it felt like water, but it was dark and it smelled strange, sweaty and brackish. She gulped for air but instead the liquid filled her lungs, making her choke. It tasted thick and malty and she thought it was going to smother her. Then her flailing hand caught the edge of something firm and she held on for dear life as the flow swept past her and dropped her hard, coughing and spluttering, in the doorway of what had once been a house.

Merryn sat up. Around her the flood lapped in dirty waves, plastering her clothes to her body, washing all manner of objects past her: a broken chair, a child's toy, even a dead cat. The smell, sweet and rich, was everywhere, filling her nostrils. Her chest hurt from coughing. Her mind felt blank with shock. She did not seem able to think. It was like pushing at a closed door. She struggled to her feet.

There was another roar of sound, even louder than the first, and she looked up to see a solid wave of blackness rolling toward her. If she had had even the slightest flicker of breath left it would have been the first time in her life that she screamed. Then someone caught her hard about the waist, drawing her beneath him, sheltering her with his body. The wave broke over them, followed by the crack and scrape of falling masonry. The house was coming down.

It was her final thought.

IT WAS PITCH-BLACK and cold and wet, and Garrick could see nothing, but he could move and he could breathe. He ached all over but miraculously he appeared to have broken no bones. In his arms, Merryn was still breathing, too. Garrick felt relief, huge and overwhelming, and gratitude, and another emotion that he did not want to define but that grabbed his heart and squeezed it tight like a giant fist. He had reached Merryn in time. He had been able to save her. *Thank God.* He pressed his lips to her hair for one heartfelt moment and breathed in the scent of her, long and deep. Her softness, her sweetness, steadied him. He felt an enormous, primitive need to protect and defend her, to hold her and keep her safe.

Very cautiously he shifted his grip on her so that she was settled more comfortably in his lap, her head in the crook of his shoulder. Merryn instinctively nestled closer to him, seeking the warmth and comfort of his arms, murmuring something he could not hear. She was not heavy but for a small woman she was no lightweight, either, and Garrick had suffered untold cuts and bruises when the house fell. His head, in particular, felt like a ball that had sustained a prolonged kicking. He tightened his arms about her, drawing her closer. The movement jarred him but he gritted his teeth against the pain.

Merryn moved again. Groaned. She was waking up.

"Where am I?" she said. She sounded frightened. There was nothing but darkness around them and the

weight of rubble pressing down on them and the taste
of dust in the air.

"It's all right," Garrick said. "You're safe." His throat
felt thick with the dirt and dust. He coughed, started
again. "There was an accident, a flood—"

"You?" She had recognized his voice and she did
not sound pleased. There was an edge to her tone that
suggested anxiety and relief together, an odd mixture.
Waking in the dark, Garrick thought, in a stranger's
arms would be terrifying. Waking to discover that she
was trapped with him only marginally less disturbing.

He felt Merryn try to move again, levering herself
upright, a maneuver that only served to press her rounded
buttocks into his groin all the more firmly. She winced.
So did Garrick, but for different reasons. For a second
the unwelcome stab of arousal was almost enough to
distract him from the pain in his head.

"What are you doing here?" Merryn demanded.
"Were you following me again?"

"Yes," Garrick said. He was not going to pretend.
They were trapped alone together in the darkness. Any
pretense between them now was impossible. "You were
going the wrong way to get to Tavistock Street," he said.
"You were upset and I was worried about you. I thought
you might lose yourself in a rookery and get into trouble.
Which you did," he added, "though not quite as I had
imagined."

There was silence. Then, "You were worried about

me?" Merryn repeated. There was an odd note in her voice.

"Yes," Garrick said. "Croft's words distressed you. I am sorry for that." He had seen the stricken look in her eyes as Croft had made his malicious remarks. Merryn did not deserve such cruelty. For a moment he felt a wave of utter fury wash through him again. He clenched his fists and wished he had planted the young peer a facer. That would have given the ton something else to gossip about.

"It is of no consequence." Merryn sounded prickly, her tone warning him to keep his distance. Garrick knew she was trying to protect herself, that she did not want him to see the depth of her hurt. He suspected that for anyone to imply that she had been bought off in the matter of her brother's death would be intolerable for her.

"Yes, it is," he said. "It is of consequence."

This time she did not deny it. She was quiet again for a moment. "You said that there had been a flood," she said. "I remember now. There was a wave of dirty water…" She still sounded dazed. She put out a cautious hand and touched Garrick's thigh, recoiling as though burned when her fingers brushed the soaking material of his pantaloons. Garrick grinned to himself as she rolled off his knee with more haste than finesse. There was a splash as she landed in the beer again.

"Why are we sitting in a pool of water?" she demanded.

"It's beer," Garrick said. "The buildings are flooded with beer."

"Beer!" She sounded startled. Then her voice changed. "That smell! I wondered what it was."

"I think the vat on top of the brewery in Tottenham Court Road must have burst," Garrick said. "I've seen it happen before when a liquid ferments and puts pressure on the vat. The hoops snap and the beer pours out in a flood."

"There was a sound like thunder, or cannon." Merryn's voice was still ruffled, a sign of her distress. "I am not describing it well," she added, "but I have never heard an explosion before."

Garrick smiled, there in the dark. How many women, he wondered, would be concerned at their lack of eloquence in a situation like this? Only Merryn Fenner would need the right word for the right occasion. Most other women he had known would be having the vapors or swooning. Not Merryn. She was more concerned with her vocabulary. He felt another rush of emotion, swift and sharp, admiration for her and something more, something deeper.

He sensed her shift toward him in the darkness although she was careful not to make physical contact again. Garrick could not see her because the gloom was stifling, like a blanket. It felt thick and heavy and it was starting to feel hot as well, as though they were inside a fermenting vat. The air seemed weighed down with the smell of the malt. Garrick could hear Merryn breathing in quick, light pants, and knew she was afraid. She was very close and he sensed she was facing him now. If he lifted a hand he thought it would touch the curve of her cheek. He wanted to touch her very much, and not just to reassure her. There was something knowing about the dark, something intimate that stripped away all layers of pretense and all formality.

"I assume that we are trapped?" Merryn asked. "Or we would not still be sitting here."

"I'm afraid we are," Garrick said. "The house came down on top of us. We are on the ground floor but there is no way out." He could see no point in lying to her. She was an intelligent woman. She would soon work it all out for herself.

"I remember the walls falling." She sounded a little more composed now but with all his senses alert Garrick could feel other emotions in her. There was the fear she was trying very hard to repress and also to hide from him, as though she was afraid it was a sign of weakness. There was anger, too. He could understand that. He was surely the last man on earth that she would want to be trapped with here in the intimate dark.

"Is there really no way out?" she said. There was a tiny catch in her voice. "I...I do not care for enclosed spaces."

"I don't know," Garrick said. "We won't be able to tell until daylight returns."

He had already been thinking about their chances of escape. With all the chaos and destruction from the explosion it was possible that it might take rescuers days to sift through all the rubble but at least the daylight might show up little cracks and gaps in the fallen masonry, a weakness or a way out. There was air in their prison, so he knew it was not totally sealed off from the outside world. In the morning he would start searching for a way to escape. Until then though the two of them were captive.

"It is night now?" This time the quiver in Merryn's voice was much clearer. Enclosed spaces combined with the long dark reaches of the winter night... Garrick could almost feel her shudder.

"Yes," he said. "It must be some time near midnight now. You were unconscious for quite a long time." He put out a hand to her. "I should have asked you before—are you injured?"

"No!" She spoke very quickly, moving a little away from him, rejecting his comfort. Garrick let his hand fall. "I don't know why I fainted," she said. She sounded defensive.

"Shock, perhaps," Garrick said. "Fear."

"That makes me seem dreadfully feeble." Now she sounded uncomfortable, as though there was more than a ring of truth in his words.

"Don't be too hard on yourself," Garrick said. "Most people with any sense would be frightened in this situation."

"Are you?" Merryn asked.

Damn it. She had such a talent for putting him on the spot.

"I have been in worse situations," Garrick said carefully.

She laughed. "You do not like to admit to fear?"

"What man would?"

"Oh, male pride..." She sounded dismissive. "If you had denied it outright I would have thought you a fool or a liar or both."

"Thank you," Garrick said ruefully.

"Not at all." She shifted. "Perhaps someone will rescue us soon."

Despite her bravado, Garrick could hear how desperately she hoped that would true.

"They'll have to tear themselves away from drinking all the beer first," he said.

She gave a gasp of laughter. "You think they would put drink above people's *lives?*"

"This is a poor neighborhood," Garrick said, "and free beer is free beer no matter how it is delivered."

Merryn was quiet. The darkness wrapped about them dense and malty and hot. In the silences, Garrick thought, he could sense Merryn slipping away from him, feel her fear creep closer, feel her thoughts turning dark. A moment later she caught his sleeve. Her fingers brushed his wrist, sending a deep shiver of awareness through him.

"You saved my life," she said. She took a breath. "I

wish it had not been you." She sounded very unhappy. "I wish it had been anyone but you."

Garrick gave a short laugh. "I'll take that as gratitude," he said. This time he did reach out and touch her cheek. It felt soft and dusty beneath his fingers. She drew back sharply.

"When it comes to life and death," he said slowly, "you cannot afford to be too particular about who saves you, Lady Merryn. That is something I do know."

There was a silence. He could hear Merryn breathing again, quick and ragged. He knew she was fighting a battle with herself against the fear that oppressed her. She gave a juddering little hiccup and Garrick felt her raise her hands, scrubbing away what must have been tears from her face. His instinct, fierce and immediate, was to reach out to try to comfort her but he held back. He knew his touch would be the last thing she wanted. Besides, he was having trouble keeping his own mind from plumbing the depths of disaster. He knew that their prospects were not good. No one knew that they were there. They could be walled up until they starved to death, they could be crushed by another fall of masonry, they could drown, they could run short of air and be smothered or they might simply go mad. Garrick closed his eyes and forced away all the images of death and catastrophe by sheer force of will. The effort made his head pound all the more. He tried to think about Merryn, about the need to reassure her. It distracted him from his own pain and discomfort.

"You do not need to be afraid of the dark," he said. "It cannot hurt you."

"I know." Her voice had eased a shade, as though talking made their captivity a tiny bit easier to bear. "I was locked in a chest once when I was young," she said. "It was so small and dark and hot, just like this. I could not move and I thought I would never be found and that I would die like the girl in a Gothic novel I had read."

"Which just goes to show how dangerous reading can be," Garrick said. "Why were you in the chest in the first place?"

"I was playing hide-and-seek with Joanna and Tess," Merryn said. He could hear her voice warm into amusement. The memory was distracting her. "I wanted to hide somewhere they would never find me," she said, "just to prove that I was cleverer than they were." Her amusement died. "Unfortunately I chose too well."

"Presumably they were cleverer than you had anticipated," Garrick pointed out, "or you would not be here." He paused. "Why did you feel you had something to prove?"

Merryn did not reply for a moment. Garrick waited. It was odd not being able to see her. He had nothing on which to judge her responses other than hearing and intuition. But the darkness seemed to have sharpened his senses other than sight. He could read all the little nuances in Merryn's voice. Her emotions were reflected in her breathing: her fear, her unhappiness and her determination not to crack and give in to weakness. He could smell her, too, the faint scent of flowers mixed with dust and beer in her hair and on her skin. He ached to touch her.

After a moment Merryn answered his question. He could hear reluctance in her voice, as though she were confiding a secret almost against her will.

"Jo and Tess were both so pretty," she said ruefully, "and I was not. All I had was my book learning."

Garrick remembered her telling him that he should address his gallantries to her sisters because she had no interest or experience in the art of flirtation.

"You look just like they do," he said. "No one could doubt that you are related."

He could feel her amazement. "No, I do not! I don't look like them at all! I am short where they are statuesque."

"You are smaller than your sisters, perhaps, but more of a perfect miniature."

She did not appear to have heard him. "And I am fair whereas Jo is dark and Tess has dark red hair."

"Blond hair is just as pretty," Garrick pointed out. "Prettier."

"And my eyes are not violet-blue."

"No, they are more like sapphires."

"And my nose is snub." Merryn sounded defiant, as though this were the clinching argument.

"True," Garrick agreed.

"Which ruins *everything*." Now she sounded fierce.

"What a good job," Garrick said, "that you do not value appearance in the least."

There was a silence. "I was jealous," Merryn said in a very small voice. "They had each other. They were friends. I was younger and I had no charm. Not a scrap of it."

Garrick found that he wanted to pull her into his arms. The impulse grabbed him fast and violently. He forced his hands to his sides. To touch Merryn now just as they were starting to build a tentative alliance to see them through this ordeal would be madness. He had to keep his distance.

"It is true that you are not in the common style," he said carefully, "but that does not mean that you are not..."

He stopped. *What, Farne?* he thought. He could scarcely tell her that she was exquisite, desirable, ravishing, even if he believed all those things to be true.

"Interesting in your own way," he finished. It sounded lame. It *was* lame. His address had clearly deserted him. He wanted to kick himself.

But Merryn was laughing. "No one could accuse you of flattery, your grace," she said dryly.

"I can see that having two sisters who are incomparables must be somewhat trying," Garrick said.

"I felt like a cuckoo in the nest," Merryn said. "You have brothers and sisters," she added, taking him aback. "Why are you estranged from them?"

Garrick laughed ruefully. "You are unfailingly direct, are you not, Lady Merryn?"

She sounded surprised. "I ask things because I want to know."

That, Garrick thought, summed Merryn up precisely. She had never learned the art of compromise, never seen why she should adopt all the little accommodations, lies and deceits that made life run so much more easily. When Merryn wanted to know something she asked a straight question.

"I am not estranged from Ethan," he said, taking her question very literally to avoid addressing the more painful truths about his family and their appalling lack of sibling spirit.

"Ethan is your half brother, is he not?" Merryn said. "The one who married Lottie Palliser?"

The word *brother* seemed to dance on the air between them for a moment and the atmosphere thickened with emotion. Garrick could sense the fragile pact between them slipping away when it was barely begun. How could it not, with Stephen Fenner's death always lying between them? And yet suddenly, fiercely, he was not prepared to accept that. He and Merryn had to survive this disaster together and he would fight for that against all the odds.

"Unfortunately Ethan is the only one who does not hate me," he said conversationally, trying to distract her. "The others refuse to speak to me."

"Oh…" Merryn almost laughed. Garrick could feel

the huge effort she was making not to allow Stephen Fenner's memory to come between them. It was the only thing that she could do, trapped alone with him in the dark. She needed comfort and reassurance, someone to talk to, and he was the only one there with her.

"Why should they hate you?" Her voice was almost normal. "You are the eldest. Did they not look up to you?"

"They took their cue from my father," Garrick said.

She digested that. "I never met him," she said. "But I heard about him. He sounded…" there was a shiver in her voice "…rather unpleasant."

"That was one word for him," Garrick agreed. His father had been the most malevolent man he had known, eaten up by raging ambition and eventually by disappointed hopes. "I am afraid that I was a great source of discontent to him," he said.

"Because you were a rake?" Merryn said. "I have heard something of your reputation." She sounded like a disapproving maiden aunt and the censure in her tone made Garrick grin. It also made him want to kiss her. That, he knew, would be as dangerous as allowing Stephen Fenner to divide them. In a moment, though, he would be sitting on his hands to prevent himself from touching her.

"That was a part of the problem," he said. "My father disapproved of my rakish ways, which was somewhat hypocritical of him since he was the greatest rake in the kingdom himself." He sighed. "More than that he disapproved of my scholarly ambitions. Those, he said, were quite beneath the dignity of a gentleman."

This time Merryn did laugh. "Yet he sent you to Oxford."

"Only because it was the done thing," Garrick said. "He did not expect me to study. That, he felt, was quite wrong and inappropriate to the station of a Duke."

"How extraordinary." Merryn sounded astonished—and resentful. "I would have given so much to be accorded the educational privileges that you and Stephen—" She stopped.

Stephen again. This time the silence was more difficult to overcome.

"You were at Eton and Oxford with Stephen," Merryn said. She sounded tentative as though she, as well as Garrick, did not quite know where this might lead.

"Yes, I was," Garrick said. Suddenly this was dangerous ground. He did not want Merryn to pursue this and yet he did not want to cut her off when this tenuous thread was all there was holding them together.

"Stephen was a very poor scholar," Merryn said hesitantly.

"Yes, he was," Garrick agreed.

"You do not try to comfort me by pretending otherwise." Merryn sounded as though she might be half smiling.

"What would be the point?" Garrick said. "You knew Stephen as well as I did. You know he had no academic pretensions."

"He was your friend." This time Merryn did not say it with any hint of accusation in her tone. Instead she sounded sad. Garrick winced to hear the pain in her voice.

"Yes," he said. "Stephen was my greatest friend." He took a breath. Was it pointless to try to explain to her? Would it be too little, too late? Would she even want to hear? "My life was bounded by duty," he said. "Stephen's friendship helped me to escape that sometimes. With him I could forget the burden of responsibility, my father's expectations, the obligations that had been weighing on me from the moment I was born." He stopped. "I was trained to be a Duke from the cradle," he said. "It was good to forget that sometimes."

"Stephen was a master at that," Merryn said. "At escaping obligations." He heard her sigh. "My father deplored his behavior. We did not have the money for him to gamble and drink away. He was a wastrel and a gamester and we could not afford him."

It was the first time that Garrick had ever heard her utter any kind of criticism of her brother. "I thought," he said, "that you idolized Stephen?"

"I loved Stephen." She corrected him. "That's different. It means that I can still see his faults. But he was kind to me and generous and the most loving brother I could have asked for." Her voice cracked. "Sometimes..." She spoke so quietly Garrick had to strain to hear her. "Sometimes I am so afraid that I will forget him," she said. "I have nothing left of his, no possessions, no paintings, nothing real to remind me… Sometimes I cannot even see his face clearly anymore. Even my memories change and fade." Her tone hardened. "I know Stephen was weak," she said. "I know he did wrong. But still he did not deserve to die."

Her words hung in the air between them, an accusation and an unspoken question, the question they could never escape.

Why did you kill my brother?

Garrick said nothing. He could feel Merryn looking at him through the dark, could feel her gaze on him like a physical touch, puzzled, frustrated, that edge of anger back now because he would never discuss Stephen's death, never bend, never tell her what happened. He ached to do so but he knew he could not. He had given his word, a solemn promise borne out of protection and penance and until he was absolved of that he had to keep silent. Each day, though, the torment seemed to grow. He had written, the previous night, after his discussion with Purchase. Perhaps when they were out of here an answer would come and then he would be free to follow his instinct. The urge to trust Merryn was even stronger now, here in the intimate dark. Only that fundamental promise held him back because he was not a man to give his word and then break it. He could not. Duty was the only thing that had redeemed him.

Merryn shifted. "Tell me about your wife," she said. "Tell me about Kitty." She sounded angry now because he had not answered her. Her words ran hot with it.

Garrick sighed. "Why do you ask?" he said. Talking about Kitty was always torture. His memories of her were so poignant, filled with regret. He had not been the husband Kitty had wanted. He had failed in that and failed her in so much else, too. He had failed to protect her when most it had mattered. The ache in his head pounded suddenly. He had forgotten about it for a short while; now it hurt.

"Did you love her?" Merryn said. Her words dropped into the dark like stones. The air was hot and still, burning with emotion now. How had they moved so swiftly from a cautious truce to this painful ground? Garrick felt as though he had taken a false step somewhere in the dark. The knowledge angered and dismayed him.

"I cared for her," he admitted. It would have been impossible not to care, he thought, nursing Kitty through her final days, seeing the misery that had torn her apart after Stephen had died.

"So you did not love her." There was satisfaction in Merryn's voice. "Did it pain you," she continued, "that your wife preferred my brother to you?"

Garrick winced. This was getting excruciating. He understood the devils that spurred Merryn on. He understood her need to do this. She had lived with nothing but doubts and questions for years. But raking up the past would be as unbearable for her as it would be for him.

"Of course it hurt me," he said.

"She loved him."

"She did," Garrick agreed. That at least had been true.

Kitty had adored Stephen Fenner, unworthy cad that he was.

"You killed Stephen for that," Merryn said. "Because you were jealous."

"*No.*" Garrick wanted to shout but he schooled his voice to calm. The images were in his head, images of Stephen, his face twisted with a cruel disdain, laughing, images of Kitty, desperate and begging. He could feel the huge, ungovernable rage rise in him in mocking resonance of that moment all those years before when everything had toppled over into tragedy.

"No," he repeated, fighting the demons back. "That was not how it was."

"You're lying." Merryn sounded impatient as well as furious now. "You *know* that there was no duel, you know you escaped trial for murder through deceit."

Her voice was so clear and vehement that it rang through the cellar like a bell, causing the walls to tremble. "Perhaps," Merryn said, "perhaps if you had tried to make amends in the past for the terrible things that you had done then I would not despise you so thoroughly as I do now." She paused. "You are a coward," she added. Garrick heard her shift, gathering herself. "I don't mean simply in the matter of Stephen's death. You're a coward because you ran away. You didn't face the consequences. You *hid.* You're spineless, no man at all."

The air buzzed with the force of her contempt.

Well, hell.

This, Garrick thought, was going too far. He understood why Merryn was behaving like this. She was angry, lonely and afraid, trapped with the one man she could not stand to be with, a man who had saved her life, a man she could not bear to be beholden to for anything. But what did she know of the consequences on him of that fateful day when he had shot Stephen Fenner? Nothing. Nor did she know what he had done to try to make amends for his actions ever since. He fought a brief, fierce battle to prevent himself from blurting out the truth.

"You know nothing," he said roughly.

"Then tell me!" There was so much anguish in her voice.

Garrick felt ripped with tension and regret. If only... "Stop this now," he said roughly. "It won't do any good."

But Merryn was beyond stopping. She had goaded herself too far. Her misery and anguish drove her fiercely on.

"I'm leaving," she said. "I'll find a way out. I cannot stay here with you. I cannot bear it."

Garrick heard her scramble to her feet, heard the frantic flutter of her hands as she brushed down her gown as though she was trying to slough off both the dust and the suffocating atmosphere. He heard stones scrape and slip away to their left and the fear grabbed him. The whole building was unstable, their safety on a knife's edge. Merryn could see nothing. She might blunder into walls in the dark, hurt herself or set off another fall of stone...

"Be careful—" he said urgently, but it was too late. He heard her stumble and caught her blindly as she tripped over a pile of fallen masonry and lurched full length back into his arms.

This time she was not limp and quiescent. She began to fight him, struggling to free herself. He tightened his arms about her in an effort to hold her still and prevent her from hurting herself, from hurting them both, but she was too fearful now, angry, panicked and desperate to be free of him. She kicked out at him, a glancing blow against his shin that jarred a bruise Garrick had not previously realized he had.

"Let me go!" He could hear the tears bubbling in her voice now and the edge of panic. "Leave me alone! I hate you!"

She broke free of his grip, her elbow catching on a pile of tumbled brick. She gave a sob, sharp and shocked, and in the same instant there was an ominous rumble as the rubble shifted and settled about them. Garrick grabbed her, following her down, pinning her to the ground beneath him.

"That's enough," he said, injecting steel into his tone. "Lie still before you bring down the rest of the house."

It was too late. Merryn writhed beneath him, sobbing, too lost in the grip of grief, anger and fear to hear him, let alone obey him. Garrick took the only other option, allowed the press of his body to trap her against the floor and brought his mouth down hard on hers.

It was harsh but damnably effective. She froze beneath

him. Her struggles ceased abruptly. It was as though she had forgotten to breathe, let alone move. For a moment they both lay still and then, as he was about to release her, Garrick felt the change in her. She went soft and acquiescent. She made a sound in her throat, a sound of desire and surrender that had Garrick's body hardening into instant arousal. He tried to resist. This was wrong, it was madness, it was the worst possible thing that he could do. But Merryn clung to him now, pressing against him, her mouth sweetly demanding beneath his own. There was a moment when he hung on the edge and then Garrick's mind—and his self-control—shattered into pieces. He gathered her close, his arms going around her, and he kissed her back with raw need, aware of nothing but the tight, painful spiral of his desire.

CHAPTER NINE

MERRYN WAS LOST in a sensual maze. The only thing that gave her comfort, the only thing that kept the shadows at bay, was this man, his mouth on hers and his arms about her, shielding her from the dark. As soon as he touched her she felt safe. She knew she should not feel like that. She knew that Garrick Farne was the last man she should turn to. Yet instinct was all she had left now. It told her that she needed the protection and comfort that only Garrick could give. It told her that she wanted him to blot out the fear.

Garrick's mouth had gentled on hers now, subtle, sweet, teasing a response from her. He drew back for a moment and she felt bereft but then his thumb skimmed her lower lip and she touched her tongue to it and heard him groan. In the hot, intimate dark the sound made her shake with sheer need.

He kissed her again, parting her lips, his tongue sliding deep. Her head spun. Such intriguing feelings… Her body felt so tightly wound, yet so hot and yielding. She realized that she wanted to be free of the clothes that imprisoned her. They felt too constricting, impossible barriers. She wanted to run her hands over Garrick's naked skin, to draw him to her, against her, inside her. She wanted his hands and his mouth on her body and just the thought of it made her tremble violently. Her stomach clenched with heat and desire.

She wanted to make love with Garrick Farne, the man who had killed her brother and ruined her family.

The thought intruded like a shower of ice. Merryn shivered with shock and self-disgust. Garrick felt her instinctive recoil and let her go at once.

"I'm sorry." She could hear that he was breathing hard. She felt him half turn away from her, as though that would lessen the desperate need that shimmered between them. He sounded as shaken as she felt. "I should not have touched you."

"I'm sorry, too." Merryn stared at him through the dark. She wished that she could see him. The madness had gone from her blood now and she felt lost and confused, ashamed, not of what she had said to him because she meant it in the deepest part of her soul, but upset at the way it had all flooded out in so unstoppable a tide.

"I am sorry for my anger and panic, I mean," she added meticulously, in case he misunderstood. "I don't know what happened to me."

"It's understandable." He sounded strained. She sensed that he was looking at her. She could hear the ragged edge to his voice, taste the malt bitterness of the beer on the air, smell the scent of his skin, a sensation that made her head spin.

"About the kiss…" She hesitated. "I can't seem to

help myself." Honesty was a habit with her, even with this man, especially with this man. "I find you very attractive," she said with painful sincerity, "and I wish I did not."

Garrick gave a crack of laughter. "Believe me, Lady Merryn," he said, "both of those sentiments are mutual."

"Why did it have to be you?" Merryn whispered. "I don't understand."

Garrick did not pretend to misconstrue her.

"You are a scholar, Lady Merryn," he said. He sounded grim. "So you will understand the concept of the chemical reaction. Sparks, heat, light leading to the explosion…"

Merryn did, but she also knew that it was more than that. Chemistry was not responsible for intuition and affinity. She rubbed her forehead, trying to make sense of her feelings. It should feel wrong to be within ten feet of Garrick Farne, let alone to touch him, and yet it did not. Rational thought drove her from him. Whenever she remembered what he had done she hated him, she was repulsed. Yet instinct, deep and inexplicable, persistently threw her into his arms. It made no sense.

She found that she was shaking. Tiredness and frustration racked her. "I think," she said, "that when we get out of here it would be best if we never see each other again."

"I think that would be a good idea," Garrick agreed, and he sounded weary to the soul. He was sitting with his back to her and he made no move to turn or draw closer.

There was quiet once more. Merryn felt horribly bereft, so lonely when the only other human being trapped with her was a man she could not approach for comfort, either mentally or physically. She wanted to rationalize her feelings away, to find an explanation for the instinct that had told her she could trust Garrick. Yet there was none.

"I expect," she said, "that our current attraction is merely a product of our situation. We are imprisoned here together and it is frightening and perfectly understandable that we should seek reassurance in one another. Besides, the beer fumes are making us both light-headed. It is a transient thing…" Her voice trailed off unhappily. If she did not believe her excuses she was sure that Garrick would not, either.

"By all means," Garrick said, "think of it in those terms if it makes you feel better. I refuse to accept that I am only attracted to you because I am drunk."

Silence again. The darkness fizzed with emotion— bitter, brittle anger, despair and longing.

"What can we do?" Merryn said helplessly.

"Nothing," Garrick said. She heard him sigh. "I am going to sleep. My head hurts." His voice sounded slurred. Now he really did sound drunk.

"You can't go to sleep!" Merryn said sharply. "Wake up!" She was remembering another of Professor Brande's lectures that she had attended the previous year, this time on medicine.

"The effects of a blow to the head may be delayed but they may also be fatal… If the patient sleeps he may not awaken…"

Panic grabbed her by the throat. She reached out for Garrick and gripped his shoulder hard.

"Don't go to sleep," she said again, and she could hear the raw anxiety edge her own voice. She grabbed his arm, shook him. "It could be dangerous. Did you sustain a blow to the head when the roof fell?"

"I don't remember…" Garrick sounded as though he was drifting away from her. "Don't worry about me," he mumbled. "I'm fine."

"I'm not worried about you," Merryn snapped. "It's purely selfish. I don't want to be left here on my own, that is all. I find after all that some company, even yours, is preferable to none."

Garrick did not respond. Merryn shook him again and heard him groan. "Leave me in peace," he said. "I'm a Duke and I can go to sleep if I like."

"You're gabbling," Merryn said coldly. She felt scared. She wondered if she should slap his face. Except she could not see where it was. "Did you not hear me?" she demanded. "If you fall asleep you may never wake up."

"That should suit you very well," Garrick muttered. "An eye for an eye, or whatever." He gave a sigh. She could tell that he was settling down to sleep.

Merryn scooped up a double handful of the sticky, warm, brackish beer and threw it in his general direction. She followed it with a second measure. There was a splash, a movement and then some very colorful swearing.

"What the devil—" At least he sounded wide-awake now. Merryn found that she was smiling. "That's better," she said.

"I'm glad that you think so." He sounded very grumpy. "Who would have guessed you could be such a shrew?"

"You should be thanking me," Merryn said. "You might have died."

"I almost did die—of beer inhalation." But he sounded himself again. Merryn's heart skipped a tiny beat.

There was a pause. She could feel his hesitation. Then he took her hand. She almost jumped at the physical contact.

"Thank you," he said.

The tears pricked her eyelids, foolish, weak tears she did not understand.

His thumb moved softly over her palm. "We *will* get out of here," he said. His voice had gentled and once again it tugged at her emotions. "I swear we will."

"Will anyone miss you if you do not return home?" Merryn asked. It had not occurred to her before, but surely someone, somewhere would raise an alarm?

"I doubt it," Garrick said. "I didn't tell anyone where I was going to be."

So no one cared where he was or what he did. Merryn thought it sounded very lonely.

"But people will surely miss you," Garrick added.

"Yes." Merryn felt a clutch of apprehension mingled with hope. "Joanna will worry when I do not return to Tavistock Street," she said. The guilt pricked her. "I was supposed to be working for Tom this evening but I told Joanna that I was attending a concert with a friend," she said. "She may not realize that anything was wrong for a few hours and even then she will have no idea as to where I might be."

"But if Bradshaw knows," Garrick said, "he may contact your sister to ensure that you are safe."

"Yes…" Merryn said. "It is possible but I think it unlikely. Tom believes me to be at a meeting of the Royal Humane Society tonight. He would hardly expect me to be in the rookeries off the Tottenham Court Road." She raised a hand to her aching head. Suddenly everything seemed intolerably complicated. It seemed very unlikely that Tom would go to Joanna and Alex, but if he did then her secret life would unravel faster than a ball of thread. On the other hand, if he did not realize that something was wrong, and she and Garrick could not find a way out, they might be trapped for days. The panic fluttered again but the warmth of Garrick's hand in hers helped her to quell it this time. She felt stronger with him near. She did not like the thought but she had to accept that it was true.

"How well do you know Bradshaw?" Garrick asked.

"Well enough," Merryn said. "He's not my lover," she added then wondered why on earth she had seen the need to mention it.

Garrick laughed. "I know that. You told me that you had never been kissed before." He had half turned toward her. "I think that I would have known it anyway," he added slowly. "When I kissed you at the ball you looked as though you had discovered a wonderful new pastime, one you had never indulged in before but would love to explore further."

"Oh!" Merryn whipped her hand from his and pressed both her palms to her burning cheeks. That had been exactly what she had felt. She had not realized, though, that she was quite so transparent.

"I did like it," she admitted after a moment. "I enjoy new experiences and it was intellectually fascinating."

She heard Garrick laugh. "Indeed! I have never before considered kissing an intellectual pastime. In what way was it…ah…intellectually fascinating?"

"Because I had no previous knowledge of it," Merryn said, "and I found it interesting to analyze my responses—"

"Analyze your responses? You mean you had time to think?" Garrick sounded slightly taken aback. "Was it better than reading a book?" he asked. "Or some other comparative academic activity?"

"That," Merryn said, "would depend upon the book. It was better than reading *Clarissa*, which I found turgid, but not quite as good as reading *Mansfield Park,* which I enjoyed a very great deal."

"*Mansfield Park.*" Garrick sounded amused. "I hope it was an exceptionally good read."

"Outstanding," Merryn agreed.

Garrick took her hand again and this time pressed his lips to the palm. "Whereas kissing me is merely… satisfactory? Interesting?"

"Very interesting," Merryn amended. Her heart thumped. Her skin was prickling. She could feel Garrick's stubble rough against the softness of her hand, chasing shivers along her nerves. For a second she felt as though she was trembling on the edge of something unbearably sweet; she wanted him to take her in his arms again, to kiss her until every other thought was banished and she was eager under his touch; she wanted to tumble headlong into whatever hot, blissful temptation waited for her.

She pulled her hand away, only to curl her fingers protectively over as though trapping the kiss.

She heard Garrick sigh. "I'm glad we straightened that out," he murmured. The teasing note in his voice faded. "I think that you should get some sleep, Lady Merryn," he said. "It will be for the best. And in the morning we will find a way out."

Merryn knew he was right. She could forget the past for a few minutes perhaps and allow herself to luxuriate in the pleasure of talking to a man whose mind seemed so delightfully in tune with her own. She could even allow herself the seduction of his kisses, a different but equally tempting sort of pleasure. But then memory would taunt her, making her stomach lurch with misery and self-reproach, and she knew that there could be no future for them. It was impossible. She should not want it.

"You always call me Lady Merryn when you want to put some distance between us," she said slowly.

"I do," Garrick agreed. She waited but he made no attempt to narrow that distance or to touch her again. After a moment Merryn settled herself down on as dry a bit of the floor as she could find, wrapped her pelisse around her and willed herself to sleep.

WHEN TOM BRADSHAW arrived at the house in Tavistock Street it was the early hours of the morning and he discovered that Lady Grant was hosting a dinner. The dining room blazed with light and it spilled out across the terrace and the gardens. Tom, lurking in the shadows, could see that Merryn was not among the assembled guests. That did not surprise him. He knew exactly where she was. And whom she was with.

As soon as Tom had heard about Garrick Farne's strange, quixotic gift to the Fenner sisters he had set Heighton to watch on Merryn and report back to him. Garrick, Tom thought, had been quite exceptionally clever in buying off the Fenner family. He had grave doubts now that Merryn would follow through on her intention to ruin Garrick because it was not in her interests to do so anymore. Tom understood all about self-interest. It was his prime inspiration. So he could hardly blame Merryn for throwing in her lot with Farne. But it did mean that he no longer trusted her and he could no longer use her.

Heighton had followed Merryn the entire afternoon. He had tailed both Merryn and Garrick to the rookeries of the Tottenham Court Road and had witnessed the beer flood. Barely stopping to sample a swift pint, he had made his way back to report to Tom.

So now Tom was in a very powerful position. He was prepared to tell Lady Grant and Lady Darent what had happened to their little sister—at a price. He was even considering revealing to them that Merryn had been working for him for two years, and then charging a higher price still for his silence, for Merryn would be utterly ruined if the truth came out. Tom was ruthless in discarding those for whom he had no further use and Merryn had served her purpose. Now she could make him some money.

He knocked discreetly at the door and asked the butler if he might speak with Lady Darent. He had thought of approaching Joanna, but there was always the danger that he might find himself confronting Alex Grant instead. That would be a very different business from blackmailing a woman of Lady Darent's apparent sensibilities. The butler gave him a supercilious look and Tom was almost certain he was going to refuse, but a hefty bribe helped the situation enormously and he was shown into the library. Nor did Tess Darent keep him waiting. It was barely two minutes later that he heard her step in the doorway and her voice.

"You asked to speak with me?"

Tom, who had been admiring the picturesque display of china that Lady Grant had arranged in a window alcove, turned abruptly. For a moment he thought he was seeing things, for in the light of the candles the woman standing in front of him looked like Merryn, sounded like Merryn and yet she most definitely was *not* Merryn. His instincts told him that even before the light shifted again and he saw that the superficial likeness was deceptive. This woman was taller than Merryn was, darker, lushly curved where Merryn was more angular. Tom realized vaguely that he had never considered Merryn beautiful, never really thought about her in such feminine terms because she had always insisted on being treated as an equal, like a man. This woman, in contrast, was lavishly, deliciously female. Tom swallowed hard.

The woman came forward into the light. "How do you do?" She extended a hand to him. "I am Teresa Darent."

Tom automatically took her hand in his. Hers was warm and soft and it seemed to flutter within his grasp. He felt short of breath and oddly out of countenance. So this was the widowed Lady Darent, whom the ton called the much-married marchioness. This was the woman who was barely twenty-eight but had buried four husbands already, whom rumor said wore them out by her insatiable demands in the marriage bed. Suddenly Tom's mouth felt as dry as cinders.

There was nothing predatory about Tess Darent. When he had heard the stories of her, Tom had imagined she would be one of those fast widows who indulged each and every one of their appetites whether it was for gambling, men or every other vice. He had thought of her as an older, wilder, more ravenous version of Harriet Knight. Now he saw her—touched her—he realized that her appeal was the opposite. She was entrancingly, fatally innocent. Every last man she met would want to protect and cherish her, Tom thought. She was irresistible, from the dimples that dented her cheeks when she smiled to the way in which she looked on a man as though he were the only creature on earth. She was smiling at him now and dimpling at him as well, as though he were a god, the most fascinating man she had ever met. Tom, who had thought he was immune to feminine wiles, could feel himself slipping and sliding somewhere very hot and tempting indeed. The combination of Tess's winning charm and lusciously rounded body made Tom feel that his collar—and other items of clothing—were simply too tight.

"And you are?" Tess prompted him, and Tom realized that he had been staring. Probably his mouth had been hanging open, too. He knew he was making an almighty hash of this and if he was not careful Tess Darent would remember him in future as no more than an inarticulate oaf she had found loitering in the library. He tried to pull himself together.

"How do you do, Lady Darent," he said. "I am Tom Bradshaw." Smooth he was not. He groaned inwardly. This was not going quite according to plan.

But Tess was still smiling. Her gaze traveled over him, assessing, thoughtful, in no way a fool.

"How may I help you?" she asked. A small frown puckered her brow. "You must forgive me, Mr. Bradshaw—" she hesitated "—but I am not accustomed to meeting with mysterious gentlemen."

"I'm not a gentleman," Tom said before he could stop himself.

Tess's lips twitched. He saw a gleam of amusement in her eyes. "Indeed?" she said. She put her head on one side, studying him. "So you are not a gentleman. Who then are you?"

This, Tom thought, was his cue to reveal his identity and that he had information on Merryn's whereabouts that he was prepared to sell to her. Lady Darent would be horrified of course, shocked and distraught, but she would see the sense in agreeing to his terms in order to buy his silence. But he could feel himself struggling. Normally he had no qualms about introducing people to a few painful facts. But with Tess Darent it seemed wilfully cruel, like breaking a butterfly. He shrugged inwardly and squared his shoulders. He could do this.

"I have come about your sister, Lady Merryn," he said.

"I have information as to her whereabouts. And other information that you may wish to…buy…from me."

He waited for the vapors, screams or swooning, but Tess Darent stood absolutely still. He was not even certain that she had understood him. He had heard gossip that she might in fact be a little short on intellect. Here was the proof, surely, in her blank expression. Then she spoke.

"How do you know Merryn, Mr. Bradshaw?" Her tone was impassive.

"She works for me," Tom said. "So you see…" He paused, smiled winningly. "I know a lot about her. I could *tell* people…a lot about her."

"I see," Tess said. She moved slightly, resting her hands on the top of the library table as though she suddenly needed to draw strength and support. Well, Tom thought, his news would have come as a shock. No doubt she was appalled, frightened and uncertain what to do next.

"So," Tess said, "let me understand you clearly, Mr. Bradshaw. Merryn works for you. You know her present whereabouts, and you wish to discuss exchanging that information for hard cash."

She did not sound shocked. She did not even sound upset. Lady Darent, Tom thought admiringly, revising his opinion, was nowhere near as stupid as people said she was.

"That's right," he said. "You might wish to consider how much my silence is worth."

"One bullet, I would think," Tess Darent said briskly. She stepped back from the library table and Tom saw that she had a tiny pearl-handled pistol in her hand. She used it to gesture him to a chair.

"I don't like blackmailers, Mr. Bradshaw," she said very sweetly, "so I suggest you reconsider." She paused, head on one side, the pistol rock-steady in her hand. "I wonder which part of your anatomy you value the most?" she pondered. "I think I can guess." Her gaze fell to his crotch. She took aim.

"Wait!" Tom said. He burst out into a sweat.

Tess paused. "Speak, Mr. Bradshaw," she said. She smiled at him. "I am listening."

CHAPTER TEN

AT SOME POINT Merryn woke, feeling cold and stiff. One of her arms was numb where she had been lying on it and when she shifted it hurt so excruciatingly that she could not help but cry out. The darkness was absolute and the night was silent. She felt as though she had woken alone in hell, the beer fumes pressing down on her like a blanket, smothering the life out of her.

A second later, Garrick was beside her, crossing the space between them, reaching for her.

"Are you hurt?" His hands were already moving over her, checking for any injury. She willed herself to accept his touch as impersonally as he offered it but somewhere deep inside she was shaking in response.

"I am a little stiff, that is all," she said. "And cold."

And so very lonely...

Garrick drew her into his arms. She could see nothing of him. He felt more familiar now, though, treacherously so, as though she had learned how to be in his arms. The brief rub of his cheek against hers was rough with a day's growth of stubble now, all evidence of the elegant Duke extinguished. The smell of him—lime cologne and the scent of his skin—was reassuring. It soothed her senses.

Merryn was too tired now to try to distance herself from him either physically or mentally. Instead she tangled her fingers in Garrick's shirt and drew him close, her head against his chest. She felt his breath stir her hair, then his body relaxed, his arms going about her more closely and holding her against him softly and protectively as though she were a child. Sleep crept around the corners of her mind again like mist. She let it claim her.

She woke again some unmeasured time later, her heart racing, the panic fluttering through her blood again as she gasped for breath. In her dream she had been thirteen years old, running through the meadow near her home at Fenners, the grass whipping her legs, her skirts tearing. She had to reach Stephen, had to get there in time because it was the only way to save him. Her heart was thumping with the effort of running but she knew it was already too late, knew Stephen was sliding away from her, dead, gone and it was all her fault… She gave a sob, coming fully awake, the tears choking her throat and the ghosts of the dream filling her mind.

Someone was holding her in a strong grip and for a moment she fought it, before she recognized his touch and all the fight went out of her.

"Hush," Garrick said. His voice was a soft rumble in her ear and it soothed the frayed edges of her fear. "You are safe. All is well."

Still dazed with sleep, her mind cloudy and dull, Merryn allowed herself to relax into his arms again. It was gentle and sweet and for a moment she clung to him. She was too exhausted to pretend to either of them. She wanted Garrick to comfort her, wanted his strength and his tenderness. For one long moment she allowed herself simply to hold him and be held and then she sat up, pushing the hair back from her face, made clumsy by both tiredness and acute physical awareness.

"Did you sleep?" she asked.

"I was honor bound not to, if you recall." There was an undertone of humor in his voice. "So no, Lady Merryn, I did not sleep."

"Thank you." Suddenly Merryn wanted to see him. She was so tired of this darkness. Except when they were next face-to-face in the full light of day it would be the moment she walked away from him forever. Her heart lurched and she felt sick and torn.

"It must be past dawn." Garrick had let her go and stood up. She heard him move a little away from her. She felt cold and repressed a shiver. "The quality of the light is different in here now," he said. "You can see the chinks of daylight appearing. Soon we may be able to find a way out."

Merryn scrambled to her feet, mad hope soaring within her. "Oh, let us try now!"

"Such haste!" Garrick sounded ruefully amused. She knew that he thought she was desperate to escape him and it was true; she was. Or perhaps it was herself she was trying to run from, and the persistent instinct that told her to seek comfort in his arms.

Garrick's movements, too, were slow and stiff. She

could see his outline now, a dark shape against the lighter blackness. He was right. The quality of the light had changed. Tiny specks of daylight were seeping into their prison, illuminating tumbled piles of brick and stone, and cold dark water lapping at her skirts. Merryn had almost forgotten how it felt to be warm and dry.

"Careful!" Garrick's voice stopped her as she stumbled against a rough pile of brick. He caught her before she tripped and for a second he held her close again, a perfect fit against his side, as though she had been made specifically to lie within his arms, safe and secure. Then he put her from him with exemplary courtesy and for some reason Merryn's heart tumbled into her soaking boots and she wanted to cry.

"I need to…" She paused delicately, unable to think of a way to express various urgent physical necessities to a man.

"I need to, too." He sounded gentle and amused, easing her discomfort. "I will move a little away and turn my back. I undertake not to turn around."

"Thank you." Teeth chattering, cold, stiff and shaking, she hurried to do what she had to do.

"I hope you are not too hungry?" Garrick's matter-of-fact tone as she rejoined him eased her embarrassment.

"I'm famished!" Merryn confessed.

Garrick laughed. "I am sorry that there is nothing we can do about that at present." He held out a hand to her. "There is less danger of you falling if you hold on to me."

After a second's hesitation Merryn took his hand. It was warm, reassuring and slightly rough. She rubbed her fingers across his palm and felt the cuts and abrasions he must have suffered when the walls had first come down. She heard his sharp intake of breath and realized with a strange skip of the heart that it was a reaction to her touch. The thought made her feel confused, heady, powerful, a little in awe to be able to do such a thing to such a man with so small a gesture. For a moment she paused in the caress, then, unable to resist, stroked his palm again, aware this time of each tiny cut and chafe, sensitive to the tension she felt now in Garrick's whole body and the way that the air between them seemed to shiver.

"Lady Merryn—" Garrick spoke very slowly, his tone was a warning.

"I'm sorry," Merryn said, allowing her hand to lie limp as a frightened mouse in his.

Garrick sighed sharply and took a stronger grip on her, drawing her forward. She followed him carefully over piles of rubble that shifted disconcertingly beneath their feet, around fallen walls, under hanging beams. Garrick seemed very surefooted, stumbling only once and biting off whatever expressive oath had sprung to his lips. Merryn followed, her hand tight in his now, every sense she possessed aware of him, of the roughness of his palm against the softness of hers, the sound of his breathing.

"Where are we going?" she whispered, and he turned his head, so close that she felt his breath feather against her cheek.

"Toward the light."

It sounded simple, but the light was elusive, skipping a little ahead of them all the time. Merryn caught her foot in the hem of her gown and almost fell again and Garrick went down on one knee and then she heard a ripping sound and the bottom twelve inches of her skirt and petticoats came away.

"What on *earth* are you doing?" she gasped.

"Preventing you from breaking a leg."

"And for that you needed to…to disarrange my clothing?"

In the growing light she actually saw him grin. He straightened up. "Don't tempt me," he said.

Merryn looked up into his face. He was standing so close to her that she could feel the heat radiating from his body. She felt her stomach swoop at the intimacy of it. She wondered if she would ever be free of the acute awareness she had for him.

For a long moment they stared at one another and then Merryn tugged on his hand. "Come along," she said again, sharply, compensating for the warmth of her feelings with the chill of her tone. "Toward the light."

She was not sure whether it was getting hotter in the darkness or whether she was starting to develop an ague.

The gloom was disorienting now, with tiny pinpricks of light dancing before her eyes, tempting her on only to lead to deep pools of stagnant beer or piles of rubble that were impossible to traverse. Their progress was excruciatingly slow and when, finally, they were confronted by a blank wall with only the tiniest hint of light beyond, Merryn could have cried out of sheer frustration.

Garrick was kneeling on the floor; she heard the scrape and chink of metal on stone and then a strange, hot breath of stale air engulfed her.

"All these houses have open cellars beneath them," Garrick said. "They lead on from one house to the next." He straightened up, dusting his palms. "I need to go down and see if they are flooded. If not we have a good chance of getting out that way—"

"No!" Merryn was shocked by the terror that hit her as hard as a tidal wave. She grabbed him and shook him. "Don't go!" she said. "It's dangerous. You might drown—" Her voice broke on a sob. She realized that she was holding Garrick so tightly that the material of his coat was scoring her sore palms. She felt frightened, an inch away from losing all control. All she knew was that he could not leave her. With him she was stronger. Without him she felt lost. And if anything were to happen to him… She could not bear the thought of it.

And then his arms came about her and they felt like steel bands, so strong and firm, and his lips were pressed against her hair and she could hear his heart beating steadily against her ear.

"Merryn," he said, "I have to go. It's the only way we can get out of here—"

"No," Merryn said. She burrowed closer into his arms. "You might be hurt—"

Garrick put a hand under her chin, forcing it up so that she was looking at him. Her heart was pattering like a trapped bird but she could still feel the steady beat of his against her hand and when he spoke, his voice was very calm, too.

"Nothing will happen to me," he said. He bent his head. His lips were very close to hers. "I'll come back for you," he said. "I promise. I won't leave you."

I'll never leave you...

The words trembled on the air between them.

Merryn prized her fingers from his jacket and took a step back. "I'm sorry," she said.

"You have nothing to be sorry for." He sounded fierce. The kiss he gave her was equally fierce, brief, forceful, setting her head spinning. He turned to go. Merryn closed her eyes and prayed hard that he would not be gone for long and that he would find a safe way out.

Barely a second later there was a scraping, sliding sound that started softly but grew to a ferocious roar, and then without warning the world was falling again, the dust thick as a cloud about them, the brick and stone plummeting down and the only constant was Garrick's arms about her and his body shielding hers as once again he stood between her and destruction.

"Garrick! *Garrick!*"

Merryn's voice sounded a very long way away and it came from a place Garrick did not want to go back to. He knew that to return would hurt; even now, with consciousness lapping at the corners of his mind, he could feel the pain eating at him in a dozen different places. But Merryn had never called him by his name before and that mattered. He did not know why, but it mattered profoundly. She sounded frightened and lonely. She was so brave. He had to help her.

He tried to move. Nothing happened. No response at all. Oh, well… At least he had tried. He started to slip back.

Something brushed his face. Her hair. He could smell the scent of bluebells—astonishing when they had been trapped with beer and dust that Merryn Fenner could still smell of fresh flowers. Then her hands were moving over him, shifting aside some of the dead weight that was pressing down on him and robbing him of breath. He felt something else against his face, something warm and wet… Tears?

"Don't die." She sounded furious. "Damn you…" More tears, though he heard her sniff as though she were trying to dash them away.

"I'm fine." The words were no more than a croak. His throat was full of dust. So were his eyes. He could not seem to open them.

"I'm not going to die." With an enormous effort he forced himself to move. A hundred muscles screamed in protest. He ignored them. "See?" He half sat. "I'm alive. I wouldn't dream of robbing you of your revenge by leaving now."

"Oh…" There was a world of emotion in her voice. Garrick cleared his throat and blinked the dust from his eyes. He could see Merryn now, kneeling beside him, a pile of stone next to her. They must have been crushed beneath it and she had wriggled free and arduously dug through the rubble that trapped him. Her hands were bleeding and filthy.

Garrick shook off the remaining debris. He was aching all over, battered from the onslaught of falling masonry, fresh cuts oozing from his arms where the sharp edges of several bricks had caught him. He felt the warm, sluggish seep of the blood. He looked around. They had been more than lucky this time. One of the roof beams had fallen from two floors above, spearing the ground not three feet away from them. He shuddered to see it.

"You saved my life again." Merryn sat back on her heels, resting her battered hands in her lap.

"You saved mine, too," Garrick said. They stared at one another. "It could become a habit," Garrick added.

She gave him a hesitant smile. "Well… Thank you. Again."

"My pleasure." He raised his brows. "Have you noticed anything?"

"Only that you look extremely disheveled… Oh!" She clapped a hand to her mouth. "I can *see* you properly!"

He could see her, too. In the narrow shaft of light that now penetrated from above she looked like a dusty angel. Her hair was almost white with dirt, a stiff, tousled halo about her face. Her skin looked unnaturally pale under its coating of grime but her eyes gleamed as bright as sapphires. She was filthy, her skirts in tatters, the skin of her hands and arms chapped and rubbed raw, but in a heartbeat she had regained all her courage and confidence. Garrick felt his heart jerk with admiration. Gently bred women were not raised to deal with disasters such as this. When danger struck they showed whether or not they had that core of steel and Merryn had shown character through and through. She had been brave beyond measure.

Her brow had wrinkled. "Why are you smiling at me like that?"

Garrick hastily wiped the smile from his face. "Um… You, too, look most…disheveled."

She frowned. "You were laughing at me. How ungallant!"

"You are right, of course," Garrick said. "A gentleman should never make adverse comment on a lady's appearance." Yet still he could not take his gaze from her. The light was growing stronger all the time, illuminating the streaks of dirt on her face and the tracks of those fierce, angry tears she had shed when she thought she might have lost him. Her hands, as small and capable as the rest of her, were punctured with faint blue bruises among the cuts. Garrick raised a hand as though in a dream, and brushed away the smudges of her tears with his thumb. He heard her breath catch and felt her skin warm beneath his touch. He pushed the filthy hair away from her face. The back of his fingers brushed her cheek and she made the softest sound in her throat and turned her face against his caress like a cat seeking the sun.

He cradled her head in his hand and drew her forward for his kiss. This time it was not a kiss in anger or passion. It was gentle and sweet but so deep that when he let her go he found he was shaking. They gazed at one another, the moment spinning out, the dust motes dancing in the light that seemed to surround Merryn like a halo, and then she turned away and her face was in shadow and instead of pulling her back into his arms and kissing her senseless, as he ached to do, Garrick let her go.

The latest fall of masonry had revealed what had once been a chimney and now it stood straight and tall among the debris of tumbled walls, offering a tantalizing glimpse of light and sky. It seemed a very long way up.

"I assume," Merryn said, looking up, "that we have to climb out of here?"

"Yes." Garrick cleared his throat. "We do."

"Then what are we waiting for?" Merryn had already started to scramble over the rubble at the base of the chimney. Before Garrick could say anything she was reaching for footholds, clambering up like a monkey, clinging to impossible ledges and giving him a most enticing view up her skirts at the same time. Garrick felt distracted, hot and confused, left behind by her sudden energy. He had to make a very deliberate effort to get to his feet. His whole body seemed to rebel against movement.

Ten feet above him Merryn stopped and looked down. A shower of grit and small stones rattled past Garrick's head and he flinched.

"What are you waiting for?" she said it again. She sounded impatient. Garrick thought that it was probably not the moment to tell her that ever since he had fallen out of a tree at the age of five, he had been afraid of heights.

"You will probably have more difficulty than I…" She had started to climb again and her voice sounded faint and far away. "Because you are much larger than I am."

"Thank you for that," Garrick said. He set his jaw. He had to do this. Was he to sit here and wait for Merryn to climb out and fetch help? That would be intolerable. She had been afraid of the dark. He disliked heights. Neither of them could pander to their fear. Another rattle of stone had him clenching his teeth so tightly they ground audibly. He knew he had to concentrate on each handhold, each foothold, on climbing steadily toward the light. He could not afford to think about falling or to allow even a flicker of fear to loosen his grip as Merryn slipped and slithered above him, one foot swinging free of the wall, her skirts filling out like a bell.

It seemed to take forever. Twice Garrick slipped and thought he would fall, and saw Merryn's face, pale and strained, staring down from above him. Finally he was up at the top, his palms slippery with sweat, his heart racing, and he could feel the air on his face and it was fresh and cold, a whole world away from the dark, dank prison below. Merryn offered him her hand to pull him out of the chimney and he took it and felt the strength in her and saw her wide smile and he looked around and the world rocked and he almost fell.

They were on what was left of a roof. Garrick felt a little dizzy. Merryn's hand tightened on his. She gave him a brilliant smile, lit up with relief and excitement. "We're free!" she said. "Isn't it marvelous?"

"Marvelous." Garrick dared not look down. As far as he could tell the roof had fallen by perhaps five or six feet during the flood, which meant that they were still a good twenty-five feet from the ground since these houses were built tall and narrow, crowding toward the sky. Instead of looking directly down, Garrick fixed his gaze on the reassuring sight of the steeple of St. Anthony's Church a few streets away. The sky behind the church tower was the palest white blue of early morning and beyond that, for street after street, he could see the skyline of London with its jumbled mixture of spires and towers, slates and tiles, stretching away to the frosty green hills beyond. The river curled like a lazy gray snake to the south, mist wreathing its banks, with tiny bridges and the smudge of roads barely visible in the dawn light. It felt very cold up here on the roof with the winter wind nipping at his exposed skin.

"You are very pale." Merryn sounded concerned. "Are you sure you did not hurt yourself on the climb—"

"I do not care for heights." Garrick bit the words out and saw her brows rise.

"Oh." Her tone changed. "Oh, dear. And we are on the roof."

"Quite." Garrick forced a smile. "My father used to take me up on to the roof of Farnecourt when I was a boy," he said. "He asked me what sort of a man I was if I could not even look down at the ground without turning green."

Merryn's face registered vivid disgust. "What a very disagreeable person your father was," she remarked. She drew her knees up and laced her arms around them. "A pity he is dead. I should have liked to give him a piece of my mind."

"That," Garrick said, "I would have enjoyed."

He could see that Merryn was looking down and he felt his stomach lurch.

"It does not seem too bad," she ventured. "There is a wall to our left that I might perhaps climb down. Or someone might come soon, with a ladder. The streets seem to be deserted but it is still early." She stopped. "You should look, you know." Her voice had changed. "I have never seen anything quite like it. So many broken walls and beer stretching away in the streets like a lake! We are cut off as though we are on an island. It is extraordinary."

She shuffled up so that she was sitting beside him on the ridge of the roof. Garrick felt his stomach heave again and tried to persuade himself that he had imagined the slight movement of the beams beneath them. This was not safe. They had to move soon—as soon as he had sufficient breath and courage.

"You did very well," Merryn added, sounding, Garrick thought, like a governess trying to encourage a dull pupil.

"Thank you." He smiled at her. The wind was teasing strands of her hair, picking out the gold beneath the dirt. "You were splendid," he said. "Is there much call for climbing chimneys in your work for Bradshaw?"

She laughed. "None whatsoever. But I did enjoy climbing trees as a girl. It provided me with somewhere quiet to read." She shivered suddenly. "It is cold out here, though. Oh, no—" She put out a hand to protest as he slid his jacket about her shoulders. "You must not! You need it yourself."

"I doubt it will give either of us much warmth," Garrick said. "It is ripped to shreds. Keep it, for what it is worth." He watched her slip her arms into the sleeves. She was a little clumsy with the cold. The coat was far too big and after a moment he turned up the sleeves for her so that her hands at least were free rather than lost inside.

"We have to find a way down," he said abruptly. "It's not safe to stay here."

Merryn scrambled up. "Look—" She was pointing to a corner of the roof some twenty feet away. "I do believe that there is a staircase."

Garrick looked and saw that she was right. Part of the roof of the next building had collapsed, leaving the top of a stair poking at the sky like a pointing finger. The house itself looked sound, still standing. Merryn started to clamber across the roof toward it.

"Wait!" Garrick called. "It may be unsafe—"

She paused, waiting for him to catch up with her, and then she grabbed his hand again. They took the vertiginous slope, easing down from the roof, sliding over slates, scrambling over stone. Garrick wondered if his future nightmares would involve endless long dark corridors full of rubble and the smell of beer seeping even into his dreams. And then they were climbing down the broken stairs. The house was silent, deserted. The staircase had sheered off at the bottom of the flight leaving a gap of perhaps ten feet to the ground below. Or it should have been the ground. Peering over the edge, Garrick saw that the floorboards were gone, snapped like driftwood, and the cellar yawned black and deep beneath them. Away to their left were the broken spars of what had once been the floor.

Merryn stopped. "We're trapped!" The disappointment was clear in her voice. She looked up the way they had come. "We'll have to go back up."

"No," Garrick said. "It's too dangerous. The staircase may come down." He looked across the gap of about ten feet to where the floor still stood. "I'll jump across," he said.

Merryn caught his arm. Her face was pale. He could feel the tension and the anxiety radiating from her. "You cannot! It is too far, too dangerous!"

There was a cracking sound beneath Garrick's feet. The wood of the staircase was buckling under their weight, too much, Garrick realized, for the damaged structure to bear. He covered Merryn's hands with his own.

"It's the only chance we have," he said. "I'll jump down and then I will catch you."

Another splintering sound from beneath them; the fragile steps seemed to shiver. Garrick saw Merryn nod.

This time she did not cling to him as she had done in the cellar but stepped back very deliberately. She raised her chin. There was a challenge in her blue eyes. He knew, and she knew, that there was only the smallest chance he could get down without breaking his neck. The floor might smash or the stair break or he could miss his footing and plunge twenty feet into the basement beneath.

"Do it, then," she said. "I'll wager you cannot and you'll be swimming about in the cellar before the end."

"Such touching faith," Garrick mocked. He eased

himself over the edge of the wooden staircase. It creaked alarmingly, shards of wood breaking off and falling into the void below. Merryn gave a little gasp as it lurched to one side like a drunk.

There was no time for hesitation. Garrick gathered all his strength and took a huge leap across the chasm to the floor below. He felt the wooden boards give beneath his feet but they held firm. He spun round to see Merryn's face, a terrified blur, as she clung to the last, cracking timber of the staircase.

"Jump!" he shouted.

She did not falter. With absolute trust she threw herself into space. The seconds seemed to spin out as she tumbled toward him and then he caught her and held her, the breath knocked from his body by the force of her fall. The whole stair splintered and disintegrated into darkness in the void of the cellar below. There was a huge splash as the wood plunged into the flood of beer, an echo of destruction that shook the entire house.

Merryn was pressed against his heart, her head sheltered beneath the curve of his arm, her hands gripping him so tight it felt as though she would never let go. Garrick kept his arms about her and looked down into her face and her smile lit him to his soul. He could feel her trembling so hard that her entire body shook. She felt hot and feverish beneath his hands, burning up with shock, excitement racking her at the same time as reaction set her shaking.

She reached up and kissed him, all heated passion

and intense relief, and Garrick thought his heart would explode. He pulled her away from the yawning chasm of the floor through the doorway into the first solid room he could find. He slammed the door behind them. It was the last coherent thing that he remembered before Merryn kissed him again and his world narrowed to her, and nothing but her, the need to protect and possess, the desire that finally could not be restrained.

"GARRICK…" Merryn breathed Garrick's name against his lips. Her hands were resting against his chest and she could feel his heart thundering against her palm. He was blazing with the same sense of victory and release that she was. She stood on tiptoe and kissed him again, winding her arms about his neck, drawing his head down to hers so that she could reach him properly. For a second she felt the hesitation in him and then his mouth came down on hers with ruthless intent, plundering, rough in his hunger for her. Her heart leaped. Garrick had saved her life twice and had stood between her and the dark when she was fearful and alone. She had turned to him to blot out all fear, to deny the past and defy the future, and now she ached for him with so powerful a need that it stole her breath and made her feel as though she would die if she could not have him. She needed this force to consume her now and wash away the darkness once and for all. She opened her lips to his and gave him back kiss for kiss, matching the fierceness of his demand.

She pulled Garrick down to the floor beside her. Here,

instead of the roughness of stone and the stinking pools of beer, she could feel the softness of carpet beneath her. It was like the most luxurious feather bed. She cupped Garrick's face in her hands and brought it to hers again. His stubble was rough against her sore palms. Her mouth was eager and open on his; she wanted to drink deep and savor the renewal of life, grasp after every sensation in her celebration of their escape. She slid her hands over the hard muscle of his shoulders, feeling the torn material of his shirt beneath her questing fingers, sliding under the linen to touch his skin. She heard him groan against her mouth.

"Merryn. Wait…" Garrick sounded dazed. He tried to pull back. "We should not," he said. "You'll feel differently when—"

Merryn cut off his words with another kiss. She did not want to wait, did not want to think. Her heart beat a mad helter-skelter. Her body seemed to be burning up. She kissed him again with renewed passion and when she felt the tension ease from him and his grip tighten on her, she knew she had won and the triumph soared even higher in her blood. She felt him shift so that he was over her and suddenly she felt very small and very feminine against such hard strength and masculinity. It was a new and devastating sensation for her but it was banished as soon as it came by other, even more powerful reactions. She felt the nip of his teeth on her neck and the press of his lips against the pulse at the hollow of her throat and she squirmed beneath him. Her gown was already in tatters; it was the work of seconds for Garrick to rip it off. His mouth closed over the tip of one of her breasts and Merryn's mind spun into a new, untried world. Desire twisted deep within her and she cried out.

Garrick's hands moved over her, stripping away her clothes, exposing her to his gaze and his touch. She felt strange, voluptuous, a creature of feeling and sensation where before she had been driven only by thought and reason. The fierce demand of her senses was like nothing she had known before. It was insatiable, a desperate need. She arched to each caress, helpless beneath the long, slow strokes of his hands. His mouth at her breast was exquisite torment, impelling her deeper into a dark spiral that wound her body as tight as a drum.

She felt him shift above her, spreading her thighs. The cool air touched her *there;* she moaned. There was an ache deep inside her that maddened her now, demanding release, and she grabbed his hips and pulled him down to her. She felt the slide of his skin against hers and knew he was naked and exultation burst inside her like the sun. A moment, and then he thrust hard, taking her with such consuming wildness that Merryn cried out in shock and fierce delight. She felt her body yield, surrendering to his, and felt the heat uncurl and spread through her, setting her trembling uncontrollably. He drove into her again, and again, his mouth ravaging hers, the rhythm of his possession a primitive beat in her blood. Her skin felt slick and hot, the muscles of her stomach jumping.

She dug her fingers into his shoulders and lifted her body to meet the thrust of his and felt herself tangle in a swirl of sensation as the world shattered. Then she was falling and falling into star-spangled darkness. She heard Garrick groan her name, felt her body clasp his as he emptied himself into her, and clung to him desperately as the only safe thing in a tumultuous new world.

She was not sure how long she lay there, her mind utterly blank for once, all thoughts and reason fled, aware of nothing but shock and pure, wicked exhilaration. She had never felt like this before, never dreamed of feeling like this. For once she let her mind lie quiescent and simply allowed herself to experience sensation. Her body felt lush and ripe and replete. She had had no notion it could give her so much pleasure. She felt stunned to discover it.

She was dimly aware of Garrick lifting her, wrapping something about her, and then she sank deeply into the softest, deepest mattress she had ever known. She was so drained by bliss that she drifted between waking and sleeping. Somewhere at the back of her mind reality stirred, but she pushed any thoughts away before they could touch her with their cold truth.

After a while she opened her eyes and looked about her. The room was lit by the strengthening glow of the dawn now. In its light she could see Garrick stretched out beside her and her throat dried to look at him. He was masculine perfection, like the statues she had studied in the London museums. But Garrick was real, hard muscle and smooth tawny skin, his auburn hair tumbling across his brow, magnificent in his nakedness.

He leaned over and pressed soft kisses against her brow, her eyelids, her cheeks, her throat. His breath stirred her hair. She could smell the scent of his skin mingled with salt sweat and dust, and her head spun.

"It should not have been like that…" His voice was soft. "I am sorry."

Dimly she understood what he meant. It had been wild and uncontrolled, no gentle introduction for a virgin to the art of love. Yet she had not wanted that. She had wanted him. She had wanted to celebrate their escape, the triumph of life over death. But now… The thoughts hovering in the shadows at the edge of her mind drew a little closer. She felt cold. Regrets, memories… She could not face them yet.

"Garrick—"

She reached for him, wanting to ward off the shade and drive away thought, if only for a little longer. She saw him hesitate. Then he brushed his lips against hers. Her heart fluttered. The shadows fled.

This time the kiss was slower, gentler. His mouth explored hers, teasing her, his tongue dancing with hers. Merryn quivered as an echo of their previous passion shook her. The heat and pleasure shimmered through her, softer this time, more persuasive, coiling through her body with seductive warmth. She reached for Garrick again but he shook his head, pushing her back against the bed, sliding his hands down her body in a caress that made her skin shiver and ache with need.

"Not now, not yet…" His head dipped to her breast and once again her mind swirled away to that hot dark place where pleasure drove her on. She felt his fingers against the soft skin of her inner thigh, parting her, touching her intimately. The heat built inside her as he stroked; Merryn dug her fingers into the bed and shifted against the covers, desperate to ease the torment.

Garrick slid something beneath her hips, raising her up. The rough silkiness of velvet abraded her. Tumbled on the bed, abandoned and unrestrained, she felt the brush of his cheek against her thigh, then the tip of his tongue at her core, trailing shattering pleasure. She arched helplessly, moaning with shock and delight. This was beyond any ecstasy she had experienced before. She felt as though her body was melting as white-hot rapture consumed her.

This time he entered her slowly while her body was still clenching with intense bliss and she gasped to feel him take her. It seemed impossible. She was tight; her climax still rippled through her belly in endless waves. She writhed beneath him and he held her hips down against the velvet and slid inside her gently, inexorably. Merryn had thought that her body could not take any further sensation but Garrick raised himself above her, pushing the tangled hair away from her flushed face, kissing her with the same deep intimacy with which he took her body.

"Open your eyes," he said softly, and her lashes fluttered open so that she met the dark molten heat in his. His body plundered hers with slow, relentless strokes, his eyes held hers. She could not break the connection between them, did not want to, captured and held by the fierce passion beneath his gentleness. With aching tenderness he drove her to the edge again and she hung there for endless moments, her body strung out with acute desire, her mind reeling with the onslaught of unimaginable pleasure. And then she fell again, shocked beyond measure, powerless, her mind and body dazzled.

Delicious exhaustion washed through her. She could not move other than to curl against him and succumb utterly to sleep, Garrick's arms about her, his body curved protectively about hers.

Merryn did not know how long she slept for but when she awoke it was to hear a hammering at the door and the sound of voices in the corridor outside and then the room was full of people. There was Joanna and Alex and Tess and a whole host of others whom she did not recognize but who were all staring at her, some in shock, some in horror, all in appalled surprise. Merryn blinked as she opened her eyes fully and the last shreds of the dream fled. Now she could not escape the thoughts that crowded back into her mind.

The room she was lying in was, self-evidently, a bordello. Either that or the owner of the house had very exotic tastes. The bed was covered in lush pink silk and draped with diaphanous curtains trimmed with silver and

gold. On the dresser lay a wicked-looking whip with a
shiny, carved handle. Rich velvet cushions lay scattered
across the room. Merryn's gaze fell on one lying on
the bedcover and she blushed. The blush spread down
her throat and across her whole body, naked as it was
beneath the pink silk cover. She turned her head very
slowly. Garrick was lying beside her still, despite the
crush of people now in the room, deeply asleep. One
strong brown arm lay possessively across her stomach,
drawing her close to his side.

No wonder he was still sleeping. He must have been
exhausted—for various reasons. The memories slid into
her head like a disconnected pattern: Garrick comforting her when she had woken in terror in the darkness
of the night, Garrick protecting her with his body when
the walls had fallen, Garrick's hands moving over her
with such sure skill and endless pleasure. Garrick. Her
lover.

She had slept with her enemy, the man who had killed
her brother.

A wave of shock and self-loathing hit her so hard that
she turned cold to her bones. The sickness rose in her
throat. She was lying naked in a bordello with a man
who was her sworn enemy. She had allowed him the
most impossible intimacies with her body. She had lost
her virginity. She was ruined.

CHAPTER ELEVEN

"FARNE."

Alex Grant's tone was colder than the polar ice, his gray gaze hard as flint. In fact, Garrick reflected ruefully, he had had a warmer welcome from Spanish guerrillas than he was getting now from Lord Grant. Which was hardly surprising. He had comprehensively ruined the reputation of Grant's sister-in-law and plunged the family into outrageous scandal. The only mystery was why Grant was wasting any time at all in speaking to him rather than simply putting a bullet through him.

"A glass of wine?" Alex asked, gesturing to the decanter that sat on the rosewood library table. "Or perhaps—" his gaze appraised Garrick's face keenly "—we should make that brandy?"

"Thank you," Garrick said. He felt a tiny amount of tension slip from his shoulders. So they were to be civilized about this. With a man such as Grant, who had allegedly wrestled a polar bear single-handed and had successfully saved his crew from certain death trapped in the Arctic ice, one could not be sure. Grant was a gentleman, of course, but Garrick was all too aware that he had broken every last tenet of honorable behavior and deserved no clemency.

"I cannot call you out," Alex said precisely, as though reading Garrick's thoughts. He strolled across to the decanter, poured for both of them and handed Garrick his glass. His gaze was still as cold as the polar sea. "Please do not misunderstand me," he continued. "The idea has some appeal." His gaze went to the pristine white bandage about Garrick's left wrist. "Though I would wait until you were recovered, of course. Killing a wounded man is not my style."

Garrick prudently kept quiet. He was not at all sure that Grant was joking.

"However," Alex Grant continued, in a level tone, "there has already been one scandalous duel between our two families. I could not countenance distressing my wife with another." He took a mouthful of brandy. "And then there is Merryn to consider. I do not believe that for me to kill you would help her in any way."

"I would like to marry Lady Merryn," Garrick said. He chose his words carefully. Others would not serve. "I want her. I wanted her from the first. I will always want her..."

He took a deep breath. There was nothing civilized about his thoughts or his desires or his need for Merryn Fenner, particularly now that he had taken her exquisite body once—twice—and burned for more.

He shifted in his chair. He knew that it was not simply desire that drove him, strong as that was. He had seen

Merryn's courage and her grace under pressure. He had held her in the darkest night and protected her from harm. He had saved her life and she had saved his. They were bound together now more tightly than they had ever been.

Regret raked him, opening old scars. He was not worthy to marry Merryn. He knew it. What could he give her, with his flawed honor and his equally damaged soul? Yet now he had to offer her marriage or be branded even more of a dishonorable scoundrel. He was trapped. There were no alternatives.

"I am aware," he said, "that my behavior has not been that of a gentleman."

"Not remotely," Alex agreed, with an expressive lift of the brows.

Garrick gritted his teeth. Grant was right of course. He had lost control with Merryn, a circumstance that had never, ever happened to him before. He had been sworn to protect her and he had done so, but then she had kissed him and the desire had exploded between them and shattered every tenet of duty by which Garrick had tried to live his life. Grant was right. He had transgressed the code. He was angry with himself for it; he felt full of violence and it disturbed him. He had not felt like this for years, since the time Stephen Fenner had died. He had thought that such powerful feelings, such dangerous actions, were behind him. Yet Merryn had smashed his cold facade and brought every emotion burning to new life.

He wanted to see Merryn. It felt as though she alone could soothe the demons in him. Yet he knew it would not be that easy. He had no notion if she would even agree to see him again, let alone marry him. The hideous scene in the brothel had haunted his thoughts for an entire day and night. Merryn, throwing on her ruined clothes in a desperate frenzy of embarrassment and horror, looking at him with loathing and disbelief.

I regret every moment of what we have done and I hate myself for it...

Garrick flinched at the memory. Everything had disintegrated into tawdriness and scandal, spilling corrosive misery over an experience that had been profoundly sweet and intense. For a brief moment they had built something exquisitely tender. And then they had lost it again.

"I make no excuse," Garrick said now, aware of Alex's steady gaze on his face. "I take full responsibility for my actions. It was unpardonable in me."

There was a silence. "Inexcusable, yes," Alex said. "Inexplicable, no."

Garrick blinked. "I beg your pardon?"

Alex shrugged. A small smile played about his lips. "Make no mistake, Farne," he said. "I do not condone in any way what happened. But I am also no hypocrite. People died in that flood. You and Merryn had been trapped for hours, facing the possibility of death together. She told us that you saved her life. Twice. " He grimaced.

"Such circumstances strain the self-control of even the strongest."

Garrick felt a little more of the tension ease from his body. "That is more than generous of you," he said, "but still I make no excuse."

"Of course," Alex said. "And I would not expect you to in all honor. So…" His tone warmed a little. "The question is what we are to do about this."

Their eyes met. Garrick realized that he had passed the test and was glad. He was starting to like Alex Grant. Owen Purchase spoke highly of the man. Under other circumstances he imagined that they might have become friends.

"I am sincere in my desire to wed Lady Merryn," he said, "and not simply because of the scandal. I have the greatest admiration for her."

A small smile played about Alex's lips. "I see," he said, and Garrick had the disconcerting feeling that Alex saw rather more than Garrick had intended.

Alex put his glass down with a businesslike snap. "You speak well, Farne," he said bluntly, "but you had best cut line with me. I imagine that Merryn is the last bride you would have sought under normal circumstances."

"That's true," Garrick said, deciding to be equally blunt. Regret scored him again. "I did not seek to wed at all," he said slowly. "I am not a good catch for any woman."

Alex looked taken aback. "Surely you jest."

"I do not mean materially," Garrick said. "My marital

history should be sufficient to dissuade any woman of sense—" He stopped.

"I'm not sure how much of that can be blamed on you," Alex said, very dryly. "Though I would not dream of speaking disrespectfully of your first wife."

There was a taut silence.

"As for Lady Merryn," Garrick said after a moment, "I am responsible for this scandal and as such I accept I have no choice other than to offer marriage to her." He looked up to find Grant's gaze fixed on him. "As I said, I have the greatest admiration for her. I like her. Very much."

"Evidently," Alex said even more dryly. He fixed Garrick with a not-unsympathetic gaze. "I do not think she will accept you, Farne."

"Because she hates me for killing her brother," Garrick said.

"It is a not-inconsiderable stumbling block," Alex agreed pleasantly. "Although…" A thoughtful note entered his voice. "I do not think she hates you, precisely." He shifted. "Her feelings, no doubt like your own, are confused. If you want her, though, you may have to force the match. Joanna and I will not stand in your way. We consider you the lesser of two evils." He flashed Garrick a smile that robbed the words of offense. "Without marriage Merryn is utterly ruined and only you can save her from that. Joanna will accept that for her sister's sake."

Garrick frowned. Alex's words were not unexpected

but they were unwelcome. "I'll not force Lady Merryn to wed me if she is unwilling," he said. "That would be the action of a scoundrel."

Alex shrugged. "Your scruples do you credit but how else can you put matters right in the eyes of the world, Farne?"

"I'll persuade her to accept my hand," Garrick said.

This time Alex actually laughed. "Persuade? Merryn? Surely you know her better than that? She is without doubt the most stubborn member of the Fenner family, and that is up against some very stiff competition."

"She is also strong and brave and spirited," Garrick said.

There was an odd expression in Alex's eyes. "Not the qualities that most men seek in their wives," he said. He paused. "I did not know Stephen Fenner," he added obliquely, "but my wife tells me he was…a charming rogue." He met Garrick's gaze very directly. "Joanna was older than Merryn when it all happened, of course. She sees things a little differently. And although she loved her brother she was not in the least blind to his faults." His tone changed. "You could consider telling Merryn exactly what happened. Intimate relationships have a better chance of succeeding if they are based on the truth."

"One day I hope to be able to tell her everything," Garrick said, "but in the end the fact is that I killed Stephen Fenner. Perhaps the details make no odds." He thought about Merryn's pain and disillusion on learning the truth. He wanted fiercely to protect her from that. But Purchase had been correct, Alex was correct. Everything had changed now that he and Merryn were to wed. He did not want a marriage based on deceit. He thought of the letter that he had sent a bare two days ago and prayed for a swift and just outcome.

Alex gave him a very penetrating look. "Only you can be the judge of what is right," he said. He held out his hand to shake Garrick's. "Good luck, Farne," he said. "I suspect you will need it."

MERRYN LAY IN HER BED watching the ripple of the winter sun across the floor and listening to the rattle of carriages in the road outside. A fire burned in the grate and beside her on the table sat a cup of cold tea. She had lain there for hours, all of the previous day, all night and now into the morning. She had not slept at all.

She could hear Tess and Joanna whispering just out of earshot.

"Merryn is totally ruined." She caught the edge of Tess's words. "Everyone is talking scandal, Jo. It is the *on dit* in all the papers this morning. Caught naked in a brothel in bed with the Duke of Farne! I can't believe…" Her voice faded away. Merryn watched a sparrow that had perched on her windowsill. It was looking through the glass, its head tilted to one side, as though it, too, was full of questions and gossip.

There was a swish of silk and then Joanna appeared

beside the bed. Her troubled blue gaze took in Merryn's untouched cup. She sat down on the edge of the bed.

"You're awake," she said.

"I haven't slept," Merryn said.

"No," Joanna said. "I imagine not."

Merryn waited. She felt odd—exhausted and yet wide-awake, her mind strangely blank and yet unable to rest.

Tess had followed Joanna across the room and was standing looking at her with a very odd expression in her eyes.

"I have to hand it to you, Merryn," she said. "Joanna and I have done many a scandalous thing between us but you…" She shook her head. "I confess myself shocked."

"Thank you," Merryn said.

"Although you do look well on it." Tess picked up one of Merryn's curls and ran it through her fingers. "How shiny the beer has made your hair! I shall have to see if I can order a barrel from the brewery. Anyway…" She remembered what it was she had originally been going to say. "You will be glad to know that although everyone knows that you spent the night with the Duke of Farne in a bordello, no one outside the family has heard the shocking news that you have been working for Mr. Bradshaw. *That* is one secret we have managed to keep."

"Thank goodness," Joanna said ironically. "No lady works for a living." She looked at Merryn, a frown puckering her brow. "Mr. Bradshaw tried to blackmail us, you know. He threatened to expose the truth about you if we did not pay him."

It was the first time that anything had pierced the lassitude that had Merryn in its grip and she shot up in bed, almost spilling her tea. "What? Tom tried to extort money from you?" She looked from one sister to the other. "What happened?"

"I threatened to shoot him," Tess said, with considerable satisfaction. "He reconsidered."

Merryn slumped back against the pillows, shocked and bitterly upset. Quite evidently she had misjudged Tom Bradshaw. She had felt so close to Tom, united in camaraderie, fighting for justice. Or so she had thought. Clearly Tom had been working for something quite different. Treacherous, deceitful Tom…

She remembered Garrick telling her that Tom was corrupt and she felt hopelessly naive. She closed her eyes for a second wondering if all her judgments were so faulty. Today she was no longer sure of anything.

Joanna patted her hand. "I am sorry, Merryn." She smiled at Tess. "Would you give me some time with Merryn alone, please, Tess? I think there are some matters we need to discuss."

Tess nodded. She gave Merryn a spontaneous hug, which brought the tears prickling Merryn's eyelids, and went out, closing the door softly after her. Merryn turned to look at her eldest sister. Joanna looked much the same as ever, stylish to a fault, although there were dark marks beneath her eyes that suggested that she, too, might have had a sleepless night. Merryn felt surprised by her sister's self-possession. She had expected Joanna to be hysterical, to rail at her for her behavior and for the shame and dishonor that she had brought on the family. Merryn had been accustomed to thinking both her sisters shallow but now, looking at Joanna's face, pale but perfectly composed, she was obliged to admit she had made a mistake, and about Tess, too.

"How do you feel?" Joanna asked expressionlessly.

"Very odd," Merryn admitted. She felt sore today, not just from all the cuts and lacerations that her body had sustained in the flood. There were other aches, other soreness that was the result of Garrick's lovemaking. The changes in her body made it impossible for her to pretend it had never happened. She felt different, aware of her physical self as she had never done before. It was odd and disconcerting and yet at the same time there was a wicked undertow of excitement and possibility about it that only served to confuse her further.

She ached more deeply, too, in her heart and soul, with a rawness that was so profound it made her want to cry. She knew she was still tired and that she was suffering from shock, but then there were other hurts that could not simply be intellectualized or explained away. How could she have done what she did with Garrick Farne? How could it have been so glorious in the moment, how could it have given her such dizzying pleasure, such excitement, such new and stunning awareness, and yet be so painful to recall now? And how could she forget it, as she had sworn she would, when she had thought about nothing else in the long darkness of the night when she had lain awake and remembered the press of Garrick's body on hers, the sense of him within her, the way that she had felt possessed and completed and utterly claimed as his?

Merryn fidgeted as a wave of heat rolled through her, making her stomach melt with a fiery longing. She had never been troubled by physical desire before she had met Garrick. She had read about lust, studied the differences between Eros, passionate and sensual desire, and Agape, deep, true love, and had thought how interesting it was and how clever language was to be able to separate and define the two. She had looked on it all as an academic exercise and had not felt anything but intellectual curiosity. But now she burned. She burned for Garrick and to learn and explore all those wonderful sensations she had only just discovered. It had been like a door opening into a richly colored fantasy world. She wanted to run through that door and greedily grasp after every new discovery.

She hated herself for it.

A wave of shame and self-reproach tumbled through her, making her feel physically sick.

You lust for the man who killed your brother…

"I am sorry, Joanna," she said. "I am sorry that I deceived you about working for Tom Bradshaw."

She saw Joanna frown. "It made me wonder," Joanna said, "whether I really know you at all." She fixed

Merryn with her big blue eyes. "You have been work-ing for Mr. Bradshaw for several years, so I understand. When I thought you were attending lectures or scientific talks you were undertaking assignments from him."

"Not always," Merryn said, feeling defensive. "I have done a great deal of study as well."

Joanna swept on as though she had not spoken. "I used to imagine you as so unworldly and intellectual. I thought that I had to protect you." She gave a short laugh. "Do you remember when John Hagan threatened to de-stroy us all if I did not become his mistress, and I went to Alex for protection? I did that for you as well as for myself, Merryn. I thought I had to care for you! It turns out you were nowhere near as naive and defenseless as I had thought."

"I think," Merryn said, with painful honesty, "that I have been extremely naive."

Joanna's gaze considered her. "We shall come to that in a moment," she said pleasantly. "For now, please permit me to get this off my chest." She drew a deep breath. "When I was abroad and thought you safely stay-ing with friends you were apparently undertaking other assignments for Mr. Bradshaw. Indeed, I am wondering if any of your friends actually exist! Last night, when you did not return home, we sent to a Miss Dormer's house because you had said you were attending a concert with her. We found that Miss Dormer did not live at the ad-dress you gave." She looked at her sister and Merryn's heart did a little dive to see the hurt and disappointment in Joanna's eyes.

"You lied to me, Merryn," Joanna said precisely. "Frequently. Repeatedly. I find it difficult to forgive."

"It wasn't like that," Merryn started to say. She felt wrenched with distress to see Joanna's unhappiness. "I thought that if I told you about my work for Tom you would stop me," she said defensively.

"So you did not trust me," Joanna said. "I am sorry for that. As the eldest I have always felt a responsibility for both you and Tess but until now I had not realized quite how badly I had failed." She made a slight dismissive gesture with her hands. "We shall leave that discussion for now. I think there are more urgent issues."

She got up and walked across to the window. The autumn sun burnished her hair to copper and chestnut and gold.

"Garrick Farne has made you an offer," she said, over her shoulder. "Alex is speaking to him. He is downstairs. He awaits your answer."

"No!" Merryn felt quick, suffocating panic. "It is impossible!"

"To marry him?" Joanna half turned toward her. Her expression was blank. "And yet you seem to have found it easy enough to sleep with him."

"It wasn't like that!" Merryn said. Her voice broke a little. She felt the tears swell in her eyes. "It is difficult to explain." Even her vaunted facility with language failed when she tried to explain to Joanna what had happened between herself and Garrick. "I was very scared," she said hesitatingly, "of the dark and of being trapped and Garrick saved my life, and the beer fumes were very strong—"

"So you were drunk," Joanna said impassively, after a moment.

"Yes… No!" Merryn said. "I'm not making excuses for myself. I will not. I cannot explain it, Jo. I was terrified and Garrick protected me and I was so grateful and relieved to be alive and he…" Her voice trailed off.

There was a long silence.

"It was a most generous way to show your gratitude," Joanna said, very understatedly.

Merryn made a little hiccupping sound that was halfway between a laugh and a sob. "I wanted him," she said. She closed her eyes. "I had no idea I could feel like that, Jo. I was desperate to have him and it was so exciting and unbelievably pleasurable. I had no notion! But then—" a tear squeezed past her closed lids "—afterward I could not believe what I had done, and I felt cheapened and sick and I despise myself for it. Such weakness—"

"You are too hard on yourself." Merryn heard a rustle of silk and then Joanna had come back to sit beside her. She felt her sister put her arms about her. Merryn could not believe it, could not believe that Joanna could forgive her when she was unable to forgive herself. It felt such an enormous comfort. She leaned in to Joanna's arms and sobbed.

"Extreme fear and indeed extreme relief can cause

us all to do strange things," Joanna continued. She was stroking Merryn's hair now, cradling her like a child. "And you are not to be blamed if you have discovered something you enjoy more than academic study." There was a thread of laughter in Joanna's voice now. "Physical pleasure can indeed sweep you away."

"And yet I cannot bear to feel that for Garrick Farne," Merryn said wretchedly. She pulled away, sat up. "Farne, Joanna!" She sniffed, rubbing her wet, sore eyes. "He ruined all our lives! How could I do such a thing? How can I bear it? I hate him! And yet—" She stopped. "I also care for him," she said forlornly. "I cannot deny it. There is something between us that I do not understand..." She shivered. "I am so confused, Jo."

"Yes," Joanna said. "I understand you might feel like that." She paused. "I suspect that you are right. You do not hate Farne, Merryn. You may hate what he did to Stephen, but you do not necessarily hate Garrick Farne himself. Quite the contrary, I suspect."

Merryn rubbed her brow. Her forehead felt hot and her head ached. Her eyes were stinging and prickled with unshed tears.

"I don't understand the difference," she said. "All I know is that it feels wrong. I feel as though it is pulling me apart."

"Maybe you will see it clearly in time," Joanna said.

"I understand that *you* might hate me for it," Merryn said bitterly.

Joanna shook her head swiftly. "Merryn dearest." There was a little catch in her voice. "We all make mistakes."

"Not ones of such monstrous proportions," Merryn sniffed.

"Once again you see things too starkly," Joanna corrected. "You met a man who roused a passionate response from you. The fact that it is Garrick Farne is—" She stopped, shrugged. "Complicated, perhaps. One might even say unfortunate. It is like fate playing a trick on you."

"I cannot marry him, Jo," Merryn said wretchedly. "It feels like a most appalling betrayal of everything I have believed for the past twelve years."

Joanna was silent for a moment. "I won't seek to persuade you," she said. "If you feel you cannot wed Garrick then I will give you all the support that you require."

"But what if there is a child?" Merryn clutched Joanna's hands convulsively, at last giving voice to the deepest fear that had stalked her through the night. She had told herself that there would not be a child, that it would not happen, but the truth was that she did not know. Oh, she understood the principles; she had read all about procreation in many different books, fiction and nonfiction, but when it came to the reality she had only just started to understand how woefully ignorant she was. She felt afraid. The fear started as a tiny pattering in her stomach and swelled to a huge panic that threatened to swallow her whole.

"I'm afraid, Joanna," she burst out. "When will I know if I am pregnant?"

She saw a shadow touch Joanna's eyes and castigated herself for her insensitivity. Joanna had spent years and years of her first marriage desperately hoping for a child and believing she was barren. Merryn had seen—but not understood then—the anguish that her infertility had caused her. Yet here she was now asking for her sister's love and support when she might have carelessly, wantonly conceived a child out of wedlock under such appalling circumstances. And yet still, it seemed, Joanna had the strength and the love to be there for her.

"It depends," her sister was saying carefully, "on where you are with your courses."

Merryn had never paid much attention to them. She struggled to remember. "I think… I believe about the middle of the second week," she ventured.

She saw Joanna pull a face. "Then that might be dangerous. It is impossible to tell. You will know in a few weeks, perhaps, or maybe a little more."

Merryn felt frighteningly adrift, as though there were suddenly no certainty left in the world. "Then I could perhaps wait and see—" She started to say, and once again saw the shadow in Joanna's eyes, and thought of all the months Joanna must have waited and been desperately disappointed. It seemed vicious and cruel that Joanna had been disillusioned each month when she had failed to conceive whereas she would be desperately waiting and hoping that there would be no child.

"I'm sorry, Jo," she said brokenly. "So sorry."

Joanna shook her head. "Do not be. I have Shuna now, and Alex and I have the prospect of more children if we are fortunate. And if we are not so blessed, well... It is enough to have their love." She loosed her sister. "I cannot tell you what to do, Merryn. You must try to make the right decision yourself. But I am always here if you need me."

"I have been so stupid, Jo," Merryn said. "I thought that I was clever—far cleverer than you—but you are wise and kind and far more generous than I."

Joanna smiled and squeezed her hands before letting her go and standing. "If you are to refuse Farne," she said, "at least do him the courtesy of telling him to his face. You owe him that, Merryn. I will send your maid to help you dress."

"I can't marry him," Merryn said wretchedly. "Jo, you know I cannot."

Joanna did not reply at once. "I know how attached you are to Stephen's memory," she said. "Probably more than either Tess or I because you were younger and he was a hero to you." She smoothed her skirts thoughtfully, as though she was choosing her words with equal care. "Stephen was very kind to you," she added, after a moment. "It surprised me, because he was not, as a rule, a kind person. Oh, he could be charming and attentive and make any woman think she was the center of his world. But—" She stopped.

"I know that Stephen could be very bad," Merryn said. "But that does not mean that he deserved to die."

"No," Joanna said. "Of course not." She shook her head. "He should never have seduced Kitty Farne, though."

"They loved each other," Merryn said defiantly. "She was unhappy in her marriage."

"Stephen seduced her long before she wed," Joanna said, and for a second she sounded very cold. "And I am not sure that he did love her. Certainly he never loved anyone as much as he loved himself."

Merryn stared. "But he must have done!" she burst out. Her thoughts were tripping over themselves, shock mingling with resentment at the abrupt way that her sister had wrenched her memories apart and set them in a different frame. "I saw them together," she protested. "He adored her! Why else would he—" She stopped.

"Why else would he take her from Garrick Farne?" Joanna finished for her. "He did it for fun, Merryn," she said gently. "He did it because he could."

"No," Merryn said. Her heart gave a little flutter of fear. If Stephen had not loved Kitty then everything that she had believed in was based on a lie. It was not possible. She could not accept it.

"I don't believe it," she said stubbornly. "I saw them, Jo! They loved each other! They were meant to be together."

Joanna shrugged. "Perhaps you are right and I am wrong," she said.

"You must be," Merryn said. She drew the bedclothes about her and held them tight. "You must be," she repeated, half to herself.

"I remember when you were in your teens you had quite a *tendre* for Garrick Farne." Joanna paused with her hand on the doorknob. "Oh, we all thought he was handsome but you…" She smiled. "You were quite bowled over, were you not?"

Merryn looked up, startled. "I did not think anyone knew about that," she said involuntarily, the color flooding her face.

Joanna laughed. "It was very clear, Merryn," she said gently, "even if Garrick himself never knew." She went out and closed the door softly behind her.

Merryn let the bedclothes slip through her fingers. So everyone had known about her *tendre* for Garrick Farne. How naive she had been to think it a secret. But in one respect Joanna had been quite wrong. She had thought Merryn's feelings had been a childish infatuation, no more, when in fact they had been so forceful and passionate, so dangerous, that they had almost consumed her.

CHAPTER TWELVE

WHEN MERRYN ENTERED the library, Garrick was standing by the window looking out over the gardens. He did not turn immediately at her entrance. She was not even sure he had heard her. She stood for a moment and looked at him, while her heart beat a violent tattoo against her ribs.

This was the man who was responsible for her brother's death yet when she looked at him all she could remember was his kiss, his touch on her skin, the broken endearments he had whispered to her as he had made love to her with such searing thoroughness and delight. In some ways she barely knew him and yet in others she knew him so intimately that the knowledge made her tremble. And it was not simply that she had so strong a physical awareness of him. Honesty prompted her to admit that something bound her to Garrick Farne so deeply that she could neither explain it nor escape it. It had been so from the start.

She saw that Garrick had done her the honor of dressing immaculately. His broad shoulders were encased in a coat of brown superfine. Buff pantaloons molded his thighs and his boots had a high polish. He had shaved closely. The stubble was gone. The thought that Garrick had done this because he was intent on proposing to her gave Merryn the oddest lump in her throat. And then he turned, and she saw that his face was pale with a livid bruise on the temple and a cut down one cheek, she saw the bandage at his wrist, and she remembered the darkness and the terror of their imprisonment and the intimacy it had forced them into, and she wanted to run.

Instead of fleeing she came forward into the room, drawing on all the strength and courage she could muster.

"Lady Merryn," he said. His voice was very deep. "You are well?"

He had taken her hands in his. Heat and awareness enveloped her instantly. She felt the abrasions of his raw skin against her fingers. Instantly she was back in the tumbled ruins of the beer flood with Garrick's body shielding hers from the falling masonry. He had defended her against all peril. Misery twisted within her. Impossible choices…

"I am…tolerably well, I thank you, your grace," Merryn said.

She saw a spark of amusement light his eyes at her formality. No wonder, when the last time they had met she had been naked in his arms while he took the most outrageous liberties with her willing body. The thought made her feel faint. She wanted to pretend it had never happened. She wanted to do it all over again. She did not know what she wanted but she felt as though she was being torn apart.

She took a deep breath. "I appear to have compromised you, your grace," she said.

The smile in Garrick's eyes deepened, warm and tender. Merryn's composure faltered, hanging by a thread.

"That is a novel way of expressing it," Garrick said. "It is generally the gentleman who takes the responsibility."

"I think we must both do that," Merryn said. "I do not blame you in any way for what happened between us."

Garrick's smile faded. He still held her hand. "How very just and fair you are, Lady Merryn," he said, "but it was my loss of control. I knew what I was doing." His eyes darkened. "You did not."

"I could have stopped you," Merryn whispered. Her heart was beating erratically, butterflies fluttering in her throat. "But I did not wish to do so."

The gentleness in his eyes was almost her undoing. "Always so honest," he said. He raised her hand to his lips and pressed a kiss against her palm. She shivered.

His tone changed. "Merryn," he said again.

Merryn wished that he would not use her name so informally and speak it in such gentle tones. Something in his voice struck the deepest chord within her and undermined all her defenses. It reminded her of the way in which he had whispered her name in the hot darkness. Of the way he had shouted it, with an edge of desperation, when he had urged her to throw herself into his arms. It reminded her of the intimate connection there was between them, the ties of memory and desire that she wished did not exist. But they did exist and she could not escape them.

She turned her face away from him, suddenly unable to meet his gaze.

He went down on one knee before her. Oh, dear, this was bad—this was like a proper proposal rather than one borne of necessity and scandal. Merryn bit her lip and forced back the unexpected tears.

"Merryn," he said, "will you marry me?"

Merryn felt the most insane urge to put a hand out to touch the crisp auburn hair that curled over his collar. His head was bent. She could see the line of his eyelashes against the straight slash of his cheek. Fair lashes, like hers. Any child of theirs would not have the thick dark lashes so beloved of artists and the fashionable ladies of the ton.

"I cannot marry you, Garrick," she whispered. "I am sorry." She closed her eyes against the pain inside her and the thought of a little girl—or boy—blessed with fair eyelashes.

Garrick had straightened up but he had not moved away from her. She felt as though his physical presence engulfed her. "May I beg you to reconsider?" His voice was strained. "Society will destroy you if you do not accept my offer, Merryn. I cannot allow that to happen."

"I do not pay any regard to the opinions of society and I never have," Merryn said fiercely.

"Yes," Garrick said. Despite everything she could hear a tinge of humor in his voice. "I do know that."

"I'll find something else to do," Merryn said desperately. She took a few agitated steps away from him. "I can see that I can no longer work for Tom but perhaps I could gain employment elsewhere—" She stopped. There was an expression on Garrick's face that could only be described as pity.

"Merryn," he said again. "Not this time."

There was a silence.

Everyone is talking scandal... It is in all the papers... Caught naked in a brothel in bed with the Duke of Farne... Merryn could hear Tess's whispered words. She knew she was the most notorious woman in London.

Ruined.

Compromised.

She liked words but she did not like this one with its overtones of suspicion and disrepute. Her reputation was sullied, her virginity lost. Even if she did not bear a child, the proof of her fall from virtue, gossip and scandal would cling to her name forever. No one would offer her employment. She knew that, in her heart. If she did not marry Garrick she would become an outcast, shunned by all except her own family. The lectures and talks, exhibitions and concerts that she had relished would become events where she ran the gamut of public gossip. She had gone from being invisible to being the most visible, the most talked about, person in the ton.

"I wonder," she said bitterly, "if it would have been different had it been a flood of champagne?"

"Much better ton," Garrick said with a faint smile, "but I fear that in the end the effect would have been the same. You would have to marry me."

"I cannot marry you," Merryn said. She took several more paces across the room.

"Merryn," Garrick said. "Please reconsider." His tone had changed. There was iron in it now, absolute, immovable. "If there is a child," he said, very deliberately, "I cannot—I will not—let it be born out of wedlock."

"But there may not be a child," Merryn said eagerly. Hope and desperation warred inside her. "We can wait," she said. "In a little while we shall see…" Her voice trailed away unhappily. She knew it would not serve even as she saw Garrick's expression.

"We wait what—a month, two?" His voice was extremely polite but the look in his eyes was not. It was furious. "Then if you are not pregnant we congratulate ourselves on a lucky escape, and if you are, we marry one another quickly, quietly, with everyone counting days and months and gossiping about us?" His mouth twisted. "That is too shabby. I will not do it."

Merryn looked into his dark, implacable eyes. She knew Garrick was correct—she could not take the risk of condemning a child to the stigma of illegitimacy, another bastard Farne offspring, like father like son. She pressed her fingers to her lips to hold back the hysteria that suddenly threatened her. Confronted with such cruel choices she felt smothered with guilt. She wanted to run.

But she could not. She had to face what she had done.

"You must marry me," Garrick said. "Good God, Merryn—" Suddenly there was raw anger in his voice. "I already have your brother's death on my conscience," he said. "I have no intention of adding to the scandal by giving the gossipmongers ammunition to claim that I have destroyed your life, too." He took her hand and she could feel the tension that gripped him. "This way I can atone," Garrick said. His voice was rough. "I tried to do that when I gave back Fenners and your fortune. I righted one small wrong. If you wed me—"

"It will not put right Stephen's death," Merryn said heatedly. "Nothing can do that."

"No," Garrick said, "but it will right you in the eyes of the world. And that way we can present the marriage as a further step toward reconciliation between our two families instead of simply a way to prevent scandal. Have you thought—" he let her go abruptly and turned away "—that many people may well imagine that you have been my mistress for some time?"

This time the silence was taut with emotion. Merryn sank down heavily onto one of the chairs. She had not imagined it for one moment. It cut her to the heart.

She remembered Lord Croft's carelessly cruel words

in Bond Street. He had implied that she had been willing to overlook Stephen's death in return for a fortune of thirty thousand pounds. How much louder, how much more salacious, would be the gossip that she was Garrick's mistress. She could almost hear the whispers, the hiss of silken skirts withdrawing from her. She could see the flick of fans as the delicious *on dit* sped through the ton. Nothing could be more scandalous than the suggestion that she had turned to the bed of the very man who had ruined her family.

Garrick was right. Marriage would at least put a respectable gloss on a deeply unrespectable situation.

"Perhaps a marriage of convenience…" She started to say. "In name only. To promote the fiction that this is indeed an alliance intended to mend the breach between our families—" She stopped as she saw the look in his eyes.

He took a step toward her, and another. "A marriage in name only," he said softly, mockingly. He took her chin in his hand and turned her face up to his. His touch was featherlight but Merryn felt it echo through her whole body. She closed her eyes for a moment against the potency of it.

"Do you think you could do that?" he asked in the same tone that had the shivers chasing down her spine. "For I could not. I warn you now—I would not even try." He bent his head until his lips brushed hers. The heat flared inside her.

"Could you do that?" he repeated, his lips an inch

from hers. His mouth took hers before she could reply and he was kissing her with skill and a mastery that set her shaking from head to toe. Her body recognized the taste and the touch of him now and responded to him with an eager need she could neither hide nor deny, opening to him like a flower to the sun. It shamed her all over again that she could be so avid for his touch when her mind was so cloudy and confused with grief and misery.

Garrick deepened the kiss and Merryn caught hold of his jacket to steady herself in a world that was spinning. The material of it slipped beneath her fingers and his arms came about her, steadying her, holding her close. His kiss was a statement of possession and intent, and Merryn recognized it as such. She would be his wife in every way possible. There was no escape.

He released her and stood back. He was breathing hard and his eyes glittered with desire.

"I already have a special license," he said. "We will be wed within the week. Oh, and Merryn—" There was an odd pause. "I should be very grateful," Garrick said, a little formally, "if you were able to honor your wedding vows."

Merryn stared at him for a moment uncomprehending. For all Garrick's forcefulness and the blazing passion between them she had sensed raw anguish in his voice then. Her heart jolted to hear it.

"Kitty," she whispered. "You do not wish for another unfaithful wife."

"It would be most unfortunate," Garrick agreed, and there was a thread of humor in his tone that did not quite disguise the hurt. "I fear I am most unfashionable in that regard. The somewhat…flexible…morals of some members of the ton do not suit my taste. Although," he added bitterly, "I can see that it would also be the most perfect revenge for you to marry me and then betray me. Life comes full circle."

Merryn shook her head abruptly. She was shocked by this insight into Garrick's pain. He had always seemed so confident and so supremely sure of himself, so unapologetic for what he had done in the past. In the dark intimacy of their confinement she had tried to provoke him by goading him about Stephen and Kitty's love. He had responded by telling her that he regretted his wife's betrayal of him every single day. She had heard his pain and disillusion then. Now, looking into his eyes, she felt it, believed it.

She swallowed hard. "I am not the sort of woman to do that," she said. "If I give a promise I keep it. I would never dishonor you."

She saw a flash of something in Garrick's eyes, some emotion so profound that she felt shaken. "Yes," he said. His tone had warmed a shade. "I believe you. You are too honest to play me false. You keep your promises."

"You did not wish to wed again," Merryn said, watching his face. She felt as though she was learning something new, stumbling along a strange path. She knew that insight was not her strong suit. Tom's betrayal had pointed that up rather painfully. But now with Garrick she found she wanted to learn and understand.

Garrick shook his head. "No. I never wanted to marry again."

Merryn understood that now. It had not occurred to her before that Kitty's unfaithfulness must have damaged Garrick so badly that he would never remarry. She had thought he had not cared. She realized that she had been wrong.

"But surely you need an heir?" she said.

"I have brothers," Garrick said. He smiled at last. "I may not speak to them but I can count on them to continue the Farne line."

It seemed a cold world to Merryn, who had only that morning come to value the extent of her sisters' love.

Garrick was watching her with those dark, dark eyes. "Do we have an agreement, then?" he asked softly.

"Yes," Merryn whispered. The word was out, no going back.

She saw him smile with relief and triumph and possession. He kissed her again and she felt her head spin and her knees weaken as the pleasure rocked through her like a sweet, hot tide.

He released her. "Thank you," he said. "I will call on you later."

He bowed to her and went out and Merryn crossed to the window and sank down onto the seat, remembering the pressure of Garrick's mouth on hers and feeling the heat still thrum through her body. Her lips felt impossibly soft and sensitive, swollen from Garrick's kisses. Her belly was aching with a tight, hot sensation. She knew how that might be eased now. She knew what she wanted.

With a groan she covered her face with her hands.

How could she marry this man and live with him as his wife when she hated what he had done?

Garrick Farne. Her husband. She felt impossibly torn.

JOANNA HAD DECREED that the winter exhibition at the Royal Academy was the event at which Merryn and Garrick would make their debut in society as a betrothed couple. The wedding was two days away.

"You cannot hide away forever," Joanna snapped, when Merryn objected. "Yes, there will be gossip but better to tackle it head-on. Trust me—I know a little about facing society's censure."

"I did not enjoy social occasions before," Merryn argued. "Why should it be different now?"

"It won't be," Tess put in. "It will be worse." She and Joanna were wrestling their sister into a brand-new yellow gown. Merryn felt like a tailor's dummy, pummeled and pushed between them. "But you have to do it, Merryn," Tess continued, "otherwise you will become even more of a hermit than you already are. They will call you the Reclusive Duchess, or something else snide and more alliterative than I can think."

"The Desolate Duchess?" Joanna suggested.

"The Dismal Duchess," Merryn said.

"Oh, yes," Tess said, smiling, "I like that one."

The sisters stood back, spun Merryn around and presented her to the mirror. "There. You look lovely."

Merryn thought that she looked like a very reluctant Cinderella with two beautiful fairy godmothers smiling behind her. Her hair had been curled and teased into precisely the sort of upswept arrangement she hated and could never maintain, even though the prettiest yellow bonnet secured it. The gown was… Well, it simply was not her style. But then she did not have a style. Shabby bluestocking was scarcely the mode and certainly would not do for the Royal Academy.

She was about to dismiss her reflection, thank her sisters politely and make the best of a bad job when she looked again and felt a small frisson of excitement. She had never previously paid the slightest attention to her appearance, never had any interest in it and yet now, suddenly, she could hear Garrick's words.

I do not even notice your sisters when you are close by...

A little shiver shook her. She looked again. Her hair, so glossy and golden, framed a face that had regained its color and gained also something of sensual knowledge and experience. Her eyes glowed deep blue. Her lips were parted on the edge of a smile. The gown skimmed her shoulders and fell like a golden waterfall from below her breast to spill about her feet. She was aware of the caress of the silk and the way it swathed her body with a soft cocoon like a lover's embrace.

She reached out one gloved hand and touched her reflection, trying to pin down the difference in her, the difference in how she felt. She thought of Garrick and the way that he watched her. She pressed her fingers to her lips in an unconscious echo of his touch. She felt alive.

"I think Merryn has woken up," Joanna said, a little dryly, from behind her.

Merryn spun around. Just for a moment, lost in a world of new and sensual discovery, she had forgotten her sisters. They were both laughing at her. They were also both looking frightfully proud of her and a little bit anxious. She felt a pang of love and gratitude and caught their hands.

"Thank you," she said. "I won't hug you because it would crush the silk."

"Gracious," Joanna said, squeezing her hand, her eyes like stars, "we will make a fashionable lady of you yet, Merryn!"

"Pray do not set your sights too high," Merryn said, laughing, and then they were all hugging each other anyway and she clung to Joanna and to Tess because everything had changed, she had changed and she was a little bit afraid, and because she had only just realized how much she loved them.

"At least you will not have to run the gamut of Garrick's family," Tess said as she disentangled herself and wiped the tears from her eyes. "I hear that they do not speak."

"Poor Garrick," Joanna said. "That must be unconscionably lonely. I wonder why they are estranged?"

"Well," Tess said, "it could be because all his siblings are the most unconscionable snobs. Ghastly, you know. He is better off without them."

It felt odd to hear Joanna and Tess speak sympathetically of Garrick, Merryn thought, and yet on a purely human basis she had to agree with them. Garrick had always struck her as the most solitary of men and in some bitter way this marriage, borne out of necessity not love, might make him more solitary still. She had always deplored the cold business arrangements of aristocratic marriages yet at least in an arranged marriage there was usually companionship if not love, mutual support and sometimes respect. Garrick had offered her his name to save her reputation. She offered him nothing. It felt wrong to enter marriage on such a basis. She gave a violent shiver. She felt small and lonely, smothered by convention. For one terrifying moment she could see her life spinning out before her in a series of images of great country houses with huge, empty rooms, spaces where she would always walk alone.

"Here…" Tess handed her the yellow coat that matched the silk gown. "You are cold."

"I am frightened," Merryn said frankly.

Joanna and Tess exchanged a look. "We will be with you," Joanna said encouragingly, "and Alex, too, although he says he is too much of a philistine to appreciate art. But I have always thought Mr. Turner's pictures most fine. I adored his painting of Hannibal crossing the Alps."

Merryn bit back the retort that would previously have sprung to her lips, a blistering comment on Joanna's appreciation of any picture that was fashionable and approved by society. Besides, that was not really fair to her sister who as well as being generous to a fault had a very fine eye for style that was all her own.

I have been very unkind in the past, Merryn thought. *I must try to do better.*

It was odd; she had thought she was happy before, keeping secrets, doing her work for Tom, harboring her hatred of Garrick Farne. Only now, with her past life in tatters and an uncertain future before her as Duchess of Farne, could she see that perhaps what she had thought was happiness had been something different, a partial life bringing interest and challenge through her work and her studies perhaps, but also devoid of love.

Shrugging off the disturbing thought, she grabbed the fur muff that matched the trim on the bonnet.

"Well," she said, smiling at Joanna and Tess, "let us go and make them talk!"

Despite her bravado, the journey to the Royal Academy in the Strand was accomplished in tense silence. The fact that the exhibition rooms were crowded with people also did nothing to soothe Merryn's nerves. Alex offered her his arm and Joanna and Tess walked ahead, arms linked, terrifyingly *à la mode,* challenging anyone, Merryn thought, who dared to look askance at them. Even so there was absolute silence for a moment as they swept into the main exhibition room before a positive barrage of chatter broke out around them. Merryn unconsciously raised her chin in exact parody of her sisters' nonchalant disdain but she was horribly aware of all the flutter of speculation and gossip, the whispers, the sideways glances. She could imagine all the unpleasant things they were saying, the comments about her fall from grace, her scrambled betrothal to save face, the delicious *on dit* of her being found naked in a bordello, a piece of scandal that surely could never be surpassed. Her face burned and the tears pricked her eyes but she was not going to give anyone the satisfaction of knowing how she felt. She had always hated to be the center of attention; this was hideous, her worst nightmare, as the fans flicked and the eyes followed her and someone tittered, a laugh full of lewd suggestiveness.

"I wish Garrick had escorted me," Merryn whispered impulsively to Alex. Although she appreciated her brother-in-law's support a very great deal she felt bereft without Garrick at her side, an odd but undeniable sensation that she had not expected.

"He is here now," Alex whispered back, smiling.

Merryn turned slowly, her heart in her mouth. Garrick had come through the main entrance doors and was walking toward them flanked on one side by a man Merryn recognized as Captain Owen Purchase. Purchase seemed to be looking at Tess with the expression of a man struck dumb with admiration.

"Another good man goes down under the onslaught of the Fenner sisters," Alex was saying ruefully.

Merryn was not paying attention, however, for on Garrick's arm was a tiny elderly lady, very stiff and upright in rustling black silk, not a white hair out of place and a truly astonishing diamond necklace glittering about her neck. They approached very slowly and by the time they were within a few paces every single person in the room was watching and once again the gossip had died to a murmur and then faded altogether.

"Is that not… Surely it is… I… Oh, dear…" Merryn was suddenly terrified.

"Lady Merryn." Garrick had stopped before her and executed the most immaculately perfect bow. He raised his voice a little so that everyone nearby could hear him. "It is my very great honor and pleasure," he said, "to introduce you to my aunt, the Dowager Duchess of Steyne. Aunt Elizabeth, my fiancée, Lady Merryn Fenner."

The Dowager's keen black gaze swept Merryn up and down as she made her curtsy and Merryn felt as though she was taking in every aspect of her appearance while leaving the verdict undeclared. The Duchess's bearing was regal, her expression haughty. Around them the crowd bobbed and fluttered, waiting. The Dowager Duchess of Steyne was a high stickler, a relic from a previous age. She was a friend of the Queen, rarely seen in public these days but still wielding the most enormous social power. It was unthinkable that Garrick Farne would have introduced his father's sister to a woman who had been his mistress, engaged in some shoddy *affaire*. All the same, the crowds waited in case the Dowager titillated their taste for gossip with the cut direct.

Merryn held the Dowager Duchess's unreadable dark gaze until she felt her nerves were at screaming point. Then something that might have passed for a wintry smile flickered across the Dowager's lips and she said, "It pleases me greatly that the breach between the Fenner and the Farne families is soon to be healed by your marriage to my nephew, Lady Merryn."

There was a whooshing sound as everyone released their breath at the same moment, turned away and pretended that they had not really been listening at all. Merryn felt herself go limp with relief. She dropped another slight curtsy.

"Thank you, your grace."

The Dowager Duchess nodded. "Charming," she said, and turned to acknowledge Joanna.

"Lady Grant," she said. "I congratulate you on the most beautiful design you created for Lady Drummond's drawing room. Exquisite taste." Her gaze moved on to Tess. "And Lady Darent…I congratulate *you* on once again being a rich widow." She turned to Alex. "Now, Lord Grant. I have long wanted to make your acquaintance."

Garrick drew Merryn slightly to one side. His broad shoulders blocked out the inquisitive crowd.

"Well," Garrick said, raising his brows, "you seem to have made quite an impression. Aunt Elizabeth is not normally so fulsome in her praise."

"That was praise?" Merryn tried for a light tone. She put a hand on his sleeve. "Thank you for what you did," she whispered.

Garrick looked down at her, a smile lightening his dark eyes again, and Merryn felt a rush of feeling that left her light-headed and a little dizzy. "It was a risk," he admitted, "but after I had explained everything to Aunt Elizabeth I trusted her to support us."

"Everything?" Merryn said faintly.

"Almost everything," Garrick amended. His gaze met hers, sliding over her, bringing heat in its wake. His smile was intimate, tender, for her alone, and it made her heart ache.

"You look very beautiful tonight, Merryn," he said.

The Dowager had turned back to them. "Lady Merryn," she said, her sharp black gaze traveling from her to Garrick and making Merryn feel as though her emotions were naked, "I have a fancy to see the Collins exhibition. You will accompany me."

Merryn shot Garrick an anguished look. He laughed.

"I will come and find you shortly," he said, a smile and a promise in his eyes. He leaned closer. "Remember she does not bite," he whispered.

"Pray do not interrupt us too soon," the Dowager snapped.

Merryn followed the Dowager's ramrod-straight figure through the archway into the next, smaller exhibition room. There were fewer people here and those that were present took one look at the Dowager's fierce expression and melted away, leaving the room empty. The Duchess stopped before a small portrait in the corner. It was a picture of a seated woman and might have been painted some fifteen years before. The subject was young, a girl of about eighteen or nineteen, exquisitely pretty, curvaceous, with dark hair curling softly about her face, limpid black eyes and a little smile just starting to dimple the corners of her mouth. A small dog sat a few feet away, gazing adoringly at the woman who looked as though she took such adoration for granted from animals and people alike.

Merryn caught her breath on a little gasp and the Duchess looked sharply at her.

"You recognize my nephew's wife, Kitty Scott? This was painted just before their marriage."

Merryn's heart was beating fast in her throat. "I… Yes, I do. We…met once or twice," she stammered. "I was only a child…"

The Duchess nodded. "Kitty was a pretty little chit. I liked her spirit but she had the most vicious temper when she was thwarted."

Merryn was shocked. She frowned, trying to match the memory of the Kitty she had known with the woman of the Dowager's description. The Kitty Farne of her recollection had been the sweetest, kindest creature in the world, always giving her sweetmeats and little gifts, ribbons and thread, asking her what she had been reading, showing an interest in all the ordinary aspects of Merryn's life that Joanna and Tess had been too wrapped up in themselves to care about. It was one of the reasons that Merryn had loved Kitty. And because Kitty had loved Stephen, of course…

The Dowager Duchess was looking at her very directly. "My nephew has suffered a gross betrayal in his life and experienced a great deal of misery and loneliness," she said. "I trust, Lady Merryn, that you will not add to his unhappiness."

I would not dare, Merryn thought. Pinned under the Dowager's cold, dark stare she felt like a specimen on a slab.

"I would never willfully cause anyone unhappiness," she said.

The Duchess nodded briskly. "I believe that. You seem a straightforward sort of gal, not in the common style." Once again that faint smile touched her lips. "Garrick says you are a bluestocking. That is all to the good since he is a notable scholar. And being a Duke is a lonely business. One needs a helpmeet."

"Yes," Merryn said. She thought of Farne House with its long, empty echoing corridors, devoid of life, of love. "Yes, I do understand that."

She looked back at the portrait, at Kitty Scott painted

on that verdant summer day so many years ago, so soon before tragedy. Kitty had not been much of a helpmeet to her husband, that was for sure.

"I am sorry," she said. "I did not realize that Garrick loved her."

The Dowager gave a dry laugh. "Oh, he did not. My brother sold Garrick into marriage to further his political ambitions. He was a blackguard, Claudius. It was a fine dynastic match and Garrick would have done his duty. A pity that Miss Scott's heart and much else was already given elsewhere." The Duchess's voice was very dry.

"Yes," Merryn said. She felt a dull ache in the region of her own heart.

Garrick would have done his duty...

Merryn did not doubt it. It was the reason that she now found herself betrothed to Garrick, because he was a man who held honor and obligation above all things.

She thought of what she knew of Garrick, the young rakehell who had been sold into marriage by his father for gain, who had been prepared to make the match work out of duty. She felt an enormous sadness. She looked up to see the Dowager Duchess watching her keenly, and with some other emotion in her eyes, something softer.

"I am sorry," she said again and she was not really sure what she was apologizing for. The Dowager Duchess actually patted her hand.

"It was not your fault, child." She paused. "But now you bear a huge responsibility. If you cannot love Garrick, you will, I am sure, do your best to honor and respect him."

If you cannot love him...

Merryn jolted to a stop, staring blindly in front of her. Garrick had taken her body and left her heart shattered, torn with doubt and confusion. She had thought that it was because of guilt and grief and the impossible choices she had to make. But that was not the whole truth. She felt breathless, frozen with shock. How had she not realized that her feelings were involved? Perhaps it was because she had never loved before. Perhaps it was because Garrick was the last man on earth that she had wanted to love. Yet she knew she did. The truth beat through her mind until she wanted to cry out to try to drown the words. It was impossible but it was undeniable. She loved Garrick Farne.

She had known it, in her heart. She had known there in terrifying dark when they had been trapped together and she had turned to him with absolute trust to hold her and protect her and keep her safe. She had known but she had turned the feelings away, reaching instead for her hatred and her grief to build a barrier and defend herself against him. Now, though, she could deny it no longer. And the thought brought a new wave of terror. Garrick had not wanted to wed her. He had been honest enough to admit that he had never wanted to wed again and without love those burdens of duty and honor and obligation that tied him to her could become the heaviest of shackles. She loved him but in return he could give nothing of his heart.

"Lady Merryn?" The Dowager Duchess sounded impatient. "You are woolgathering, my dear."

"I beg your pardon," Merryn said, blinking, pushing away the tumble of thoughts and emotions that threatened to overwhelm her. "I was thinking…" She realized that she was still staring at Kitty's pretty painted face and that the Dowager had misunderstood her.

"It was all a long time ago," the Dowager said, "and nothing to do with you, child that you were. Don't let it taint you."

Too late. She had let it taint her life for twelve long years.

Merryn shuddered. She had made so many mistakes, taken so many false steps. What if she had been wrong about Garrick from the start? What if…

What if it was not Garrick who had shot Stephen at all? What if there had been a terrible accident and Kitty had shot her lover and Garrick had taken the blame?

Merryn's heart started to hammer in long, slow strokes. She thought of the instinct that persistently told her that Garrick was an honorable man. She thought of his life raised in duty and service. She trembled at the enormity of what must have happened.

Suddenly she was possessed with the most monstrous impatience. She had to speak to Garrick, to ask him to tell her the truth. She had to get him alone. Not even she could be so direct as to ask him in front of the assembled crowd at the Royal Academy whether his wife had shot her lover by accident and he had taken the blame.

She looked across at Garrick. He was standing with Alex and Joanna, admiring a William Collins engraving, The Fishing Boys. His head was bent, his expression grave and thoughtful. He turned slightly to answer some remark of Joanna's and for a second a smile lighted his eyes and Merryn felt a rush of emotion so strong and turbulent that it stole her breath.

He *had* to be innocent of the heinous crime of which she had accused him. She was sure that she was right. She *had* to be right. Kitty had shot Stephen and Garrick, out of duty and honor, had protected her.

Something urgent in her stance must have communicated itself to Garrick because he looked up and his gaze tangled with hers. For a moment they stared at one another while the crowd spun past them in a blur of color and noise. Garrick excused himself from Joanna and Alex and came across to her.

"What is it?" he said, raising his brows. His brown eyes were very steady. He took her hand, entwining his fingers in hers.

"I need to speak with you alone," Merryn whispered.

The Dowager bent a very disapproving look upon her. "Not before the wedding, Lady Merryn. That would be quite improper. You shall be chaperoned at all times." She looked around, summoning Joanna and Tess with the merest glance.

"It is time to take Lady Merryn home," she instructed, making Merryn feel like a child. "I need hardly add," she said, fixing Merryn with a very hard stare, "that the slightest sign of *inappropriate* behavior will destroy all the good work we have achieved tonight." Her gimlet eye slid around from Merryn's flushed face to Garrick's rueful one. "Is that clear, nephew?"

"As crystal, aunt, I thank you," Garrick said. He raised Merryn's hand to his lips and placed an irreproachably proper kiss on the back. "Good night, Lady Merryn," he said. "I will call on you tomorrow."

As the coach trundled home Merryn sat between Joanna and Tess, the least proper chaperones in the world, she could not help thinking, and contemplated how on earth she was going to get Garrick alone now that she was watched over as closely as any virginal debutante. That was not her only difficulty. She could foresee that Garrick, who had guarded his secrets so well out of duty and honor, might not necessarily be willing to tell her the truth. She was going to have to make him talk.

Merryn's heart was suddenly thumping, shivers of equal nervousness and excitement skittering across her skin. She understood now the power she had over Garrick. She understood how much he wanted her. She wondered if she dared to use his desire against him.

She had every intention of being very inappropriate indeed.

CHAPTER THIRTEEN

IT WAS THE night before the wedding.

Garrick sat in the library at Farne House. One candle burned on the desk before him beside a half-empty brandy bottle. The faint light reflected in the speckled pier glass above the fireplace and barely penetrated the darkness of the cavernous interior of the room, rank upon rank of shabby mahogany bookcases with uncut books on their shelves, dusty and ancient, a testament not to his father's love of literature but to his need to impress. Tonight the Farne Dukedom hung like a lead weight about Garrick's neck. Tonight he was not sure he could go on without someone to stand by his side and share that huge responsibility. He realized that he had wanted that person to be Merryn. No one else could take her place. But now—he flicked the letter lying on the desk before him—now he had either to let her go or be confronted by a hollow sham of a marriage with no true intimacy. There could be no honesty between them. His hopes were dashed.

He looked down at letter although he already knew the contents off by heart.

"We cannot accede to your request. It was agreed

many years ago that no one should know... Think of the child... For her sake, keep your promise..."

Sometimes Garrick felt as though he had done nothing but think of the welfare of the child for twelve years. She was the only reason to keep silence. He had robbed Stephen Fenner's daughter of her father before she was even born so he had taken on himself the responsibility of fatherhood, of protecting her, keeping her safe. He, whose childhood had been so steeped in misery, had sworn that hers, despite its appalling start, would be better, happier than his own. And it had been. Stephen and Kitty's daughter lived with her aunt in a family where love was plentiful. She was happy and healthy. She had a settled home. And Garrick would never do anything to put that happiness at risk.

Kitty's family, the Scotts, had been adamant from the start that no one should know Kitty had had Stephen's child. Her reputation had already been sullied. It had been impossible to keep the affair a secret, too. Lord Scott had hated Stephen for ruining his daughter. The events of that day when Stephen had died had utterly destroyed his family. They had wanted nothing more to do with the Fenner family for the sake of both Kitty and her child. They had forbidden Garrick ever to speak and he, equally devastated by what had happened, had given his word.

The grief hit Garrick then in a blinding wave. He had a choice, of course. One always had a choice. And perhaps if he had not been the man he was, he would sacrifice this older promise for the sake of his future with Merryn. But he could not. When Stephen Fenner had died he had sworn to do everything in his power to protect the innocent and the weak and to make recompense for taking a life. He could not abandon that principle now simply because there was something he wanted more. He could not be that selfish.

So instead he must sacrifice his chance of happiness with Merryn. They would both pay for his sin in taking Stephen Fenner's life. He reached for the brandy but then pushed it away in a moment of self-loathing. It was not the answer no matter how much it called to him to give temporary release.

Merryn. He could not even think about her now without so sharp an ache in his heart that it stole his breath. He trusted her. He hated deceiving her. He wanted to tell her the truth. He was trapped.

He would still wed her. He needed her too much to let her go. That was selfish, he knew, but it was time for him to take something for himself and he wanted her more than he had ever wanted anything in his life. He wanted to have her shining spirit, her honesty and her courage and integrity to illuminate his darkness. Yet the danger was that this secret, the truth he could not reveal, would always come between them and in the end it would dull even Merryn's brave spirit. And that would break his heart.

Perhaps he should let her go. That would be the unselfish thing to do, not tie her to him for a life that was fettered by grief and regret. But if he released Merryn from the betrothal her reputation would be ruined forever. So he was trapped, destined to hurt her either way.

A draft stirred the candle flame, sending shadows scurrying along the walls. The grandfather clock struck a quarter to twelve. Garrick turned, shoving the letter into the desk drawer. Someone was standing beside the door, a shadow in the deeper shade of the darkness.

Merryn.

How long had she been there? The anxiety crawled down his spine that she might have seen the letter.

"You should not be here." He stood up as she came toward him. She was cloaked in black, a wraith. "How did you get in?"

"The way I always got in." She put back the hood of the cloak and the candlelight shone on the spun gold of her hair. Garrick felt an irresistible urge to touch and clenched his hands at his side. Something softened, opened and trembled deep inside him. He fought it. It was pointless now to acknowledge how much he needed her when he could not be honest with her.

"You are in a state of undress," she said, allowing her gaze to drift over the shirt open at his neck to the coat he had discarded on the chair. "That could be useful."

"You should go," Garrick said. His voice sounded rough. Was it because he was so desperate for her to stay?

Her clear blue gaze searched his face. It felt so candid whereas he felt old and soiled and worn.

"I wanted to talk to you," she said, "but no one will let me see you alone. I had to buy Tess a copy of the new edition of *La Belle Assemblée* to distract her before I could creep out."

"We are not meant to be alone together because it is not proper," Garrick said. He sounded pompous even to his own ears. Merryn laughed.

"Stable doors, horses bolting," she said. She loosed the cloak. It slid from her shoulders a little, revealing nothing but bare skin. Garrick stared.

"I came to ask you about the duel," she said. "But I expect you knew that. I expect you had realized that I cannot marry you without knowing the truth."

Garrick had realized it. He knew Merryn was too honest to tolerate any deceit. The irony stole his breath. Merryn would not marry him without knowing the truth. He had to marry her and could not tell her.

"I know," she said, when he did not speak. "I know you will refuse to talk. You always do and I wonder why." Her gaze was very bright. "At first I thought it was because you were guilty and too arrogant to admit to any wrongdoing. But now…" Her gaze drifted over him. "Now I wonder."

Garrick felt the anxiety tighten in his gut. "Merryn," he said, "please don't do this."

She shrugged. "I thought you would refuse. I have asked you time and again and now I am tired of asking. So instead I thought I would seduce the truth from you."

The cloak slipped a little farther. She was holding the ribbons across her breasts now. Her shoulders were completely bare, all pale creamy skin and delicate curves and hollows. Garrick's mouth dried. Was she wearing anything at all beneath the cloak?

"Have you been drinking?" he demanded, willing his errant body into stillness while every instinct he possessed demanded that he reach out and grab her.

Her gaze drifted to the brandy bottle. "No. But I see that you have."

"Not enough to be incapable."

"Oh, good." She gave him a smile he had never expected to see on her lips. It was full of wicked knowledge, not Merryn at all. And yet the Merryn who had lain with him on the velvet bed of the bordello had been just such a wanton. Their wild lovemaking had woken her to physical pleasure. And they had released something in each other that could not be satiated. That desire stalked him now.

Merryn's lowered the black cloak another inch, revealing the curves of the tops of her breasts. Garrick's body, supremely indifferent to the control his mind was trying to exercise, sprung to even greater attention.

"This is madness." His voice sounded so rusty that he had to clear his throat. "Seduce the truth out of me? I have told you the truth."

"Not all of it." She drifted closer. The cloak swung out, the hem brushing his leg. He caught a glimpse of bare thigh beneath and his mind spun. Dear God, she really was naked beneath that cloak. Her scent, that elusive fragrance of bluebells, enveloped him. He imagined he could feel the warmth of her skin. His head swam with memories of the wild wicked passion they had shared.

"Awaken a virgin to pleasure—" he ground out.

"And she wants more." Her gaze drifted to his, glittering blue with desire. "Quite." She smiled at him.

"So this is all about sex," Garrick said. "You could try waiting until after our wedding. You only need exercise self-control for one more day."

We have reversed roles, he thought. It was usually the rake who seduced and the lady who protested.

She came close to him, putting her hands against his chest. Her breath tickled his ear. He thought she could easily let slip the velvet ribbons, and then the cloak would come tumbling off. He prayed it would not—and simultaneously hoped that it would.

"It's not about sex," she whispered. "It's about honesty." She drew back a step. Her gaze held his. "There was complete honesty between us when we made love before," she said. "I do not believe that you could make love to me again and lie to me, too."

"I assure you," Garrick said, reaching for cynicism as his last defense, "most men would have no problem with that at all."

"Most men, perhaps." Her gaze was fearless. "But not you."

Dear God, it was a mad idea, but as he watched the

cloak slide farther down her shoulders, Garrick had the disconcerting suspicion that it might just work. She was right in that he had been building defenses against her from the very first, blocking her out because there was such a valiant integrity about her that he had known one day he must fall before it—and that he could never allow himself to do so.

"I have never lied to you," he said painfully, truthfully, knowing it was no real answer because he had omitted to tell her so many things.

"We'll see." She had turned away, seemingly indifferent. The velvet edging at the neck of the cloak was below her shoulder blades now, the rich black a stark contrast to her white skin. Garrick's body tightened unbearably. His throat was dry and his entire body shaking with the need to exercise such self-control over his raging lust.

"Merryn," he said, a last-ditch attempt, the last plea of a soldier overwhelmed by opposing forces, "no—"

Too late...

She turned back to him and allowed the cloak to slide down her body so slowly that he almost groaned aloud. She was not naked but the gown she had chosen—if it could be dignified with such a name—was designed specifically to inflame rather than quench his desire. For a start it was transparent white, clinging to her breasts, so high and firm, showing the nipples dark through the gauze. It skimmed the gentle curve of her stomach, caressed her rounded thighs and drew Garrick's gaze irresistibly to the shadowed valley between them.

No underwear. She wore no underwear at all.

His body hardened into painful arousal.

"Where did you get that gown?" he said, and he barely recognized his own voice.

"I borrowed it from Tess's wardrobe." There was defiance and a hint of anxiety in her voice. "I wanted something that would not be too difficult to remove."

God almighty. Garrick thought he might just explode with lust.

The velvet cloak slipped and slithered sinuously down to pool at her feet.

This was the moment, Garrick thought, that a gentleman would pick up the cloak, wrap her in it, propel her out through the door and call a carriage to take her home.

He looked into her eyes and saw nervousness there as well as bright, burning desire. In that moment he knew that she was afraid. She thought he would reject her. She thought that he would laugh at this mad plan she had gambled everything upon and send her away. Despite the harlot's gown and the attempt at wantonness she was too inexperienced to know if her strategy would work.

A huge tenderness filled Garrick to see the anxiety in her eyes. He gave a groan, caught her bare shoulders and pulled her to him, kissing her with a famished desperation that was as much a product of his despair as of his lust. She made a gentle humming sound of pure satisfaction and anything-but-pure desire and pressed close to him, her breasts soft and yielding against his chest. He kissed her with hunger, with craving, and felt his self-control shatter and his emotions reel. This was wrong, the very last thing that he should do when he had a stark choice to make between letting her go and tying her to him in a barren marriage. Yet instead of releasing her he held her locked against him; he drove his hands into her hair and covered her face with tiny, frantic kisses.

"I need you…" He spoke hoarsely, the words torn from him. She had no idea of the depth of his longing and his desperation. She was the only light in his darkness and he knew he did not deserve her. Yet miraculously she was not going to turn him away. She lifted a hand to his cheek; her lashes fluttered, she smiled at him. Garrick felt as though a fist had smashed straight into his heart, transmuting his raw hunger into something far more frightening and profound.

He held her for a moment longer, his face pressed against her hair, shudders convulsing him deep inside. Then she made a slight movement, bringing her lips back to his, and he abandoned thought and kissed her long and deep, her bare skin hot and smooth beneath his hands, her mouth eager and demanding under his. Garrick reached out, swept all the household accounts from the long mahogany table, the piles of paperwork it had taken him so long to compile, picked her up and sat her on the edge of the table. Her head fell back, the golden hair spilling about her like a drift of corn in the sun. Garrick's lips nipped and kissed the soft line of her shoulder and down to the slopes of her breast. The hunger drove him hard. He fought the urge simply to spread her and take her. That was not good enough for Merryn, that he should sate his lust on her. He wanted her pleasure more than his own, wanted to bind her to him with every bond of physical desire he could use. Yet he knew he wanted more than that; he wanted to smash the barriers between them and claim her soul as well as her body.

He pulled back. "Do you want me to stop?" he demanded roughly.

"No." Her word was a whisper. "Don't stop." He felt her make an effort. "But…"

"Yes?" He paused, his lips hovering over the ruffle that edged the neckline of the scandalous gown.

"The gown…" She sounded dazed, bewitched. "It was supposed to come off."

Garrick took the neck of the gown, gave it one sharp tug and freed her breasts.

"Oh!" Her eyes opened wide in shock and pleasure, and Garrick's body quickened in response.

"Oh," she said again, this time on a whisper, as he took her nipple in his mouth, licking, sucking until she squirmed. She arched to the touch of his lips, bent back like a bow, and Garrick allowed his hands and mouth to plunder her, caressing, demanding, roaming now over the soft skin of her breasts and brushing the quivering tautness of her belly. Her skin felt hot and so sensitive. She vibrated beneath his touch. Garrick watched her face,

dreamlike in its delight and discovery, and felt humbled
by the openness with which she gave herself up to him,
utterly exposed, utterly vulnerable. Desire tugged at
him again but he leashed it, repressing his own needs
ruthlessly as he continued to pleasure her until she was
visibly trembling and crying out helplessly to him.

The gown, obliging as ever, fell open as he pulled it
up. He parted her thighs, his fingers finding her core,
stroking, sliding deep. The caress wrenched a gasp from
her and Garrick covered her lips with his again, a reassurance as well as a demand. He felt her respond; she
reached for him then, to draw him close, but he held her
off for a moment, fumbling with his breeches with hands
that shook so much he thought he would never manage
it. He was utterly undone, aching, desperate, yet the need
to treat her gently even in the center of this maelstrom
of desire had him exercising a fierce restraint.

He felt Merryn stiffen slightly at the first touch of his
body against hers, as though she had suddenly realized
how vulnerable she was in this position. He opened her
gently, pushed upward, and felt her body start to yield
to him.

"Open your eyes," he whispered.

He saw the precise moment that Merryn caught their
reflection in the mirror, the dark, erotic image of herself
seated on the edge of the table, thighs pale, widespread,
skirts about her hips, breasts bare, her golden hair falling
about them both like a silken curtain. She gave a keening
cry and he slid deep inside her and felt her body sheathe

him so tightly he almost came. He held still for a moment and felt her ripple and clench about him and the bliss was so intense he thought he might fall. He grasped after control against the barrage of sensation that assaulted him, withdrawing from her a little. He stroked her again and felt her whole body tighten in response. She grabbed his hips and pulled him into her, and Garrick could resist no longer. He claimed her, sinking deep, pulling out, driving them both fiercely onward. Possessiveness flared in him, the need to claim her surrender and to know she was irrefutably his. Yet alongside his triumph was a vulnerability that terrified him. She could bring him to his knees. She had already done so. He was lost.

It was his last thought. Merryn's body clenched and released him again, sending shards of exquisite pleasure tumbling through him. It tore a harsh groan from his throat as he finally relinquished control and emptied himself into her. The pleasure flowered through him, a flood tide of passion that swept him to madness, a sweet delight he had never imagined. He drew her close and held her to his heart for a timeless interval.

Finally he released her. He was still breathing so hard he could not speak. Merryn lay back on the table, the books and papers scattered about her like petals in a storm, the candlelight shifting and shimmering over her body in bars of light and shadow. She made no effort to move or to cover herself and seeing her lying there so abandoned, so beautifully decadent, made Garrick want her all over again with a hard, fierce need that drove him to despair.

So it had not been enough. He had almost lost his mind. He had been driven to the edge by the force of his release. He had taken Merryn, mastered her body again, claimed her undeniably as his, and yet… And yet something was missing. It prowled along the edge of his consciousness, taunted him from beyond his understanding.

He wanted more. This was not enough.

Merryn shifted. As he watched her, his cock twitched and the lust tightened in his gut. This time he ignored them. He scooped her up in his arms and carried her across to the nearest chair, sitting down with her on his lap, pushing the tangled hair away from her face.

"Was that what you wanted?" he demanded.

She turned her head and a slow smile played across her lips. "Not precisely, your grace. Though…" she gave a languorous little wriggle that made Garrick grit his teeth against the new onslaught of temptation "…it was very, very nice." She sat up a little. Her hair fell like a rich golden curtain about her face, hiding her expression.

"I had planned to stop at a crucial moment and ask you some questions," she said.

Garrick gave a snort of laughter. "You planned to stop?"

She cast him a sideways look. "I see that I miscalculated."

"You did," Garrick said. "That was never going to work."

"I realize that now. In my inexperience I misjudged the situation." She stood up, moving away from him in a tangle of swirling hair and pale limbs. She lifted the cloak and swung it about her shoulders. It enveloped her. Her fingers were steady as she secured each little fastening. Only when the entire garment was sealed up to her neck did she look up and meet Garrick's eyes. It felt odd to see her distance herself from him so deliberately. He wanted to take her upstairs to his bed, to hold her in the darkness of the night as both protection and protector, to make love to her again, to keep her with him all night and for as many of the following days and nights as he could. Merryn, on the other hand, looked as though she wanted to leave. Something cold and hard settled in Garrick's stomach. Fear crept down his spine.

"I was going to ask you," Merryn said slowly, "if it was Kitty who killed Stephen. I think she did. I think there must have been a terrible accident and that you took the blame."

The shock slammed into Garrick with physical force. Lost in the welter of his feelings for her he had almost forgotten her quest to seduce the truth from him. But Merryn, of course, would never forget. Merryn was completely single-minded. And she was so close to the truth now—so close and yet so utterly wrong.

The silence stretched so taut that the ticking of the grandfather clock seemed almost to split his eardrums.

"You are mistaken," he said hoarsely, when he could speak. "Kitty did not kill Stephen."

"I don't believe you," Merryn said. She was holding the material of the cloak tight about her neck now, like a shield. What he saw in her eyes now was different from all the other times she had confronted him. There was no anger anymore, no frustration. There was nothing but shining hope, so pure and confident, and—he shuddered to see it—love. Garrick could not bear for her to love him, not with what he had done. Not when he was so undeserving. Not when he was about to smash her hope and her faith once and for all. He could taste bitterness in his mouth.

"I have been looking at things the wrong way around," Merryn said. "You are good and noble, Garrick. You have always done your duty—"

Garrick knew he had to stop this now, before Merryn stumbled onto the truth. He felt as though his heart was snapping in two. "I am neither of those things," he said gruffly. "You are deluded, Merryn. I am neither good nor noble and I thought I had just proved that to you."

She shrugged an indifferent shoulder. "I have no complaints that you could not resist me," she said. She took a step closer to him and placed a hand on his arm. "I love you," she said softly. "It is that simple. And I could not love you if you were the cold-blooded murderer you claim to be."

I love you...

Garrick flinched. "No," he said. He shook. This was

too much; he could not accept it. Once he would have given so much for the love of a woman like Merryn Fenner, before Kitty's betrayal, before Stephen's murder. Now it was too late. He had killed a man and destroyed too many lives to deserve such generosity of spirit, especially from Merryn. The images danced before him, vicious memories. Kitty screaming, Stephen dying, lives changed in a second, hideous consequences stretching over the years. Those could never be wiped out by Merryn Fenner's love. It was impossible. He looked into her face, saw her determination and the clear, pure love in her eyes and felt his heart snap.

"No," he said again. "Merryn…" He cleared his throat. "You think that you are in love with me," he said, "so you want me to be all that is good and heroic. The truth is that I am not. I never was and I can never be."

She shook her head. "I cannot believe that—"

"Believe it," Garrick said harshly. "Because I killed your brother and in the end that is the only thing that matters and it will always come between us."

She shook her head. "No—"

Garrick thought savagely of the letter. There was only one way to end this, he thought. He had to tell her what he had done, what Stephen had done, but keep Kitty's secrets.

"Merryn," he said. He knew he was going to break her heart and shatter her illusions, but there was no other way. "Please listen to me," he said. He tried to make his voice as gentle as he could even as he knew there was no gentle way of telling her. "I did kill Stephen," he said. "There was no duel. You were right about that all along. I found Kitty and Stephen together. There was an argument. Stephen tried to kill Kitty and I shot him. That is why I am not the honorable man you want me to be."

He saw the shock explode in her eyes. She backed a step away from him. There was an anguished, frozen moment. Merryn's face, so rosy with animation a moment before when she had laid her heart beneath his feet, was now so pale he was afraid that she would faint. Her eyes were dull, opaque. "No," she said again. She pressed her hands together and Garrick saw how much she was shaking. He wanted to touch her, to take her in his arms, to offer comfort for the grievous hurt he had inflicted but the torment in her eyes warned him to stay away.

"I'm sorry," he said. "Merryn, I am so sorry—" But he could tell she could not even hear his words.

Her voice was a whisper. "Stephen loved Kitty. I *know* he did! He would never hurt her." Her voice rose. "He would never hurt the woman he loved." Her eyes were wild. "You're lying to me. You must be!"

Garrick watched the hurt curl within her like a flower scorched in the sun, bending, withering. It was worse than ever he had imagined. He had thought Merryn would be distraught to be so disillusioned about her brother. Not for one moment had he believed that she would meet his words with so flat a denial. It was as though she simply could not accept what she had heard.

Or did not want to accept it. Perhaps, despite what she had said about recognizing Stephen's weaknesses, she had still seen her brother as a hero. Garrick's heart ached for her. He watched her fingers tighten on her cloak until the knuckles showed white. She backed away from him toward the door.

"It was not meant to be like that," she said and she sounded lost. "They were supposed to run away together—" She stopped. "Stephen would never do that," she repeated. Her voice sounded raw. She was so open a person that now she had no defenses to hide behind, no way to conceal her pain.

Garrick watched her face crumple. "It cannot be true," she said. It was more a plea than a protest, begging Garrick to deny what he had told her. He said nothing, clenching his fists at his side.

Merryn paused as though she were hoping for a reprieve and the moment stretched out unbearably, a torture to Garrick beyond whatever he had imagined.

"I thought you had some honor at the very least," she said. "You gave Fenners back. You saved my life. Now you defame the memory of a dead man." The candles fluttered in the draft from the door. She was gone.

Garrick took the letter from the desk drawer, threw it into the fire and watched it burn. He did not need it to remind him of his obligations. They felt like locks on his soul.

CHAPTER FOURTEEN

IT WAS THE MORNING OF the wedding, very early morning, dark and cold.

Merryn was sitting in her bedroom. Beside her on the bed the Fenner estate records lay scattered like snow. She had sought them out for comfort, hoping to find among the old documents something to anchor her to the past as she remembered it, to the happy days of her childhood, to the memories of that last summer. But it was too late. Something had changed. Everything had changed.

When she had fallen in love with Garrick she had wanted to exonerate him. She had wanted him to be a hero. But he was not. He really had killed Stephen and he had claimed that it had been because Stephen had tried to murder Kitty in an argument. Such a terrible slander, that Stephen had tried to kill the woman he had loved. It was surely impossible.

She did not believe it. She did not want to believe it. She could not believe it because it would mean that everything she had done to help Kitty and Stephen had been a terrible mistake, based on no more than a lie. And that she could not bear. She tried to close her mind to it. Except that she could see Joanna's face and hear Joanna's words.

I am not sure that Stephen did love Kitty. Certainly he never loved anyone as much as he loved himself...

A sob caught in her throat. Garrick had killed Stephen. She did not doubt it for one second now. She had wanted him to be innocent, to have taken the blame for Kitty, because that way he could have been guiltless and she could have absolved him. But once again she had been naive. And even if he had killed Stephen to protect Kitty—she allowed herself to think about it for one second and the crack in her heart gaped wide with pain and fear—there had been no duel, Garrick had lied for years and covered up the truth, he had run away rather than having the courage to face justice, so how could she ever respect him or trust him or love him again? Garrick had been right—he was not the man she wanted him to be.

Merryn's agitated fingers scattered the papers on the bed, catching the edge of one of the estate books and sending it tumbling to the floor. She had read through all the papers and the books days ago, when she had been looking for evidence against Garrick. She had found nothing of note other than the rather odd reference to a meeting between her father, the Duke of Farne and Lord Scott in the days after Stephen's death. Now she could see that something was poking out of a corner of the book, a document that had been half hidden beneath the cover, one she had not seen before.

It was her father's will.

She had never read it and she wondered if Mr. Churchward had included it in the papers by accident. Lord Fenner had declared on his deathbed that none of his daughters should have sight of it and it had remained with Mr. Churchward ever since. Merryn had assumed that her father had been so ashamed of the poverty of the estate that he had not wanted to distress them with it. She read the dry legal language. There had been so little for Lord Fenner to leave because by now the estate had been bankrupt. It was why all Stephen's possessions had been disposed of, why Merryn had not a single memento to remember him by.

"To my daughters…" A few sticks of furniture, the ugly little table that Joanna, for all her elegance and style, still kept in the hallway.

"To the servants…" A few shillings scraped together in return for a lifetime's service.

"To Lord Scott of Shipham Hall in the County of Somerset, the miniature of my son Stephen…"

Merryn gave a little gasp of pure shock and pressed a hand to her mouth. Why would her father have left his daughters not one item to remember their brother by and yet give the precious miniature of Stephen to a man they barely knew? It was extraordinary. It made no sense at all.

She stared at the words until they danced before her eyes. Why had her father given away so cherished a keepsake as Stephen's miniature? Lord Scott must surely have hated Stephen for ruining his daughter. What possible reason could there be to give him so precious a token? Merryn rubbed her temples where a headache pounded. She would never be able to ask her father that question now. He was dead and gone, as was the Duke of Farne. Only Lord Scott remained of those three men who had met after Stephen's death for whatever mysterious purpose. Lord Scott…

He was the only man who could help her now.

Merryn moved quickly and quietly after that, gathering together a few items for her journey, filling one small portmanteau since, unlike her sisters, she did not need a baggage train when she traveled. The house was quiet. Tess and Joanna, no doubt worn-out with discussions about her trousseau, were asleep. Merryn tiptoed down the stairs, passed the dozing night porter, closed the main door very softly after her and went out.

The streets were cold at this time of the morning. A very pale gray dawn was barely starting to creep in from the east, turning the clouds soft as a pearl. Merryn reached the White Lion in Holborn with barely five minutes to spare before the Bath Flyer departed. The coach was not full. It was too late in the year and the roads too bad. No one wanted to travel on the roof.

The guard was checking his watch. With profuse apologies Merryn wedged herself into a gap between a buxom lady and a stick thin girl and then they were away.

GARRICK HAD NOT SLEPT and when Pointer knocked softly on the door he was lying fully clothed on his bed staring up at the ceiling. He knew before the butler spoke exactly what he was going to say. Pointer's long, thin face looked even more lugubrious than ever, his nose twitching with sympathy.

"Lord and Lady Grant are here to see you, your grace." His nose twitched again, this time in disapproval, as he took in the frowsty room and Garrick's unkempt appearance.

"Would you like to shave before you meet them, your grace?" Pointer's voice implied that only the ill-bred would decline such an offer to make them look halfway presentable for company.

"No, thank you, Pointer," Garrick said. He grabbed his jacket and shrugged himself into it. It was barely light. Lady Grant was known for keeping late hours, which was one of the reasons that the wedding had been set for the afternoon. Only the direst of emergencies could have impelled her from her bed at dawn.

Garrick knew exactly what that emergency must be.

He ran a hand over his hair to smooth it down and went out onto the landing. Farne House looked even more like a barracks at this time of day with the gloomy light barely wreathing the high ceilings and failing to reach the dark corners. Over the past week Pointer had employed a veritable army of servants to clean and scrub and polish in anticipation of the arrival of the new Duchess of Farne. The result had been to make a neglected

Gothic horror of a house look like a shining Gothic horror of a house. Garrick felt a pang for the servants and for all their hard work. There would be no new Duchess to approve their industry now.

Alex and Joanna Grant were waiting for him in the library. Pointer had lit two branches of candles—Garrick doubted that his father had ever been so extravagant as to require more than one—but the effect was to give the huge barnlike room a quality of even greater gloom, the bookcases looming over the space in oppressive shadow, the speckled mirror only serving to make the room look twice as large and twice as lonely.

Joanna Grant, neat as a pin in a striped gown and matching spencer, was perched on the edge of vast armchair but she jumped up as soon as he entered the room. Her face was white and strained.

"Your grace—" she said, and her voice broke.

"It's all right," Garrick said. "I know. Merryn does not wish to wed me."

His record was deteriorating, he thought. At least his first wife had waited a month before leaving him. This one had not even made it to the altar.

"I'm sorry, Farne," Alex Grant said. He sounded, Garrick thought in vague surprise, as though he genuinely meant it. "It's worse than that, though," Alex added, as his wife shot him an anxious look. "Merryn has run away. She left no note. We do not know where she is."

Garrick thought of Merryn alone in the dark on the streets of London and felt the fear grab his throat. This was his fault, he knew. He had callously rejected her love. He had told her the truth about her brother's perfidy and she had been unable to accept it. It was little wonder that she had run rather than wed him.

"Oh, if only we had not forced her to marry!" Joanna said. One hand was pressed against her lips, the other held in Alex's strong clasp.

"We did not," Alex said. He gave his wife's hand a squeeze. "Joanna, you told Merryn you would love and support her whatever she chose to do. You could not have done more." He turned back to Garrick. "I do not think," he said slowly, "that Merryn has run away to escape the wedding, Farne."

Garrick looked up sharply.

"I am not saying that she wanted to marry you," Alex continued, crushing the flare of hope that Garrick had felt for one brief moment, "merely that there is something else behind this."

Joanna was staring at her husband, her eyes a bright vivid blue with both distress and surprise. "You did not say this to me earlier," she accused.

"Yes, I did," Alex said dryly. "You were not in a state to listen to me."

Garrick could imagine how it might have been in Tavistock Square with both Joanna and Tess Darent in hysterics over their sister's disappearance. He gave Alex a brief sympathetic grimace. Alex actually smiled.

"Well!" Joanna said. "If Merryn is not running away to escape an intolerable match—" she looked at Garrick

"—I beg your pardon, your grace, but this is no time to beat about the bush—then what *is* she doing?"

"I think I might know," Garrick said slowly.

They both looked at him.

"Before we were trapped together in the beer flood," Garrick said, "Lady Merryn warned me that she was working to ruin me."

Joanna's face puckered. "She wants to *ruin* you? Oh, this is much, much worse than I had thought!"

"Joanna, darling," Alex said gently, "wait until we understand everything before you have the vapors." He looked at Garrick, his dark eyes narrowing. "Was this because of her brother's death, Farne?"

"Yes," Garrick said. He looked at Joanna. She did not have any of Merryn's blind obstinacy or her quest for truth and justice, he thought, but she did, unexpectedly, have some of her sister's strength of character. She was not having the vapors after all.

"I am sorry, Lady Grant," he said gently. "The facts of the case are well-known. I killed your brother and I have never tried to pretend otherwise."

"No," Joanna said. Her blue eyes, so like Merryn's, swept his face with surprising perception. "And yet you have never spoken of what happened." She paused. "Did Merryn ask you about it?"

"Yes," Garrick said. "She asked me several times."

Joanna pressed her hands to her cheeks. "You refused," she whispered.

"I could not tell her the whole truth," Garrick said. "I

should have realized that she would never settle for half measures." He rubbed a hand over his face. He could see that so clearly now, now that it was far, far too late.

"Merryn will not wed you without knowing everything," Joanna said. She gave a little exasperated sigh. "Oh, that is *so* like her! She has probably gone on some wild-goose chase to try to unravel the past. She is too stubborn and too principled. She can never see that sometimes it is better to let matters lie."

"But Merryn cannot live like that," Garrick said. "I have to find her. The only problem is that I have no notion where she might have gone."

"Perhaps Bradshaw might know," Alex suggested, leaning forward. "She might have shared her plans with him when they worked together. He seems to be a man quick to capitalize on anything that might work to his advantage."

Garrick looked at him. "I had not thought of that," he admitted. "And there is only one way to find out."

Alex pulled a face. "If he has a vested interest, he may not tell us."

"We could try to persuade him," Garrick said.

Alex laughed. "I like your thinking, Farne, but Bradshaw is a tough nut to crack."

"We could send Tess," Joanna said. "He is terrified of her."

Alex looked at Garrick, raised his brows. "Worth a try," he murmured.

Garrick was thinking fast. "We'll all go," he said.

"Lady Darent can try first. If Mr. Bradshaw proves obstinate…" He shrugged and saw Alex smile.

"Will you come back with us to Tavistock Street to fetch Tess?" Joanna asked. She sighed. "It may take a little while for her to be ready, I'm afraid." She smiled at Garrick, a limpid smile that for some reason made him feel very, very wary. "And while we wait for her," Joanna said, "you can explain to me what it is you refused to tell Merryn about Stephen's death." She paused. "I never hero-worshipped my brother," she said, very precisely. "I know he was an unmitigated scoundrel, if that makes it any the easier for you."

Garrick hesitated. "Lady Grant," he said, "I cannot. I am under oath not to tell—"

He fell silent at the steely look in Joanna's eyes. "Then you will explain to me as much as you can," she said.

Alex laughed. "Best admit defeat, Farne," he said. He gave Garrick a consoling slap on the shoulder. "You thought it was just Merryn, but it is not," he said. "All the Fenner women are as stubborn as mules. Since you are to be a member of the family—" he smiled "—it is best you understand that from the start."

HARRIET KNIGHT WAS IN A bad mood and had been for a whole week, since the news of Garrick Farne's precipitous engagement and imminent marriage to Lady Merryn Fenner had reached her ears. It had fired her temper and Tom had reaped the benefits of that in several ways but now, as he sat in his office chair in a state of great disarray with a partially naked Harriet squirming on his lap, he reflected that this must be the last time. He had extracted every last ounce of useful information from Harriet and some delightful sexual favors as well, but now he had urgent business to deal with. His bags were packed, sitting in the corner of the office, and he was traveling to Somerset later that day. His departure, he thought, would give him the perfect excuse to break matters off with Harriet.

"Thomas..." Harriet had been kissing his neck, her hands roving over his bare chest but now she slapped his face to regain his attention, and none too playfully, either. What a shrew. The sooner he was rid of her the better.

"You are not paying attention to me," Harriet scolded. "You are thinking about your work."

Tom silently admitted that he had been. He, too, had been in a permanently bad mood since Merryn had had the stupidity to be trapped in the beer flood with Garrick Farne and had ended up betrothed to him. His manipulation of her had been working so well. She had found out much useful information. Then everything had gone wrong. His attempt to blackmail her family had misfired spectacularly and he had ended up having to do his own dirty work after all.

Tom frowned, trying to think past the sensual barrage that was Harriet's determined seduction. He knew that he had only one option left now. He had to go to

Somerset and finish this job himself. Harriet started to lick and nibble at his chest, her tongue scampering over his skin and distracting his attention again. It was arousing, as was the fact that he was very close now to bringing down the Farne Dukedom. He had wanted that for a long time.

Harriet slapped him again, a little harder this time, punishing him for his lack of attention. Little witch. He caught her wrist and held it tightly. She kicked him, her bare foot catching his shin so that he winced. There would be a bruise there tomorrow. He tried to kiss her but she wrenched her head away and bit him on the lip. Hard. Her eyes were bright with malice and excitement. Tom tasted blood. He gave a roar, tumbled her off his knee and onto the rug. She dragged him down with her, and they rolled over, Harriet's hair flying as she struggled like a wild thing in his arms, scratching and pummeling him. He held her arms above her head to prevent her from hurting him and she laughed up at him, eyes blazing with lust now and he pulled down his pantaloons and plunged into her and she screamed with excitement.

The door opened. Tom, buried deep inside Harriet, froze. His mind was utterly incapable of coherent thought. His body, so much more unsophisticated—so much more predictable—wanted to shaft Harriet until he was thoroughly satisfied. He wished he had locked the door. He wished his unwelcome visitor would take the hint and go away.

Then he noticed the beautiful silver slippers in his line of sight and the embroidered hem of the matching silver silk gown.

"Dear me," Tess Darent said. Her voice was mild and sweet. "I see you are *very* busy, Mr. Bradshaw. Perhaps I should call back later?"

Tom felt himself start to wither. He did not dare look up. He had a very bad feeling now, replacing the transcendent bliss of a few moments before. He could sense his plans diminishing with the same rapidity as his erection.

Harriet was screaming now. Tom wanted to cover his ears because it was so piercing.

Then matters got considerably worse. The door opened again and Tom saw the very shiny top boots beside Tess Darent's slippers. Two pairs. A masculine voice said, "For pity's sake, Bradshaw…"

Someone hauled him to his feet. Tess was helping Harriet to stand and tidy her clothing. Tom turned. On one side of him was a man he did not recognize. He did not like the look on his face. On the other side was Garrick Farne. Tom liked Farne's expression even less. And when Farne spoke, the smooth courtesy of his tone did not in any way cloak the iron beneath.

"Good morning, Bradshaw," Farne said. "Do I take it that you will be making a formal offer of marriage to my late father's ward?"

"Certainly not," Tom said.

Harriet threw the sherry decanter at him. Then she started to cry. "I don't want to marry him," she sniffed. "I want a rich old Duke."

"I'll find one for you, Lady Harriet," Tess said, patting her hand comfortingly. "I'm very good at that sort of thing."

Farne glanced toward the traveling bags, sitting guiltily in the corner of the office. "Were you planning on leaving town, Bradshaw?" he inquired silkily.

Tom, normally a fluent liar, found that his imagination appeared to have failed him under Tess Darent's clear blue gaze.

"We are looking for my sister," she said very sweetly. "Once before you had information on her whereabouts, Mr. Bradshaw, so I wondered if you might help us now?"

Tom started to sweat. "I have no notion—" he began feebly.

"I expect Lady Merryn has gone to Somerset to find out about your by-blow, Garrick," Harriet said maliciously to Farne. "I told Mr. Bradshaw all about the baby—"

It seemed to Tom that Farne moved so quickly then that one moment he was standing and the next Farne had him pinned in his seat with one hand at his throat. Tom tried to squirm and almost choked.

"My illegitimate child," Farne said. His eyes were very intent. "Tell me what you know about that…"

Sherry dripping down his face, a bitter taste in his mouth, Tom knew that it was going to be a very bad morning indeed.

CHAPTER FIFTEEN

By the time the carriage had reached Maidenhead they were all getting on famously. Merryn had discovered that the elderly gentleman seated across from her was a piano tuner on his way to tune a Broadwood grand for Lord Tate in Newbury. The fat lady on one side of Merryn was a Mrs. Morton, the widow of a very prosperous greengrocer, and the thin girl on the other side was her elder daughter Margaret, and they were traveling to spend the Christmas season with relatives near Barnstaple in the hope that Margaret would be able to catch a suitor.

"I did so wish Margaret to marry into the ton," was Mrs. Morton's constant refrain. "Goodness knows, her dowry is large enough but she did not *take*. And now—" she cast her daughter an exasperated look "—I very much fear that she will have to settle for a man who has to buy his own furniture rather than one who inherits it."

"Well, that can be a blessing in so many ways," Merryn said soothingly. "You have no notion, Mrs. Morton, as to the ugliest pieces of furniture we were obliged to have in our house when I was young simply because they had been in the family for so many years."

As the day progressed, gray and drab with the hint of snow in the air, Merryn sat and watched the countryside unroll. As a child living in North Dorset her life and those of her sisters had been bounded by the nursery, the schoolroom and the village of Fenridge and its immediate neighbourhood. There had been few visits up to town. Stephen was the only one who had traveled and that distinction had made him even more fascinating in Merryn's eyes. She had never traveled farther than Bath. The first time she had met Kitty was when Garrick had brought her to Starcross Manor as his wife. Merryn wondered now what had made Garrick make the infelicitous choice of taking his wife on honeymoon to a house a bare five miles from that of her lover. Kitty, she thought, with a sudden rush of feeling. Kitty would have asked Garrick if they could go there. Kitty had done it to be near Stephen.

For the first time in years Merryn felt hatred for Kitty Farne. Sweet, pretty Kitty Farne, who had had both Stephen and Garrick dancing to her tune. She had been so jealous of Kitty, not because Kitty had had Stephen's love but because she had had Garrick's attention, too. It had not been fair. Her thirteen-year-old self had been so jealous and resentful.

The coach passed Reading making good time and with plenty of stops to change the horses. At Newbury the piano tuner descended. Just outside Hungerford there was a close encounter with a private chaise driven by a reckless young man who shaved past them with only inches to spare.

"These young Corinthians," Mrs. Morton said, generously handing around some boiled sugarplum sweets. "Do you have any brothers, Lady Merryn?"

"I had one," Merryn said. "He died. He was a noted whip."

The motion of the carriage started to soothe her into sleep. It was warm and stuffy inside, even warmer as Mrs. Morton had thoughtfully brought a spare blanket and insisted on lending it to her. Gradually the hours of the journey seemed to blur into one another as darkness fell. There was their arrival at Bath in a snow flurry, a room at the White Hart Inn where Merryn lay wakeful listening to Mrs. Morton's snores through the wall, another carriage in the bright cold morning, this one considerably inferior in comfort to the mail coach. Finally she and Mrs. and Miss Morton rolled into the tiny seaside village of Kilve in Somerset, in the early afternoon and Merryn bespoke dinner and a bedchamber and arranged for a pony and trap to take her the final few miles to the village of Shipham.

It was a cold afternoon with a bitter winter wind off the sea that was edged with snow. Merryn huddled in the trap and shivered deep inside her winter pelisse. Now that she was here, she had no notion what she was going to say to Lord Scott. She thought she should have sent a note first. She should not have succumbed to this impatient desire to learn the truth. Except that it felt as though the whole of her future hung on understanding the past and now she was so close she could not wait.

The carter set her down at the entrance to Shipham Hall. Merryn put her hand on the metal gate that fenced the carriage sweep. The house stood back a little from the road, an Elizabethan manor, half-timbered, a modest family home. Merryn could hear children's voices somewhere in the garden, the shrill calls and cries as they played, wrapped up in hats and scarves and muffs, running through the little box tree maze that was surrounded by lawns to the west of the house. A nursemaid in a crisp white apron, cap and coat who looked little older than a girl herself was running after them, laughing, throwing herself down on the snowy lawn and holding her side where she evidently had a stitch. Merryn could see an older child—seven or eight, with brown hair in a long plait, holding the hand of a toddler. There was another small child, a boy of about five, and another older girl who was fair. She had lost her bonnet and the cold winter sun shone on her hair and it was the exact silver gilt color of Merryn's.

The nurse held her arms out to the baby girl, who toppled forward into them, laughing. The older girls were walking together now, up the icy steps that led to the terrace. Their heads were bent as they talked, solemn and preoccupied. Merryn could hear a woman's voice from within the house, calling to them.

"Susan! Anne! Come inside and wash your hands before tea!"

Merryn's heart stuttered a little. She peered closer at the girl with the silver gilt hair.

To Lord Scott of Shipham Hall... A miniature of my son Stephen...

"Susan! Anne!" The woman's voice was louder. She came out onto the terrace, a tall woman in an old flowered gown, her hair beneath the lace cap a rich brown with just the faintest hint of gray. She was smiling. She took each child by the hand. And as they turned back toward the door, Merryn saw her face and the world stood still.

For a moment it felt as though she was looking at Kitty Farne, Kitty grown older and grayer and more lined but still with that pretty rounded face and smiling demeanor. Merryn knew that she must have made some involuntary movement because the little group on the terrace saw her and stopped. The child called Susan was looking straight at Merryn now. Her eyes were a clear, vivid blue, the blue of Merryn's eyes, the blue of Joanna's. She smiled hesitantly and Merryn saw that she had dimples in her cheeks just like Tess's. Merryn's fingers were tight about the iron fence now. The hard metal bit into her hands through her gloves. She could hear a strange roaring sound in her ears, as though she was about to faint. Down on the lawn the nursemaid was still playing with the babies. Merryn could hear their calls and their laughter but they seemed to come from a very long way away indeed.

Panic possessed her. She wanted to run, away from the sunlit garden and the child with the same blue eyes and golden hair that she possessed. Suddenly the images in her memory started to unreel like a spool of cotton. It was odd, she thought, how the tiniest details that one forgot in time could come back at any moment. For now she was remembering how very rounded Kitty had looked on the last afternoon she had seen her. Kitty, the thirteen-year-old Merryn had thought, had looked fat. She had even wondered if Kitty, unhappy in love, had been eating too many sweetmeats.

Kitty, Merryn thought now, had looked pregnant.

She willed her legs to move but they felt heavy, leaden. She found that she was trembling deep inside her pelisse, racked with shivers. She felt cold all over, cold all the way through. This, then, was Stephen's legacy, a child whose existence none of them had guessed, a child whom Garrick must surely have known about but whom he had gone to great lengths to keep from her. She felt a vast desolation seep through her, as bleak as the winter night. She thought of how much she loved Shuna, Joanna's daughter, and how much love she would have lavished on this other niece she had never known and she thought that her heart would break in two.

And then she heard the crunch of carriage wheels on the road behind her and felt a frisson of premonition touch her neck. She turned very slowly. She knew it would be Garrick. She knew that he had come, as he must, to protect Kitty's family and Kitty's child, just as he had done for the past twelve years.

Garrick jumped down from the curricle and took several steps toward her. The snow was starting to fall all

about them now in huge white flakes. Garrick looked
tired, his eyes strained, the stubble once again shadow-
ing his cheek. Merryn realized that he must have driven
through the night.

"Merryn," he started to say. He put a hand out to her
but Merryn stumbled back. She was aware of nothing
but the most excruciating pain.

"You knew," she said. "You knew how desperately
I missed Stephen. I had nothing of him left, not one
thing." Her voice broke. "And all the time you knew that
Stephen had a child. You were going to marry me and
you were never going to tell me." The snow was swirling
about her now and she brushed it angrily from her face,
brushed away, too, the hot tears of fury and despair. Out
of the corner of her eye she could see the woman who
looked like Kitty coming down the steps now toward
them. She saw Garrick's gaze flick toward her and then
back to Merryn's face.

"If we could talk," he began but he fell silent as Merryn
shook her head in a tiny gesture of repudiation.

"I don't want to talk to you," she said. "I never want
to see you again."

The woman had reached the gate now. "Garrick!" she
called. She was smiling. "We did not know you were
coming," she said. "You should have sent word." She
looked at Merryn. Her smile started to fade.

Merryn turned and walked away. She felt numb and
cold. All she could think of was Stephen, and the child
that was his, and of Garrick's silence. It made perfect

sense, she thought. Garrick had told her that there had been an argument. He had discovered that Kitty was pregnant with Stephen's child. Perhaps Kitty and Stephen had told him they were to elope together and so Garrick had shot Stephen through jealousy and revenge. And then he and Kitty's family had formed a conspiracy of silence to keep Kitty's child a secret from her father's relatives forever.

Misery twisted in Merryn again, as violent as a knife. She had not known she could feel like this. It hurt so much, the anger and the raw pain. And yet there was something else there, too, a tiny voice that in the face of all the evidence whispered that she was wrong, that the man who had protected her and stood between her and death could not behave in such a way. It whispered to her to think again, to keep faith, because she had loved Garrick for a reason and although her faith was battered that love had not completely died.

There had been three shots, she remembered. There had been two bullets in Stephen's body, but what had happened to the third? Garrick had told her that Stephen had tried to kill Kitty and she had wanted to disbelieve him because she had been so sure that Stephen and Kitty had loved one another. But if she had been wrong then Garrick had defended Kitty. He had tried to save her from Stephen. And if Kitty had been pregnant then perhaps Garrick had taken her abroad to shield her from the scandal as later he had tried to shelter and protect her child…

The hot tears scalded Merryn's throat. The instinct that had prompted her to trust Garrick with her life, with her heart, started to unfold within her again, tentatively and a little fearfully. She knew she would have to go back, be brave, confront Garrick and hear the truth at last. And if that truth meant that all she had believed about Stephen and Kitty had been based on a lie then she would have to finally confront that, too.

THE TRACK ALONG THE CLIFFS was wild and lonely on a winter afternoon. Eventually the path descended through patches of sea clover and thrift and the short springy grass and Merryn came down onto the beach below Shipham and stood for a moment inhaling the salt-laden air. It was so cold it felt as though it cut her lungs. Her tears had gone now. She felt numb and tired. She sat down on a rock at the edge of the sands. In a moment she thought she would turn and go back. She would find Garrick. She would listen to what he had to say.

There was a crunch on the shingle beside her. Merryn jumped and spun around. For a moment she thought she was imagining things. Tom Bradshaw was standing behind her, Tom in his London clothes looking debonair and tough and not particularly friendly.

"Hello, Merryn," Tom said. He smiled, his dazzling, charming smile, but his eyes were opaque.

"What on earth are you doing here, Tom?" Merryn said.

"I followed you from the house," Tom said. "I wanted

to talk to you." He half turned away from her, driving his hands into his pockets. "Quite a shock, isn't it," he said conversationally, "to discover that not only did Garrick Farne kill your brother, but he stole his child, too."

"Stop it," Merryn said sharply. "Don't say that."

"I suppose he'll present it to you as being frightfully honorable," Tom said, grinning. "Impossible choices, a promise of silence given on his wife's deathbed, a child he knew could never bear his name because she was born too soon to have been his…" He shrugged. "You should appreciate all that, Merryn. I seem to recall that you were always frightfully keen on honor and justice and all those high-flown ideas."

"What do you mean?" Merryn said, frowning. "How do you know all this, Tom?"

"Oh, I had it all from a friend," Tom said. Merryn could tell that he was enjoying himself hugely. "She thought that the child was Farne's own by-blow," he added, "but I soon found out the truth, that it was his wife's little bastard, not his own and after that…" He shrugged. "Well, the rest of the story was easy enough to come by. Servants talk, you know, when the price is right and you know whom to ask. And there are some servants here with long memories, people who recall Garrick Farne bringing the child here. They remember your father and the Duke of Farne and Lord Scott making a devil's bargain to hide the truth and bury Kitty Farne's shame with her. Your brother's, too," Tom added thoughtfully. "He was scarcely a lily-white innocent in all this, was he?" He looked at her. "Shall I tell you all about it?"

Tom's eyes were bright and pale. Merryn realized with a pang of shock how much he was relishing this story and how much he enjoyed seeing her unhappiness. She had known that Tom Bradshaw was ruthless. She had even known that he could be cruel but she had never realized before that he enjoyed seeing others suffer. She clenched her fists. Her fingers, even inside her leather gloves, were almost numb with cold now.

"I don't want to hear it," she said. "Not from you. If there is more to tell then Garrick will be the one who tells me, not you."

"How charmingly loyal," Tom sneered. "Even in the moment when you could think the worst of him, still that stubborn spirit of yours clings to the belief that he cannot be bad through and through."

"I know he has more integrity than you," Merryn said furiously. She jumped to her feet. "You tried to blackmail my family," she said. "You pretended to work for justice when instead you were only out for yourself. You—" She stopped dead. "You used me," she whispered.

Tom laughed. "My, but it's taken you so long to realize that!" he said. His smile broadened. "You are quite right," he said. "I fed your hatred of Farne. I manipulated your every move. I used you to get the information I wanted."

The cold settled icy and deep in Merryn's stomach. "Why?" she said. "Why, Tom?"

"Because I'm going to bring down the Farne Dukedom," Tom said. He smiled again but his eyes were cold. "I want to ruin Garrick Farne. He has everything that should have been mine."

He half turned to face the sea. The wind caught at his hair, ruffling it. The tide was creeping closer, eating up the beach, smoothing and sculpting the sand. Merryn's footprints had already disappeared.

"I am Claudius Farne's son, too," Tom said, "but unlike Garrick I was not born to privilege."

"You?" Merryn took a step back. "But…your father worked on the Thames! You told me all about it—" She stopped because Tom was not paying her the slightest attention. He was looking out to sea where another gray snowstorm was sweeping in and ruffling the whitetops of the waves.

"My mother was a housemaid," Tom said. His gaze came back to her but Merryn still had the oddest feeling that he was looking through her rather than at her. "She had known my father—the man who gave me his name—from childhood. They wed when she was already pregnant. As for the late Duke—" his shoulders moved beneath his jacket "—he took and used the household staff as though they were his private property. What was one more maid to him? What did it matter if she were willing or not? He offered my mother nothing. She was turned off without a penny, branded a whore."

"I'm sorry," Merryn said. The wind took her words

and whipped them away. The storm was moving closer now, snowflakes swirling across the sand.

Tom took a tiny golden locket from his pocket. For a moment the gold caught the light, gleaming like treasure on a dark day. He raised his arm and threw it with all his strength across the sand. "My mother stole that when she was thrown out of Farne House," he said. "It was a portrait of him. He did not give it to her. He gave her nothing." The locket shimmered for a moment against the sand and then vanished. "When he died," Tom said, "I thought that he might finally acknowledge me in some way." His face twisted. "I had waited and waited for his notice. It was foolish of me, for of course I was nothing to him. I was less than nothing."

"It was after he died that you showed me the documents relating to Stephen's death," Merryn said and saw him nod. She felt bitter and foolish. She could see now how cleverly Tom had influenced her, providing information, spurring her on while pretending to have his doubts, using her because in her quest for justice she had been blind to all else.

"I have all the evidence I need now," Tom said. "I know there was no duel. I can prove it. I'll reveal the whole truth and I'll make sure Farne will hang."

"No!" Merryn said. She thought of the children in the garden, of everything that Garrick had worked to protect. She remembered Garrick's words to her at the ball: *"If you pursue this the innocent will suffer..."* She could see the impossible choices he had made and the hard decisions he had taken. "I'll stop you," she said. "I'll testify against you if I have to. You will *not* hurt that child and…" she took a deep breath "…I will not let you ruin Garrick."

Tom laughed harshly. "You were always so righteous," he said. "What does your brother's little bastard matter to me?" He put his hand into his pocket and took out a pistol. "I might have known you would fall in love with Farne," he said. "He is an idealist like you."

The snowstorm reached them with a sudden violent swirl of sound and the blizzard enveloped them. Tom took aim and Merryn turned, taking a hasty step back, tripping over her skirts. A wave caught her, knocking her off balance. She went down, feeling the sand shift treacherously beneath her feet. In a flash of blinding fear she remembered the locket shimmering on the surface of the sand and then vanishing below it. She was on the edge of a quicksand and had not realized it and now, as another wave buffeted her, she heard the greedy sucking of the waves about her feet. It was terrifying. It felt as though there was nothing but emptiness beneath her, no firm foothold, nothing but the quicksand dragging her down, devouring her. And in front of her was Tom Bradshaw, with a pistol.

She waited as time seemed to spin out in endless moments.

And Tom stood there, watching the sands take her, and made no move to help her at all.

CHAPTER SIXTEEN

GARRICK HAD LOOKED everywhere for Merryn, asked everyone he had seen and had drawn a blank at every turn. With each empty road and every negative response his anxiety for her had grown, desperation lending his steps even greater speed as he had searched everywhere he could think.

All he could see was Merryn's stricken face and the blank shock in her eyes as she had reproached him.

"I had nothing of him left," she had said of her brother. And he had remembered the long, dark night in the beer flood when she had told him that sometimes she could not even remember Stephen's face, that he was slipping away from her even as she desperately tried to hold something of him to her, to keep his memory alive. He knew that this business of the child was one thing that she could never forgive him for. She had said that she never wanted to see him again. He understood that. But even so he had to know that she was safe.

He had been searching for her since the previous day, tracing her steps to the White Lion in Holborn where the landlord remembered her taking the Bath Flyer, driving hell for leather on the Bath Road, calling at the White

Hart in Bath, following her trail to Shipham, becoming more and more anxious for her with every mile that passed because he knew that when she discovered the whole truth as surely she would now, it would shatter her illusions once and for all and destroy her world. Bradshaw had been as slippery and deceitful as Garrick had known he would be, swearing that Merryn knew nothing of the child and that he himself had no interest in the scurrilous gossip that Harriet had carried to him. Garrick had sensed the man was lying about something but in his haste to find Merryn he had let Bradshaw go.

Now he paced the courtyard of the inn in Kilve. As a last resort he had assumed that Merryn would return there intent on taking a carriage home, intent at least on getting as far away from him as possible. He had waited ten minutes, in an agony of impatience and doubt, and a further ten barely able to contain his feelings. And now, another five minutes later, he knew that something was wrong. He could feel it. The unease prickled along his skin and nagged at his mind.

The ostlers were unharnessing his carriage horses, leading them to the stables and rubbing them down. Suddenly Garrick made up his mind.

"Saddle me up your best horse," he said abruptly to one of the gaping grooms. The anxiety grabbed at him again. "Quickly, man!"

The ostler was looking dubious. This was a country inn, after all.

"The best, your grace?" he queried.

"Now!" Garrick snapped.

The best horse was perhaps not quite as highly bred as those in the Farne stables. In fact it looked suspiciously like an Exmoor pony and he was afraid that his weight would prove too much for it. However it was no broken-winded nag, Garrick saw to his relief, and it proved game enough when he turned it on to the coast path and gave it its head. The stones flew from its hooves. The thunder of the surf was in Garrick's ears and the whip of cold air on his face, and the ride should have been exhilarating had fear not held him tight in its grasp now, a dark formless dread that told him that something was terribly awry.

He saw the blue of Merryn's gown from the cliffs and immediately changed his course to go down onto the beach. There was someone with her; Garrick could not see clearly what was happening but they were by the water's edge. Merryn appeared to be on her knees...

Then two things happened at once. He recognized Tom Bradshaw when Tom began to run. And Merryn did not move.

With a muffled oath Garrick set the horse to the edge of the cliff, scrambling and slithering down the precipitous slope until they reached the beach. Thank God, he thought, this was an Exmoor pony. It looked as though it took such inclines in its stride every day of the week. It was not even pulling for breath. He urged it to a gallop and the little creature responded, the sand flying. On the way he passed Bradshaw running away as fast as he could. Bradshaw took a shot at him, the bullet flying so close that it passed through the horse's mane. Garrick did not even pause. His entire being was focused on Merryn, on reaching her in time, on saving her. His heart was thumping.

He reined in six feet back from the edge of the water so that the horse did not become mired in the quicksand, too. He cut the reins.

"Keep still," he said to Merryn. "Don't move." There was no time. She was already up to her thighs in the sand, then her hips, her waist. Her face was white as chalk, her eyes huge, terrified. But he could not allow himself to think of that. He could not allow himself to think of her fear, or feel his own. He had to concentrate. He knotted the reins into a loop with hands that were absolutely steady.

"Listen to me," he said, and saw her give a tiny nod. "I'm going to throw this to you. Slip the noose around your body and hold on tight."

Merryn did not respond. Her eyes were blank.

"Do you understand?" Garrick said. He injected a hint of steel into his voice. "Merryn."

She nodded. "Yes."

Another wave broke around her and Garrick saw her slip an inch deeper, two inches. The sand was almost up to her armpits now. In seconds she would be gone. The fear clawed at his throat, paralyzing him for a brief second. To lose Merryn now would be intolerable, eclipsing everything else that had happened in his life, driving out light and love forever. When Purchase had confronted him about his feelings for Merryn he had denied that he loved her. He had believed it. He had thought himself too tarnished and bitter to love. He recognized his mistake now in the seconds before he was about to lose that love forever.

He could see the horror in Merryn's eyes. It filled her whole being. The sand sucked at her and she slipped another inch. She opened her mouth to scream. Garrick knew she was on the very edge of hysteria and that if she gave in to it she would be lost. She would sink in an instant and be smothered, drowned in sand.

"Merryn," he said. "I love you. Don't leave me now."

Her gaze jerked up to his. Her breathing calmed a fraction.

He threw the makeshift rope.

She caught it and slipped the loop over her head and the breath left Garrick's lungs so fast he felt dizzy.

"Hold on!" he shouted.

The snow was swirling, blinding him now. He pulled harder than he had ever pulled in his life before and felt the resistance. He pulled again, almost wrenching his arms from their sockets, and then another wave broke and he felt the sands shift and move and Merryn came free to her waist, then her knees, and then she was sprawling on the sand in a tumbled heap, half conscious, as Garrick lifted her with hands that shook so much now he could not keep them steady. He held her close against his racing heart and pressed his lips to her hair.

"I am sorry," he said. "If you cannot forgive me—"

"Be quiet, Garrick," Merryn said very clearly. Her eyes opened. She reached up and cupped his face in her hands and kissed him and then Garrick was kissing her back, over and over, desperate, famished kisses as though he would never let her go.

THEY DID NOT TALK on the way back. The horse was tired now and carrying a double weight and Merryn felt colder and more tired still. Garrick had wrapped her in his jacket and though she murmured a protest and tried to shrug it off he just fastened it all the more closely about her and after a moment she accepted his gift. The coat was warm and smelled of Garrick and she turned her face against the collar and drank in the reassurance of it. She found that for once she did not want to speak at all. She felt simultaneously too full of emotion to be able to grapple with it, yet utterly drained and exhausted. She had questions—she would come to those soon enough and this time, she knew, Garrick would answer—but for now she was content to lie quietly in Garrick's arms as he encouraged the little horse back to the village.

It was only a matter of minutes before they were back in Kilve's broad high street and turning through the arch into the courtyard of The Smugglers Inn. Garrick handed the shivering pony over to the ostlers, gave it an appreciative pat, lifted Merryn down again and carried her into the inn. This time her protests were stronger.

"Put me down," she snapped, wriggling in his arms. "I am perfectly capable of walking. I am not an invalid!"

Mrs. Morton chose that precise moment to appear from the parlor and seemed extremely flustered to see Merryn clasped in the arms of a man.

"Lady Merryn!" she exclaimed.

"Mrs. Morton," Merryn said as Garrick gently restored her to her feet. "This is—"

"I am Lady Merryn's husband," Garrick lied smoothly, shooting Merryn a swift look that positively forbade argument. "Garrick Farne, at your service, madam." He executed a perfect bow.

"You did not tell us you were married!" Mrs. Morton exclaimed, seemingly torn between indignation that Merryn had kept such a prime piece of gossip from her and a certain admiration for Garrick's evident style.

"I am afraid that Lady Merryn has not quite got used to the idea yet," Garrick said, before Merryn could respond. His hand tightened warningly on hers. "Our relationship is only of recent standing."

Merryn opened her mouth—saw his expression—and closed it again. Garrick, she thought, looked extremely forbidding. "Come, my love," he added, shifting his grip to her arm. "You are chilled to the bone. I will ask the landlady to draw a bath for you."

The landlord appeared at the moment, with promises of spiced wine and hot food and when he addressed

Garrick as "your grace" Mrs. Morton's mouth fell open, her eyes became as huge as dinner plates and she hurried off, presumably to acquaint the rest of the inn's occupants with the news of their august guest.

"I don't know what you had to do that for," Merryn said as the landlord ushered them into a private parlor where a fire roared in the grate.

"Because," Garrick said, "I had no wish to make you the butt of yet more scandal."

"I think," Merryn said, "that my reputation is probably beyond saving now."

"Probably," Garrick concurred.

There was a little silence.

"Did you mean it?" Merryn said. Her voice trembled.

Garrick did not pretend to misunderstand her. "Yes," he said. "I meant it. I love you with all my heart." There was so much of pity and regret in his eyes. "But I also meant what I said in London." His voice was lacerated by pain. "I can never be the man you want me to be, Merryn."

The landlord knocked at the door and came in with the spiced wine and a tray piled high with food. Garrick poured for her and passed her a glass. He moved away again immediately and Merryn knew that despite their passionate embrace when he had saved her from the quicksand he would not touch her again. Only she could put matters right now if she had the strength and courage to face the past.

She took a sip of the spiced wine, feeling the rich liquid burn a line of fire down to her stomach, feeling it warm and soothe her.

"When I discovered that Kitty had been pregnant," she said, "I wanted to believe that I had been right about you from the start, Garrick. I wanted to believe that you had killed Stephen in cold blood, out of anger and revenge. It would have made perfect sense. Your best friend had betrayed you with your wife. There was an argument. You shot him. I wanted to believe that you had lied to me when you told me Stephen had tried to kill Kitty." She stopped, rubbing her fingers over the delicate tracery of the goblet, over and over. "Except by then I had already come to know you." She looked up. "I had already come to love you. And I knew you would not lie."

She looked at him. His mouth was hard, his eyes shadowed.

"Tell me what happened," she said.

Garrick came to sit close to her, not touching, but near. There was a long silence. Merryn waited. Garrick started to talk, slowly, reluctantly. It felt as though the words were dragged out of him, gathering fluency only when he seemed to forget that she was there and lost himself in the dark memory of the past.

"I found them in the maze at Starcross Hall," he said. "Kitty had been expecting me—I had been up in London on business but then I received a note from her asking me to come down to Somerset on a matter of urgency. I set off as soon as I could." He raked a hand though his hair in a quick, anguished gesture. "Perhaps she planned for me to find her with Stephen to force a confrontation. To this day I do not know. But whatever she had planned, it had gone wrong. I heard them arguing violently as I tried to find my way through the maze toward them." He stopped. Merryn watched the play of emotion across his face like light and shade—anger, pity, regret. "Kitty was crying," Garrick said, "and pleading with Stephen to run away with her. She said that they could make a new life together, the two of them with their child." He glanced at Merryn's face, then away. "That was the first that I knew she was pregnant." Merryn saw him look down at his clasped hands, the knuckles gripping white. "Stephen was laughing at her," he said tonelessly, "and taunting her. He said that he had no intention of running off with her, that he had never loved her, that she was nothing more than a whore and that if she was sensible she would pay him to keep his mouth shut about the baby and pretend that it was mine all along."

Merryn gave a little moan, covering her face with her hands. For a moment it was as though her heart had stopped. Her memories were splintering now, dissolving, reforming into a new pattern. In her mind's eye she could see Stephen, hear his voice echoing down the long garden corridor of Fenners on the last morning of his life. He had been dressed for riding and was halfway out of the door already, the sun behind him, lighting him up so that she could not see his expression.

"Congratulate me, little sis! I am on my way to make my fortune!"

She had thought that it was odd that he had seemed so happy because only the night before she had heard him arguing with Lord Fenner over money. He must have had Kitty's note, telling him of her pregnancy, begging him to elope. And he had known he had no intention of doing so and every intention of threatening to broadcast her disgrace unless she paid him off. Kitty, who had been fathoms deep in love with him. Kitty, whom he had betrayed...

Garrick was still talking in that rough, painful tone.

"The next thing I heard was Kitty screaming," he said. He glanced at Merryn, looked away. "She had a pistol. I don't know why. I have often wondered. Maybe she did not trust Stephen from the first and that is the saddest thing of all. Anyway, she swore to kill him if he abandoned her."

Merryn felt the anguish rake through her, raw and sharp. The tears clogged her throat, tears for Kitty, so disillusioned and alone.

"There was a shot," Garrick said, "and I forced my way through the hedge to the center of the maze and I found them." He stopped, breathing hard. "Kitty had shot Stephen in the shoulder. She was mad with grief and distress. Stephen was on the ground. He was bleeding copiously and swearing at her. He was still taunting her, telling her that she was so stupid she could not even kill him. He had his own pistol leveled at Kitty and he said he would show her how it should be done." Garrick stopped. "We both fired together," he said. "Stephen's bullet hit Kitty in the arm. Mine killed him."

Merryn sat dry-eyed and frozen. *Stephen,* she thought. *You blackguard. You utter scoundrel.* The tears prickled her eyelids and closed her throat, tears of bitterness and disillusion. There was a sharp pain in her chest, a crack in her heart, stealing her breath. All pretense had been stripped away now and she had to accept the fact she had always known in her heart of hearts and yet had chosen to deny: that her brother had been worse than a wastrel and a rogue. He had been arrogant, vain and dangerous. He had played with people's lives, with Garrick, with Kitty, with herself, as though they were counters in a game.

She buried her face in her hands again as the shivers racked her.

She felt Garrick move and then he pressed her glass of wine into her hands, holding them steady as she drank obediently and once again felt the warm liquid flower within her giving her warmth and strength. She raised her head and looked at him. The lines of grief and unhappiness were etched so deep in his face that she wanted to reach out to him and smooth them away.

"I'm sorry, Merryn," he said. "I wish I could say it was not true."

"You took Kitty away to protect her," Merryn said. "I thought you had run to escape trial."

"I thought I would have had a good chance of acquittal

if I had stood trial," Garrick said. "I wanted to stay, to face justice for what I had done." A muscle worked in his jaw. "But it was impossible. Everything would have come out—not merely Kitty's *affaire,* which we could not hide, but her pregnancy, too…" His voice fell. "She would have been utterly ruined and the future of the baby, too." His face twisted.

"I would have given the child my name if I could have done," he said, and Merryn could hear the rawness in his voice. "I would have done anything for her to be mine—" He stopped.

"You could not claim her as your own because it was too late," Merryn said. She watched the way that his fingers tightened around his wineglass and wanted to ease that pain in him. "Kitty was already pregnant when you wed her."

"Three months gone," Garrick said, "and I had been out of the country until a month before our wedding." He shook his head. "Even so, I thought there might be a way, if I took Kitty abroad where nobody knew us. I thought we could pretend and that I could give the child my name."

"But if the child had been a boy," Merryn said, "he would have been your heir."

Garrick shrugged. For a moment a hint of amusement lifted the harsh lines of misery on his face. "That would not have mattered to me," he said. "God knows, it was not the fault of the child—it was innocent in all of this—and there have been bastards aplenty in the Farne line before. Ethan…"

There had been Tom, too, Merryn thought. Soon she would need to explain to Garrick about Tom but not until everything else had been laid bare between them.

"My father, though," Garrick said, his voice bitter and hard. "He would not stand for a bastard inheriting the Farne Dukedom. He had too much arrogance and pride. It was our final quarrel. And in the end—" His shoulders slumped. "It did not matter because Kitty had no will to make a future with me after Stephen had died. Susan was born prematurely and Kitty slipped away. It seemed as though she had no reason to live."

Merryn took his hand and laced her fingers tightly in his. She felt his surprise and his instinctive move to draw away from her before he relaxed and let her hand rest in his.

"You had a reason to live, though," she said softly. "You had Susan."

Garrick looked down into her face. "She had lost her mother," he said, "and I had robbed her of her father before she was even born. What else could I do other than to protect her?" His fingers tightened painfully on Merryn's. "I could not keep her with me," he said, "in exile, alone. Besides Kitty's family wanted her." He raised a hand to Merryn's face and touched her cheek. "Just as you wished for something to remember Stephen by," he said, "so they wanted to have something of Kitty, something good and unspoiled and true that need not be tainted by the scandal. So I gave Susan to them and I promised to keep the secret of her parentage. I swore never to speak a word to anyone to protect her always." Again his fingers brushed her cheek, his touch full of regret. "I did not know you then," he said harshly. "I did not know how much I would come to love you and how desperately I would want to tell you the truth. When we were to wed I wrote to Lord Scott begging to be released from my oath. But he..." He stopped.

"He forbade you to tell," Merryn said. Her voice shook. "I understand. No one had cause to hate the Fenner family more."

She thought of the way that she had hated Garrick in the beginning with such a blind passion that it could not be quelled. Kitty Scott's family had had equal reason to hate.

It was then that Merryn realized that she was crying, silently, big fat tears dropping onto the arm of the chair like the snowflakes outside. She rubbed them away with her fingers. Garrick took her damp hands in his and his touch was warm and comforting and for a moment she clung to him before he freed himself and moved away. She could sense the loneliness in him again, the solitariness that she had seen from the first, that had set him apart. She remembered the way he had rejected her love for him because he believed that what he had done had made him a pariah, unworthy of love. First she had hated Garrick Farne with a passion, she thought, and then she had wanted him to be a hero and neither was fair to the man he was, the man who had been forced to make terrible choices and had lived with the consequences ever since. Now at last she saw Garrick as he truly was: an honorable man who had been in an intolerable situation, who had made mistakes and tried to make reparation, too.

"I don't understand why you blame yourself, Garrick," she said carefully, wanting to reach out to him, to breach that frightening coldness and give him the comfort that she knew he needed in his soul. "You acted to protect Kitty and her daughter. Everything you did, you did for their sakes, out of honor."

Garrick shook his head. There was stark unhappiness in his face, so sharp it cut Merryn to the bone. "Don't seek to give me absolution, Merryn," he said. He turned away from her as though he could not bear for her to look on him. "You were right all along," he said briefly. "I *was* jealous of Stephen. When I discovered that he had bedded Kitty I hated him for his careless arrogance and the way he could simply take whatever he wanted." He shook his head. "Every single day," he said, "from that moment to this, I have thought that I need not have killed him. I could have put a bullet through his shoulder or shot the pistol from his hand..." His voice fell. "But I did not. And I will never be sure that I did not act through jealousy and revenge."

Merryn got up slowly and crossed to him, putting her arms about him. He did not respond. She could feel the resistance in him. "You have tortured yourself every day, Garrick," she said softly. "You had no time to think, no time to do anything other than to react. And if there was an element of anger and jealousy—" she shook her head "—then every day since you have atoned for that by protecting Kitty and then her daughter from harm."

She felt a tiny slackening of the tension in him. "I acted out of duty," Garrick said. "What else could I do?"

"You acted out of honor," Merryn corrected. "What else would a man like you do?" She freed him, stepped back. There was something that she had to tell him now. "Listen to me," she said. Her voice shook. There were tears in her eyes. "We all do wrong," she said. "There is something you do not know."

Garrick had heard the painful note in her voice. He turned toward her.

"I was Kitty and Stephen's go-between," Merryn said.

There was a silence. Garrick stared at her, dark eyes narrowed. He looked incredulous. "You?" he said. "But you were a mere child—"

"I carried messages for them," Merryn said. "They could not trust the servants so they used me. It was easy," she added. "No one suspected me."

Her mind was opening now like a window into the past, and the memories she had repressed for so long because of her grief and guilt came tumbling out. That summer had been hot, the fields yellow and dry under a baking blue sky, the sea a perfect cobalt-blue. She could see Stephen, lounging on the grass under the plane trees in the garden at Fenners, calling her over, teasing her, smiling at her.

"Merryn, be a sweetheart and take this letter to Lady Farne for me…"

His laughing blue eyes had been narrowed against the sun. He had smiled, a smile for her alone.

"Don't tell anyone… It's our secret…"

It had been so exciting to be so important. She had rubbed her dirty palms on her even dirtier skirt, hauled up her stockings and taken the letter from his hand. She could feel it even now, smooth and cool against her hot skin. She had sped across the fields to Starcross Manor, tumbling over the stile, with the dry stalks of the meadow grasses whipping her legs. Kitty had been waiting for her. She had sent the maid for lemonade and Merryn had gulped it down thirstily. Kitty had written a reply but she had not sent Merryn back at once—that was one of the things that Merryn had grown to love about her. Kitty always took the time to talk to her, to ask her what she was reading, to give her little presents of ribbons and bookmarks and quills. She was kind. And later Merryn knew that she was unhappy, that she had been forced to wed when her heart was given somewhere else. Given to Stephen.

"You were only a child," Garrick repeated. He rubbed his forehead as though it pained him. "You cannot have known what you were doing."

"I knew exactly what I was doing," Merryn said. "Do

not make excuses for me, Garrick. I was thirteen years old. I thought it was romantic. I *wanted* them to run away together." She gulped in a breath. "You said that Kitty wrote to you," she said. "It was the reason you came down that last day, the day you found them together. But it was not Kitty who wrote to you, Garrick. It was I." She looked away, her words wrenched from her. "I loved you," she said. "Oh, I was only young but I felt it so passionately! You know me now—" a small sad smile cut through her grief "—you know how wholeheartedly I give myself up to every thing I believe in. It is my greatest weakness, I think. And I thought that if Kitty and Stephen were to elope then you might notice me at last." Her breath caught. "I was almost fourteen," she said. "I thought that in a couple of years I would be old enough for you."

She stole a look at Garrick's face and the shock and the dawning horror she saw made her feel sick. She gave a despairing gesture. "So I wrote the letter. I lured you to Starcross Manor." She struggled to control her voice, raked by the agonizing grief of what she had done. "I thought it would force a confrontation," she said. "I knew you were a good man, a generous man. I thought you would let Kitty go. But instead…" She put her hands to her face then let them fall. "That was why when you told me in London that Stephen had tried to kill Kitty I could not believe you," she whispered. "I did not *want* to believe you. It was not meant to be like that." She stopped, her throat dry, her heart aching. Garrick was standing absolutely still. He had not moved, had not spoken. His face, dark and drawn, was turned away from her. Merryn felt her soul wither.

"I'll go now," she said and her voice broke.

She was shaking. She was not sure how her legs carried her to the door. The handle slipped under her fingers as she fumbled with it.

Then Garrick's hand closed over hers, holding it still. "Merryn," he said softly. His arms came about her and as she felt their strength she turned her face against his chest and her grief burst out and she cried and cried while Garrick held her as gently as though she were a child.

"Hush," he said, stroking her hair. "Merryn, sweetheart—"

She raised her face to his and he kissed her lashes, brushing the tears from her wet cheeks, kissing her trembling mouth.

"I'm sorry," she said brokenly. "I'm so very sorry."

"To think that you have lived with that all these years," Garrick said, his voice rough with emotion, "never knowing what happened, desperate to understand."

Merryn clung to him. "I could not let it go," she whispered. "When you came back I had to know. I had to find out what had happened, what had gone wrong."

"And I thwarted you at every turn." Garrick sounded bitter, regretful. His arms tightened about her.

"I blamed you because I could not face my own culpability," Merryn said, the words tumbling out. She wiped the streaming tears away with the back of her fingers. "I knew I had done wrong but I could never tell anyone…" Her voice trembled. "Oh, Garrick…"

They stood for a long time, wrapped in each other's arms, lost to all else, drawing strength and love from one another. After a while Garrick loosed Merryn enough to look down into her face.

"Merryn," he said, "will you marry me?" He smiled, brushing the tumbled hair gently back from her flushed cheeks. "I asked you before," he said, "and you did not want me. If you have changed your mind—"

"With all my heart," Merryn whispered, reaching up to kiss him.

Garrick patted the pocket of his coat. "I brought the special license with me. Was that very presumptuous of me?"

"Frightfully," Merryn said. She looked at him under her lashes. "When?"

"I thought tomorrow?" Garrick said. "If you are in agreement and if the vicar of Kilve agrees."

"What do we do until then?" Merryn said, more softly still.

"Well," Garrick said, "you need to take a bath for you have almost been drowned in a quicksand and threatened, and sustained any number of shocks and it is remiss of me to have kept you from your bed for so long…"

Merryn smiled. "I bespoke a bedchamber but it was

the last one available," she said. "I am afraid that you will have to sleep in the taproom."

"And have Mrs. Morton assume that we were already in marital difficulties?" Garrick said. "I thank you, no. I have no wish for her to press on me her sovereign cure for impotence, nor for my alleged shortcomings in the bedroom to be broadcast to all of her acquaintance."

Merryn was betrayed into a giggle. "She could help you," she said. "She told me in the carriage that she has a range of remedies to cure all ills."

"Thank you," Garrick said, "but I do not recall you having any complaints before." He scooped her up in his arms and strode to the parlor door. Out in the hall, Mrs. and Miss Morton were lighting their candles at the bottom of the stairs. Mrs. Morton gave a little shriek to see Merryn once again clasped so tightly in Garrick's manly grasp.

"Good night, Mrs. Morton," Merryn called as Garrick took the stairs two at a time.

"I do not believe those two are married at all," she heard Mrs. Morton hiss to her daughter. "And they call themselves the Quality!"

UP IN THE PRIVACY of a tiny chamber under the eaves of the inn Garrick stripped the blue gown from Merryn's body, peeling off her underclothes with gentle hands, shaking out the sand that seemed to have penetrated every fold of her dress and clung to her skin, making it salty and rough. He concentrated very hard on the practical task, trying to ignore the delicate curve of her breast as she stepped out of her shift, trying to blot from his sight the luscious arch of her hips, the long, pure, tempting line of her bare leg. He had been quite enough of a brute keeping her downstairs in the parlor, cold and filthy, while they talked. He felt racked with remorse. The best way to make it up to her, he thought, was to see her safely into bed, make sure she was wrapped up warm and tight so that she did not catch an ague, and then retire to the taproom for a long, frustrated wakeful night alone and Mrs. Morton's impotence aids be damned. This was no time to be thinking of ravishing Merryn. He would wait until she was recovered from her ordeal, wait until they were wed, wait until he had the marriage lines and they were respectable as the Duke and Duchess of Farne. He looked at Merryn as she rolled the stockings down her legs and felt the heat rise over his body, felt the color sting his cheeks and his eyes burn and he turned away so that she did not see the evidence of his arousal.

A hipbath stood in the corner, the scented water steaming. It smelled divine of lavender and herbs and he heard Merryn give a little greedy moan. She skipped across the room, all rosy skin gleaming in the firelight, and slipped beneath the water with a sigh of pure physical pleasure. Garrick gritted his teeth hard and turned his back. Unfortunately that brought the wide bed into view, with its fresh white sheets turned down so very invitingly. Garrick stomped across to the window and stared out into the snowswept darkness. That was better; a cold winter night should chill his ardor.

There were splashes, more sighs of bliss and then Merryn's voice, deceptively innocent. "Garrick, please could you help me wash my hair? I cannot reach…"

With a tortured sigh Garrick turned back and walked across to the bath, dropping to his knees beside her. Her skin was pink from the heat of the water now. Her shoulders gleamed wet and pale in the firelight, the shadows leading down to the hollow between her breasts and lower. Garrick's mouth dried to sawdust. He wrenched his gaze away so violently it hurt.

Merryn placed one hand on his arm, compelling him to look at her. Slowly, very slowly, her blue gaze came up and met his. Her eyes were burning as deep and rich as sapphires with a flame in their depths. The moment spun out like a golden thread between them and Garrick thought he had never been so aware of her, of every inch of her beautiful body begging for his touch. And then she smiled at him and his heart expanded under the radiance of it and she held out her arms to him and he swept her up out of the water and laid her down before the fire, following her down. For a while they lay there, his breath shortening, his arms about her, his palms flat against the smooth skin of her back. Then she gave a little sigh and raised her lips to his and he kissed her with passion and hunger, as though he were starved. Her hands were moving over him now, tugging at his shirt, eager and clumsy with haste. She pressed her lips to the point of his shoulder and bit down, making him groan, then feathered tiny kisses across his chest and lower over the taut skin of his belly. She was all quicksilver and fire and impatience, fumbling with the fastenings of his breeches. They defeated her and she made a soft sound of irritation and he covered her hands with his, showing her how it was done. He kissed her again, the passion and greed easing into tenderness, running his hands into her hair, nipping at her throat and lower to her breast, tugging the nipple to a tight aching peak. Her eyes were closed, her breathing quick and sharp as she held him, digging her fingers into the hard muscles of his shoulders, sliding her hands down his naked back. He kissed the hollow of her throat and the cleft between her breasts. She tasted sweet as honey with the tang of salt still faintly on her skin and he licked the underside of her breast up to the nipple and heard her moan. He watched the play of the firelight over her skin, stroking her in graceful curves, tracing the lines of her body until she arched beneath his touch.

"I love you," he said, kissing her again with aching gentleness and saw her smile. She reached up and touched his face.

"Garrick, my love…"

He carried her to the bed and laid her down on the cool white sheets, kissing her belly, gently parting her so that she lay naked, open and spread to him. With shaking hands he cast off the rest of his clothes and came over her and slid into her with triumphant tenderness. Now at last there were no shadows to darken their lovemaking and no secrets between them. Garrick poured out his love for her and felt Merryn meet it and return it, matching his movements with her own, wider, deeper, faster, stroke for stroke, equal at last until they plunged into brilliant ecstasy and he claimed her at last in all love and honor. They slid into the deepest and most peaceful of sleeps and Garrick wrapped his arms about Merryn and knew he would never let her go.

IT WAS ALMOST NOON when Merryn woke and then it was only because it sounded as though the inn was in complete uproar. She bent over to kiss Garrick softly and he murmured in his sleep, his mouth curving into a smile of love and gentleness. They had made love again and again through the night, Garrick possessing her with a triumphant passion that had awed her to her soul.

The sounds from the inn courtyard became louder and more chaotic still. Throwing on her nightdress—and how had that come to be left in so tangled a heap on the floor—Merryn hurried to the window and stared out.

The courtyard was in chaos with no less than six coaches all busily disgorging people, portmanteaux, servants, silver, furniture, wall hangings, brightly wrapped presents and one small white dog. Merryn gasped.

"Darlings!" Joanna appeared beneath the window, staring up. Behind her stood Alex with Shuna in his arms. A crimson hood framed Joanna's face. There were snowflakes in her hair. She looked, Merryn thought, like a fairy princess. Merryn, her hair tousled, her feet bare, wearing no more than a crumpled robe, immediately felt shabby. Garrick came to stand behind her, dropping a kiss on her hair.

"I am so pleased that you are here!" Joanna called. "Are you wed yet?"

There was the sound of footsteps on the stairs and then the door burst open. With great presence of mind, Garrick scooped Merryn up and tossed her back into the bed, sliding in beside her. A moment later Tess stood in the doorway. Behind her was Alex, Shuna and the Duchess of Steyne, her tiny upright figure wrapped in the most extraordinary traveling furs. Then a tall, dark and shockingly handsome man appeared. Merryn thought he looked vaguely familiar. She heard Garrick gasp.

"Ethan?" he said, and Merryn heard the uncertainty and the pleasure in his voice, the hesitation of a man who had been accustomed so long to being alone and now could not quite believe what was happening to him. A dark-haired woman ran into the room and threw herself against Garrick's naked chest, planting a kiss on his lips in a way that made Merryn feel absurdly possessive.

"Garrick darling, I never had the chance to thank you," the woman said. She spun around on Merryn, catching her in her arms.

"Merryn!" she said. "You lucky, lucky girl!"

"Lottie!" Merryn said, dazed. "What on earth—"

"I sent for them," Joanna said. She had appeared in the

crowded room now. She was looking slightly sheepish. "I hope you don't mind," she said.

Garrick grabbed Merryn's hand in his. "Of course not," he said. "But…"

His face, Merryn thought, was a perfect reflection of everything that she was feeling: bewilderment, astonishment and dawning joy.

"But I don't understand," Merryn said. "What are you all doing here?"

"We have come to celebrate your wedding, of course," Joanna said. "And then we thought we might travel on to Dorset and open up Fenners for Christmas." She looked at Garrick. "Did you not tell her that we planned to follow you down?" she asked.

"I apologize," Garrick said smoothly. "We had rather a lot to talk about."

"And to do, by the looks of it," Lottie said, her bright brown gaze taking in the tumbled sheets of the bed.

"But you hate the country," Merryn said to Joanna. "You and Tess and Lottie—none of you can stand it."

"Well, this is different," Joanna said. "It is Christmas and you are newly wed, Merryn darling, and there is much to celebrate." She looked at them. "You *are* married, aren't you?"

"Not yet," Garrick said.

"Then you had best get your clothes on and get down to the church, nephew," the Dowager Duchess proclaimed. "At once!"

"Give us an hour," Garrick murmured, drawing Merryn back under the sheets.

"A half hour," the Dowager declaimed. "And then I will come back."

Garrick, ignoring them, rolled Merryn over, and started to kiss her. "Out!" he said briefly, over his shoulder. "If you please, Aunt Elizabeth," he added punctiliously.

There was a gasp from the Dowager. The room emptied as though by magic.

"I am sorry," Merryn said, looking up at him. "It seems that when you marry me you marry my family as well."

"I am content," Garrick said. He bent his head to kiss he again. "Very content," he said, as his lips left hers.

"I really did not want my sisters at my wedding," Merryn said, miserably. "And Lottie as well! They are all so beautiful and stylish—"

"I didn't notice," Garrick said. He stripped the crumpled nightgown from her body. "You know I can see no one else when you are by." His hands started to move over her, with love, with tenderness. "Darling Merryn," he said, "shall we leave them all here and elope?"

Merryn giggled. "It is very tempting," she said.

"But poor recompense for the love they have shown us, I suppose," Garrick said. He raised himself on one elbow. "Will you mind very much being at Fenners for Christmas?" he asked. "I know it may be difficult for you—"

Merryn silenced him with her fingers against his lips. "It will not be difficult," she said, "if you are with me." She pulled him down into her arms. "It is a time for new beginnings," she said.

EPILOGUE

Christmas Eve

"Mr. Churchward has sent us a letter," Merryn said. It was very late on the night before Christmas and she was sitting before the fire, wrapped in her new husband's arms. The room was warm and intimate, lit only by the glow of the flames and the one candle that burned on the dresser. Apple logs and pine scented the air.

Garrick was in a state of delightful undress in just his shirt and pantaloons. Merryn was wearing the most delicious little concoction of gauze and lace that Tess had given her as a Christmas present. She had pressed it on Merryn in advance of Christmas Day, whispering that Garrick might enjoy it, too, and indeed its effect on him had already been most gratifying. Merryn felt beautiful and very, very loved. It was lucky, she thought, that Joanna had had the delicacy to give them an entire wing of Fenners to themselves. Although she suspected that the rest of the family might be celebrating Christmas with its promise of love and renewal and hope for the future in much the same way that she and Garrick had.

She unfolded Mr. Churchward's letter and it rustled a little as she spread it out and started to read.

"He apologizes for disturbing us with business matters at such a time as Christmas," she said. She paused. "Poor Mr. Churchward—is there a Mrs. Churchward, do you think, to share the festive season with him?"

"If there is I doubt she can be as happy at this moment as I," Garrick said. He raised a strand of Merryn's shining hair to his lips and kissed it before he let it slide softly through his fingers. "Must you read that?" he murmured, brushing the hair aside, his lips moving to the soft skin of her neck.

Merryn pushed him gently away. "Listen. He says that Tom Bradshaw has disappeared." A shiver touched her. She dropped the letter into her lap. "Do you think he will ever come back?"

"I'll have him arrested for attempted murder if he does," Garrick said, so ferociously that Merryn felt reassured. She picked up the letter again and started to read. Then she stilled. Garrick felt her sudden immobility and looked up.

"What is it?" he said.

"Mr. Churchward—" Merryn stopped. Her voice was a little rough with emotion. "He says that he has had a letter from Mrs. Alice Scott of Shipham about her niece, Miss Susan Scott." Her breath caught. "He says that Mrs. Scott wishes to discuss the possibility of us talking together to see if Joanna and Tess and I might meet Susan—" Her voice broke. Her eyes filled with tears. "You wrote to her, didn't you?" she whispered. She pulled back and stared into Garrick's dark eyes. They were soft and so full of love that she thought her heart would burst. "Even though they rejected your pleas you wrote again," she said. "You did not give up."

Garrick took her hand in his. "It mattered to you very much," he said gruffly. "I had kept Susan from you so long and I could not forgive myself." He pressed a kiss against her fingers. "I would have tried again and again," he said, "so that I could give her back to you. I wanted to make you happy."

Merryn touched his hair in the most tender of caresses. "It was the nicest thing you could possibly have done," she said. "The best present you could give me."

She bent to kiss him, her tears salt against his lips. Garrick drew her down beside him on the rug and kissed her back and then everything became very sweet and pleasurable as the letter was forgotten in the outpouring of love and healing and happiness between them.

Much later, Merryn lay with her head pillowed on Garrick's bare chest and her fingers entwined with his.

"It is almost midnight," she whispered. "Almost your birthday, Garrick Charles Christmas Farne." She felt his chest move as he laughed and turned her head to kiss him. "What can I give you," she said, "in return for your generosity to me?"

She felt Garrick's arms tighten about her with a fierce protectiveness. "I have everything I could ever want here in my arms," he said and Merryn rolled over to look at him, utterly awed by the fierceness of the love she saw in his eyes.

Garrick scooped her up and carried her over to the vast four-poster bed then went across to snuff the candle. He picked up the letter, somewhat crushed and creased by now, smoothed it out and read the final paragraph.

"'I must also take this opportunity to apologize for an oversight on my part,'" Mr. Churchward had written. "'I realize that when I sent the Fenners estate papers to Tavistock Square I mistakenly enclosed a copy of Lord Fenner's will which should have remained confidential in my office. I do hope,'" Mr. Churchward had underlined, "'that the perusal of this did not cause any difficulties…'"

Garrick paused, a smile starting to curl his lips. He let the letter drift down onto the table. Mr. Churchward, he thought, never made mistakes. He would have known that Merryn would find the reference to the miniature and would set out to unravel the truth. Mr. Churchward, Garrick thought, was a very unlikely Christmas angel but he had given them a gift beyond price.

* * * * *

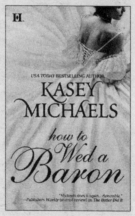

REQUEST YOUR
FREE BOOKS!

2 FREE NOVELS
FROM THE ROMANCE COLLECTION
PLUS 2 FREE GIFTS!

YES! Please send me 2 FREE novels from the Romance Collection and my 2 FREE gifts (gifts are worth about $10). After receiving them, if I don't wish to receive any more books, I can return the shipping statement marked "cancel." If I don't cancel, I will receive 4 brand-new novels every month and be billed just $5.74 per book in the U.S. or $6.24 per book in Canada. That's a saving of at least 28% off the cover price. It's quite a bargain! Shipping and handling is just 50¢ per book.* I understand that accepting the 2 free books and gifts places me under no obligation to buy anything. I can always return a shipment and cancel at any time. Even if I never buy another book, the two free books and gifts are mine to keep forever.

194/394 MDN E7NZ

Name	(PLEASE PRINT)

Address	Apt. #

City	State/Prov.	Zip/Postal Code

Signature (if under 18, a parent or guardian must sign)

Mail to **The Reader Service:**
IN U.S.A.: P.O. Box 1867, Buffalo, NY 14240-1867
IN CANADA: P.O. Box 609, Fort Erie, Ontario L2A 5X3

Not valid for current subscribers to the Romance Collection
or the Romance/Suspense Collection.

Want to try two free books from another line?
Call 1-800-873-8635 or visit www.morefreebooks.com.

* Terms and prices subject to change without notice. Prices do not include applicable taxes. N.Y. residents add applicable sales tax. Canadian residents will be charged applicable provincial taxes and GST. Offer not valid in Quebec. This offer is limited to one order per household. All orders subject to approval. Credit or debit balances in a customer's account(s) may be offset by any other outstanding balance owed by or to the customer. Please allow 4 to 6 weeks for delivery. Offer available while quantities last.

Your Privacy: Harlequin Books is committed to protecting your privacy. Our Privacy Policy is available online at www.eHarlequin.com or upon request from the Reader Service. From time to time we make our lists of customers available to reputable third parties who may have a product or service of interest to you. If you would prefer we not share your name and address, please check here. ☐

Help us get it right—We strive for accurate, respectful and relevant communications. To clarify or modify your communication preferences, visit us at www.ReaderService.com/consumerschoice.

MROM10R

Try these Healthy and Delicious Spring Rolls!

INGREDIENTS

2 packages rice-paper
spring roll wrappers
(20 wrappers)

1 cup grated carrot

¼ cup bean sprouts

1 cucumber, julienned

1 red bell pepper, without
stem and seeds, julienned

4 green onions
finely chopped—
use only the green part

DIRECTIONS

1. Soak one rice-paper wrapper
   in a large bowl of hot water
   until softened.

2. Place a pinch each of carrots,
   sprouts, cucumber, bell
   pepper and green onion on the
   wrapper toward the bottom
   third of the rice paper.

3. Fold ends in and roll tightly
   to enclose filling.

4. Repeat with remaining
   wrappers. Chill before
   serving.

Find this and many more delectable recipes
including the perfect dipping sauce in

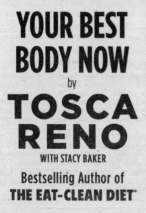

NICOLA CORNICK

77487	ONE WICKED SIN	___ $7.99 U.S.	___ $9.99 CAN.
77440	WHISPER OF SCANDAL	___ $7.99 U.S.	___ $9.99 CAN.
77395	THE UNDOING OF A LADY	___ $7.99 U.S.	___ $8.99 CAN.
77389	THE SCANDALS OF AN INNOCENT	___ $7.99 U.S.	___ $8.99 CAN.
77377	THE CONFESSIONS OF A DUCHESS	___ $7.99 U.S.	___ $8.99 CAN.
77303	UNMASKED	___ $6.99 U.S.	___ $6.99 CAN.

(limited quantities available)

TOTAL AMOUNT	$ _____
POSTAGE & HANDLING	$ _____
($1.00 FOR 1 BOOK, 50¢ for each additional)	
APPLICABLE TAXES*	$ _____
TOTAL PAYABLE	$ _____

(check or money order—please do not send cash)

To order, complete this form and send it, along with a check or money order for the total above, payable to HQN Books, to: **In the U.S.:** 3010 Walden Avenue, P.O. Box 9077, Buffalo, NY 14269-9077; **In Canada:** P.O. Box 636, Fort Erie, Ontario, L2A 5X3.

Name: _____
Address: _____ City: _____
State/Prov.: _____ Zip/Postal Code: _____
Account Number (if applicable): _____

075 CSAS

*New York residents remit applicable sales taxes.
*Canadian residents remit applicable GST and provincial taxes.

HQN™

We *are* romance™

www.HQNBooks.com

PHNC1210BL